"THE EAGLETS ARE IMPATIENT," HENRY SIGHED.

"Because the eagle has kept them in the nest too long," Eleanor replied.

"You turned them against me," he accused. "You are at the source of all my troubles."

"Had you been the husband I wanted, I would have loved you to the end."

"You wanted to rule."

"Aye. We both wanted it."

"And between us, we bred the eaglets." With that, he turned away at the door and looked back at her. "Oh, God, Eleanor, why was it not different? What would I not give for just one loving son."

Then he was gone.

She laughed quietly. Poor Henry, the great King, the seducer of women, the lover whom none could resist. He had failed where she had succeeded, for she had one son who loved her. . . .

THE REVOLT
of the
EAGLETS

by

Jean Plaidy

FAWCETT CREST • NEW YORK

THE REVOLT OF THE EAGLETS

This book contains the complete text of the original hardcover
edition.

Published by Fawcett Crest Books, a unit of CBS Publications,
the Consumer Publishing Division of CBS Inc., by arrangement with G. P. Putnam's Sons

ISBN: 0-449-24460-1

Printed in the United States of America

First Fawcett Crest printing: November 1981

10 9 8 7 6 5 4 3 2 1

The King's chamber at Winchester castle was painted with allegorical pictures representing his life. One of these was a painting of an eagle and four eaglets. Three of the eaglets were attacking their father while the fourth looked on. The King is said to have remarked: "The four eaglets are my sons, who will persecute me until I die. The youngest of them, my favourite, will hurt me most. He is waiting for the moment when he will peck out my eyes."

KINGS OF ENGLAND

WILLIAM THE CONQUEROR

WILLIAM RUFUS   HENRY 1   Adela

William (drowned)   Matilda   STEPHEN

HENRY II
m. ELEANOR OF AQUITAINE

William (died young)   Henry   Matilda   RICHARD   Geoffrey   Eleanor   Joanna   JOHN

THE KINGS OF FRANCE

Louis VI

Philip (died)

LOUIS VII m. Eleanor of Aquitaine   m. Constance   m. Adela

Marie

Alix

Alice

Marguerite m. young Henry

Agnes

PHILIP

Alice betrothed to Richard

News of Murder

It was the first day of the year 1171 and in the Castle at Argentan they had been celebrating the passing of the old year and welcoming in the new. The King was in a good mood anticipating with pleasure his return to England and re-union with his mistress Rosamund Clifford. Since his wife, Queen Eleanor, had become aware of her existence, there was no longer the need to keep the liaison secret. Not that he, King of England, Duke of Normandy and the rest, was afraid of his wife, although she could be formidable. His anxiety had been that she might take some revenge on Rosamund before he could prevent her doing so. Eleanor must learn that he was master, but it was a conclusion which she had evaded for the nineteen years of their marriage.

Yet he supposed theirs had not been an entirely unsatisfactory union. She had provided him with four sons and two daughters—a good tally—and not only that: her rich lands of Aquitaine, which she had brought to the marriage, had extended his possessions and made the King of England the most powerful man in Europe.

He had much on which to congratulate himself. He had brought that justice back to England which under the reign of weak Stephen the country had lost; he had managed to cling to his possessions overseas; he had skilfully arranged the marriages of his children—all but six-year-old Joanna and five-year-old John—to bring him the utmost advantage, and he was in fact feared and respected throughout his kingdom—and others.

Although on this New Year's Day he was in a benevolent mood, all men knew that his notorious temper could be aroused at any moment. Then his pinkish skin would become dull red and his eyes would grow fierce, his nostrils flare until he would resemble the lion to which he was so often compared. He had never been able to control those tempers, nor did he see any reason why he should. When he was angry

9

he wanted men to know it. His rages were terrible. During them he lost all control of his actions and would vent his fury on any inanimate objects which happened to be at hand, often causing damage to himself. He had been known to roll on the floor and gnaw the rushes at such times.

Eleanor had said: "One day when you are in one of your rages you will do yourself a mischief."

He remembered the glint in her eyes, and he had cried: "You would not be displeased if I did, my lady, I fancy."

She had not denied it. She had always been defiant, never showing fear of him, constantly reminding him that though he might be King of England, she was the Duchess of Aquitaine.

He doubted she would care if he were dead. In fact the event might please her. There was their son to follow him to the throne. Young Henry, already crowned King, handsome, with all the charm imaginable, already binding men to him by the sheer attractiveness of his personality. It was unwise to crown a son King while his father still lived. Becket had been against it.

"Ah, my Lord Archbishop," muttered Henry, "was that perhaps because *you* were not the one to perform the ceremony?"

Young Henry was now leaving boyhood behind him. He was sixteen. Boys did grow ambitious at such an age. The King admitted to himself that he did now and then feel uneasy and had asked himself whether he had acted thoughtlessly during the preceding year when he had allowed his son to be crowned.

Well, it was done; and if he, the King, were to die within a few weeks—which was not unlikely for he was constantly leading his armies against some rebel who had thought to take advantage of his many commitments—then England would have an undisputed King who had already been crowned and bore the title.

He would not allow such thoughts to disturb him on this day. He would think of home and Rosamund and their two boys and the domestic peace he could find with no one but her. He was glad Eleanor had walked through the maze of trees that day and discovered the Bower where he had hidden Rosamund. He was tired of Eleanor. It suited him well that she should go to Aquitaine; he hoped she would stay there; he no longer desired her. She was nearly twelve years older than he was; and there was no need to get more children by her, when they already had six and in any case she was now past the age of childbearing. It was good to be rid of her spiteful tongue, for she made no effort to control it now that she had a reason in Rosamund for hating him. As if she, a woman of such worldliness, could have expected him to be faithful to her! That was not exactly the case. Like so many women of her kind she would accept the casual adventure. The fact that galled her was that he could actually love someone as he loved Rosamund, and let her continue to bear his children, that she was someone to whom he could go for peace and comfort, someone who could be to him a wife as his Queen could not be. That roused her venom and set her thinking of how she could most effectively revenge herself on him.

Let her try.

Rosamund was so different. He brooded on how he had first seen her in her father's castle in Shropshire where he had rested on some expedition into Wales; she had been an innocent young virgin; he had desired her and there had been no one to deny him—not Sir Walter Clifford, her father, nor the fair Rosamund herself; and ever since . . . she had been as a wife to him. A dear docile creature never complaining of his infidelities, never seeking prizes for herself, always there when he needed her to comfort him.

He was fortunate in Rosamund and now that Eleanor was away he could safely bring her to Court. He hoped his wife would never come back to England.

A shout from below broke into this pleasant reverie.

He called out: "What goes?"

One of his attendants was hurrying to him.

"My lord, riders are coming to the castle."

He was at the window. Riders, yes. And they came from England. Trouble! It could only mean trouble. Who had risen against him now? Well, it would hasten his return and the sooner he would be with Rosamund.

He was in the hall when they came in. They threw themselves at his feet and he cried impatiently: "What news? What news?"

"The Archbishop of Canterbury is dead, my lord."

"Dead!"

"Murdered, my lord, in his own Cathedral."

"Oh, my God, no. This cannot be true. Who has done this deed?"

"Four of your knights, my lord. Reginald FitzUrse, William de Tracy, Hugh de Morville and Richard le Breton."

"*My* knights," he said.

The messengers bowed their heads.

"Why did they do this?" muttered the King. "What can have made them commit such a crime?"

The messengers remained silent. They dared not tell him that the knights had said they had done the deed at the King's command.

"Thomas . . . dead!" went on the King talking to himself. "It cannot be. It must not be."

"My lord," said one of the messengers, "the deed was done but three days ago and we came with all speed, knowing it would be your wish to be acquainted with the fact."

"Go . . . refresh yourselves . . . leave me with my grief," said the King. He called to his servants. "Bring me sackcloth. I shall change my robes. This for me is a day of mourning."

Thomas . . . dead! Old friend and now enemy, dead! So many memories came crowding into his mind. The jokes they had shared when Thomas had been his Chancellor and best friend. "Do not make me your Archbishop," he had said, "for that will be the end of our friendship." Was that a premonition? For how right he had been and what bitter enemies they had become. What had he said to those four knights that they should have taken their swords and stormed the Cathedral? What part had he played in this?

Solemnly he took off his royal robes and wrapped himself in a cloak of sack-cloth.

"Leave me," he said, "Leave me to my grief."

He went into his bedchamber and buried his head in his hands.

"I did not want this," he murmured again and again.

He dropped his hands and stared before him, not seeing the tapestried walls but the past . . . and the future.

Thomas was too well known a figure for his death to go unnoticed. Unnoticed! There was no hope of that! There would be an uproar. It would spread throughout Christendom. Thomas would be as tiresome in death as he had been in life. He would become a martyr. Henry was not afraid of any general, but he was terrified of martyrs.

What had he said to those knights? He remembered well the occasion when they had been present. He had heard that

Thomas had threatened to excommunicate all those who had been concerned in young Henry's coronation and as none had been concerned more than he himself that meant him also; and one of the bishops—it must have been Roger of York— had said that while Thomas Becket lived he would never have a peaceful kingdom. And then a sudden rage had possessed the King. He had cursed them all. He had maintained them and they were false varlets. He could hear his own voice now shouting to those cringing men. "You have left me long exposed to the insolence of this low-born cleric and have not attempted to relieve me of him."

They had taken those words to heart, those four knights; they had interpreted them as a command to murder. It must be so, for they had made their way to Canterbury and there slain Thomas in his Cathedral.

"That this should have happened!" he cried; and he was thinking: They are going to blame me. The whole world is going to blame me. Those four knights dealt the blows but I shall be named the murderer.

What could he do? He could see the Pope and the whole world rising against him. They were going to make a martyr and a saint of Thomas and the more reverence they showered on him the stronger would be the odium poured on the one they would blame for his murder.

He needed time to think. His actions now were of the utmost importance. He had come a long way in the last twenty years, when, as son of Matilda, daughter of Henry I of England, and the Count of Anjou, he had had a not very steady grasp on the crown of the Dukes of Normandy. He had married the richest heiress in Europe and had taken the crown of England and there was not a man who could stand against him. The King of France feared him; he had defied the Pope, he had had his way and it had brought him great power.

But now he was in danger, and all through Thomas à Becket. The Church would sing the Archbishop's praises, for Thomas had been slain in the battle between Church and State which had been raging for years and would doubtless go on. And Thomas would be a saint and a martyr.

"You always tried to get the better of me, Thomas," he muttered and a grim smile appeared on his lips. "And I always fought you ... often in jest and latterly in earnest and you have to learn that I always win."

13

And now in death you play this trick on me!

A great deal depended on what he did now. First of course he must insist that the knights had misconstrued his words. He must show everyone that no one mourned the death of Thomas à Becket more deeply than the King.

He would shut himself into his chamber; he would let it be known that so stunned was he by the news that he must be alone to mourn. He would not come down to eat; he would take only what was necessary to keep him alive—he had never been a great trencherman so that was no difficulty—he would wear nothing but his robe of sack-cloth and all must understand that he wished to be left to prayer and meditation.

Fortunately the position of Pope Alexander was not very secure and the papal Court was at Tusculum. Alexander had to be careful whom he offended and he would not wish to arouse the enmity of the King of England.

First Henry would send the messengers back to Canterbury with the news that the King's one-time Chancellor and Archbishop of Canterbury was to be given burial worthy of his rank.

How to approach the Pope needed a great deal of consideration. It was no use pleading complete innocence. No one would accept that. That there had been friction between himself and Thomas was a well-known fact. Yet there must be no delay in writing to Alexander before others got in with their accusations.

He took up his pen and wrote:

"To Alexander by the Grace of God Supreme Pontiff, Henry, King of the English, Duke of the Normans and Aquitainians and Count of the Angevins sends greetings and due devotion."

There was no harm in reminding Alexander of the power he held over so many territories.

"Out of reverence for the Roman Church and love for you ... I granted peace and the full restitution of his possessions, according to your order, to Thomas, Archbishop of Canterbury, and allowed him to cross over to England with a fitting revenue.

"He, however, brought not peace and joy but the sword, and made accusations against me and my crown. Not being able to bear such effrontery from the man, those he had excommunicated, and others, rushed in upon him and, what I cannot say without sorrow, killed him.

"Wherefore I am gravely concerned, as God is my witness,

for I fear that the anger I had formerly conceived against him may be accounted as the cause for this evil deed. And because in this deed I fear more for my reputation than my conscience, I beg Your Serenity to encourage me with your advice in this matter."

He despatched messengers to Tusculum and waited.

How quickly life could change. He had just been congratulating himself on having control of his subjects, of having rid himself of Eleanor; he had been delightedly planning a little domestic peace with Rosamund, and Thomas à Becket must be murdered! Why could not Thomas have died of some flux, some bodily disorder? No, he could not do that, though it seemed he was ailing. He had to die in the most spectacular fashion from the sword thrusts of the King's knights.

Trust Thomas to plague him to the end.

He thought of Eleanor who would very soon hear the news, for he was sure it would be ringing across the length and breadth of Europe. He could picture her sly smile, for she would know how discomfited he would be. In her malice she would doubtless feed the rumours with tales of his quarrels with Thomas, for at one time he had confided in her a great deal. She had never liked Thomas. In the days of the great friendship between the King and his Chancellor when Eleanor herself was still a little enamoured of her husband, she had been jealous of Thomas because she had known that the King preferred his conversation to that of anyone else.

"A curse on the Queen," cried the King.

He must not give way to anger now. He needed all his wits about him. He thought of all his vassals, those who unwillingly accepted him as their suzerain. They would be ready to whisper against him, the man who must surely be cursed because he was guilty of shedding the martyr's blood.

He stayed in his room most of those days. He was not seen at the table. His servants and knights spoke in whispers. "The King is deeply affected by the death of Thomas à Becket," they said.

When messengers arrived they were summoned immediately to his presence.

They had stories to tell of what was happening in Canterbury. On the night of the murder, it was said, there had been a violent storm. The lightning was horrifying and many were terrified of the thunder which broke right over the Cathedral. A blind woman had stooped and kissed the stones which were stained with Thomas's blood and lo, her sight was restored.

People were flocking to Canterbury, the sick and the maimed. It was said that Christ had given Thomas the power of healing.

It was worse than Henry had feared.

There was news too from Tusculum.

The Pope had shut himself away as soon as he had received the news of the murder. For eight days he had remained in seclusion that, as he said, he might mourn his beloved son. When he emerged he gave orders that no Englishman should be admitted to his presence.

Meanwhile the Archbishop of Sens had denounced Henry King of England as the murderer and the King of France joined the Archbishop in his accusations.

Henry knew that it was only a matter of time before he would be excommunicated.

This was disaster. But he was not a man to give way in adversity. In fact it was at such times that he showed his greatest skills. He had done what he could. He had written to the Pope honestly stating what had happened. He could only plead his sorrow and show that he mourned the death as sincerely as did everyone else.

There was nothing more he could do to convince the world of his innocence; and if they refused to believe him then he must make them aware of his might.

He had ever sought to add to his dominions and for long had had his eyes on Ireland.

This seemed an appropriate time to show the world that it would be unwise for any to underestimate him. His knights had murdered Thomas à Becket and he might be thought responsible, but let none of them forget that he was the great-grandson of the Conqueror.

He decided to spend his days in plannng an invasion of Ireland.

The young King Henry received the news in the old Saxon Palace of Winchester.

He was feeling somewhat displeased with his lot. It had been a great experience to be crowned King of England and he would never forget that ceremony which had taken place last June, some six months before. How wonderful it was to be a king! Those about him feared to offend him; they remembered that his father could not live forever and that one day there would only be one King of England. He was very surprised that his father had allowed him to be crowned and had made a king of him when it was quite clear that so many people liked the son better than the father.

Young Henry knew that he was more handsome than his father. They told him he resembled his paternal grandfather, the Count of Anjou, who had been known as Geoffrey the Fair. Looks were important, although his father would never accept that. Young Henry would never get his hands chapped and rough because he refused to wear gloves. He liked to see them adorned with rings. He was not like his father at all; he tried to charm people, something the older Henry never bothered with. But it was important, reasoned Henry the younger; it made people like one, it bound them to one; they were likely to be loyal if they had an affection for a ruler. No one had a great affection for his father. They might respect him as a great ruler and fear him, but love him? Never!

He knew how people were with him. They flattered him because he flattered them; there had been many a hint that those about him would be happy enough when there was only one King to rule England.

Not that he had been allowed to do much ruling yet. He had quickly realized that his father had had no intention of giving him power, only a crown. He was in fact becoming more and more disgruntled every day.

He wished he could see his mother, but of course she had always been more fond of Richard than she was of him; as for his father, it sometimes seemed as though he wanted his affection. Let him do something to get it then. Let him give the son he had made King some land to rule over; let him be King in fact as well as in name. As if the old man would give up anything he once laid his hands on!

"Your father is the most acquisitive man on earth," his mother had said to him. "He'll never take his hands from anything once they have held it."

What hatred there had been between those two! He and his brothers had sensed it; in secret they had ranged themselves on their mother's side against him. She had loved them and although Richard was her favourite she had shown that she cared passionately about them all. It seemed that the more she hated their father, the more she loved them.

The King had treated her badly. He had had no right to

bring his bastard Geoffrey into the nursery! The son of a common whore who had followed the camp and borne the King a son—and that son was brought up in their mother's nursery! It was too much for any proud woman to endure and when that woman was Eleanor of Aquitaine, naturally there would be trouble.

She had said to him: "Henry my son, your father has made a king of you. He did it only to spite Thomas Becket, I'm sure. He knows that old fellow will be beside himself with rage because he was not here to crown you. He'll regret it, but his regrets will be your blessing. As he has made you a king, he must not be surprised if you act like one." And she had laughed loudly at the thought; and ever since he had resented his father's parsimony; because of his mother's words he had come to dislike his father even more than he had at first. His mother had always pointed out to them all their father's shortcomings; and the only one who didn't listen to her was Bastard Geoffrey. He worshipped the King; and when their father came to the nursery he would try to get his attention, which he invariably did, for the King always listened to what Geoffrey the Bastard had learned and nodded his approval.

Now young Henry believed he had done it to annoy their mother. There was so much one understood as one grew older.

"Your father will use you all like pawns in a game of chess," said their mother. "Look how he has married you without your leave!"

It was true. Young Henry had a wife, Marguerite, the daughter of the King of France. At this time she was in Aquitaine with his mother, being brought up by her until the time when she should come to him and share his bed, roof and crown. She herself had not yet been crowned and the King of France was very angry about that, but his father had promised that she should be, and when she was, he supposed their married life would begin.

He had so few opportunities for displaying his kingship that when he did get one he was determined to use it. He had done so quite recently when Thomas à Becket had come to see him.

He had refused to see the old man. He had felt a little uneasy about that but he had persuaded himself that he could do nothing else. Roger, Archbishop of York, had arrived to see him and to tell him that the Archbishop of Canterbury was on his way.

Young Henry had been pleased to hear this for he had had a great affection for his old teacher. He and young Marguerite had been put in his care many years ago before Thomas's exile. He had been stern and they had had to spend long sessions on their knees. Marguerite used to say her knees were sore with praying, but they had loved him in spite of his strictness and the stern talks he used to give them, for there was a merry side to his nature and suddenly it would burst forth and they would all be very gay together.

He remembered that day when they were told that Thomas à Becket would no longer instruct them because he had quarrelled with the King and as a consequence he had fled to France.

That was long ago. Marguerite had broken down and wept; and Henry had almost done the same. And no other teacher had been quite the same.

But Roger of York had scorned Thomas à Becket.

"My lord King," he had said, "you cannot receive that man. Had he had his way you would never have been crowned."

"And why not?" he had demanded in his new arrogance.

"Because the Archbishop of Canterbury did not believe you should be crowned. He is a man who thinks he knows best on every matter."

"It is because he did not perform the cermeony."

"Mayhap that had something to do with it, but he had declared his disapproval and is threatening to excommunicate all those who took part in it."

"That's insolence," Henry had cried, for he was very sensitive about anything that touched his pride in his new office.

"He's an insolent fellow. If you receive him he will preach to you. He will tell you to give up your crown."

"I will tell him to be gone."

"Better to tell him not to come. My lord King, if you will allow me to express an opinion, for the sake of the dignity of your crown you cannot receive a man whose aim is to snatch it from you."

"Indeed I cannot."

"Then you should have him warned that you will not receive him."

"I will," declared Henry, and had done so, but almost immediately he regretted it. It seemed so churlish to turn his old teacher away.

But Roger of York was right. Now that he was King he could suffer no indignity.

He let his mind dwell on the glory of the coronation when the crown had been placed on his head in the solemn ceremony and later at the banquet his father the King had served him.

Men looked on amazed at such at sight. The idea of a king—and such a king—bowing to his own young son was incongruous.

One of them had said to him afterwards: "What a sight it was. The King himself to kneel to you!"

"Why should not the son of a Count kneel to the son of a King," retorted Henry; and that remark was repeated, for indeed it was true. Young Henry was the son of the King of England and the King of England was only the son of the Count of Anjou.

Ever since, he had been deeply aware of his title, and with each day his resentment grew.

Six months a king and still treated like a child! It would not do. He would speak to his father. So he said now. It would be a different matter when he stood before him. Then he would be afraid of nobody as men were, be they prince or serf, that the dangerous colour would flame into the face and the whites of the eyes redden and the terrible temper rise up like a roaring lion ready to destroy all those who crossed him.

"One of these days when your father is in one of his rages it will be the end of him." That was his mother's voice, quiet, mocking, putting thoughts into his head which would not otherwise have been there.

Messengers at the castle. They always excited him. What news were they bringing? A message from his father? Was he to join him in Normandy or wherever he was? Was he to place himself at the head of a troop of soldiers? Was he going to be given land and castles of his own at last?

"My lord," said one of his knights, "there is a messenger from Canterbury."

"From Canterbury, but my father is across the sea."

"He comes not from your father, my lord."

"From Canterbury! From the Archbishop! But I will not see the Archbishop. I have said I will not receive those who do not please me."

"My lord, he has doleful tidings."

"Then bring him to me."

The messenger came. He bowed low. "My lord, this day I bring you sad tidings. The Archbishop of Canterbury has been murdered in his Cathedral."

"Murdered!" cried Henry. "How so?"

"Four of your father's knights have killed him."

"Killed him . . . in the Cathedral!" The boy's eyes were misty. It could not be so. And yet he might have guessed it. Thomas had quarrelled with his father and the King allowed none to do that with impunity.

"Tell me in detail," he commanded; and the story was told.

Henry went to his bedchamber. He could not shut out the terrible sight those men had conjured up. Thomas à Becket lying on the stones of the Cathedral in a pool of blood.

"I refused to see him," he said to himself, "but I did not wish this to happen. Oh, God, how thankful I am that I had no part in it."

Then he thought of the old days when Thomas had taken him into his household and given special attention to the son of the King. The Archbishop had told him stories of his father, how they had been great friends and roamed the countryside together before he had become Archbishop and was merely the King's Chancellor. Pleasant merry stories, showing the King in a different guise. It was clear from the manner in which Thomas had talked of Henry that he had loved him. He had been as much aware of Thomas's love as he had of his mother's hatred. And yet his father had murdered Thomas.

Oh yes he had. Young Henry knew that everyone was thinking it even if they dared not say it. Four knights had struck the blows but the whole world would know on whose instructions.

"It will be remembered against him," he mused. "The people will turn from him because of it. And to whom will they turn? Surely to the one whom he himself had crowned their King."

Eleanor Queen of England was content to be in her beloved city of Poitiers. This was the land she loved; the land of mild breezes, warm sun and song. It was here that the Courts of Love belonged; it had been impossible to transplant them in the colder climate of England and with a people who had little patience with the laws of chivalry and dreams of ideal love. The King of that country was typical of the people he ruled, thought Eleanor scornfully—lusty, unimaginative, seeing something decadent in lying in the sun and making beautiful verses in honour of lovers.

This was where she belonged and she never wanted to see England again. She might tell herself that she never wanted to see Henry also, but that was not true. He stimulated her as no one else could; he probed her emotions to their depth; she could never be truthfully aloof from him. Once she had loved him fiercely and now as fiercely she hated him.

Often in her gardens she would be thinking of Henry when handsome troubadours strummed on their lutes and gazed at her with love and longing which must be feigned, for she was nearly fifty years of age and although she had been an exceptionally beautiful woman and still was, she had lived her life adventurously and time had left its marks on her. She remembered those early days when they had loved passionately and she had divorced Louis King of France in order to marry him. He had been as eager for the match as she was, but that may have been because she could bring him Aquitaine and he was a glutton for land. Sometimes she thought that he dreamed of conquering the whole world. Still if Aquitaine had been the main attraction he had hidden the fact and those early years of their marriage must have brought some of the satisfaction to him that they had brought to her. The strong physical attraction had been there—there was no doubt of it; but he, the lusty King, who all his life had taken what he wanted when he wanted it, had soon been unfaithful. She could laugh now at her fury when she had discovered it through the little Bastard Geoffrey he had brought into her nurseries.

What a glorious battle there had been then and how she had enjoyed it; it had pleased her to see the rage which possessed him because in some way it weakened him. When his temper was out of control and he kicked inanimate objects, when he lay on the floor and rolled about in an agony of rage and tore the dirty rushes with his teeth, he betrayed himself. That magnificent power and strength which was normally his were lost somehow in the man who might control armies but was not in command of his own nature.

She could not stop thinking of him and oddly enough her hatred of him absorbed her as once her love of him had done. Once she would have done everthing in her power to advance him; now she would employ the same energy to destroying him.

How she loved this city. Her city! And he, Henry, was Duke of Aquitaine, but he should not remain so. That title was for her beloved son Richard; and when Richard became Duke of Aquitaine he should be so in truth. Henry was quite content to bestow titles on his sons as long as it was understood that no power went with them. His was to be the governing hand, as young Henry—proud to be called a King—was realizing.

But it would not always be so. Already the people of Aquitaine were getting an inkling of the relationship between the King and the Queen; and there was no doubt where their loyalty lay. They demonstrated whenever she rode out that they regarded her as their Duchess and they would never submit to the fiery arrogant Angevin who regarded himself as the conqueror of Europe. No, they loved their Duchess Eleanor, the lady of song and learning, the adventurous Queen whose conduct had often scandalized the world, but even these scandals had only endeared her to her own people of the South.

Often she went up the ramparts of the castle and surveyed with pride and emotion the city below her. She would gaze at the beautiful Notre Dame la Grande, and the baptistery of Saint Jean and feel young again. She remembered too when the magnificent Cathedral of Saint Pierre had been built. There were so many memories here of other days; and looking back did she regret the passing of her youth?

How could she, when the years had brought her her beloved sons? And chief of these was Richard.

She had always loved beauty in the human form and in her eyes her son was her ideal. Some might say he lacked the regular-featured handsome good looks of his elder brother Henry, but the strength of his character showed in his face, and although Eleanor loved all her children and determined to bind them to her, Richard was the one who had the cream of her devotion.

Richard was tall, his limbs were long and he was noted for the long reach of his arms. His hair was neither red nor yellow but of a colour in between, and his eyes were blue. From an early age he had shown great daring and such a strength of purpose that once he had made up his mind to complete a task he never swerved until it was done. In horsemanship, archery and all other sports he excelled, and what so enchanted the Queen was that he was equally skilled in verse making; he could sing and play the lute with the best of her troubadours. Now that she felt this fierce hatred for her husband she concentrated her love on her children and Richard especially.

He returned her love. To her he confided his ambitions. He enjoyed hearing of her adventures in the Holy Land and she loved to tell them, dramatizing them, setting them to verse and glorifying them by song. They were romanticized and made enchanting stories and she and the lovers she had taken during that wild adventure were the heroine and heroes of a story as entertaining and romantic as that of Arthur, Guinevere and Lancelot.

"Oh what a beautiful city this is," she would say. "My city that shall be yours, Richard. This city on a hill. Did you know that Marcus Aurelius built an amphitheatre here to hold twenty-two thousand spectators? The Saracens were routed here when they swept across France. Standing here on these ramparts you can sense it all, can you not?"

And Richard would understand as once she had thought his father would have done. For in the early days of their marriage Henry had loved literature and works of the imagination. But he had coarsened; his love of power and his lechery had done that.

"When he enters a town," said Eleanor to her sons, "he does not see the magnificent façade of a cathedral; he does not hear the melodious ring of bells. He looks over the women and decides which he shall take to his bed to make sport with, not caring whether she be willing or not."

"Let us hope he does not come to Poitiers," said Richard.

"We will do our best to keep him away."

"Why, my mother, even you could not do that."

"Think you not? What if I were to make the people here dislike him so that they refused to have him?"

"That would be the very greatest inducement for him to come. He would ride into the town with his knights and soldiers in such force that none would dare stand against him."

"You are right, my son. Even so, I do not intend that my subjects should be kept in ignorance of the kind of man he is."

"Let us not think of him," said Richard. "We are happy without him."

And so they were.

"Let us plan a masque for tomorrow," she said. "Could you write some special verses for the occasion? What think you?"

He thought it was an excellent idea and he would set about the task at once.

So life flowed on pleasantly in Poitiers. There was many a

masque, many a banquet; with her were her sons Richard and Geoffrey and even the latter was something of a troubadour; there was Marguerite, daughter of Louis and wife to young Henry, who was still in her care. Richard's betrothed Alice, another daughter of Louis but half-sister to Marguerite, for Marguerite was the daughter of Louis's second wife and Alice of his third, was being brought up at the English Court. Since Eleanor could not be a happy wife she could at least be a contented mother. Her sons loved her and so did her daughters. Even those whom she had deserted still had an affection for her.

These were Marie and Alix, the two she had borne Louis when she was his wife. She had loved them dearly when they were babies but she had been too adventurous a woman to devote herself to children. Marie and Alix were married now—Marie to the Count of Champagne and Alix to the Count of Blois—but they had inherited her love of literature and consequently they could best satisfy this at the court of Poitiers and whenever it was possible they visited her.

What joy it was to have her attendants hurry to tell her that they had arrived and then to go down to the courtyard to drink the welcoming cup with them. She believed that they bore her no rancour for her desertion of them. They, like her other children, enjoyed hearing stories of her wildly adventurous life. Marie was perhaps the more attractive of the sisters. She was beautiful and had a spontaneous wit which enchanted everyone including her mother. Marie wrote exquisite poetry herself and it gave Eleanor great pleasure to see the affection between the two most loved of her children, Marie and Richard.

It was into this happy court that the messengers came from England with the news that Thomas à Becket, Archbishop of Canterbury, had been murdered in his Cathedral.

Eleanor's eyes shone with excitement. "Murdered!" she cried. "And by the King's knights! We have no doubt who is the true murderer."

Richard and Goeffrey stared at her in horror. How wise they were! she thought. Wise enough to know the importance of this news!

"The whole of Christendom will rise in horror against the one responsible for this crime," prophesied Eleanor. "They will all cry shame on the murderer of such a man."

She laughed aloud. She could not stop herself.

It was going to be amusing watching the effect of this deed, for she knew it would be great. It would reverberate throughout the world and could bring no good to the man she hated.

Now was the time for his enemies to rise up against him.

She looked at her sons and said slowly: "The time will be soon at hand when you should claim what is due to you. The time is ripe for action."

Princess Alice

The first shock was over. Henry emerged from his chamber of mourning and laughed at his fears. Was he not capable of holding what he had won? Was he going to be afraid of what penance the Pope might try to extract under threat of excommunication?

He was named as the murderer of Thomas à Becket and because people were becoming more and more convinced that Thomas was a saint they were regarding him in horror.

He would maintain the fact that he had never meant his knights to murder Thomas, meanwhile there was the business of being King to be attended to.

Now more than ever he needed to show the world that he was ready for any who should come against him.

Duke Conan of Brittany had died suddenly and it was evident that there might be trouble there, for Conan had been holding Brittany for Henry's son, young Geoffrey, who as a boy not yet thirteen years old was not capable of governing himself.

No sooner had Henry heard that certain Breton nobles were stating their refusal to do homage to him than he set himself at the head of a troop of soldiers and marched on Brittany. He felt better immediately. Whatever the outcome of Becket's death he was still the King of England and surely not even the Pope would dare attack him.

With his usual skill, in a short time he made those Bretons realize that he was their master. His son, Geoffrey, was as yet too young to take up his role as ruler but his father would hold the land for him until he was of age.

That lesson accomplished he was ready for whatever might come. He was seriously thinking of Ireland. This was the answer. He would not brood in one of his castles waiting for excommunication; he would go into action and add to his possessions, thus making himself more powerful than ever.

It was while he was settling affairs in Brittany that he

received a message from Count Humbert of Maurienne who asked if the King would receive him as he had a proposition to lay before him.

Knowing that Count Humbert was a widower with two daughters Henry guessed what might well be the nature of his business and when he considered the Count's possessions, Henry was not displeased.

He received him with honour and begged him to state his business.

"As you know, my lord King," said Humbert, "I have no son but two daughters, and it would be a great honour to me if you would accept the elder as a bride for your youngest son."

Henry pretended to be taken aback. In reality he was far from it. He had already thought very seriously of what Humbert could bring into the family. This was very important. His daughters, Matilda and Eleanor, were both suitably placed—Matilda to the Duke of Saxony, Eleanor to the King of Castile; as for Joanna, she was a child yet, being only six years old; and daughters were little problem. They could usually be married advantageously. It was not always easy with sons, for their father was expected to provide them with lands. Young Henry would be King of England—he was already crowned—and as the King of England would have Normandy and Anjou; Richard would have Aquitaine and he had provided Brittany for Geoffrey. But what of baby John? His patrimony had always been an anxiety. When he had been born Henry had looked at his little face and thought: Another son, what land shall I give him? He had nicknamed him then Jean Sans Terre; and the name had clung. He was often called John Lackland.

Here was an opportunity to provide him with territory to rule over. For the chance of marrying his daughter to the son of the King of England—albeit that son had three brothers older than himself and therefore one might say had no chance of reaching the throne—a mere Count of Maurienne would be ready to give a good deal.

He narrowed his eyes and studied the Count. "Well, my lord Count," he said. "I believe your daughter to be a comely child in good health and I would welcome her into my family, but I must look to my son's welfare. What dowry would she bring?"

"For such a marriage," said the Count, "I would be prepared to bestow the greater part of my lands. I have as you know, my lord, a younger daughter, and for her I must reserve a little of my territories, but as she could not hope to make such a brilliant marriage as her sister, naturally she would have to take a far smaller portion."

"There is the County of Belley," said Henry. "And the valley of Novalesia."

"And Rossillon-en-Bugey, my lord. Aix, Aspremont, Rochetta, Mont Major . . ." The Count went on counting them off on his fingers.

The King sat nodding. "And you have a claim on Grenoble, I believe."

"I have, my lord, and that too should pass to my elder daughter."

"It seems a fair enough proposition," said the King.

"I should ask that the bridegroom brought five thousand pounds to my family," added the Count.

Five thousand pounds! For so much! It was a fair bargain and Henry's eyes sparkled at the prospect of the lands which would come into the family on the marriage of John to the daughter of Humbert of Maurienne.

"Of course your son is but a child as yet," went on the Count.

"Almost six years," agreed the King, "but bright for his age and there is no reason why we should not get them betrothed. We'll not bed them yet but it is well for them to know that we think of them."

It was a bargain.

John should be Lackland no longer.

It was this kind of bargaining which pleased the King and made him forget the gathering storm over the death of Becket.

While he was congratulating himself on this match, disturbing news was brought to the castle. Two papal legates had already crossed the borders into France on their way to deliver a message to the King of England from the Pope.

Henry was well aware of what that message would contain. His spies had heard that the Pope wished him to observe his humility which meant of course to do some penance for his share in the murder of Becket. To do this would be to admit publicly his guilt and that was something he was not prepared to do.

He must leave for England at once before the papal legates could reach him. There he would give orders that any messenger from the Pope should on setting foot in England be seized as a spy.

Then he would make plans for his campaign against Ireland. The conquest of that country could not be achieved in a few weeks. It would doubtless be a campaign of some duration and while he was engaged on such an enterprise he could hardly be expected to give his mind to other matters. The longer the lapse of time between the murder and the reckoning the better.

So . . . to England.

His first visit was to Rosamund, now installed in the royal apartments at Westminster. As ever her beauty surprised him and he marvelled, as he had never ceased to do, that he could have loved her so long. The years had added a serenity to her charms; and he thought how much more attractive she was than a more clever and ambitious woman would have been. Of course he was comparing her with Eleanor.

She was pleased to see him and for the first day and night there was nothing but this delight in each other.

She told him of the fears she had while he had been away. He responded with assurances that in the strategy of war he was always one move ahead of his enemies; and that never had he forgotten her and his joy in returning to England was because he would find her there.

They talked of their boys who were now growing up. Young William would soon be of an age to come to Court.

"Never fear," said Henry, "the boys shall be as my legitimate sons, for, Rosamund, in my eyes you are indeed my wife."

"But not, my lord, in the eyes of God and the State."

"What matters that if you are so in my eyes? I will tell you something that has been in my mind of late. I have no love for the Queen—nor she for me. Why should I not rid myself of her?"

"How so?" asked Rosamund with a note of fear in her voice.

"Why should I not divorce her?"

"It would never be permitted."

He was astonished. It was rare for her to suggest that anything he wanted would not be possible.

"If I willed it, it should be," he said a trifle impatiently.

"There are the young King and his brothers."

" 'Tis no affair of theirs. Their position could not be altered."

"On what grounds would my lord be given his divorce? If it

30

were consanguinity then would not the young King and his brothers be illegitimate?"

The King sighed. " 'Tis so," he conceded. "If it were on grounds of adultery that would not affect my sons. By God's eyes I doubt I'd have difficulty in proving something against her. Louis could have divorced her for adultery. She took as her lovers her own uncle and a Saracen. Any woman who could do that . . ."

But for a man to accuse his wife of adultery when he was in bed with his mistress was in a measure ludicrous. Moreover a divorce on such grounds would mean neither party could marry again. So therefore it was clear that the King was not speaking seriously when he declared he would divorce the Queen.

Rosamund was uneasy. She supposed that there must come a time in the life of any woman in her position when she must ask herself what her future would be. Rosamund was not concerned with her material future. She knew that the King, even if he ceased to be in love with her, would always provide for her and their sons. It was not that which worried her.

With everyone else Rosamund had shuddered at the news of Becket's murder. She knew how deeply the King had been involved with the man. Many were the times when he had come to her distraught, angry, sad—and all because of Thomas à Becket. He had talked to her often as though he were talking to himself . . . he would ramble on sometimes about the great friendship they had shared and at others the hundred ways Thomas had found to plague him. Once he had said: "There'll be no peace for me while Thomas à Becket is Archbishop of Canterbury. I would to God I were rid of the man."

When she had heard that Thomas had been killed she could not get those words out of her mind. And she kept seeing Henry on those occasions when he had given vent to his rage against the Archbishop. Then he had frightened her with the violence of his fury and only her loving solicitude had prevented his giving way to it. She soothed him at such times by agreeing with him, offering him sympathy, making him realize that whatever he said, whatever he did, she believed him to be right.

And now . . . Becket.

She could not stop thinking of him. She had heard what had happened at the Cathedral after the death. How pilgrims were already visiting the place, the sick and maimed. They believed that if they kissed the stones on which his blood had been shed they would be blessed and perhaps cured of their sins.

For once she could not say to herself or to the King: You were right in what you did.

Thomas à Becket was between them.

He sensed the change in her. It frustrated him, put a barrier between them. She smiled and was as gracious and loving as ever; he was as ardent; but something had changed in their relationship and they were both aware of it.

There was not the same comfort with Rosamund as there had been.

In the palace at Westminster he visited the nursery. There were only the two youngest of his children there at this time—Joanna in her seventh year and John in his sixth. The fact that he had just made a marriage contract for his youngest son had awakened his interest in him and he wanted to tell the little fellow about his good fortune.

When he strode into the nursery a hushed awe fell upon the place; the nurses and attendants curtsied to the floor and the children watched in wonder. Henry cast a quick glance over the females—a habit which never left him—to see if any of them were worthy of his passing attention; and perhaps because his mind was busy with the change in Rosamund, or perhaps because he was not greatly impressed by any of them, he dismissed them.

The children were looking at a picture book and with them was a girl of some eleven or twelve years. They all rose. The two girls curtsied and young John bowed.

What a pleasant trio. The King felt his mood changing as he surveyed them. His son John was a pretty creature and so was his daughter. In grace and beauty though he had to admit that their companion surpassed them.

He remembered suddenly who she was. Of course she was Alice, daughter of the King of France, and she was being brought up here because she was betrothed to his son Richard.

"I trust you are pleased to see me," said the King.

John smiled; Joanna looked alarmed but Alice replied: "It gives us great pleasure, my lord."

He laid his hand on her soft curling hair.

"And do you know who I am, little one?"

"You are the King," she answered.

"Our father," added John.

"You are right," said Henry. "I have come to see how you are all getting on in your nursery. Come, Joanna, it is time for you to speak."

"We get on well, my lord," murmured the little girl shyly.

He picked her up and kissed her. Children were charming. Then he picked up John and did the same. When he set him down he looked at Alice. She blushed slightly. "And you, my lady," he said, "I must offer you like treatment, must I not?"

He lifted her in his arms. Her face was close to his. The texture of children's skin was so fine, so soft. Even beauties like Rosamund could not compare with them. It gave him great pleasure to hold this beautiful child in his arms. He kissed her soft cheek, but he did not put her down. He went on holding her. He looked into her eyes so beautifully set. Richard, he thought, you have a prize in this one. The idea of monk-like Louis siring such a perfect little creature amused him.

John and Joanna were looking up at him. He held Alice against him and kissed her again, this time on the mouth.

"You kiss Alice more than you kiss us," said John.

Henry put the girl down. "Well, she is our guest so we must make sure she knows she is welcome."

"Is Alice our guest then?" asked John. "They say she is our sister."

"She is to be your sister and she is our guest." He took one of her ringlets and curled it round his finger. "And I want her to know that there was never a more welcome one in my kingdom. What say you to that, little Alice?"

She said: "My lord is good."

He knelt down, feigning to hear her better, but in fact to put his face closer to her own.

"I like you well," he said; and he patted her face and his hands went to her shoulders and moved over her childish unformed body.

He stood up.

"Now I will sit down and you shall tell me how you progress in your lessons." He looked at John whose expression had become a little woebegone.

"Well, well, my son," he said, for his spirits were higher than they had been since he had heard of Becket's death, "we'll not go too far into the subject if it is not a pleasant one, for this is an occasion for rejoicing."

He took Alice's hand in one of his and Joanna's in the other and led the way to the window. He seated himself there. John leaned against one knee and Joanna against the other. "Come, Alice, my dear child," he said, and drawing her between his knees held her close to him. "Now," he said, "we are a friendly party. John, my son, I have come to see you because I have some good news for you."

"For me, my lord," cried John starting to leap up and down.

"You must not do that," said Joanna.

"Oh, we will let him express a little joy, daughter," said the King, "for it is a most joyful matter. I have a bride for him."

"A bride," said John. "What is that?"

"He is too young to understand," said Alice.

"Of course," said the King tenderly stroking her arm. "But you are not, my little one. You have been betrothed have you not . . . to my son Richard?"

"Yes, my lord," said Alice.

"You are too young as yet to go to him," went on the King and was amazed at the relief he felt. It would be unendurable to allow this beautiful child to go to some bumbling boy. Richard of course was handsome, but he was too young yet.

"It will be soon though," said Alice.

"No," said the King firmly. "There is some time yet."

"What about me?" said John.

"Listen to our young bridegroom. Joanna, Alice, my dears, listen to him!"

"You said it was *my* bride, father."

"So it is, my son. I have found you a bride who will bring much good to you and us, and her father and I have agreed that when you are old enough you shall be married. Her name is . . . why, she has the prettiest name in the world. What do you think it is? Alice! The same as my dear daughter here. Alice, I have already grown to love that name."

She smiled delightedly. A little dimple appeared in her cheek when she did so.

"You are a dear child," he said, "and I love you." He held her tightly against him and kissed her warmly on the cheek.

John was asking impatient questions. How big was his bride? Could she play games? Was she pretty? Was she good at her lessons?

"She is all these things," said the King, "and she is very happy to be my daughter and your wife."

John laughed delightedly. He was a charming little fellow, his youngest son. The others had always resented him in some way. That was their mother's influence he was sure. It was

34

very different in the nursery now. He must visit it more often.

Of course his illegitimate son Geoffrey was no longer there. He was being tutored in knighthood. A fine boy, Geoffrey. He had always preferred him to Eleanor's brood. But his son Henry was so handsome that he would have liked there to be a closer bond between them. As for Richard he was so much his mother's boy that it seemed they could never feel anything but enmity for each other.

John was different—the youngest child whose love for his father had never been tainted by his mother's venom.

From now on John would be a favourite of his. He would visit the nursery frequently, and it would not be a duty but a real pleasure. The main reason was that enchanting little creature Alice. A little beauty in the making if he knew anything and from the experience he had had he should know a good deal.

Dear sweet creature, what good she had done him. She had stopped him thinking of the changed attitude of Rosamund and chief of all the murder of Thomas à Becket.

He would be ready to sail for Ireland in August. So far he had kept the papal legates at bay. They would not let the matter rest there he knew. What would they want of him? Some sort of penance he supposed and if he refused to make it—excommunication. It was not good for a King to suffer that. His subjects were superstitious and if they feared that the hand of God was against him they would turn from him and even those who remained loyal would lose heart. He believed that when men went into battle they must be well equipped for the fight, not only materially but spiritually. They must believe in victory if they were to achieve it. This had been one of the firm beliefs of his great-grandfather, William the Conqueror, who insisted on seeing good in omens when other men feared they might be evil. I only believe in omens when they are good ones, his grandfather, Henry I, had said; and he had proved himself to be one of the most astute rulers ever known.

Therefore he wanted no excommunication. But time was a good ally. The longer the delay between the murder and the bringing home of the guilt the better. Passions cooled and as long as there were not too many miracles at the shrine of Canterbury, he could weather this storm as he had so many others.

Ireland now faced him.

He was on his way to Portsmouth when news came to him that the old Bishop of Winchester was sick and thought to be dying, and was asking to see the King.

There was nothing Henry could do but visit the old man; one did not refuse a dying request.

Poor old man! He was indeed in his last extremities. No doubt he was ready to go, for he had been blind for a long time.

He was the brother of Stephen who had usurped the throne which should by rights have belonged to Henry's mother, Matilda; and the Bishop of Winchester had been one of his brother's main props, although there had been a time when he had been so exasperated by Stephen's folly that he had been almost ready to turn to Matilda. That was long ago and wrong had been righted for he, Henry Plantagenet, grandson of King Henry I, was King of England.

He found the Bishop very close to death but he seemed to revive a little when he realized the King had come.

"My lord King is good to answer my last request."

"My dear Bishop, much as I dislike requests from my clergy, I hope it will not be the last from you."

"Ah, you see me, my lord, both frail and full of years, and you can have no doubt—as I have none—that my time is come."

"May God bless your soul, Bishop."

"And yours, my lord. You will know why I wished to see you, why I wished to speak with you before I left this earth for ever. I fear for you, my lord."

"Be of good cheer. I have taken care of myself and my kingdom for many years. Fear not, I shall go on doing so whatever befalls."

"It is what may befall, my lord, which makes me fearful."

"Have you brought me here to utter gloomy prophesies, Bishop?"

"My lord, you know I refer to the murder."

"Few refer to anything else now. I am a little weary of the subject."

"You must be very sick at heart, my lord."

"The Archbishop is dead. Nothing can bring him back. When a man has a kingdom to govern he cannot indulge in prolonged mourning because a subject is no more."

"Thomas was no ordinary subject."

"Archbishop of Canterbury no less, though for some years he preferred to forget it."

"You cannot deceive a dying man, my lord. You are sick at heart and fearful of consequences."

"Why should I be, pray?"

"Because, my lord, you are guilty of murder and that the murder of a saint."

"My lord Bishop you forget to whom you speak."

"I am dying, my lord. Nothing you could do to me now could harm me. I will speak the truth in death."

"Is it not a cowardly thing to do—to say in death that which you feared to say in life?"

"I would say it if I had ten years more left to me. I tremble for you, for you have murdered a saint."

"My lord Bishop," said the King affecting weariness, "my knights misunderstood me. I raged against the man. Who would not? He plagued me. He frustrated me at every turn. I forgave him. I allowed him to return to England after his exile and what did he do? He tried to raise the country against me."

"He did no such thing. That was what his enemies said against him. He was always your friend."

The King was silent for a few moments then he burst out: "I had no part in his death. I did not wish him dead."

"My lord," said the Bishop lifting his hands, "your knights killed the Archbishop because you had led them to believe you wished it. You cannot deny that and you are responsible for his death. I fear your expiation will be terrible."

Hot anger seized the King. He clenched his fist and wanted to crash it into those sightless eyes. But this was a dying man and a terrible fear and remorse quickly overcame his fury. He remained still with his fist raised.

"Repent, my lord," murmured the Bishop. "Ask God's forgiveness for this terrible deed."

The Bishop was suddenly still. The King called out: "Come hither. The Bishop is dying."

He was glad to escape from that chamber of death. He was afraid and fear made him angry.

"Thomas," he muttered, "are you going to haunt me for ever?"

He must escape. He must shut out of his mind memories of Thomas, memories of the dying Bishop.

Normally he would go with all speed to Rosamund; now he

thought the innocence of the children in the royal nursery could appease him better.

When the Kings of Ireland heard that Henry Plantagenet had landed they made haste to swear fealty to him. The chiefs and kings of such places as Waterford, Cork and Limerick were all eager to avoid a war. They trembled before the might of the King of England. They were Celts, tall and elegant men and their complexions were ruddy. Their tunics were of roughly spun wool and their weapons of war were very primitive for they had nothing but swords, short lances and hatchets. Although they were quarrelsome they often appeared to have little heart for a fight; they were passionately fond of music and many of them played the harp. Their houses were of wood and wattle; their country was green and fertile, the climate warm and damp. Henry liked what he saw of it and recalled to his followers that both his grandfather and great-grandfather had planned to conquer the place, but their commitments in England and Normandy had made it impossible for them to do so. Now he, who had ever wider territories to control, was on the point of doing so.

At Waterford he received the homage of the petty princes and arranged that they should pay him a small annual tribute as a token that they accepted him as their suzerain.

It was November by the time he came to Dublin. He took up his headquarters in the wooden palace there; and he sent his two commissioners, Roger de Lacy and William Fitzalden, to parley with Roderick, the King of Connaught, who was the chief of all the petty princes. They met on the banks of the Shannon where Roderick made it very clear that as he considered himself the true ruler of Ireland he had no intention of abdicating in favour of Henry of England.

When Henry received the message he was furious. Everything had gone so smoothly until this time. He would have liked to go into battle immediately to show the little King that he was master, but his soldier's eye saw at once that the mountains were too steep and the weather too wet to enable him to embark on a successful campaign. He cursed Roderick—the only one who had stood out against him—and swore that as soon as the weather changed he would be ready to make him wish he had acted differently.

Christmas came. Henry was not sorry that he must celebrate the festival in Dublin. Time was getting very near to the anniversary of Thomas's death and he knew that in

England and France people would remember. It was as well therefore to be far away at such a time.

Those of the Irish who had decided to accept him as their ruler paid great honour to him. They even built him a palace outside the walls of the city. It was constructed in a very short time and was made of wattle. Henry was very proud of it. There should be a great celebration on Christmas Day, he said, and he would invite all his new and loyal subjects to join him at his table.

Then he set his cooks to produce a magnificent meal such as would impress these people so much that they would talk about it for years to come and Roderick of Connaught would hear of the riches of the new lord of Ireland.

There was merrymaking and much laughter and Henry listened with grave appreciation to his new subjects' songs and performances on the harp.

Shortly after the festivities he arranged that the Bishops of Ireland should swear fealty to him and when this had been done he wrote to the Pope asking Alexander to accept him and his heirs as the rulers of Ireland.

All was going well with the exception of the tiresome Roderick who was constantly affirming his determination to stand against the King. Henry planned to take by force what Roderick would not give him, but the weather was still too treacherous for him to launch a campaign. The wind howled up the river; the rain fell in torrents; it was clear to the most inexperienced soldier that no campaign could be successfully carried out in such conditions.

January passed and February had come, but the weather continued to be against them and there was nothing he could do but wait.

All through March he waited and just as he was preparing to finish Roderick's resistance for ever, ships arrived from England.

They had disturbing news.

On the anniversary of Thomas's death, the pilgrims had streamed into Canterbury. Many of them declared that they were cured of their infirmities at the shrine of the martyr. Everyone was saying that Thomas was a saint.

Worse still the Pope had sent Cardinals Theodwine and Albert to Normandy to find the King.

"Why do they wait in Normandy?" demanded Henry. "Why do they not come to England?"

There was a simple answer to that. They did not come to England because they knew that they would be arrested as a danger to the peace if they set foot there.

Instead they waited for him in Normandy.

"Then they must needs wait," was his answer to that.

"They are saying, my lord, that if you do not go to Normandy with all speed they have the Pope's authority to lay all your lands under edict."

"By God's eyes," muttered the King.

He knew of course that he had to go. If he did not he could lose Normandy.

Thomas was continuing to plague him in death as much as he had done in life—and that was saying a good deal.

He shut himself into his apartments. What must he do? It was more than a year since Thomas's death and the martyrdom was as fresh as ever. Moreover, there were all those miracles at the shrine and he had too many enemies.

He dare not delay. There were many waiting to snatch his lands from him. He could not conquer the whole of Ireland as he had planned. Roderick of Connaught would have to wait.

Leaving Hugh de Lacy behind with a garrison to hold what he had gained he sent messengers to the Cardinals telling them that he was sailing at once for England and would in due course arrive in Normandy.

That Christmas the young King Henry decided to remind everyone at his Court that he was indeed their King. His father had sent him to Normandy when he went to Ireland, where he was to act as a kind of regent. "A regent," stormed Henry to William the Marshall, "why should I be a regent? I am a king in my own right."

William the Marshall, the Earl of Salisbury's nephew, who had held a post of knight-at-arms to young Henry for some years, was his closest friend and companion. "In due course you will be so in every way," he reminded him.

"Not while my father lives, William."

"My lord," answered William, "it is unwise to mention the King's death."

"How can I help mentioning it? It can only be when it happens that I shall be free."

William the Marshall looked over his shoulder fearfully but Henry burst into laughter.

"Have no fear. The people here are my friends."

"A king never knows who are his friends."

"I know that there is not a king in Christendom who has more enemies than my father. His nature is such to arouse enmity."

"I would venture to contradict you, my lord."

"Have a care, William. Remember I am your King."

"And you are my friend also. If I must flatter you as so many do I should cease to be that. What do you wish, my lord, my flattery or my friendship?"

"You know, William."

"I think I do, so I will risk saying that if all men do not love your father there are few who do not respect and fear him; and sometimes it is better for kings to be respected and feared than loved."

"The old man has bemused you with his rages."

"I beg of you, do not speak of him thus. He is your father and our King."

"I am not likely to forget that. But know this, William, he shall not keep me in this state for ever."

"My lord, you are young yet. You have won men's hearts by your nature but you could not afford to stand out against your father."

"I did not say I would do that, William. I merely say that I want to be a king in more than name."

"But there is already a King of England."

Henry sighed. "Come, let us think of other things. This is my first Christmas as King and I intend to celebrate it as such. This Court shall have no doubt about my rank."

"This court, my lord, knows exactly your rank. You are its King, and it is the first time in England's history that she has had two Kings."

"It was my father's wish that it should be so, and he can have no one to blame but himself for it. Come, I am determined that my first Christmas as King shall be remembered for ever, so that people will know how merry life will be when there is only one king in England. And I will tell you something, my friend, when I am King and have a son, a crown shall not be put on his head until I am dead."

William the Marshall was silent, but he wondered, as many had begun to, how Henry II could have made such a major blunder as to have had his son crowned King while he still lived.

"I have it," cried Henry. "I shall invite all the knights, counts and nobles together with men of the church to my banquet. They shall have gifts which will prove to them that

I shall be a generous king. My father is the most parsimonious man alive. He hates giving anything away. He will never relinquish his hold on one castle while he lives. I will show my subjects here how different I shall be. I want to be as different from my father as I can possibly be. I regret that I share his name.

"Would you rather have been a William?"

"That was my eldest brother. There are more Williams in England and Normandy than any other name, I'll swear. They are all named after my great-great-grandfather, William the Conqueror. You are one of them, my friend."

"I'd say there are as many Henrys."

"Nay, William, I'd wager it. I have an idea. At my banquet I shall separate all the Williams and they shall dine with me in one room. No one who is not a William shall sit down with me. Then you and I will count them and see how many Williams are there. I'll wager there will be more than a hundred."

Henry was excited at the prospect and William joined in his enthusiasm, realizing that in planning his Christmas celebrations Henry forgot his enmity towards his father.

He was delighted to discover that there were one hundred and ten knights named William and many of other ranks. He was the only Henry among the Williams who crowded into his chamber. This was called the feast of the Williams.

When his father heard what had happened, he was displeased by what seemed to him childish frivolity. He also heard rumours of his son's growing dissatisfaction with his state and this was more disturbing than his irresponsibility.

Young Henry left for England soon after Christmas. That banquet had been a great success. It was all very well for his friend William the Marshall to tell him to beware of flatterers. He *was* popular, good-looking, charming—all things that his father was not, and what William called flattery was in fact the truth.

When he had been at Bures his mother's uncle, Ralph de Faye, had come to see him bringing with him his friend, Hugh de St. Maure, and they had said what accounts they would take back to his mother of his kingly ways.

He had been enchanted by this kinsman and his friend. They had declared themselves quite shocked by the manner in which his father tried to treat him.

"You might be a child of ten years old by the way the King

behaves towards you," they said. "Why, you are in your seventeenth year. You are a man."

It was true; he was a man and treated like a boy!

"You should make your dissatisfaction known," Ralph told him.

He knew he should. But how? It was all very well to talk about defying his father when he was not there and quite a different matter when one was confronted by him. Young Henry remembered how the face could flush, the eyes seem to start out of their sockets and the terrible fury begin to rise. Any wise man kept away from that.

Still, they were right. Something should be done, but it would have to be more subtle than confrontation with his father and a demand that he be given his rights.

In the meantime he was going to England and that was where he liked best to be because in England he was a king; and when his father was absent he could delude himself into thinking that he ruled the land.

He was not allowed to delude himself for long. He had not been at Westminster more than a month or so when his father arrived.

Face to face with the older Henry the younger lost his courage. It had always been so. Much as he might rage against him to his friends, his father only had to appear and he was immediately subdued.

"I hear," said the King, "that you passed a merry Christmas at Bures."

"I think my . . . our subjects were pleased by the display I gave."

The elder Henry nodded slowly.

"You seem to have a fondness for my Norman subjects. That is well because we are leaving shortly for Normandy."

"We . . ." stammered young Henry.

"I said we, by which I mean you and I."

"You will need me to stay in England while you are in Normandy."

"My justiciary Richard de Luci has my complete trust."

"Father, I would rather stay here. I have had my fill of Normandy."

The King raised his eyebrows and his son was alarmed to see the familiar tightening of the lips and flash of eyes which warned any who beheld it that they must be wary, for those were the danger signals.

"I thought you would wish me . . ." began young Henry.

"I have told you what I wish. You will be ready to leave for Normandy. I desire your company there, my son."

"Yes, my lord," said the young King quietly.

This was humiliating. Henry secretly raged against the Pope. He had to keep himself under control. He was in a very tricky position. That he, Henry Plantagenet, should be summoned to meet the papal legates was insulting. Yet what could he do? He must act very carefully or the whole world would be against him.

He would have to deal very subtly with those emissaries of the Pope and he wanted to be completely free of anxieties while he did so. Ireland was safe he believed, even though it was not yet fully conquered. He himself would be in Normandy. Eleanor was in Aquitaine; and he was certainly not going to leave young Henry in England. He would have to be watchful of that young man. He was beginning to see what a great mistake he had made in crowning him king. Why had he done it? To spite Thomas à Becket. To have the boy crowned by Roger of York. Yes, it had been done partly to humilate Thomas à Becket. Thomas . . . it always came back to Thomas!

Now he needed some comfort before he left for Normandy and he would go to Rosamund.

He thought there seemed something lacking in her pleasure. She was as deferential as ever, as determined to please and yet there was a certain sadness about her.

He awoke in the night and felt the weight of his trials heavy upon him. He stroked her hair and kissed her into wakefulness.

"My Rosamund," he said, "I doubt I was ever in such a position as I now find myself."

She was wide awake at once, ready to listen, to offer comfort.

"Before I gained the kingdom which was mine by right I had very little but my hopes. I was sure then of my success. Then I achieved it and my troubles began. It is the fate of Kings of England ever since the Conqueror. Our lands are too far flung for us to be able to keep them in order. This I accepted. I knew that any moment I must hurry to Normandy to subdue this or that traitor, and then come back to England because I was needed here. But never was I summoned before."

"Can you not refuse to go?"

"I would have the whole of Christendom rise against me. I

would to God these miracles at Canterbury would stop. I do not believe in them. They are a fabrication of my enemies."

He was aware that Rosamund shuddered. Even she had changed since the death of Thomas à Becket.

"You believe that, Rosamund?"

She was silent.

God's eyes, he thought. Even she believes Thomas is a saint and I am guilty of his murder.

He sat up and looked at her in the faint light of the crescent moon. Beautiful Rosamund whom he had loved for years, and been faithful to in his way, even she thought him guilty.

"How could I have known that those stupid knights would take me literally?"

Still she was silent.

"Why do you not speak, Rosamund?" he asked.

"What do you wish me to say, my lord?"

"I wish you to say what is in your mind, not to utter words which I should put into your mouth."

She raised herself and wound her arms about his neck.

"Then I would say, my lord, that in Normandy you should admit that these men thought they were acting on your wishes."

"All the world knows that already."

"And that you would give a great deal to undo what is done and that you take responsibility for this fearful crime."

"I . . . take responsibility!"

"If you do this, they will ask some penance. And when it is made then you will have expiated your sin in behaving as you did."

He looked at her in dismay. She was saying what the rest of the world was saying about him. He had wanted her to cling to him and to tell him how he was maligned, that he was completely and unquestionably innocent.

He was disappointed.

She knew it.

He looked down at her and saw that there were tears on her cheeks.

"I am afraid," she said.

"Of what?" he demanded.

"Of sin."

"Sin?" he cried. "What means that?"

"You and I," she answered. "You have a Queen and I have lived with you as your wife. I have your sons who were born in sin."

45

"By God's teeth and eyes, Rosamund, what has happened to you?"

She answered: "It has long been in my mind and since the murder . . ."

He turned away impatiently and lay staring into space.

She closed her eyes, for she felt that something had gone for ever out of their relationship.

The King rode away. His thoughts were of Rosamund, which relieved him of thinking what lay ahead in Normandy.

She had changed. Before, she had no other thought than for him. He had needed her and she was there. Now she was concerned with her soul. Something had entered her life which was more important than he was. He would not have believed that possible from his gently devoted Rosamund.

And this had happened at the moment when he needed her most. She had failed him. Soon she would be talking of going into a convent. Women like Rosamund thought of that when they reached a certain age just as men went on crusades or pilgrimages to the Holy Land. He could never do that. He had too much to keep him where he was.

He understood Rosamund. He loved her; she had brought him great joy and comfort; but it was inevitable that in due course such a good woman would contemplate her sinful life and regret it.

He sighed. The subject was almost as depressing as what awaited him in Normandy. He would turn his thoughts to other matters. Soon he must take John from his nursery and get him betrothed, but that must wait. He would go along though and see how the children were progressing. It would be a pleasure to see young John and his sister Joanna . . . and of course little Alice.

He found Alice alone in the schoolroom.

"My lord." She started up when she saw him and curtsied while the deep colour flooded her cheeks.

"So you are alone?" he said, and an excitement gripped him. She was more enchanting than he had imagined.

"Joanna and John are riding. I stayed behind. I had a lesson to complete."

"And how goes this lesson?" he asked. He picked her up in his arms and kissed her. "Alice, you are a witch," he said.

"Oh, no, my lord." She looked frightened.

"I mean that you bewitch me with your beauty."

She looked frightened.

He walked with her to the window seat and sat down holding her on his knee.

"How old are you, little Alice?" he asked.

"I shall soon have seen twelve winters, my lord."

" 'Tis a charming age. I have seen many more winters than that."

Twelve! he was thinking. Some girls were mature enough at twelve.

"And you are to be my daughter. I begin to feel sorry for that."

She still looked frightened. "If I have offened in some way, sir . . ."

"Oh, yes," he said, "you have offended me, Alice, because since I saw you last I have thought of you constantly."

"If you will tell me where my fault lies . . ."

"It lies in these pretty curls, this soft skin, these inviting lips which make me want to kiss them like this . . . Alice."

"Oh, my lord."

"Yes, and oh, my lady! Alice I would that you were not affianced to my son. If you were not, by God's eyes I would ask your father that you might be affianced to me."

Her eyes opened very wide. "How could that be, my lord?"

" 'Tis not impossible."

"But . . ."

"Oh, you have not yet seen twelve years out and I have seem many more. But years are of no matter. You would find me a very loving husband."

"But you have a Queen, my lord. Richard's mother."

"Kings have been known to rid themselves of queens whom they do not love."

"Do you not then love the Queen?"

"I hate the Queen, Alice. I hate her as much as I am beginning to love you."

He watched her steadily. She was not frightened now. She was becoming excited. He tried to stem his rising desire. He could not. She was a child. She was betrothed to Richard and she was the daughter of the King of France. Even he could not sport with a king's daughter as he would a kitchen wench. There had been girls as young as this one—though he had always had more pleasure from mature women. He did not know when he felt so delighted in anyone—not since he had first seen Rosamund. And she had not been much older than Alice. Rosamund had displeased him; she had failed him in a way that he had never expected she would.

"Alice," he said, "if I loved you, do you think you could love me?"

"I must," she said, "because you are Richard's father and will be mine."

"Nay I meant not as a father."

"How so, my lord?"

Was that a little coquetry he saw in her eyes? If it were so, if this innocence was a little feigned his resolutions would crumble; he would act first and think after. Louis would much rather his daughter were Queen of England than Duchess of Aquitaine which was all she would be if she were married to Richard.

He put his face against hers and his hand was on her budding breast. "Does it please you to be so fondled?"

"Why yes, my lord."

"And that I should be the fondler?"

"Yes, my lord."

"I, rather than any other?"

She nodded.

"Why so?"

"Because you are the King and our lord and master."

"A right goodly answer," he said with a laugh. "And would you be ready to obey me in all things?"

"Yes, my lord."

"And do all that I ask of you?"

"But yes."

"Alice," he whispered, "methinks you are a wise little girl. You know something of the ways of the world, do you?"

"A little, my lord."

"And would know more I warrant. Alice, I am going to be your tutor."

When he had seduced her in a gentle and expert manner his conscience worried him a little. But he soon stilled it by reminding himself that he would look after the child. He would definitely see if he could divorce Eleanor and if he could he would make Alice his wife. Her innocence was delightful; it was not going to be difficult to make her adore him. He would teach her as he had taught Rosamund and if he married her—which he might well do—she need have no qualms about her sins. And if he did not, well then in due course she would go to Richard.

But he did not want to think of her belonging to anyone but himself.

He loved his little trusting Alice. She was just what he

needed at this time; he could forget the ordeal which was awaiting him. He could forget frustrations, irritations and the anxiety which was beginning to grow within him about his sons.

"My darling Alice," he whispered to her on parting, "this is our secret. Tell no one what has taken place between us. I trust you. And one day soon you shall be my Queen and I will put a crown on your head and we shall go everywhere together."

She was ecstatic with wonder. He was so powerful, so clever. She had not liked what she had seen of Richard very much. But the King would save her from that marriage. Of course he would. He was going to marry her himself.

The King and Queen

The King set out for Normandy accompanied by his son who made little effort to disguise his displeasure. The boy was distinctly sullen, but his father's thoughts were occupied with too many other matters to concern himself greatly with young Henry.

He could not stop thinking of the adorable Alice and what a pleasure it would be to get back to her. He would take her from the nursery and install her in the palace. There would have to be some secrecy of course. He had to think of Rosamund to whom he was still devoted; but Rosamund must know that he could not have married her even if he divorced Eleanor, although he had once contemplated this and mentioned it to her. Perhaps he had been wrong in that and it was due to this that she had become obsessed by the idea that she was living in sin. He remembered tenderly so many aspects of their relationship. He still needed Rosamund but he wanted Alice with an intense desire which could not be held in check. Alice, daughter of old Louis, King of France! That old monk! It amused him really. Alice—conceived not in passion but because of the duty to France to get a child. And this perfect creature had been produced for his pleasure. If I made her Queen of England Louis would not object. Only Eleanor stood in his way. It might well be that Eleanor would like to marry again. She had always been a very energetic woman. What was she doing in Aquitaine surrounded by her troubadours? How many of them did she take to her bed? Women like Eleanor were never too old.

There were other less pleasant matters to take his mind off a future shared with an eager-to-please Alice minus sour Eleanor and a docile understanding Rosamund in the background of his life.

No sooner had he landed in Normandy than messages arrived from those Cardinals Theodwine and Albert to the effect that they were waiting for him at the Monastery of Savigny.

In ill humour so that all men feared to approach him lest he fly into a temper over the slightest fault, the King rode to the monastery. That he, the King of England, should be so summoned was inconceivable. And yet not so. He had to face the fact that the Pope was more powerful in Christendom than the King of England. Was that not what the quarrel between himself and Thomas à Becket had been about?

Inwardly he cursed the Pope, as coldly he greeted the Cardinals. He had come far, he told them irritably, and at great inconvenience, to see them. He had been engaged on an important campaign in Ireland. Out of respect for and honour to His Holiness he had come, but he would like them to state what it was the Pope wished of him without delay for matters of importance demanded his attention.

"This," Cardinal Theodwine told him, "is of the utmost importance, my lord King. It concerns not your temporal power but the very existence of your soul."

Henry was a little shaken. He never doubted for a moment that he could outride any earthly storm, but the thought of the unknown could arouse fear in most men; and living the life he did how could he be sure that he might not any day come face to face with death? It was never far from the battlefield and a King might become a victim of the assassin's lance or arrow at a moment's notice. Every night retiring to his bed, he would be justified in fearing that he might never see the light of day.

Thomas had been cut down in the full flush of spiritual glory. A curse on Thomas! There was no escape from him.

"What will be required of me?" he growled.

"It would be necessary to perform some penance."

"Penance! I! For what reason? Do you hold me guilty of this murder?"

"Those who did the deed were your men. They acted on your orders."

"I gave no such orders, nor shall I permit it to be said that I did."

"My lord, it will be necessary for you to swear to that."

"Necessary! Who makes such rules? You forget, sir, that you speak to the King of England."

"We act on the instructions of His Holiness the Pope."

"I tell you I am master here."

"We come from the spiritual master of us all," answered the Cardinals.

"I would remind you that these are my lands and you would be well advised to remember it."

He was fighting to control his temper. He could feel the blood rushing to his head.

Cardinal Albert said: "We will leave you, my lord, to consider what must be done. We will confer again tomorrow."

In the chamber they had set aside for him he clenched his fists and bit them until they were red and blue with his teeth marks.

"By God's arms, eyes and teeth!" he cried. "Thomas, you will not let me rest. I would to God I had never seen you. Why could you not have died in your bed?"

He was too wise and shrewd to believe he could defy the Pope. If he did, as soon as he left Normandy the rebellions would start. He would have to stay here to hold them in check. And what would be happening in England while he did that? He had his enemies there. Excommunication, a loss of his lands. No, he must be wise. There was nothing for it. He must give way.

It was in a chastened mood that he met the Cardinals on the next day.

"Well," he cried, "what is it you desire of me?"

"We desire this, my lord. You must hold the Holy Gospels in your hand while you swear that you did not order nor wish the death of Thomas à Becket, Archbishop of Canterbury."

Henry was thoughtful. Of course he had wished it. Who would not have wished the death of a man who caused so much trouble? He had demanded of his knights why they did not rid him of the tiresome cleric. But, he assured himself, I did not wish the *murder* of Thomas. He was my dear friend, and I would to God he had not been so brutally killed in the Cathedral.

He took the gospels in his hands. It's true, Thomas, he thought. I would we were together again as we used to be when we roamed the countryside together. I always wanted that. It was only when you became my Archbishop that there was this trouble between us.

They were demanding of him some sort of penance. Why, if he had no part in the murder? It was easier to grant what they asked than to swear on the holy book.

"My lord, the Pope asks that you support two hundred knights for the defence of Jerusalem for a year."

"I will do this," said Henry. It was always simple to promise money for there were invariably so many reasons why such promises could not be kept.

"You will allow appeals to be made freely to the Pope."

Now they were tampering with the Constitutions of Clarendon over which he and Thomas had quarrelled. Well, if it must be, it must. He would have to extricate himself from this unpleasant affair as quickly as possible and get on with the important business of safeguarding his realm.

"You must restore the possessions of the See of Canterbury so that they are as they were before the Archbishop left England."

"Yes," he agreed.

Finally, English Bishops must not be asked to take the Oath he had demanded of them at Clarendon; and those who had taken it must be freed from any obligation to keep it.

He must put an end to this humiliating situation. He must make his peace with the Pope.

He could have murdered those Cardinals. He could have gone into battle against the Pope. But he was not called the most shrewd king in Europe for nothing. He knew when concessions had to be made and this was one of those occasions.

He had settled the matter, he believed once and for all.

And Thomas, my beloved friend and hated enemy, you in your shrine at Canterbury have defeated the King of England on his throne. The battle is over, Thomas, and I can say with truth that I wish with all my heart that it had never been necessary to indulge in it.

He left Savigny with rising spirits. He was free of Thomas.

There was news from Eleanor. Richard was now of an age to be officially declared Duke of Aquitaine, and she believed that the ceremony of establishing him as such should no longer be delayed.

He agreed with her. Let Richard be the acknowledged Duke of Aquitaine. When he considered what he had done to Richard's betrothed it soothed his conscience a little to agree readily to his acquisition of Aquitaine. Eleanor was for once pleased with him, and when they met at Poitiers she was quite gracious to him.

Richard viewed him with suspicion. It was almost as though he knew how his father had betrayed him with Alice. But no, Richard had always disliked him and he had always disliked Richard. It seemed strange that a man could feel so about such a good-looking son of such promise, for Richard excelled in horsemanship, swordsmanship and chivalry far more than any of his brothers. He was a poet too, so perhaps it was because he was very much his mother's son that his father could not like him.

With the thought of Alice always in his mind now he liked him even less as he must one whom he had wronged so deeply, for if he were completely honest he could not rid himself of the thought that it might be neccessary for Alice to be Richard's bride after all. He would delay it as long as possible. In any case it was a matter about which he did not wish to think.

It was a grand ceremony at Poitiers where this fifteen-year-old golden boy took the abbot's seat in the Abbey of Saint-Hilaire where he accepted the lance and banner of the Dukes of Aquitaine, the insignia of his new office.

How the people cheered! And Eleanor looked on, softened for once by her affection and pride in this favourite of all her sons.

"The people love him," she told Henry exultantly; and she added slyly: "He is no foreigner to them. He belongs to Aquitaine."

Which was a reminder that they had never accepted Henry Plantagenet as their Duke but had taken him on sufferance merely because he was the husband of their Duchess.

Never mind. Let her gloat. She would learn in time who was the master. Once he had divorced her . . . Was it possible? He was already framing his apologies to Rosamund. "I must marry Alice, Alice is royal. It is necessary politically for me to marry the daughter of the King of France."

But first he must rid himself of Eleanor. He wondered how she would react to the suggestion.

In the meantime there was the occasion of Richard's crowning as Duke. Then next a ceremony was to take place at Limoges where he would receive the ring of St. Valerie, which was held sacred as it was said to have belonged to the city's patron saint.

There with the ring on his finger, the handsome golden-haired boy received, at the altar of the cathedral, the sword and spurs according to the ancient orders of chivalry.

To see him standing there in his silk tunic, the golden crown on his head and the banner of Aquitaine in his hands, Eleanor was more deeply moved than she had been for many years; and she saw in this young man the highest hopes for his future and her own.

And beside her stood her husband—coarse, ugly in comparison with his handsome son. And she revelled in the hatred she bore this man whom once she had loved and who had dared in the early years of their marriage, when she had been prepared to offer him her undivided love, to betray her with any light woman who came his way.

My pride and your lechery have broken this marriage, she thought. They have made enemies of us and by God and his Saints, I swear, Henry Plantagenet, that I shall not rest until I have destroyed you and set up my sons in your place.

After the crowning of Richard as Duke of Aquitaine Henry made his way back to Normandy and on the way called on the King of France.

Louis was some fourteen years older than Henry and looked his age, yet a certain dignity had come with the years. He had grown accustomed to wearing the crown of France which in his youth he had accepted so reluctantly. He had fathered several children: Marie and Alix by Eleanor before the divorce which had made it possible for her to marry Henry; by his second wife Constance, Marguerite, who was married to young Henry, and another girl named Alice who had died young; by his third wife Adela he had had his only son, Philip, the delectable Alice who was now Henry's mistress, and Agnes.

Only one son and all those daughters, thought Henry, but daughters were good bargaining counters. Louis should be pleased, for was not his daughter Marguerite a prospective Queen of England and nothing would please the King more than if Louis's daughter Alice were to be one, too.

The rift between Louis and Henry, which had been widened by the quarrel with Thomas à Becket, had by Henry's show of penitence been partially removed. Louis received the King with honours.

They did not mention the Archbishop but Henry knew what Louis's feelings were on that matter. Hadn't he given shelter to Thomas in his realm and done everything to provoke the King of England by the attention he paid to his rebel priest?

Louis had not done this out of spite towards Henry. He merely had a natural indulgence towards anyone connected with the Church and for that reason he had supported Thomas against the King. Louis had wanted to be a monk and by God's eyes, thought Henry, it would not have been a bad thing if he had been, except of course that if he had been he would never have sired the charming Alice. No, no, it was better that Louis should have been forced out of the pious life he craved by the death of his brother.

How much enmity did Louis still bear towards him for having taken his wife? Doubtless, thought Henry grimly, he was glad to be rid of her. He himself would be glad to be rid of her now. But that had happened many years ago and here they were two kings, natural enemies in a way because Louis must always resent the fact that Henry was lord of a greater part of France than he was himself since his marriage, and Henry could not forget that for the lands he possessed in France he must pay homage to the King of that country.

Normandy, Anjou, Maine, Aquitaine, Brittany, they were all vassal states of the King of France and even though he was their ruler (though his sons were nominally so) still he must swear fealty to Louis.

They were wary with each other and talked of State affairs. But at length Louis began to complain because, although Henry's son had been crowned King of England, Louis's daughter Marguerite, who was the wife of young Henry, had never been accorded this honour.

"What means this?" he asked. "Is it that you do not regard my daughter as the young King's wife?"

"It is nothing of the sort. I have always said she shall be crowned at a convenient moment and crowned she shall be."

"Then why has this coronation not taken place?"

"Because the moment has not been ripe."

"I see not why this should be."

Henry surveyed Louis—father of his dear little Alice. What would Louis say if he told him that he loved his young daughter, the betrothed of his son Richard, that he had already deflowered the girl and was determined to keep her as his mistress and if possible marry her?

He laughed inwardly at the thought and at the memory of that lovely childish form.

"It shall be as you wish," said Henry. "I will send the young people to England without delay. Henry shall be crowned again and this time Marguerite with him."

Louis nodded. The King of England was in an acquiescing mood.

"I should like the Archbishop Rotrou to accompany them to England and perform the ceremony."

"My dear brother, a foreign Archbishop to perform such a ceremony. It has never been done."

"The alternative would be Roger of York would it not?"

"Roger of York crowned my son."

"He was a traitor to the Archbishop of Canterbury," said Louis firmly. "I would not wish my daughter to be crowned by one who had played false such a great good man."

Henry was silent; his fingers had begun to twitch. So this one-time monk, this husband of Eleanor at whom she had jeered in the first days of her marriage to Henry, this rival King would tell him how to run his kingdom! By God's eyes . . . he thought and then: But he *is* the father of my little Alice. I must go carefully. When I divorce Eleanor and openly take Alice to my bed I shall need the support of her father.

"I would not wish Roger of York even to attend the ceremony," went on Louis. "Nor the Bishops of London and Salisbury. They were all enemies of the saintly Archbishop and did much to bring about his sorrowful end. In my eyes they would contaminate any ceremony they attended."

Thinking of little Alice Henry said: "It shall be as you wish. The young people shall be crowned and the ceremony performed by Archbishop Rotrou."

Louis was a little taken aback. He had expected protests. There was a subtle change in Henry. It is because of the death of the martyr, thought Louis. He is truly penitent.

Henry went on to Normandy and the young couple sailed for England for their crowning.

Henry had decided that he would spend the coming Christmas in Chinon in Anjou for he was making a complete tour of his dominions to assure himself that his fortresses were at full strength. He sent a message to Eleanor asking her to join him for Christmas at Chinon. He thought he might sound her as to the possibility of a divorce.

She expressed willingness and he decided that this should be a family gathering. He wanted to give the impression that he had done what he could to keep his family together.

Henry and Marguerite should join them too. A message was accordingly sent to them commanding them to make their preparations to leave at once.

The young King was angry. He liked being in England where he was the King, and where life was particularly enjoyable when his father was not present. It seemed an admirable arrangement for his father to stay in Normandy while he governed England. He was surrounded by sycophants who assured him that England could not have a better King and he believed them. He was fond of Marguerite; she was a pleasant little Queen and he liked to ride out with her beside him and listen to the acclaim of the people. Young monarchs were always so appealing.

But to go to Chinon and be under the shadow of his father was the last thing he wanted.

"I shall not go," he told Marguerite, but of course he had to change his mind. His friends told him how unwise it would be to disobey his father.

"I'm not a King," he complained to Marguerite. "I just have a crown, that's all. Can you imagine my father's giving away any little power? But he won't always be here. He'll go off one day with all his sins on him when he's in one of those tempers of his. Men have fallen down dead when they are in such a state as he gets into. I don't think it will be long now, Marguerite."

Marguerite was sure it wouldn't.

There came another message from the King. His good friend the King of France, he wrote, had expressed a desire to see his daughter, so the young couple must leave without delay and before they came to Chinon they must stay a while at the Court of France.

"I should like to see my fahter," said Marguerite.

Young Henry was secretly pleased. He could pretend he was not really obeying his father in leaving at once but gratifying his wife's whim to see her father.

And so they left England as soon as the winds were fair enough and most joyfully did Louis receive them at his court which at that time he was holding at Chartres.

Louis loved his children dearly. He asked news of little Alice.

"Poor child," he said, "she is young to be brought up in a strange land."

"We all suffer it, my lord," answered Marguerite, for indeed she herself had been brought up in the same foreign court, although much of her time had been spent in Aquitaine with Queen Eleanor.

Louis nodded. " 'Tis the lot of royal princes and princesses. Tell me did you see the child before you left?"

"I did see her, Father. She seemed happy enough."

"Thank God. Soon she will have her wedding day. She is almost ready."

"Yes, and Richard is very handsome I believe. Not so much so as Henry, but he is very good-looking."

"And you are happy with your young Henry, my child?"

"Yes, Father."

"And when Alice is Duchess of Aquitaine she will not seem so far from me. Your husband seems not very pleased with his lot, Marguerite."

"His father angers him gravely. He treats him as a boy."

"Is that so?" Louis smiled faintly. He could not help liking to hear criticism of Henry Plantagenet. Deep down in his heart he had always borne a grudge against him for taking Eleanor. Life had been more peaceful without her, but he often thought of the first time he had seen her. What a beautiful young woman she had been! And what vivacity she had had! She had been so clever. Half the Court had been in love with her. He sighed. He should have known he would never keep her. She had not been faithful to him. How long before she had deceived him? Was her uncle the first on that never to be forgotten journey to the Holy Land? And the Saracen? Had she really contemplated marrying him? He would never forget the shock she had given him when she had demanded a divorce. The Pope had persuaded her against it then but when she saw Henry Plantagenet she had fallen so deeply in love with him that she had determined to marry him.

Henry had only been Duke of Normandy then and as the owner of Aquitaine she had been richer than he was. Henry was nearly twelve years her junior. Strange that she, so fastidious, taking such care with her appearance, setting the fashions, caring for her body with unguents and perfumes should have become so wildly enamoured of rather stocky Henry who wore his clothes for convenience rather than ornament and never bothered to wear gloves when he went out in the most bitter weather so that his hands were red and chapped. Of course he had a power, a strength which Louis completely lacked. He had charm too, particularly for women. He emanated strength and power. He supposed that was what they liked.

But the two Kings were inherent enemies. There could scarcely be any other relationship between them. Any Duke of Normandy must almost certainly be at odds with the King of France. The Franks had never forgiven the Vikings for raiding their land and making things so unpleasant for their ancestors that to stop their sailing up the Seine to Paris they had been bought off with that northern province which was called Normandy. That went back to the days of Rollo but it rankled still. There was one thing to be grateful for; the Dukes of Normandy like the Counts of other provinces had remained vassals of the King of France.

And this descendant of the Norman Dukes—this Henry Plantagenet—had taken his wife as ruthlessly as Rollo had taken a piece of France; Louis was not a vindictive man, but he would not be displeased to see Henry brought low. Moreover he was deeply shocked by his treatment of Thomas of Canterbury.

Had such a man been my subject, thought Louis, I would have counted myself indeed fortunate.

Now he listened to the complaints of young Henry and Marguerite.

"Your father has made you a king," he said. "Why did he do that, if he had no intention of allowing you to behave like one?"

"I believe he did it to spite Thomas à Becket."

"My dear son, you should not say such a thing."

"But it is true, my lord. He hated Thomas. He would have done anything to discountenance him."

Louis shook his head and crossed himself. "May that great saint bless us all and intercede for us with God," he said.

"I loved him well," remarked Henry, and he was trying not to remember that he had refused to see Thomas when he had wanted to call on him because he had acted on the advice of Roger of York.

"All good men loved him," said Louis.

They were silent for a while, thinking of Thomas.

"It is the greatest tragedy that ever befell England," went on Louis, "and no good will come of it."

"I thank God that I had no part in his murder," said Henry fervently.

"There are others, I doubt not, who wish they might say the same. Well, my son, you have your troubles, have you not?"

"Yes, and I fear I shall continue to. But I will not be treated as a child for ever."

"Nor should you be. Your father should give you complete control over England if he wishes to stay in Normandy, or over Normandy if he wishes to dwell in England."

"So say I, but he will not do that."

"And will you endure this?"

"No," cried Henry firmly, "I will not." But when he thought of his father's face, eyes narrowed, colour flaming under his skin, he knew in his heart that he was going to find it very difficult—and very likely impossible—to stand out against him.

"You must tell him what is in your heart," said Louis.

"Yes," answered Henry, feeling that that was more easily said than done. "I fear he will not listen though."

"He must. You are no longer a child. You are a man; you have a wife; soon you will have sons. And your father made you King."

"I will ask him," said Henry. "I will tell him exactly what I feel."

"And if he will not agree, you should not stay at his Court, for what good can you do there? If you are to be given no authority what matters it whether you are there or not?"

"Where should I go?"

"Where should you go but to the home of your father-in-law. If the King of England continues to treat you as a child and will not listen to your arguments, come to me here. I fancy that might put him in the mood to do something."

Henry seized the hand of his father-in-law and kissed it fervently.

Louis was right. If his father would not respect him then revolt was the answer.

The King and Queen had arrived by their separate ways at the castle of Chinon, there to spend Christmas. With the Queen came her son Richard, the new Duke of Aquitaine, and his younger brother Geoffrey, the Duke of Brittany. Young Henry and Marguerite were on their way to join them.

Eleanor and Henry took stock of each other. She has aged, thought the King. By God's eyes she is an old woman now. He was comparing everyone with the tender youth of Alice. But he must admit there was still some quality about Eleanor. No one was quite as elegant and regal as Eleanor and never would be. She could marry again mayhap if they were divorced. Her child-bearing days were over though, so she could not bring heirs to a new husband. And Richard was now the Duke of Aquitaine.

Eleanor thought: He has grown older, toughened even

more than before by events and weather. Thomas's death shook him, for somewhere in his flinty heart there was a spark of love for that man.

Once it had been so strong that she had accused him of loving the man unnaturally. Henry had laughed at that, for if ever there was a man who wanted women that man was Henry; yet she had noticed that he was a little thoughtful. We do not all know ourselves, she thought, not even you, Henry Plantagenet, who think yourself almighty.

She had determined that the Christmas should be passed in great revelry. It was not often nowadays that the King and Queen of England were together. She had brought with her the finest of her poets and musicians and had ordered them to devise an entertainment which should surpass all others. Henry was not completely immune to the charms of literature. There had been a time when he and she had been in harmony and he had enjoyed good literature and music almost as much as she did. But when her influence had been removed he had thought less of the artistic way of life; he had become absorbed in the need to conquer and of course indulge his lechery.

Yet at this Christmas she would try to remember the good times they had had together. In the early days of their marriage she had doted on him. She had wished to see him supreme; she had been proud to have him crowned Duke of Aquitaine. But how their marriage had soured! It had started when he brought the bastard to her nursery and she knew that in those early days of their life together he had been unfaithful to her.

Well it was all in the past and love had turned to hatred, for hate him she did. She hated him for being able to beget children which she could not conceive. Of course she had had a good start of him. Almost twelve years his senior. Well, she was not too old to hate and it amused her to see how this great man was in so many ways a fool.

His children either disliked him mildly or hated him fiercely. Richard, of course, had always had a fiery resentment against him. She had engendered that. Richard was her dearest one and he must think as she did. Geoffrey listened to his brother and was beginning to see his father as a tyrant. And now Henry the eldest was growing restive. My dear husband, she thought, what a fool you were to crown Henry! You should have known that there is room only for one king in one kingdom.

Henry and Marguerite joined them the day before Christmas and Eleanor immediately detected the smouldering resentment in her eldest son.

She took him to her chamber as soon as she could and when they were alone asked him how he had found the King of France.

"Very well and friendly towards me," answered Henry. "And willing to be more friendly."

"So should he be. Are you not his son through your marriage with his daughter?"

"I found him kind and sympathetic."

Eleanor laughed. "It would seem, my son, that you are drawing comparisons. You found him more kind and sympathetic than your own father, eh?"

"I did," he answered defiantly. "My father regards me as a child."

"Oh 'tis not that. He is a man who can never take his hands from that which they have once grasped. You will never be anything but a pawn in his game, Henry, I can tell you that. That is what he would wish us all to be."

"I will never accept that."

"Nor should you. You should speak to your father."

"I know, but it is difficult. He is so fierce. He has such power."

"He wants you to fear him. He want us all to fear him."

"You do not, I know."

"I never did. And I should like my sons to be the same."

"He has such power and his rages are terrible. When he is in one of them he could order anything to be done to us."

"It's true. Methinks sometimes he uses his rages in an attempt to cow us all."

"Except you, my lady."

"I was Duchess of Aquitaine when he was only Duke of Normandy. Perhaps that was why he was so anxious to marry me. I know him well. He will never *give* you what you want, Henry."

"Then am I to remain as I am until he dies?"

"Unless you take what you want."

"How so?"

"Sons have done it before now!"

"It would mean . . . war . . . war against my father! Is that what you mean?"

"I do not mean that you should go straight from here and gather together an army. Though doubtless you could do that

63

for he has his enemies . . . many of them. I mean that you should think of these things. He will not give you what is yours by right. Well then, you could think carefully—and be in no great hurry—of how you could best take it."

"You are right, my lady," cried Henry. "You have given me great hope. You and the King of France."

"The King of France would be a very powerful ally," said the Queen. "You should remember that."

Henry and Eleanor had separate apartments at Chinon and during the sojourn there, they had had little time for private conversation but there were two matters on which the King wished to speak to her. One was straightforward; the formal betrothal of their son John to Alice, daughter of the Count of Maurienne, after which ceremony the little girl would be taken to England to be brought up there. The other he must approach in a subtle manner. That was the possibility of a divorce.

It was soon agreed that they should lose no time in bringing about the betrothal of John and arrangements should be put in hand so that this could take place in early February.

There remained that other matter.

The King approached it uneasily. "We have seen very little of each other of late, Eleanor," he began.

"Do not tell me that is something you regret for I shall not believe you."

"I fancy that it is not a matter which has caused you great grief."

"I could not deny it with truth," she answered. "In fact I have considered myself well rid of you."

"Then I think we are of one mind. Our marriage can no longer be fruitful on account of your age."

"And perhaps of yours?"

"Oh come, Eleanor, you know·I am twelve years younger than you."

"And doubtless have sons and daughters preparing to be born all over your kingdom."

"There might be a few. But let us not waste time in senseless vituperation. You and I no longer have need of each other. Our marriage is at an end. We shall never again share a bed."

"A particular article of furniture on which you set great store."

"It is a necessary part of marriage. The procreation of children. What else is marriage for?"

"And when one partner is beyond child-bearing she is to be discarded. Is that what you are saying?"

"Discarded! I used no such word. I want us to look at this sensibly."

"Then please say outright what you mean."

"It is this. There may be someone whom you would like to marry."

"And there is without doubt someone whom *you* would like to marry." Eleanor burst into loud laughter. "I know the lady well. Your fair Rosamund. That's it, is it not? Her youth too will pass ... is passing. And then you must find someone even younger, must you not? Rosamund. Foolish simpering Rosamund! She never raised her voice against you, did she? You liked that. Every woman—and man—must applaud you. Everywhere you go, you must be treated not as a king but as a god. And now you would marry Rosamund. Is that what you want? You would legitimize her bastards and mayhap try to set them up above my sons. That, my lord, is something I shall never agree to. So put marriage out of your mind. I shall never allow a divorce."

He was faintly relieved that she had no inkling of his relationship with young Alice. Most certainly she had not, for if she had she would never have been able to keep it to herself. She would have burst out with it, and doubtless made trouble. What trouble she could make! The betrothed of Richard! The daughter of Louis! What had he done! No sooner had he extricated himself from the trouble over Thomas à Becket's murder than he had seduced the not yet twelve-year-old daughter of the King of France.

But Eleanor was right. He did think that there was one set of rules for him and another for the rest of the world.

He was the King of England and controlled large areas of the Continent. He would do what he wished and none should dare condemn him.

But he had had to humiliate himself over Thomas and he had seduced the daughter of the King of France.

He must be very careful for it was clear that Eleanor would never divorce him, which meant that he could never make little Alice his wife.

Castles for John

In Montferrand in the Auvergne, Count Humbert of Maurienne had arrived with little Alice who was to be betrothed to Prince John, and there, the little six-year-old Prince, who had arrived from England, was formally betrothed to the Count's daughter.

It was a charming ceremony. Henry felt quite tender towards his youngest son. This one's mind had not been poisoned by his mother. It shall be different with John, Henry promised himself. He was delighted with the arrangement when he considered the fine dowry, John's bride was bringing him and all for a payment of five thousand marks ... and this to be paid in instalments, the last of which would not be due until the marriage.

Henry was extending his Empire far and wide.

There was one discordant note. After the ceremony there were to be celebrations in several towns, for Henry wished everyone to know what good this marriage would bring by giving his family control of more provinces. They were to spend a few days at Limoges and it was while they were there that Count Humbert began to ask himself what John was bringing to his daughter. It was true that young Alice would have the King's son for a bridegroom and that King the most powerful in Europe, but John had three elder brothers who had already been promised the cream of his father's possessions. His fears had been roused when he had heard the youthful bridegroom referred to as John Lackland.

Being a forthright man he decided to speak to the King about this matter.

"You have not yet told me, my lord, what possessions your son John will bring to the marriage."

Henry was silent for a few moments. He was thinking: The ceremony has been performed. He cannot withdraw now. But he could. How often had betrothals taken place and there had been no marriage!

He had no doubt that Humbert would listen respectfully to whatever he said and if he had nothing to offer John he would go back to his dominions and make some excuse why the marriage should not take place.

He thought quickly. "John," he said, "shall have the castles of Mirebeau, Loudon and Chinon."

"I am pleased to hear it," replied Humbert smiling and satisfied. "Those will be a goodly heritage, and with what my daughter brings to the marriage they will be very comfortably settled indeed."

Henry congratulated himself that he had overcome a difficult situation with great ease.

He had in fact aroused a hornet's nest.

The Court was talking about the portion that John was bringing to the marriage, and there was a certain amount of malice in the talk, for the three castles which Henry had designated to John had already been given to his son Henry as they were situated in Anjou which, with Normandy and England, was the inheritance of the King of England. Therefore the King had robbed Henry to pay John.

When Eleanor heard, she burst out laughing.

"Now, my son, you understand your father's ways. Promises to him are made to be broken. Next you will hear that he has bestowed the crown of England on someone of his fancy."

"I'll not endure it," cried Henry, almost in tears.

"Nor should you," answered his mother.

"What can I do?"

"Your brother Richard would know what to do. When he heard he said: 'By God, if he tries to lay his hands on Aquitaine, I will place myself at the head of any army and march against him.'"

"Go into battle against my own father!"

"It has been done before."

"Oh, no!" cried Henry.

"You lack Richard's spirit," said Eleanor watching closely.

"I do not," retorted Henry. "I am the King of England, remember."

"No one will remember it if you allow your estates to be filched from you."

"I will go to him. I will tell him I will not have it."

"Go then," said the Queen.

He stood before his father.

"Father, I must speak with you."

"Say on, my son."

"The castles you have given to John belong to me."

"You are mistaken," said the King. "These are mine. They are still mine. They always will be mine."

"But I am the Count of Anjou ... and ... and these castles are part of my lands."

"You have titles which I have given you. I can take them away if I wish. You must rmember this, Henry. There is one King of England, one Count of Anjou, one Duke of Normandy while I live."

"You have given me these titles."

"They are titles ... nothing more. If I were to die tomorrow then England, Anjou, Normandy would be yours. But I am not dead. Nor do I intend to die so that you can possess now that which if you wait long enough will in due course be yours."

"I am no longer a boy," cried Henry.

"Then why behave like one?"

"I am not behaving like one. I will not be told to do this and that. I want lands to govern. If you want Normandy give me England. Let me stand on my own."

The King laughed scornfully. "Do you think you could hold these dominions together?"

"I do. I do."

"I do not and I know. You have to learn to rule."

"How old were you when you became Duke of Normandy and King of England?"

"I had learned to govern when those honours came to me."

"I will learn. I have learned."

God's eyes, thought Henry, what a mistake to crown this boy King! I never made a greater mistake in all my reign— except it were to make Thomas à Becket my Archbishop of Canterbury.

"You will do as I wish," he said shortly.

"Others think I should not be treated in this way."

"Who thinks this?"

"The King of France. Some of my knights think it too."

"So you discuss our affairs with a foreign king?"

"Louis is my father through marriage."

"And doubtless would like to see trouble in my realm. Louis is our enemy ... our natural enemy. We can make truces and peace with him through our marriages, but the fact remains that he is the King of France and I am the King of England and as such we are enemies. As for your knights, I would know who these fellows are who speak and act treason. I will tell you this, son. They will no longer be your knights."

"I tell you I will not be treated in this way. If you are a king, so am I."

"Through my grace."

"It matters not through whose grace. I am a king and known as such."

It was true.

The king was silent for a while. Then he said: "If you will be a king you have lessons to learn. You shall begin without delay. I shall keep you at my side and when you have learned your business you can be of great use to me. Mayhap then you will be left in charge of certain of my dominions when my presence is needed elsewhere. Till then you will do as I wish. Go now. I have finished what I have to say."

Young Henry went away with a dull anger in his heart. It was not appeased when he heard that certain of his knights had been dismissed from his service and sent back to England with a warning that they had been treated with leniency on this occasion, but should they displease the King again that clemency would not be repeated.

Then the King declared that he was leaving Limoges for Normandy and that his son Henry would accompany him.

Eleanor took leave of her son for she was travelling back to Aquitaine with Richard and Geoffrey.

"Depend upon it," she whispered to young Henry, "he will keep you at his side so that he will have his eyes on you. You will endure more restraint then ever."

"I'll not endure it," declared Henry.

"The King of France said he would shelter you, did he not, if you found the situation with your father intolerable?"

"My father says he is our enemy."

"And who is your real enemy, pray? Is it not the one who has robbed you of part of your inheritance? Might not his enemy be your friend? You are no longer a child, my son. It is time you woke up and took what is yours."

"He will never permit me to have it."

"There are many against him. Why should you not take what he will not give you? Think about it."

Henry did think and grew excited thinking. But the King was determined that he should accompany him to Normandy.

Marguerite went back to visit her father before she returned to England and the two Henrys left Limoges for Normandy.

Father and son rode side by side. I shall have to watch him, thought the older Henry. I believe his mother has been urging him to rebellion. I begin to believe I never had a greater enemy than my wife. But the boy is young; I will soon subdue him. At the same time he was saddened by the situation. How pleasant it would have been to have had an affectionate son, one whom he could trust. He had always hoped that would be the case with Henry. Richard he knew would never care for him. His mind had been poisoned at too early an age. But perhaps if he could make this boy see reason they could work together, side by side and he could teach him to be a great king. If England were to be a great power she needed a strong king. Surely the people realized what could happen with a weak one? They had seen what the rule of Stephen had done to the country. Many of them had lived through those years of civil war when Matilda and Stephen had wrestled for the crown and then ineffectual Stephen had followed. Men such as the Conqueror, Henry I and Henry II were what the country needed. And this boy would be the third Henry; he must match up to the first two. Could he be taught? Could he be made to see that he must curb this personal vanity for power, for that was what it was? What a handsome boy he was and one had to admit he was possessed of a great charm of manner when he was not sullen as he was now. Good looks were an asset in a king; Stephen had had them; but one could get along very well without them if one had strength and that inborn genius which gives a man some secret magnetism to arouse the respect and fear of men. When he looked back on the preceding reigns it was so easy to select those who had ruled well and those badly and the two great Kings were two of a kind and he trusted he was in the same category.

He must make young Henry see this.

So he talked to him as they rode, in a friendly fatherly fashion. He tried to convey to the boy that he wanted to teach him to be a great king, and it was partly for this reason that he did not wish to put a great strain on his inadequate powers now. But even he knew that he could not bear to take his own hands from the reins. It was true that once he had acquired possessions he could not bring himself to part with them.

He curbed his temper in his effort to win the boy's affection. He tried to joke pleasantly while he instructed him. He began to believe that at last he was making some headway.

The younger Henry listened to his father and his resentment grew every day. How strong he is! he thought. He will live for years. I shall be an old man before I have a chance to rule and while he lives he will never give way one little bit. I am a king. There are many who would rather follow me. Nobody loves him. They are afraid of him. That is the only reason why they do not revolt. But if they had a leader, a leader they loved, respected, admired . . . what then? When he was riding beside his father revolt seemed impossible. But when he was alone he kept thinking of his mother's words. She was powerful. Aquitaine would rise for her against her husband if she wished it.

He began to grow excited. If he could get away he could go to the King of France, and there he could rally men to his banner. His mother would help him, for she hated her husband. Why should he wait on his father for years and years until he was an old man without ambition?

His father seemed to sense that rebellion in him. He kept him at his side and at night he insisted that they share the same room.

"It will show all what good friends we have become," he said jocularly.

Young Henry said nothing. He was afraid of betraying his thoughts.

He had sounded one or two of his friends. Would they be ready to follow him? They were cautious. They greatly feared the King's rages. Already he had dismissed certain knights from his son's suite with dire warnings of what would happen to them if he ever found them speaking treason. And yet the young King had great charm; his mother hated his father to such an extent that she had been heard to swear that she would never live with him again. It was said that when she had gone off to Aquitaine she had declared she would never return. There was certainly some truth in this because the Archbishop of Rouen had warned her that if she left her husband the Church would blame her and this could lead to excommunication.

Eleanor cared as little for the Church as her husband did and had ignored the Archbishop's reproof. But it showed how much she disliked his father and that she would be ready to help her son against him.

Moreover the King was still under the shadow of suspicion which had risen from the murder of the Archbishop of Canterbury. There had been whispers that Heaven would not allow him to prosper.

In the circimstances there were some who were ready to support the young King against the old and the former, discovering who these were, made his plans for escape.

They had reached the château of Chinon. It had been an exhausting day's ride and the older Henry was very tired. He said they would retire early and get a good night's sleep before setting off early in the morning.

No sooner had his father fallen into a deep sleep than young Henry rose from his bed, dressed hastily and made his way to the stables. There horses were saddled and waiting and he and a few of his trusted knights rode with great speed towards the French border.

When the King awoke to find his son had gone his rage was intense. He roared at his attendants, cuffing them right and left. Why had he not been told? Who had aided his son? Who had gone with him? By God's eyes, they should be sorry they had ever been born.

But he was quick to realize that he was wasting his time giving way to his fury. His son would have gone to the French border. He had hinted as much. He would seek sanctuary with Louis which was the last thing Henry wanted him to do.

He shouted instructions. They were leaving at once and they would change direction. They were going to the French border. He sent riders in several directions and mounting the fastest of his horses he set out on the chase.

Young Henry however had had a good start and although his father made every effort to catch up with him, he failed to do so and after two days Henry arrived at the Court of France.

Louis was delighted to see him. At the evening's banquet given in Henry's honour, he sat at the right hand of the King of France. He told young Henry that he would support him in his claim for Normandy for he thought it fair to do so. The young man had sworn his oath of allegiance to Louis his suzerain and therefore the King regarded him as a vassal. If he wished to gain territory which by right belonged to him then his cause was a just one and the King saw it as his duty to aid his vassal.

Young Henry was delighted. He had taken the first step and it had been comparatively easy.

When the King of England heard that his son was at the

Court of France and being entertained with honour by the King of France, his anger flared up.

He sent a message to Louis in which he said that the King of England demanded that his son be sent back to him.

Louis's reply was: "I do not understand this message. The King of England is with me. If by the King of England you mean the King's father, then I do not regard him as the King of England. He was I know formerly King of England but he resigned his crown to his son, and is no longer King."

When Henry received this message he bit his lips and hit this thighs with his clenched fists until he was bleeding and bruised.

He was angry as much with himself as with his son and the King of France.

He had no doubt now that his greatest act of folly had been to allow his son to be crowned King.

The news reached Eleanor of Aquitaine where she was holding one of her Courts of Love in which her troubadours sang romantic songs and brought their literary efforts for her to judge.

The messengers came from the Court of France and she stopped the singing that she might hear the news without delay.

When she heard that her son Henry had successfully escaped from his father she laughed with pleasure.

"Rejoice," she cried. "He is my true son after all. He has decided that he will no longer endure the bonds of tyranny. Ah, how I wish I could have seen my husband when he received that news. I doubt he ever fell into a greater rage. No more singing. I wish to be alone with my sons."

When the troubadours had left in a somewhat crestfallen manner she turned to Richard and said: "You know what this means?"

"It means that we are going to war against my father."

"Henry must not be foolish. He will not be, I am sure. Louis will guide him. I doubt not that there are many who will rally to his banner. And you, my sons—yes, you too, Geoffrey, must join him without delay that he may know that he has you to support him."

"We should leave immediately," said Richard, his eyes gleaming at the thought of battle and particularly that it should be conflict against the father whom he hated.

73

Geoffrey was eager too. At this time he always wanted to follow Richard.

She smiled from one to the other.

"This is the moment. Your brother will shortly be King in very truth."

Geoffrey said: "Our father is a very great soldier, Mother."

"He was. Don't forget that he murdered the Archbishop of Canterbury. That is something which will never be forgotten. There is a curse on him for what he did to that saint. All men know it. You will see he cannot prosper now. That is why the time is ripe to attack him. You see, the King of France who I have good reason to know is the mildest of men, is ready to help your brother against him. Louis thought highly of Thomas à Becket. He loathes his murderer. Louis will see himself as the instrument of God who is to strike down the man who has offended all Christendom and Heaven too."

"Our mother is right," cried Richard. "I will be ready to start for the Court of France tomorrow."

"Then I will accompany you," replied Geoffrey.

Eleanor embraced them both and they prepared to start.

Eleanor watched them from the topmost turret of the castle.

How brave they looked seated on their horses, their pennants waving in the breeze. She watched until she could see them no more.

In her chamber she wrote verses on the sadness of parting with loved ones. How she missed Richard! She wondered whether he missed his life with her. He had always been a warrior in the making. Had he forgotten the pleasant hours they had spent together? Was he content to leave her now and march against his father?

She could not settle to write. She wanted action now. She should have been riding out with her sons. She pictured herself on her horse, her standard bearer riding before her, going into battle against the man she hated.

She was laughing to think of what he would say and feel when he heard that his sons Richard and Geoffrey had joined their brother Henry against him. And that would not be all. Aquitaine was ready to rebel against him. Brittany was doubtless the same. What of Anjou? Normandy she supposed would be loyal to him.

It was so exciting. She could not stay in the castle. She sent a messenger to her uncle, Raoul de Faye, begging him to come to her as she was in need of his advice.

Eleanor was very fond of this uncle though not quite in the same way as she had been of that other uncle, Raymond Prince of Antioch who had been her lover; but she had relied very much on Raoul de Faye who pleased her by his dislike of Henry Plantagenet and who had done a great deal to arouse young Henry's antagonism against his father.

Raoul quickly arrived in answer to her summons. He was delighted when she told him what had happened.

"This will be the end of that arrogant husband of yours," he declared. "There is scarcely a man living who does not hold him guilty of Becket's murder. This will be remembered against him and even those who have been his most loyal supporters until now will begin to change their tune."

How pleasant it was to walk in the gardens with Raoul, a charming and handsome man. She forgot when she was with him—for he paid her the most delightful compliments—that she was no longer young and that her notorious beauty was considerably faded for she felt young in the company of such a man, and because she could gloat over her hatred for her husband she was happy for a while.

This would give him little time to dally with his Rosamund, she told Raoul.

"I doubt not he will find women here and there to amuse him in the manner to which he is accustomed."

"He will do that, but he will not rest in peace long."

"I have heard that the people of England are murmuring against the heavy taxes he imposes."

"They always did. But they remember the reign of Stephen when brigands roamed the country and took from them their possessions. They prefer to be robbed by the King with his taxes than that their money should be taken from them by roaming robbers."

"They will forget the robber brigands and remember only the robber king."

"He has staunch friends in England."

"Never mind England. We will drive him out of Aquitaine, Anjou and Normandy."

"My dear uncle, you will help in this?"

"You may be assured that I shall do my best to stir up rebellion against him from all sides. Louis will be with us. We cannot fail to win."

"Then my son Henry shall have England, Normandy and

Anjou, Richard Aquitaine and Geoffrey Brittany in very truth."

"The writing is on the wall for Henry Plantagenet," said Raoul de Faye.

When he had gone Eleanor could not settle. She remembered the days when she and Louis had set out on their crusade to the Holy City. What excitements there had been then—discomforts too, but they only brightened the high lights. Wonderful days of youth and vitality!

But she was not so old. At least she did not feel old. She could not expect to go into battle, but she could join her sons; she could advise them. No one could say she was not a woman of experience.

Why should she not?

The more she thought of it the more she liked the idea. She would go to the Court of France. It was ironical that she should be turning from Henry to Louis when once it had been the other way round. But Louis was turning out to be more astute than she had ever believed possible. He had fathered several children so was not so much of a monk and since the birth of his son he had been quite ready to go to war for the good of his kingdom.

It would be amusing to see Louis again.

When she made up her mind to do something she became obsessed with the need to accomplish it. Now she had decided that she would join her sons.

It would not be wise to let people know that she had left Aquitaine. There might be a revolt in the Duchy so she would slip away quietly. But even then she might be seen.

Then the idea occurred to her. She would disguise herself as a man and leave Aquitaine with a party of knights. She would be dressed as one of them.

When Henry heard that Richard and Geoffrey had joined Henry he shrugged his shoulders. Foolish boys, all of them. What did they think they were going to do? Young Henry was peevish, thinking because he had been crowned King he could replace his father. If the boy had stayed with him he would have learned something of what it meant to be a king, then perhaps he would not be so ready to take on the responsibility. As for Richard and Geoffrey they had been goaded by that she-wolf of a mother of theirs. They were all children really. He would summon them and give them a few lessons in what he expected of them.

He was soon to realize the matter was more serious than he had believed. The rebellion of his sons was regarded as a call to arms to all those discontents throughout his dominions. The shadow of Becket hung heavily over him. Superstitious men believed that the martyr who was capable of performing miracles would surely help those who took up against his murderer.

Henry was fully aware of this and when he heard that Count Philip of Flanders had captured Aumâle and, after a siege, the castle of Driencourt he could no longer remain complacent.

Louis had marched forth with young Henry and they were besieging Verneuil. Those loyal and faithful supporters, Hugh de Lacy and Hugh de Beauchamp, could be trusted to hold fast, but when after a month's siege food became short in the town the inhabitants threatened to surrender.

The King then decided that he must take action.

He led his considerable army to Verneuil.

The reputation of the King of England as the greatest living general still existed; and many of the men in the opposing army, particularly those who had deserted him in favour of his son, trembled at the thought of his approach. If God and Becket were not on his side then the Devil would surely be.

Louis realized that in a face-to-face fight with Henry he could not win. From a hilltop he saw the approach of Henry's army and he was greatly disturbed. All his distaste for battle returned to him and he sent messengers asking for a truce until the following day.

Normally Henry would not have accepted this, but his son was with the army of the King of France and he wished to teach him a lesson rather than that any harm should befall him. After all he understood the boy's desire for power. Hadn't he had similar desires when he was his age?

So he agreed to the truce. That night, Louis's soldiers—out of control as they had been on the notorious occasion of Vitry-the-Burned—sacked the town; and when morning came they were already in flight.

When Henry saw the burning town his fury was great. He set off immediately in pursuit of Louis's army but although he inflicted great slaughter on its rear he did not catch up with Louis and young Henry.

Now it became clear that revolt was springing up all over his dominions. It was necessary for him to send a force without delay to Brittany where fortunately he was quickly able to put down the insurrection.

It was a great blow to him to hear that Robert, Earl of Leicester, the son of the man who had been one of his most loyal supporters, and his Chamberlain, William de Tancarville, had left England for France and had joined young Henry.

This was serious, and when Louis, who had been greatly upset by the affair at Verneuil, suggested that they meet to discuss peace, Henry was ready.

He was considerably hurt to hear that his three sons had accompanied Louis to Gisors, the spot where the conference was to take place, and that they had come to support the King of France against their own father. He wanted to be on friendly terms with his sons and to start again to build up a pleasant relationship with them. His offer was generous considering that they had taken up arms against him. It was true, he recognized, that there was some justice in their demands, but it was none the less depressing to sit with his own sons on one side of the conference table and himself on the other. Young Henry had become defiant—perhaps he always had been—but now with the backing of the King of France he was not afraid to show it. Richard gave him cool looks of hatred; and his two elder sons were training their brother Geoffrey to follow their example. Life had indeed become sour, when those who should have loved him and worked beside him had turned against him.

He promised certain concessions. Henry could choose whether he wished to live in Normandy or England; Richard should have more revenue from Aquitaine, and Geoffrey from Brittany.

How galling that they should retire with the King of France to discuss with him their own father's proposals!

They left Gisors without seeing him again. His terms were unacceptable, they said. It seemed nothing would satisfy them but that he, the King, at the height of his powers, should hand over everything to his sons.

Frustrated and angry he fell into a great rage and declared that if the cubs wanted war they should have it.

Eleanor, disguised as a knight, was riding towards the French frontier. She had received little news of the fighting but her hopes were high that her three sons, with the help of Louis, would be victorious over her husband. She would not deceive herself; Henry was a great general; she had not been

78

wrong in that respect when she had assessed him all those years ago. He was one of those men who are born to command and conquer. But no man should conquer her. If he had been her good and faithful husband, they would have worked side by side and she would have brought up her children to love and respect him. But his lechery was going to prove his downfall.

What would happen now? Louis, with young Henry, Richard and Geoffrey beside him would conquer Anjou and Normandy; she felt certain that there would be traitors in England to rise against her husband. But they would not be traitors, for they would support the new King, the young King, her own son Henry.

How she would laugh at Henry the old lion. "Did you not crown your son, Henry?" she would taunt. "Was it not at your command that the ceremony took place?"

Sly, cunning he was, but he had made two great mistakes, one when he became involved in the murder of Becket and the other when he had crowned his son while he himself still wanted to hold the crown and all that went with it in his greedy hands.

"We must be nearing Chartres," she said to the knight who rode beside her.

"It will soon be in sight."

She had forbidden them to address her as "my lady". Not until she reached Louis's Court should her identity be guessed.

She imagined his surprise at seeing her. Poor Louis, who had loved her so devotedly once. He had never wanted the divorce even though he knew she was unfaithful to him. He would have been her creature as Henry never would.

In the distance a band of riders appeared on the horizon, and Eleanor recognized them as men in the service of her husband.

"We will call a greeting and pass on," she said, "and if they should ask whither we are bound we will say we are travellers who are on our way to Poitiers. Let us be civil with them and elude them as soon as possible. But it may be that a mere greeting will do."

How wrong she was! She had had no news so she did not know that war was in progress between her son Richard, Duke of Aquitaine, and his father and it would immediately be assumed that the knights were on their way to join Richard. Therefore they would be the enemies of the King of England.

79

The party was three times as strong as Eleanor's and it very quickly became clear what was about to happen.

"Halt," cried the leader of the party. "You are Poitevins, are you not?"

"We are," replied one of Eleanor's knights, "and on our way to Poitiers."

"You will not reach it. You are our prisoners. The Duke of Aquitaine is at war with our King."

Eleanor was horrified. This could mean only one thing. She was Henry's prisoner. And how long could she keep her identity secret?

Henry was becoming very disturbed. This was no minor revolt. Trouble was springing up in every direction. He thought he knew why. God was angry with him. This was Thomas's revenge. Of course he was guilty of his murder. Of course he had wanted him dead. He had more or less commanded those knights to kill him. At least he had upbraided them for not doing so. What could be clearer than that? And ever since ill fortune had been his lot. His own sons were turning against him and all over his kingdom there was discontent. Everyone connected him with the murder of Becket and to make matters worse, miracles were being performed at Canterbury and the story of them was being blazoned throughout his dominions.

That traitor Leicester was in Flanders doubtless making plans to invade England with foreign help and take it from him that it might be presented to his son. And now another blow, William King of Scotland had chosen this moment—as might be expected—to cross the border. Thank God he had some loyal friends. He could trust Richard de Luci to keep the Scots at bay. They were nothing more than a parcel of savages and although they could lay waste the country in most barbaric fashion they would have no chance against a well disciplined army. But he needed Luci elsewhere.

This was a ruler's nightmare, when his dominions were so scattered and trouble arose in several places at once.

One of his men came in to tell him that a knight was without who wished to have urgent speech with him.

He commanded that he should be brought to him. Fresh trouble? he wondered. Where would the next rebellion be?

But this man's news was different.

"My lord," he explained, "we were riding near to Chartres when we came upon a party of Poitevin knights. We were of

80

the opinion that they were riding to join the enemy so we captured them."

The King nodded. The right act but scarcely one to report to him.

"There was one among them, my lord, who aroused our suspicions. We formed the opinion that she was a woman."

A woman. The King grimaced, but the knight's next words made him stare at him in amazement.

"She proved to be the Queen, my lord."

"The Queen! My wife!" cried Henry.

" 'Twas so, my lord. She admitted it and there was indeed no doubt."

Henry started to laugh. He stopped abruptly. "Where is she?"

"We have brought her to you, my lord, not knowing your wishes."

Henry went to the knight and slapped him heartily on the back. "You did right," he said. "By God's eyes, I promise you I'll remember you for this deed. She is here then. Bring her to me. I would have speech with my captive."

It was indeed Eleanor. She stood there before him, anger in her eyes, defiance, hatred, everything he remembered so well.

"Leave us," he commanded. Then he stared at her and gave vent to loud laughter.

"So you have joined the army, eh?"

"It behoves all men and women to fight against tyranny."

"Brave words from a prisoner. Captured, eh? Where were you going?"

"To join my sons."

"And you were going into battle with them against their father?"

"Nothing would please me more."

"You are a little old for such activities. These are not the days when you rode out to the Holy Land and had great sport on the way with your uncle and the infidels. You see what happens? You are captured before you reach your objective. I'll wager you were on your way to the Court of France. Did you hope that now that you are old your first husband might be more to your taste than he was in your lustier days?"

"It surprises me not that Henry the Lecher's thoughts run always in one direction. My project was to gain for my sons that which is their right."

"You talk nonsense. I am the King. What I hold I hold by

81

right and conquest. You are a foolish woman and you shall learn this for you are my prisoner and I swear that you shall never again be free while I live to make discord between me and my sons."

"What do you mean? You will throw me into a dungeon?"

"What I intend to do you will know ere long."

"Do you think your sons will allow you to insult their mother?"

"My sons will learn, as their mother will, who is the King and ruler of them all."

She came towards him, her arm uplifted. He caught her in his strong grip and she cried out in pain. Their faces were close, hers distorted by hatred, his triumphant. He thought: My luck has changed. This is the greatest good fortune. She can make no more trouble for me. And when the world knows that she is my prisoner they will realize that Henry Plantagenet is still the man he was and even the wrath of Heaven does not dismay him.

He shouted to the guards at his door.

"Take this woman," he said. "Keep her in close confinement. Guard her. It will go ill with any if she escapes."

Eleanor looked over her shoulder at him as she was dragged away, but the venom in her expression only made him laugh.

Those were uneasy months which followed. Richard de Luci with Humphrey de Bohun, now Constable of England, had held back the Scottish invasion and had been able to establish a truce with William of Scotland. Henry had held at bay the rebellions which had sprung up over Normandy and Anjou with alarming frequency.

He was constantly afraid that Eleanor would get away. He was determined to take her to England and see that she was incarcerated in a prison there from which she could not escape.

He could not help feeling that some power was against him and it occurred to him that until he confessed his guilt in Thomas's murder and asked forgiveness for this ill luck would be his.

There was a glimmer of brightness when the Earl of Leicester who had landed in England was completely routed by Henry's supporters. The King was exultant. This would show young Henry that he could not defeat his father as easily as he believed. And what were his sons thinking now that he held their mother captive?

While he was congratulating himself that he was going to suppress all those who rose against him, urgent messengers arrived from England.

At first the King listened to their warnings but decided that his presence was needed in Normandy; but as they became more insistent he realized that it would be folly for him to stay in Normandy to protect his possessions there while he lost England.

He made up his mind that he would cross to England without delay taking with him his captive Queen for he imagined what havoc she could cause if left behind. She might prevail on someone to release her and if she were free he could expect trouble from her direction. The safest place for Eleanor was in the stronghold of some castle and her guardian should be someone whom he could trust.

He would also take with him Marguerite, young Henry's wife, who by good fortune was in his custody, for her very relationship with his son would make her his enemy.

He had another matter very firmly in his mind. He must stop this chain of disaster. He would no longer pretend he was guiltless of Becket's murder, for it seemed very likely that the events of the last year were due to what had happened in Canterbury Cathedral. It seemed to him that not until he obtained absolution could he hope for better fortune.

His kingdom, as well as his soul, was in peril.

He must save them both.

He was thoughtful as he rode to the coast. He fancied that what he was about to do would be smiled on by Heaven and once it was done—distasteful as it was—he would cease to be plagued by ill luck.

A gale was blowing and he could see the fear in his companions' faces but he was determined to delay no longer. He was going to do what should have been done a year ago and only when it was completed would he be safe from his enemies.

"My lord," said his advisers, "we cannot sail in this wind."

"We are putting to sea without delay," he told them.

They were dismayed but they dared not disobey and when they were ready to sail it seemed that the wind changed. It was behind them and blew them across the Channel. The King was pleased.

"You see," he declared, "you may always trust my judgement."

Exultantly he went to see the Queen.

"So here you are!" he said. "Far from your troubadours! You will not find your jailers so ready to sing to you."

"Think not," she answered, "that my sons will allow me to remain your prisoner."

"They must take care that they may not soon be in like case. By God's eyes, I will teach all what it means to rebel against me."

"Take care that they do not teach you what happens to tyrants."

"You are too bold, Madam, for a woman who is in the hands of her enemy."

"Not for long."

"For as long as I shall live, my lady."

"It was an ill day for me when I first set eyes on you."

"Take pleasure, Madam, in knowing that that day is even more regretted by me."

How strong he is, she thought, with grudging admiration. Every inch a king. And her mind went back to the days when she had determined to marry him and how she had longed for the time when they could be together.

"I can assure you that your regret could not be greater than mine," she told him. "But you are a deceitful man for you led me to believe that once I was important to you."

"It was before I learned to know you."

"Aye, and I also had bitter lessons to learn. If you had not been such a lecher we might have worked together."

"You, Madam, are scarce in a position to criticize others for that fault. Before our marriage you took strange bedfellows."

"Never such a tyrant as my second husband."

"We waste time, and I have none to spare. I sent for you to tell you that you are to be taken to Salisbury Castle and there you will remain until it pleases me to change your residence. But think not that you will go free. You have offended me too much. You have proved yourself to be a traitor, and though you are my wife shall be treated as such."

It occurred to him that he might bargain with her for a divorce. Would that be wise? To have her free to communicate with his sons? No. This was not the time to speak of divorce when he was currying favour with Heaven by doing penance for his part in Becket's murder.

He must be quiet about that matter for a while. Moreover

what if he procured a divorce? Could he marry Alice? And what of Rosamund? Clearly it was better at this time to say nothing of divorce—not to *think* of divorce. His mind must be free to consider Becket's murder and the fact that he deplored it and repented for any part he might have had in bringing it about.

He watched his wife through narrowed eyes. Traitor! Any King was justified in imprisoning a traitor who threatened his realm . . . even though that traitor should prove to be his own wife.

"I will say farewell," he said. "The audience is over."

"I will not be dismissed in this way. There is much I have to say to you."

"You will be dismissed when I dismiss you and I have no interest in what you may wish to say to me. Say it to the walls of your prison." He summoned men-at-arms. "Take the Queen away," he said. "Let her go to Salisbury and there be placed under confinement."

Eleanor protested vehemently. But it was useless. Her arms were seized by the men-at-arms and she was taken from the King's presence.

The King's Penance

The King rode on to Canterbury. As he came in sight of the
Cathedral the bells rang out and he dismounted from his
horse, and there, on the road, he took off his kingly garments
and wrapped himself in a coarse woollen gown. He took off
his shoes and walked barefoot into the city.

Into the streets the people came to see their King for once
in his life dressed as a humble pilgrim and behaving as one.
Looking sad, solemn and truly penitent he came to the
Cathedral. There he was received by the Bishop of London,
Gilbert Foliot. Foliot was feeling very uneasy for he had
always been jealous of Becket and had been one of his
greatest enemies. However the King did not remind him of
this, so intent was he on his own act of penitence. The King's
feet were bleeding from the rough stones of the road and the
people looked on in astonishment to see him behave so
humbly.

"Take me to the spot where he was struck down," said
Henry and when he was conducted there, he knelt and laying
his head on the stones wept that his tears might be on the
very place where Thomas's blood had been shed.

The Bishop of London then mounted the pulpit and spoke
to all present explaining to them the meaning this strange
spectacle.

"All you here present know that Henry, King of England,
invoking, for the salvation of his soul, God and the Holy
Martyr, protests before you that he neither ordered, wished
nor wilfully caused nor desired in his heart the death of the
martyr. But as it is possible that the murderers availed
themselves of some words imprudently escaping him, he
declares that he seeks penitential chastisement of the bishops here assembled and consents to submit his bare back to
the discipline of the rod."

The King then rose and addressed the assembly.

"What the Bishop has said is indeed what I have commanded. I trust my humble penance will be acceptable to God and the late Archbishop. This day I have restored to Canterbury the dignities and rights of the Church; and I have ordered that lights shall be kept burning at the tomb of Thomas à Becket. A hospital shall be built at Southwark and this shall be erected in honour of God and the Blessed Martyr Saint Thomas."

The Bishop hastened to add that he would associate himself with the building of this hospital and would grant special indulgences to any who contributed to it.

He was fully aware that he should be sharing the King's penitence for had he not said, after the murder of Thomas à Becket, that his body should either be thrown on a dunghill or hung on a gibbet? This was a very uneasy day for the Bishop of London.

The King now indicated that he was ready for the act of penance and in the midst of bishops, abbots and the priests of the chapter of Canterbury, he went into the crypt where the tomb was situated.

There he removed his clothes and knelt exposing his bare back while each bishop took a whip and struck the King three or four blows.

"As thy Redeemer was scourged for the sins of men," said each bishop as he administered the whip, "so be thou scourged for thy own sin." The bishops having whipped the King, the priests took the whips and did likewise.

When this was over Henry continued to pray for Thomas. He toured the Cathedral stopping at the shrines to say his prayers and ask forgiveness of his sins; there he remained through the rest of the day and for the night.

The next day he heard Mass and drank holy water which contained a drop of Thomas's blood.

He then left Canterbury.

His anxieties and the effort of the last hours had affected him deeply. He was suffering from a low fever, but he wished to travel to Westminster and insisted on doing this and when he reached London took to his bed for a day.

It was in London that news was brought to him that the King of Scotland had been taken prisoner.

The King leaped from his bed. Great exultation was in his heart. This was a sign. A sign from Thomas!

"Thomas à Becket," he cried, "so you and I are friends once more. Now you will work with me. I shall be invincible. Thomas, you will guard my kingdom for me."

It seemed as if this were indeed the case for within a few weeks of the King's penance rebellion was quelled throughout England.

Henry was certain that it was as he had believed. Heaven . . . and Thomas . . . were pleased with him.

He went to see Rosamund who was installed in his palace now that no secret was made of their relationship. He was still thinking in terms of divorce but he did not want to go too closely into that as yet. Eleanor was safely confined at Salisbury Castle. Let her stay there until his dominions were safe and he could devote his thoughts to some way of getting rid of her. It was not a situation which demanded an immediate solution. Rosamund was as always tenderly waiting to perform her wifely duties; what greater pleasure could he get from their relationship if he married her? But of course he could not marry Rosamund. He had no intention of doing so. If he obtained the divorce it would be for the sake of his dear little Alice.

And now with Rosamund and Alice to appease his sexual hungers and Saint Thomas and Heaven working for him on the battlefield he had much in which to rejoice.

Rosamund's sons were doing well. He would find places for them that would delight their mother.

"I think God cannot be displeased with me," he told Rosamund, "for the sons I have out of wedlock are good boys. There is Geoffrey, son of the whore Hikenia, who is more faithful to me than my sons in wedlock. And there are our two boys."

"Sometimes I tremble for them," said Rosamund.

"Why should you? They have their father to look to their future."

"But bastards, my lord."

"A King's bastards! Remember that."

Rosamund sighed.

She bathed the wounds on his back made by the whips of the priests and wept over them.

"My lord, that they should have dared do this to you!"

"They dared not do aught else. It was at my command, remember."

Her touch was gentle; her ointments soothing. Dear Rosamund! He thought then that if she had been his Queen he would have been a faithful husband . . . well, a more faithful one. But even while she tended to his wounds and later when they made love, he was thinking of Alice.

"Now I am at peace with Heaven, Rosamund," he told her. "Thomas and I are as we were long ago when he was my Chancellor. We are good friends. He will guard my kingdom for me when I am away. He will intercede with me in Heaven. I have done my penance. My tears have touched the spot where his blood was shed. It is a wonderful feeling, Rosamund, to have admitted a sin and to have gained remission."

"I think of it often," she answered.

She was a little mournful, which made him impatient. Soon she would be talking of going into a convent. He wanted none of that. He came here to be amused and it pleased him that she should be content with the lot to which he had lifted her.

"My sins sit heavily upon me," she said. "Methinks that I am in need of forgiveness."

"You Rosamund! What have you ever done that was not gentle and loving?"

"I have lived in sin and borne bastards."

"You have eased the lot of your King and obeyed him. That is your duty, my dear."

She sighed and did not answer.

Later he thought her penitent mood was not such a bad thing. If he ever divorced Eleanor he would want to marry Alice. Then nothing could suit him better than that Rosamund should go into a convent to expiate her sins and leave him with a free conscience to marry Alice.

So he would not entirely dismiss this matter of the convent. It was as well to encourge her sinful feelings in case they could be of use later.

He smiled tenderly. He could always trust his Rosamund to please him.

From Woodstock to Westminster to see his little Alice. He was delighted with her.

"You have grown, my little love. Why you are almost a woman."

"Does that please you, my lord?" she asked anxiously.

"You could never do anything but please me."

How delightful she was! She was developing passion. There was no need to coax her to the act now.

"You have missed me, little one?" he wanted to know.

She assured him that she thought constantly of him and spent many hours at the turret window watching for him to come.

"Never tell anyone of what is between us."

She would not, she assured him.

But he wondered whether some of the household suspected. It was never easy for a king to keep the secrets of his private life.

How different she was from Rosamund! She had no sense of guilt, only a desire to please him. He was the King and therefore whatever he did must be right.

He told her that he had seen her father.

"Did you tell him that we were going to marry?"

He stroked her arm gently. "Nay, little one. That I cannot do until I rid myself of the wicked Eleanor."

"Is she very wicked?"

"More wicked than you can understand. She has turned my children against me and would go into battle and kill me if it were possible. Oh, do not fear, she is my prisoner now. No harm can come to me through her. I shall divorce her and then . . . you will see."

"There is talk," she said, "of you and Rosamund Clifford."

He laughed heartily.

"You must not be jealous, sweetheart. She was once my mistress."

"Am I your mistress?"

"Nay, you are my wife-to-be."

"So I shall truly be the Queen."

"You shall be so, when I have rid myself of that old she-wolf."

"Did you love her once?"

"Nay never. I loved her lands of Aquitaine."

"What will you love me for?"

"For your beauty, your innocence and because you love me."

That satisfied her. Children were easily pleased. She never doubted that he would marry her.

So would I if it were possible. Is she not the daughter of the King of France?

And he laughed exultantly, wondering what old Louis would say if he could see his daughter lying naked in his bed.

And Richard? It might well be that she would have to go to him one day. She was his betrothed, and if there was no way of ridding himself of Eleanor . . . Richard was growing up.

Very soon now he would be demanding his bride and old Louis would be shaking his fist and asking what the King of England meant by holding his daughter in one of his castles.

He seemed to have conveyed something of his thoughts to her for she said: "My lord, what of Richard? Have you seen him?"

"Nay," he answered. "He is my enemy. He fights with his brothers against me."

"Not against *you!*"

"It is hard to believe that a son can so wrong his father." A sly smile played about his mouth at the irony of the situation. Richard wronged him in the battlefield and he wronged Richard in the bedchamber. Serve the young cub right. He wondered what he should say if it so happened that one day Henry would be obliged to relinquish Alice to him and he knew she had been his father's mistress.

But he would not give her up. She was too delightful. Moreover she was the daughter of the King of France.

What an important figure in his life was that King of France. There could not be two men more unlike. Louis the monk, Henry the lecher—and both had been husbands of Eleanor.

He would come to some arrangement. Louis would surely prefer to see young Alice Queen of England rather than Duchess of Aquitaine.

"I can never like Richard," she was saying, "because he has not been good to you."

He covered her flower-like skin with kisses.

"My little Alice," he whispered. "Do not think of Richard. He is not for you nor you for him. How could that be when I have decided that no one but myself shall ever use you in this way?"

He was content. The future could be good with Thomas watching over him from on high; he would rid himself of Eleanor; Rosamund could be by subtle hints jostled into a nunnery and this adorable Alice, daughter of the King of France, could be his Queen.

Confident that he had made his peace with Heaven and that St. Thomas à Becket was guarding his realm for him. Henry set about safeguarding his overseas dominions. He could not really believe that his sons were fighting against him and there came to him a great desire to be loved by them. If they had been good obedient boys what help they would have rendered him! That they should have banded together with his enemy the King of France against him was the basest ingratitude. Of course it was all due to the insinuations of their wicked mother. During their childhood she had done everything she could to turn them from him. What a viper! He gloated on the fact that she was in his power now. Never while he lived should she go free.

Was it some misplaced sense of chivalry which was forcing his sons into battle now? Had they some scheme for rescuing their mother? He wanted to meet them, to talk to them like a father, to make them understand. He loved the boys, particularly Henry. How proud he had been of his eldest son when he was growing up. That charm of manner, those good looks. He had wanted to tutor him into becoming a great king, for only a great king could hold these dominions together. Surely they knew what had happened under Stephen.

He must put an end to this conflict. He must win back his sons. He could not have them ranging themselves with his enemies. One thing he was determined on. Young John should never feel the pernicious influence of his mother.

Now he would be invincible for since he had made his peace with Heaven, there was a feeling of confidence throughout his army. God was no longer against him. He, the greatest and most powerful of kings, had humbled himself at the shrine of St. Thomas à Becket and had actually ordered his priests to chastise him.

What greater penitence could he have shown than that, what greater love for Thomas?

"Thomas, guard my realm while I go forth to battle for my sons."

The Rebellious Cubs

Young Henry laughed aloud when he heard of his father's penance at the shrine of Canterbury.

"How could he so humiliate himself?" he cried.

His good friend, William the Marshall, pointed out that he thought it was a clever move on the King's part. It might well be that he was truly penitent in which case his conscience would be clear. On the other hand if it were a gesture it was a clever one for now it would seem that the King had escaped from the shadow of guilt which must hang over him until he confessed his part in the murder.

"I believe," said Henry suspiciously, "that you have a fondness for my father."

"Who can help but admire him?"

"Those who are his friends cannot be mine," said Henry meaningfully.

William the Marshall was sad. For so long they had been close companions, but since his coronation an arrogance had settled on the young King; he seemed to believe that the act of crowning gave him strength which he had not possessed before. The more experienced and logical William was fully aware that his father had given young Henry a title only and he believed he would be wise to accept this fact.

But Henry, being young and unsure of himself, turned rather to those who would flatter him than to those who would tell him the truth. Thus as the bonds of friendship between himself and William slackened he became more and more bound to that flamboyant knight, Philip of Flanders.

Philip it was who had sent his Flemings to England in the hope of wresting the country from the elder Henry. That was a forlorn hope as had been proved and the old King's superior generalship had soon routed the foreigners and put an end to their hopes of an easy capture of England.

Now Philip was young Henry's constant companion. He assured him that he was ill-treated by his father. He pointed out that he, a king, lived in a much poorer state than the sons of mere knights. Philip was flamboyant, gay, one of the best knights in France, noted for his chivalry and skill in jousting. Henry had had little experience of this sport which was becoming more and more popular and under Philip's influence became very enthusiastic about it.

He visualized the freedom he would have when he was King and his father vanquished. He promised himself that life would be one round of tournaments and triumphant rides. He was more than ever determined to have what was, his friends assured him, his right.

It was a great blow that he and his friends had not succeeded in winning England. They must shelve that project for a while but that should not prevent their attempting to take Normandy, and the best time to start was while his father was settling matters in England.

Philip of Flanders agreed with him. Philip was ambitious, and young Henry had promised him estates in England when the plan to subdue the father and place the son firmly on the throne succeeded.

It was great good fortune that they should have the backing of the King of France. Louis had changed since the days when he had been Eleanor's young husband deploring the fact that his lot had been a crown instead of the priestly robes. He had a son—young Philip—who was now some nine years of age and the birth of his son had made a great difference to his life. From his previous wives—and he had married three times—he had had only daughters and when on that joyous August day in the year 1165 his wife Adela had given birth to a boy, so great had been his exultation that he had the news proclaimed in the streets of Paris and bells rung throughout his dominion. He had a son and heir to his dominions. It was God's blessing on a man who had always tried to do his duty in that way of life to which he had been sent against his will.

Adela had been fertile, giving him two more children— young Alice and Agnes, both girls. He would have rejoiced in another son, for Philip was a delicate boy. But he must be thankful. He had his son. Alice was in England now, the betrothed of Richard of Aquitaine, and soon he must insist that that marriage take place. What was Henry's motive in seeking to delay it, for it did seem that he ignored any suggestion that the two should be brought together? Perhaps he wished to bargain a little over Alice. Louis would not suffer that. The younger people had been betrothed.

In the meantime, Louis realized that Henry's position was not a happy one and with the King of England's sons ready to go to battle against him, this seemed the time for France to exploit her advantages.

Young Henry was at his Court and with him was Philip of Flanders. A clever young man, this Count—energetic and eager to vanquish old Henry. And he was right when he said that the objective should be Normandy.

"There should be no delay," said Flanders to Louis. "For depend upon it if we are to strike we must do so quickly. When the old warrior has settled his English affairs he will cross on the first favourable wind."

Louis agreed that the objective should be Rouen, the first city of Normandy, for if Rouen fell it would have such an effect on the rest of Normandy that conquest would be made easy.

They would surprise the city and lay siege to it. This they did with great effect and the people of Rouen waited in their town for the coming of Henry, who, they were sure, could not delay long when he knew what was happening to their city.

Throughout his life Louis had been plagued by his religious training which had more than once intruded on his military designs. The siege was progressing favourably but it seemed likely that the coming of Henry to the rescue would not be long delayed. Louis then remembered that the Feast of St. Lawrence was at hand and he did not see how he could do battle on such a day, so he declared a truce. There should be no fighting for a whole day and night. Rouen might consider itself released from siege for a day.

When this news reached the city the people went wild with excitement. It was an example, they said, of Louis's ineffectual generalship. The King of England must be on his way to save them and every hour was important to them. The folly of the King of France must surely have saved them.

So delighted were they that there was singing and dancing in the streets. They believed that the siege of Rouen was all but over. They threw open the gates of the city and some of the knights staged a tournament in the fields outside the city walls.

The French soldiers watched the proceedings with dismay, but none was more put out than Philip of Flanders.

So incensed was he that he forgot his reverence for the crown of France and stormed into the King's tent. Louis looked pained, but he was well known for his mildness and he bade the Count of Flanders have his say.

"My lord King," cried Philip, "the King of England is on his way. He cannot be long delayed. You may depend upon it news had reached him of the state of siege which exists in Rouen. In permitting this truce you give him an opportunity to come in time to save the city."

"If he comes we will face him."

"We shall lose Rouen."

"St. Lawrence in whose honour we have called this truce will aid us."

"And what of St. Thomas à Becket whom he will summon to his aid?"

"St. Thomas would never aid him."

"But he has done penance at his shrine. He has allowed himself to be whipped."

"He is his murderer."

"It was not his hand that struck the blow and see what success he has had in England since his penance."

Louis was a little shaken. He had great faith in St. Thomas à Becket. But it was he, Louis, who had given the Archbishop sanctuary in France and it had never been necessary for him to do penance at his shrine.

"My lord King," implored Philip of Flanders, "if this truce goes on through the day and night we shall lose Rouen."

"I have given my word and said my prayers to St. Lawrence."

"St. Lawrence can do nothing against the King of England," said Philip almost impatiently, and he added: "My lord, might it not be that this opportunity comes through St. Lawrence? The city gates are wide open; the knights are sporting in their tournament. Could this not be the time to go into the attack?"

Louis was horrified. "I have given my word."

Philip of Flanders tried to hide his scorn. All his life the King of France had lost opportunities on the battlefield. Was he now doing the same?

Philip wrung his hands. He went away and left the King of France saying his prayers to St. Lawrence. Shortly after Philip returned to the King's camp and with him came young Henry. The young King threw himself on his knees before the King of France.

"My lord, hear me," he cried. "My kingdom is at stake. We can take Rouen now if we surprise the city. Soon my father will be here with his troops. We must take the city before he comes."

"I have declared a truce," persisted Louis.

The two young men joined in their entreaties. They pointed out to him what victory would mean. Was he going to throw it away because of a promise? It might be that if he did not give way many French soldiers would lose their lives.

"Then," he said, "let us exploit the situation. Let us make ready to take the city while the gates are open to us."

Before he could change his mind Philip and Henry hurried away to give orders that immediate preparations should be made for capturing the city.

Rouen might have been taken with the utmost ease but for the fact that a group of young men had dared two of their number to climb the church tower. This they did and as they were poised there, they could see beyond the city to those fields where the French army was encamped and it was obvious to them that preparations were in progress for an immediate attack.

Coming down they told what they had seen and within a few minutes the church bells were ringing out a warning. This was the sound for alarm. The knights at their tournament heard it; they hurried into the city; the gates were closed; boiling pitch was prepared and carried to the battlements. Everyone was ready for action and determined to hold Rouen with an even greater determination because of the perfidy of the French in violating a truce which they had proclaimed.

Thus when Philip of Flanders and young Henry led the attack they were repulsed. The surprise was lacking; the citizens were ready for them and their little strategy might never have been.

All through the night the battle raged and the next day the watchers from the city's walls gave a great shout of joy for the King of England's army was seen approaching. The siege would soon be over.

In a short time the English were within sight of the French and the battle was about to begin. Louis, who was not averse to besieging a town, disliked the thought of hand-to-hand battle. He had never lost his revulsion to bloodshed and he now heartily wished that he had never embarked on the campaign to take Rouen. When he heard that the English had already attacked his rear-guard and inflicted severe casualties, he was so sure he could not win in a hand-to-hand fight that he sent messengers to Henry to ask for a truce and request that he might retire with his troops some miles from the town where he and the King could parley.

Not realizing at this stage that the French had perfidiously broken the truce they had made with the citizens of Rouen and secretly not wishing to do battle with an army in which his son was fighting against him, Henry agreed to allow the French to withdraw.

He was not surprised nor was he displeased when news was brought to him that during the night they had fled and had not stopped riding until they crossed the borders of France.

Henry laughed aloud. It was always good to force a retreat without the loss of blood. That was an easy victory. He only had to appear, to strike terror into his opponents. This would teach young Henry a lesson. He would see that it was not easy to oppose his father.

What rejoicing there was when he entered his city of Rouen! He praised those valiant men and women who had withstood the siege. He sent for the young men who had climbed the tower and when he heard their story he embraced them.

"You did well," he said. "It shall not be forgotten."

Whether it would or not remained to be seen, for Henry was one who often forgot his promises; but he could always make people happy because they had won his approval to such an extent that he made the promise.

He went into the church and gave thanks to God, and St. Thomas à Becket, for he was certain that it was the Archbishop who had sent those men up to the tower and had saved his city of Rouen.

Richard, the King's second son, was not yet eighteen. More warlike than his brothers, he exulted in the necessity to take up arms. He was determined to excel on the battlefield and to hold Aquitaine against his father. He hated his father. It was true that his brothers were impatient with the old King, that they believed he had cheated them of their inheritance, that they had taken up arms against him, but none of them hated him as Richard did.

All his life he had seen his father as the devil—the evil genius of their life. His mother had believed this and she was wise and clever and he loved her even as he hated his father.

He longed to be with her, but she was her husband's captive. When Richard thought of that he was so filled with fury that he longed to kill his father. And he would, he promised himself. How gleefully he would cut off his head and send it to his mother. She would appreciate that. Together they would make a ballad of it; they would sing in harmony.

He had a double mission now—it was not only to defeat his father and become true ruler of Aquitaine but to set his mother free. He wished that he were older. He was a born fighter but no one took so young a man seriously, and his father had created an aura about himself; he was becoming known as the invincible lion. Yet he was ageing, and it would not always be so. The King of France was against him; so were his other sons, Henry and Geoffrey. Surely he could not stand out for ever against such opposition? And when the Archbishop had been murdered it seemed as though the whole world was against him. Could people have admired him for performing that humiliating penance? Richard could not believe this could be so. Surely he had demeaned himself, and yet since he had done it, he had had great success in England. Attempts to take it from him had failed. But it would be different in Normandy and Aquitaine. He was not going to win there.

He exulted to think of the armies of the King of France and men such as Philip of Flanders. Henry would soon be in command of his kingdom. So must Richard be in command of his.

How he enjoyed riding at the head of troops, his pennants flying.

"My best loved son," his mother had said, "you were born to lead men. I thank God that you are the one to inherit Aquitaine. Indeed I would never have allowed my native land to go to anyone else."

They were supposed to rule it jointly, he and his mother but since she had been her husband's prisoner she could not be said to have a say in the governing of the land. The people of Aquitaine loved her but they did not take all that kindly to her son. With his fair hair and bright blue eyes he did not appear to belong to the south. There was something alien about him and they sensed this. They only accepted him because he was his mother's son but they were always aware that in him there was a strong strain of his Norman ancestry.

He was a poet; he loved music. In that, he was his mother's son. But they could not forget that his father was Henry Plantagenet whose mother had been the granddaughter of the Norman Conqueror.

So, when he rode through Aquitaine trying to rouse men to his banner in order to preserve his inheritance from his avaricious father, the knights of Aquitaine were not eager to join him.

News was brought to him that his father, having assured himself that England was safe, was on his way to Aquitaine to settle matters there. Richard realized that he was very like his brothers in that while his father was at a distance he could rage against him but the thought of coming face to face with him in battle struck terror into his heart. The old King's reputation could not be forgotten. All men were aware of it and the sturdiest quailed before it. He had that rare quality possessed by his grandfather and great-grandfather which had often resulted in their winning a battle before it had started simply by filling their enemies' hearts with fear and the certainty that they could not win against such a man.

Richard now surveyed his company. He could see the fear in their faces. He suspected that if they knew that his father was marching on them many would in sheer terror desert.

He called a messenger to him and told him to ride with all speed to the army of the King of France which he believed was in Normandy. "Take these notes," he said, "and give one to each of my two brothers and one to the King of France."

He watched the messenger ride away. He felt safe now. They would not let him be defeated. They would send help.

His father had still not come but he was approaching. Richard watched for the messenger's return. With him must come aid. Perhaps his brothers themselves. If they had taken Rouen they would be flushed with victory and that would be the best news he could receive, for it would mean that they had defeated his father and the myth of his invincibility would have been exploded.

But no soldiers came, and the messenger returned.

"Alas, brother," wrote Henry, "we were not successful at Rouen, but were forced to fly before our father's troops. Now there is a truce and we wait to discuss terms with him. But one condition he has laid down is that we must send no aid to you."

Richard clenched his fists in quiet rage. In some measure he possessed the Angevin temper but instead of being hot like his father's it was cold. Richard would never lie on the floor and gnaw the rushes; he would never grow scarlet so that men believed he might drop to the ground in a fit. He grew pale; the blue eyes were like steel; but his anger was none the less fierce because it was cold.

He felt that anger now. For here he was a boy in age, with a small army, and he must stand alone against the greatest general of the age—his own father.

He himself might do it. His followers never would.

He knew he had no alternative but to retreat before his father. When he discussed the state of affairs with his most skilled knights they agreed with him.

"The men would never stand and fight your father's armies," they said. "They would tremble with fear at the prospect and desert before your father arrived."

It was true. There was nothing to do but retreat.

What bitter humiliation! Henry marched through Aquitaine, extorting obedience from all. Richard marched south but he could not go on marching for ever. His men were deserting him. Soon there would be but a handful of them left.

At length he realized that he could retreat no more. He must face his father.

The meeting took place and when Richard looked into that strong face with its curly hair—a little greying now—clipped square on the forehead, the flaring nostrils, the leonine aspect, his emotions were mixed. The hatred was there; fear too; and he knew why men quailed before his father.

He knelt and put his face on the ground in a sudden access of wretchedness. He was beaten and he knew that he was too young as yet to stand up and face this man. He had been guilty of great folly and, although he hated his father more fiercely than he could ever hate anyone else, he must respect him.

Henry watched him in silence. My son, he thought. This handsome boy is my son Richard, the betrothed of Alice.

He felt a sudden tenderness for him—perhaps because he was his son, perhaps because he had taken his bride from him.

"Rise, Richard," he said.

And when the boy stood so that they were face to face—and Richard must look down on him for he was several inches taller than his father—he put his arms about him and embraced him.

"It is a sad thing," he said, "when a son takes up arms against his own father."

Richard said nothing. A slightly sullen expression touched his lips.

"Sad," went on the King, "and useless. You are a good fighter, they tell me, Richard. But there is more to battle than brandishing a lance, my boy. There's subtlety and strategy. A good general knows when he should retreat and when he should advance. Well, let us say this: You knew when to retreat did you not, and when to show humility? Suffice it that you have been a worthy general. Now we will talk."

He put his arm through Richard's and they walked together.

"I like not these quarrels," said the King. "Your brothers have come to their senses. I shall see them ere long. We are to have a meeting and it might be well if you joined us. I have much to say to you all, for I am not of a mind to endure these family quarrels."

"We are men," said Richard. "And men cannot be treated as boys."

"Both boys and men are given the treatment they warrant. Remember that and we shall understand each other. Now, my son, know this. There is now peace in Aquitaine. You are its Duke but the titles my sons hold, they hold under me. Remember that and we shall remain at peace."

The King ordered that a banquet should be prepared and at table he kept his son beside him; and all noticed that he showed a certain fondness for him and that Richard was subdued through seeming sullen.

The next day the King sent for his son.

"Go now and join your brothers at the Court of the King of France," he told him. "You will say that you have decided that there shall be no more strife in Aquitaine, and that you, like them, are now aware of the folly of your ways. Like them, you are at peace with your father. We shall all meet soon and then I shall tell you what my proposals are."

Richard took his farewell of his father and rode towards the French border.

Henry was thoughtful. He could not comtemplate Richard without thinking of Alice. The boy had said nothing of his bride. Did he never think of her?

Henry thought of her constantly.

102

In Salisbury Castle, the Queen received news of her sons. She had been more than a year in captivity and her first humiliated rage had passed. She had become accustomed to her imprisonment which was not by any means rigorous. At first she had thought that Henry would attempt to murder her. Perhaps he would. He wanted to be rid of her. Or did he? Was that just a sop to Rosamund? He could not marry Rosamund. The people would never accept it. But being Henry of course he might attempt what others would be afraid to do.

All her hopes were in her sons. If they could win their battle against their father, their first duty would be to free her. She could trust them to do that. What a great day that would be when the tables were turned, when Henry was the prisoner of his wife and sons. How she would taunt him!

But it was not yet. There was still fire in the old lion. *Old* lion. She had to remember that he was twelve years younger than she was!

She went to the topmost point of the keep and looked out across the moat. She was allowed the freedom of the castle but if she attempted to cross the drawbridge she would be stopped by guards. At first she had planned escape, but nothing had come of it. She was too well guarded. Bribery was useless. All her guards knew that if she were allowed to escape, Henry's fury would be unleashed and the greatest punishment would be inflicted on them.

She had always been an intriguer and now her chief pleasure was in following her bent. How strange that she, the adventuress who had travelled to the Holy Land, who had taken her lovers, who had divorced the King of France that she might marry Henry Plantagenet, should now be a prisoner, confined to one small space, looking out day after day on the same horizons!

She would outwit him though. In time she would be the victor. This thought kept her spirits up. Every day when she awoke she thought: This could be the day. Today a messenger may come riding from my sons . . . from Henry or from Richard . . . with the good news. Perhaps they would send her <u>his</u> head to gloat over. No, not that. She did not want him dead. She knew that the world must be a duller place for her without him. It had always been so. Nothing had ever excited her quite so much as her tussles with him. She thought of the days of their passion. She had never really had a lover to compare with him. There was a power about him and it was this which appealed to her. She had believed in the first days of their marriage that she would love him with a deep abiding passion all her days. The passion had remained but it had become a passion of hatred.

She remembered her anger when she had first become aware of his infidelities. That was when he had introduced his bastard Geoffrey into her nurseries. The son of one of his light o' loves to be brought up with the royal children! And that same Geoffrey was fighting with him now, ever-faithful to him, and it was said that he loved him dearly. "Bastards can be faithful," she had said. "They have to be grateful. They have no rights. It is different with those who have just claim to lands and titles."

Let him drool over his bastard! It was his legitimate sons to whom he would have to answer.

"Oh, God," she prayed, "deliver him into their hands."

She had her spies. They came to the castle on various pretexts and found the moment to speak to the Queen.

Some of her attendants had friends who gave them news. She had with her some of the women from her native Aquitaine and they spoke the Provençal language. They would sing the news to her in this language as though it were a song. Perhaps there was no need for this, but it appealed to her sense of intrigue, and enlivened the days of captivity.

How delighted she had been when she heard that Richard was holding Aquitaine and that he was rousing the knights of that fair land against his father.

Then came the news of the siege of Rouen. How like Louis! she thought.

She talked to her women of the old days when Louis had turned away from a fight because he had no stomach for it.

"He could have faced the King of England, fought with him. But he had to run away. He was always more of a monk than a man. Though in the early days of our marriage I made almost a man of him. And my sons . . . Henry and Geoffrey? What of them? They should have stayed to fight. But to give in, to call a truce . . . and then be content to listen to his terms. And what will those terms be, I ask you? Henry Plantagenet will never take his hands from land or castle. Once his greedy claws have seized it, he will never let it go. My son Richard had more spirit than his brother. You may depend upon it, he will never give in."

But he did give in. She pictured his cold anger when he realized that he was no match for his father. The people of Aquitaine had not trusted so young a boy and they feared the rage of Henry Plantagenet. So the war in Aquitaine had petered out even as it had outside Rouen.

"It would seem he has but to appear and people are afraid of him. Why should they be?" she asked, but she knew. He had a quality which she would never forget. She wished that he would come to see her in this prison in which he had placed her. How she would have enjoyed a verbal battle with him.

She railed against fate. He was too strong, he still retained the vigours of youth; and the boys were too young. In time it would not be so and as they matured so would he grow old. She must wait till the years clouded the lion's eyes; then his cubs would savage him.

If she could but be there with them, to advise them, perhaps to cajole Louis. Could she do that now? How she longed to be free!

She was excited by an unexpected piece of news.

It was given to her in a song. A great King loved a young girl . . . a very young girl . . . who was betrothed to his son.

She listened. It could not be so.

Alice!

Why, she was but a child. But not too young to satisfy his lust.

So it had come to children! And the betrothed of his son! Richard's bride!

What did he plan? To pass the soiled beauty over to Richard when he had finished with her?

That must not be.

Then another thought came to her. He wanted a divorce. He had suggested as much.

Oh, my God, she thought, does he want to marry Alice?

She had satisfied herself that he would not marry Rosamund. The people would not want her as their Queen and he was king enough to know that he must above all things keep the approval of his people. But Alice, the daughter of the King of France! That was another matter.

Dallying with Alice! The lecher! She could picture his face clearly; the speculation in the tawny eyes, the nostrils flaring suddenly as they did in moments of intense emotion.

How much does he want to marry Alice? she wondered. Enough to murder his wife?

How simple it would be. Who would miss her? Her children? But they were his also and he was the master. What was going on behind the lion's mask? How safe was she?

She felt she must act quickly.

She would get a message to Richard. She had friends enough to be able to do that.

She was framing it in her mind.

"Demand that the King sends your betrothed to you. It is time you and Alice were married. He must do this. Tell the King of France that you want your bride."

She was alert.

She would have to take very special care now.

It was the last day of September—mild and misty—when Henry sat at the conference table facing his sons, Henry, Richard and Geoffrey.

In his heart was triumph tinged with a certain sadness. It was unseemly that a father should be called upon to make peace terms with his sons; on the other hand it was gratifying that he had brought them all to heel—every one of them— Henry, with his grandoise ideas of what belonged to him, because his father had had the magnanimity to allow him to be crowned King; Richard, cold hatred gleaming in his blue eyes, too young and inexperienced to realize how unwise he was to show it; and Geoffrey who seemed still a boy. Fine lads all of them—and all here because they had conspired against their father.

He could not help being proud of them. They were all good looking. Henry was the most handsome; it had been said of him that he was the most beautiful Prince in Christendom; Geoffrey was almost as good looking, taking after his grandfather of Anjou who had borne the same name. Richard was different. None the less, good looking but in a different way. Taller than his brothers and more skilled in equestrian arts; one day when he was more experienced he would be a formidable foe to meet on the battlefield.

These boys he had sired; the thought filled him with some emotion and the sternness faded from his eyes. All the same he was going to let them know who was the master.

"My sons," said Henry, "it grieves me that we should be sitting here in this way. I remember well those days when you were in the nurseries of my castles and what joy I took in your growing up. You have been ill-advised and have offended against the laws of God and man in taking up arms against your father. But I do not forget that you are my sons and because of this I will be lenient. First we will make a solemn vow that we all forgive our enemies and restore to their rightful owners those castles which we have taken during the conflict with each other. You may have made promises to my enemies to join with them against me. You must now declare yourselves free from all promises and undertakings."

He watched them quietly. Henry and Geoffrey faintly sullen, Richard a little defiant. But all of them—even Richard—knew that they had no alternative but to agree to the King's terms.

"Henry," he went on, "you shall have two castles in Normandy and an allowance of £15,000 Angevin money. Richard shall have two in Poitou and half the revenues of that land." He turned to Geoffrey. "And you, my son, are soon to marry Conan's daughter, Constance. You shall now have half the marriage portion and when the ceremony takes place the whole of it."

Inwardly the brothers were dismayed because they knew that the castles offered to them were of no strategic importance and in making these gifts their father was in fact taking from them every vestige of that power for which they had been fighting.

"You have a young brother," went on the King, his voice softening a little. Young John was the best of the bunch. *He* had not risen against his father. At eight years old he was an engaging little fellow. Thank God, he had escaped his mother's influence. "He is my son too," went on the King. "From him I have had no sign of disobedience. I gave him three castles as you know well." He permitted his lips to curve in a sardonic smile. Was it not these three castles over which there had been all the trouble? "A poor inheritance for the son of a king. Now I shall give him one thousand pounds a year in England and the castles of Marlborough and Nottingham. He shall have two hundred and fifty pounds a year from his Normandy lands and the same amount from his property in Anjou where I shall give him one castle. He shall also have one in Touraine and another in Maine. You would not wish your brother to be a pauper, I know, simply because he had the misfortune—or as it has turned out it may be the good fortune—to be born after yourselves."

They were dismayed. The trouble with their father had started because he wished to take from them to give to John—although the cause went deeper than that—and now they were worse off than when they had begun. But they could not protest, they knew. They could see the purpose in his face; and no matter how they might fulminate against him in his absence, face to face with him they knew his strength, and they feared it. He had had no hesitation in putting their mother into prison. They knew full well that any resistance to his wishes and they would end up in similar circumstances. He was, after all, according to his standards, acting very leniently towards them since they had all taken up arms against him.

"There is one thing more," said the King, "I must have an assurance from you that you will not ask any more of me and that you will not withdraw yourselves or your service from me."

This was perhaps the most important part of all but they knew it was impossible to evade it. They were here in this little village of Mont Louis near Tours and he could, if he wished, seize them. They were virtually his prisoners, for he was their master.

He was smiling at them.

"Then we are friends," he said. "Richard, Geoffrey, you will do homage to me which will show that you are indeed my loyal sons and I your liege lord."

His two sons knelt and swore allegiance to him and when this was done, young Henry prepared to do the same.

His father smiled at him quizzically. "Nay, Henry," he said. "Are you not a king and a king of England? You could not then pay homage to me."

A great fear touched the young man then. He said in a sudden panic: "You are my father. I will swear allegiance to you as my brothers have done."

But the King shook his head. "Nay, my son." He laid his hand on young Henry's shoulder and pressed it hard. "I shall expect loyalty from you and you will give it, for if you did not there could be terrible consequences . . . for you. But you will keep your vows. You will remember that I am your father, that it is from these hands that your good fortune flows. You shall be beside me. You shall be taught how to become a king in very truth and I shall be your tutor."

Young Henry smiled faintly, but he was uneasy.

* * *

Now that he had made peace with his sons the King decided that he would keep them with him for a while that he might instill into them the need to keep to their promises.

Ruefully he reminded himself that they were his sons. He had not always kept his promises. What if they had taken after him in that respect? He imagined they had. They were fighters all of them; whether they would make good kings he was unsure. But they could doubtless be tutored. He wanted young Henry to carry on in the way he had, for he had followed to some measure the rules laid down by his two great predecessors. Could he rely on Henry to do the same? Not at this stage. Henry was too easily led; he gave too ready an ear to flatterers. That was a trait which was of no use to any king. One of his best men had been Richard de Luci, his Chief Justiciar; he could trust that man as he would few others and never had his trust been misplaced and never had Richard de Luci flattered him. Sometimes his frankness might have angered the King but only momentarily. He thanked God he was too good a ruler to run from his best friends because of a bit of plain speaking. Young Henry must learn this. He was constantly in the company of men who fawned on him. He was turning from William Marshall who was a good friend and a worthy knight. People like Philip of Flanders attracted him. Henry would be the first to admit that such men could be attractive, entertaining, amusing; but one did not attach too much importance to their friendship.

Young Henry had much to learn and where better could he learn it than at his father's side?

And as yet he would wait and see where he would send his sons. Perforce for a time they should ride with him. It was good to make them think of him as a father, to repair some of the damage that she-wolf had done. He should have barred her from the nurseries. What an unnatural woman! How different it would have been if Rosamund had been his Queen . . . or Alice. Alice was young yet for bearing children. Sooner or later he would get her with child he doubted not. And then . . . ? That could take care of itself when the matter arose.

They had ridden through Anjou to Normandy. He had wanted the people to see his sons riding with him. Henry on one side, Richard on the other and young Geoffrey a pace or two behind. "See, we are united." That was what he was saying to the people. "Any who have rebellion in their minds get rid of it quickly. I am invincible . . . but with my sons beside me I am to be feared more than ever."

Yes, it was good to ride through his dominions with his sons as companions.

In December they came to Argentan.

"Here," he said, "we shall spend Christmas. It is good that we should all be together."

It would be a merry Christmas. How wonderful it would be if little Alice were here with him as his Queen. Other women could not completely satisfy him. This was how it had been in the early days with Rosamund.

His foresters from England sent eighty deer to Argentan because, they said, there were no deer that could compare with those of England. The King must celebrate his Christmas with his sons and the deer of England.

He liked the gesture, although food had never been his great concern. He was glad though that it was recognized that this was a special Christmas.

He rode often with his sons and a few days before Christmas when he was returning to the castle he said to Richard: "You look woebegone, my son. Are you not well?"

"I was thinking of my mother," said Richard.

The King's face hardened. "Alas, she has a lesson to learn."

"It is a hard one, my lord."

"As traitors' lessons must be."

"You have been kinder to your sons than to your wife," said Richard.

"It is for me to decide what shall be the punishment of those who betray me."

"She did not fight against you."

"How could she . . . a woman?"

"She but came to join us, her own sons."

"That she might instill in you the wish to rebel against your father."

"If she were at fault could you not forgive her now as you have us?"

"Nay," he said, "I could not."

"But should you not be kind to your wife?"

"By God's eyes, Richard," cried the King, "would you presume to tell me my duty?"

"Nay, father, I think your heart will tell me that."

"It does, my son. And the message it gives me is "Keep that woman under restraint. She is a she-wolf who would teach her cubs to devour their father."

"Their father would not allow that."

"By God's hands, teeth and eyes he would not. But enough . . . enough I say. Be silent! Or I might change my mind regarding you. You would not wish to share your mother's fate."

Richard *was* silent. The familiar signs of anger were rising. Richard was too bold, decided the King. The lad would have to be taught a lesson. Of all his sons Richard made him the most uncomfortable. But perhaps that was because of Alice.

They feasted well on the deer from England and after the banquet the musicians played to them. Richard sang a song of his own composing which was about a knight who was betrothed to a fair maiden whom a wicked ogre had imprisoned in a castle. The song was about the knight's love for his lady and his determination to face any odds in order to rescue his bride.

The King felt faintly uneasy and more so later when Richard was seated beside him and his son said: "Father, I am no longer a boy. Like the knight in the song I am betrothed."

"Oh yes . . . to young Alice. I hear she is a comely girl."

"It is time we were married."

The King nodded. "Very soon," he said soothingly, "very soon."

"I am of an age to have a wife."

"You have much to do, my son. I have plans for you. We have far-flung dominions and such need protecting. I am fortunate in having four sons who have overcome their folly and have now learned what is best for them. I can see you will be a great fighter, Richard, a leader of men."

"I feel that too, Father, but I shall also need a wife. I believe the King of France is of the opinion that our marriage should take place at once."

"The King of France has never been a man of good judgment. Leave me to decide, Richard, when you shall have your bride."

"And that will be soon, my lord?"

"It will be when I think fit, my son."

"You have seen my bride, Father?"

"Yes, she has been in the schoolroom with young John and Joanna."

"Do you think she will make me a good wife?"

"I think she could well make a good wife."

"Then the ceremony must soon take place. I am determined on it."

The King was silent. Then he clapped his hands and asked for another song.

An uncomfortable fellow, Richard. Different from the others. Stronger in a way.

But he was not going to have Alice. He was not parting with her. Something would have to be done. When he returned to England he would try to think of a plan.

The King's Choice

The King had no intention of wasting time on Christmas revelries. He wanted to go to England but before he did so he must make sure that his possessions here were safeguarded. He could trust his sons . . . for a while. Their vows had been too recent for them to dare break them yet. He told young Henry to go to Rouen and let it be known there that he came with his father's blessing. Richard should go to Poitou and preserve order there; Geoffrey should go to Brittany and act in the same manner there. He himself would ride through Normandy and make sure that the dukedom could safely be left in the hands of trusty custodians.

The young men, all relieved to have escaped from their father's vigilance, departed on their various ways.

The young Henry could not resist riding to the Court of France on the pretext that his wife, Marguerite, wished to see her father. Louis received them with the utmost honour, for he was delighted that the young man should come to see him, and Henry, smarting from the humiliation which surrender to his father's wishes had given him was appeased to be received thus by the King of France.

Louis wanted to hear about the meeting and expressed himself horrified when he heard of the old King's terms.

"My dear son," he said, "you see he has robbed you of your rights."

"I see," replied Henry, "that I am in no better case than before my rebellion—in fact even worse."

Louis nodded. "It will not always be so."

"But I have sworn not to rise against him."

"Events will show you how to act," said Louis.

"You do not like my father, my lord."

"Like him? Who likes him? He is not a man to be liked. He is a great general. He is victorious in battle. But there is more in life than fighting."

"It plays a large part in the life of a king, it seems."

113

"Alas! How much happier a man would be living peacefully with his children around him."

"My father would not allow me to pay homage to him. He accepted this from my brothers but he said that as I was a crowned king it would not be meet for me to pay it to him."

Louis was thoughtful. "Did he not then?" he ruminated and shook his head slowly.

"It shows, does it not, that he regards me as a king?"

"The paying of homage is double-edged," said the King of France. "The knight swears to serve his master, his master swears to protect his knight. It could well be that your father did not wish to give his word to protect you."

"Why not, think you?"

"It may well be that he has his reasons."

"What reasons could there be?"

"Your mother is his prisoner. She showed that she was ready to rebel against him. You have shown that, my son."

"And so did my brothers."

"But they have not been crowned king."

"What do you fear for me?"

"That since he is not bound to protect you he could imprison you as he has your mother."

"Do you believe he would do this?"

"I would believe anything of Henry Plantagenet."

The young King was alarmed but Louis laid his hand on his arm. "Take care, that is all. Make sure that you are never in a position such as your mother's."

"How could I make sure of this?"

"You can never be sure, of course. But if your father accepted your homage and in return swore to protect you, you could feel much happier."

Henry was afraid. No, he did not trust his father. Could it really be that he would imprison him? Why had he not done so, if that were the case? He had captured his mother when she was disguised as a knight. That was different.

He continued to be uneasy.

At the French Court he met Philip of Flanders with whom he had been on terms of friendship since Philip had helped him to try to invade England. That endeavour had gone awry but Philip was not worried.

They jousted together. Philip was a master of that art. Tilting was his passion. One needed so much equipment that Henry could not afford to take much part in it. Philip laughed at him. "And you a king!" he cried. "Never mind. I will help you. I can supply you with all you need."

It was a wonderful pastime. Henry would have loved to linger and enjoy it. His father would have called it a waste of time. He thought of nothing but governing his realms; he had always said that he dared not take his hands from the reins for one moment. Serve him right. He should let his sons take their inheritance and govern for him now that he was getting old, let him go to England and live like a king. But he had never cared for things which meant so much to Henry. When he rode out with a lance it had to be in a real battle; when he spent money it had to be to equip his army and to build some castle. It was work and duty all the time with him. He missed so much in life. Young Henry did not however intend to miss these pleasures if he could help it.

Tilting, feasting, enjoying the company of women—they were the good things of life.

He wished he could live like Philip of Flanders.

Philip told him that he was contemplating a trip to Jerusalem. He thought it would be a great adventure to travel to the Holy Land and strike a blow for Christianity.

How Henry would have liked to accompany him. He imagined telling his father of his desire. He could see the lights of contempt flashing into the leonine face. "Fight for the Holy Land! You have a kingdom here to fight for, my son."

Yet his mother had gone. She had had great adventures. How sad that she was a prisoner. And to think that his father was her jailer!

He was at the root of all their troubles.

Even then he remembered that he was supposed to be in Rouen. Reluctantly he and Marguerite took farewell of Philip of Flanders and he presented himself to his friend and father-in-law Louis of France, in order to receive his blessing.

"Take care," said Louis. "Beware of Henry Plantagenet. Make sure that he does not treat you as he has his wife. If he should send you to England do not go until he has accepted your homage and promised his protection. If you do not you could be his prisoner, for in England he has the power to do that which he would hesitate to do elsewhere."

Henry thanked his father-in-law and left for Rouen.

It seemed that they had been a very short time there when a command came from the King. His son and daughter-in-law were to join him at Bures for he wished them to accompany him to England.

The young couple were dismayed.

"It is as my father said it would be," cried Marguerite. "He wants you to be in England where he will make you his prisoner."

Young Henry did not know what to do. To disobey the summons was unthinkable and yet what would it mean to go?

"Your father said that if he would accept my homage it would be difficult for him to imprison me."

"I see that," replied Marguerite.

"The only thing I can do is to implore him to allow me to swear fealty to him."

"Try that," advised his wife, "and if he refuses you will know you have to be on your guard. We might try to escape. My father thinks that if you have not sworn fealty as soon as you are on English soil you will be at his mercy."

"I am at his mercy now," grimaced young Henry.

"But at least he cannot go against his vows so quickly."

"He can and will do anything he wishes. But at least I think he would wait awhile. I shall implore him to accept my homage. We shall then see what his reply is."

When they reached Bures the King was impatiently awaiting their arrival. He embraced them warmly, asked after their health, particularly that of his daughter-in-law, for he was wondering whether she had become pregnant yet, and then told them that he was planning to sail for England immediately.

Young Henry asked if he might see him alone and permission was immediately granted.

"My Father," he said, "I cannot believe that you love me as you do my brothers, and this makes me a most unhappy man."

"Why should you have such a notion? Are you not my eldest? And if you have rebelled against me so have your brothers. I have forgiven you and if you are a good son to me you can be sure of my love. How many fathers would have forgiven treachery such as you and your brothers showed towards me? And you say I do not love you!"

"You have refused to accept my homage."

"Well, is that not because I have made you a king?"

"It is but a title."

"Aye, but a title! There cannot be two kings in one realm. I

116

made you a king, my son, so that when I die there will be no question as to who is my successor. You hold the title until you take the crown and that you can only do when I am not here to wear it."

"I am a king but in name. You are our sovereign lord. Yet you will not accept my homage. I can see no reason for this except that you do not love me."

'My dear son, if you wish to pay homage to me and take our oath of fealty then so shall it be."

"Oh, Father, then you do indeed love me."

They embraced and the King said with emotion, "It pleases me to see you in this contrite mood."

Tears of relief were on young Henry's cheeks. If his father would accept his homage then he was safe.

"I will arrange that this little ceremony shall take place without delay," said the King, "for I see that until it does you will think that I remain indignant towards you. You shall be treated as your brothers and then we shall be good friends. For that, my son, is to both our interests."

Henry went to Marguerite and told her what the King had said. She was pleased.

"But make sure he keeps his promise. You know his nature. He does not always think it necessary to keep a promise."

This one however the King did keep.

The holy relics were produced and, placing his hands on these, young Henry swore his oath of allegiance to his father.

"I will bear you faith against all men and as long as I live shall seek no harm either to my own men or to those of the King, my father, who have served in the war when we stood against each other. I will abide by your counsel in all my actions."

The King listened, his expression softly affectionate.

When the oath was taken he embraced his son.

"From now on you and I are the best of friends and that is good news for us and our dominions."

Shortly afterwards they sailed for England.

The King's first indulgence was to visit Alice. She was no longer the child she had been when she first became his mistress, for she had matured quickly. He grew more and more deeply enamoured of her because he was discovering greater depths of sensuality in her while she yet remained docile and undemanding. He had once thought Rosamund gave him all he needed but she lacked the voluptuous indulgence which was becoming more and more apparent in Alice. Alice was the perfect mistress. There was no doubt about that. He realized that during their most passionate moments Rosamund had in a manner of speaking glanced furtively over her shoulder to see whether the recording angel was in attendance. Love such as this should fill the moments; there should be no thought of the reckoning. If that came it must come later.

He wished that he could spend more time with Alice.

"But now I am in England," he told her, "I shall see you more often. Will you always be so eager to see me?"

She assured him that she would.

He did not tell her that her betrothed Richard was asking that she go to him. He did not believe in spoiling such moments. Besides he had other matters with which to occupy him. He was particularly interested in his son Henry, whom he determined to keep beside him. This was not only because he did not trust him; he genuinely wanted to tutor him in the art of kingship. Young Henry had many good qualities. He was very good looking and quite charming. He had these assets which had never been his father's. But he was frivolous and lacked his father's dedication. He did not yet understand that to govern a kingdom—and particularly one which was so wide-spread—a ruler must never allow pleasure to stand in the way of his duty to his crown. He thought fleetingly of his Alice. Well, he compromised, hardly ever. And if the secret came out that he had taken Richard's betrothed as his mistress, he would overcome that as he had other troubles. He would insist on a divorce. He would offer Louis marriage for his daughter . . . marriage to the King of England. And nothing would please him more.

Besides, when one had years of good rule behind one, one could take risks which an inexperienced man could not take.

So he would deal with this matter of his delightful Alice when the time came.

One of his first duties in England would be to visit the shrine of St. Thomas, to pay homage to the saint who was now his good friend and working on his behalf in Heaven. There was now a new Archbishop, Richard, Prior of Dover, who had been unanimously elected and had held office for nearly a year. On the day he had been elected news had come from the Pope that Thomas à Becket's name had been added to the list of saints.

Richard it seemed would not be a troublemaker, and for

this the King was grateful. He could congratulate himself that everything had worked out very well.

As he travelled to Canterbury with young Henry beside him he received sad news from Count Humbert of Maurienne. His little daughter Alice who had been betrothed to Prince John had died suddenly. The King was momentarily dismayed and then it occurred to him that with John's better prospects he might make a more advantageous match. It so often happened that these betrothals came to nothing. Children were affianced in their cradles and so it was small wonder that events occurred while they were growing up to prevent their marriages ever taking place.

John was now a free bargaining counter and his father would be alert for a more advantageous proposition.

And now to Canterbury.

The King watched his son as they rode. Too handsome, a little petulant still. And how insistent he had been that his homage should be accepted. Why was that? Had he really learned the folly of his ways?

He was surprised to find within himself a softness for his family. He would have liked a gentle wife—Alice of course— and a brood of sons and daughters who admired and loved him and thought only to serve him. Surely that was not asking too much? It was natural that fathers and sons should work together.

Something had gone wrong in the family. He had from necessity had to absent himself for long periods at a time, and Eleanor . . . It all came back to Eleanor. It was a great pity that he had ever married her. But was it? What of Aquitaine? She had been the richest heiress in Europe and he had been counted lucky to get her.

If he divorced her, he would lose Aquitaine. A sobering thought.

But this was not the time to think of that matter.

They were approaching Canterbury.

"See my son there before us, the tower and spires of the Cathedral. I can never see it without emotion."

"That is not to be wondered at, Father," replied young Henry, "considering what happened there."

"It pleases me that I have made my peace with Thomas à Becket. We are now friends as we were in the beginning of our relationship. You and I are friends too, my son. Our strength is in our unity. Always remember that. I want you to know it and all England to know it. That is why I am going to make it known that you and I have sworn the oath of allegiance to each other. Who would dare come against us when we stand together?"

"All know that we are friends, Father."

"Those close to us, yes . . . but I want all to know, so I am going to make a public declaration, that none may be in any doubt."

"What do you mean by this, Father?"

"Never fear, my son, you shall see."

Henry did see.

The King spent some time with his new Archbishop and declared himself pleased with him.

He told the Archbishop that he wished him to summon all the bishops of Westminster and he himself should accompany them. He would command all knights and barons to be present for he had something of importance to impart to them.

"What is this conference, Father?" asked young Henry.

"You will see in good time," he was told.

There in the hall of the palace the King and his son were seated side by side on the dais and the elder Henry addressed the company.

He had summoned them for an express purpose.

"You see me here with my son," he said, "and that there is amity between us. You know full well that but a short time ago the situation was very different. But I have excellent news for you. My son, King Henry, came to me at Bures and with tears and much emotion he humbly begged for mercy. He asked me to forgive him for what he did to me before, during and after the war. In all humility he begged that I, his father, would accept his homage and all allegiance declaring that he could not believe I had forgiven him if I did not. I was touched by this. My pity was great for I saw how remorseful he was to so humble himself before me. I put aside my grievances against him and I allowed him to pay homage to me. On holy relics he swore that he would bear me faith against all men and abide by my counsel and that he would order his household and all his state by my advice and henceforth in all things."

The young King felt a violent resentment rising in him. It was true that he had promised this but that his father should have arranged this public declaration was humiliating in the extreme.

He had brought him here that the leading men of the nation should know that although he bore the title of King there was only one King of England and every man among them—including his son—was his subject.

His resentment flared up. He wanted to stand up and cry out that he had begged his father to accept his homage not because he had wished to serve him, but because he feared what might happen to him if he did not make such a declaration.

He would not endure such treatment. He had sworn his oath but he would await his opportunity.

The King felt it was good to be in England. He would always be King of England before anything else and this land was more important to him than any other, born and bred in Anjou though he had been. To lose England would be the greatest disaster which could befall a descendant of the Conqueror. There would be no danger of this if it were not for the fact that he must guard his lands so far away.

He kept young Henry with him, trying to win his affection. He was sorry for the young man and, though he was suspicious of him, wanted to be a father to him. He was learning that even a king could not command affection. He had tried to explain why he had made that public declaration of Henry's homage to him. It was not to humiliate him. It was to show the people that they had sworn to be friends.

"Was it not enough," asked young Henry, "that I had given you my oath?"

"It was better that all should know you had given me your oath."

"I felt humiliated."

"Never be humiliated because you do your duty to your father. Be proud that you had the courage to confess your fault and glad that your father had the magnanimity to forgive you and take you back into his heart."

He would have his son sit beside him at table and ride beside him in battle. He would have had the young man sleep in his room if it were not for the fact that Henry was a husband and he himself often preferred another bedfellow.

Alice, dear sweet Alice! She was changing; her body filling out as she was growing out of childhood into womanhood.

One day when he visited her she had disturbing news.

"My lord," she said, "I believe I am pregnant with your child."

He felt a mingling of horror and pleasure. Something would have to be done now. What? How could he write to the King of France and tell him he had got his daughter with child? How could he tell Richard that his affianced bride was about to be a mother?

He looked at her and drew her to him holding her fast so that she might not see the expression in his face.

He had known that there was this possibility and had refused to look it straight in the face. He knew that when it happened there would be some change in his way of life, for Alice could not stay at the palace and bear a child which would be known to be his. And even if it were not—what a scandal there would be if the affianced bride of his son Richard should be in such a condition, when she had not been married and nowhere near her affianced husband for years.

How much was whispered already? His visits to this palace would have been noted. There must be many who were aware of his relationship with Alice. It was true, that none would dare expose the secret for fear of his anger, but they would whisper of it.

"What must I do?" asked Alice.

"Leave this to me, my dearest," he said.

She was happy to do that. What a wife she would make! She did not ask how or where or why. She was just content to leave it to him, so sure was she of his ability to solve all her problems.

He turned the matter over in his mind. If he could divorce Eleanor now . . . and marry Alice . . . But there was no time. He imagined the difficulties there would be in the way of his divorce. He just could not do it. If only Alice were not the daughter of the King of France how easy it would be! Just another bastard to add to the many he had already fathered. But the daughter of the King of France! The betrothed of his son! This was a very delicate situation.

Alice clearly must not stay at the palace. It would be quite impossible for her to have the child there. Where then could she go? She must be whisked away before her pregnancy became obvious. And where to send her?

If only he could marry her. But how could he? There was only one way in which he could and that would be if Eleanor were to die.

That was impossible. If she died mysteriously he would be immediately suspected. It would be Thomas à Becket all over again. And what of Aquitaine? That would go to Richard and he himself would never be accepted there. That was quite out of the question. Moreover he was not that kind of murderer. He could kill a man in battle; he could have people put to death if they offended him, but he could not murder his wife.

He smiled wryly. He remembered so much about her. He had been enamoured of her once. What a tigress she was— and a great lover! They had had some good times together in the early days. Something bound them together even if it was only hatred. He liked to think that she was still on the Earth—best of all in a prison of his choosing.

Dearest Alice, he thought, as much as I would like to make you my wife that is not the way. I would this had not happened and that we might have gone on in the old manner until such a time as I could devise a plan. Now we have to formulate one with all speed.

He studied the problem from all angles and it seemed to him that he could find only one solution.

He set out for his Palace of Woodstock.

Rosamund was, as ever, delighted to see him.

He embraced her warmly and told her how as ever she gave him great comfort. She quickly realized that he had not come to spend a few peaceful days in her company. He had a problem and he thought she could help him.

"There is something I have to tell you, Rosamund," he said. "Let us walk in the gardens for there we can be quite alone."

Through the paths with their carefully tended bushes they walked arm in arm.

"I need your help in this matter, Rosamund. It concerns the Princess Alice."

He was aware that she flinched. There had been rumours then and they would have reached her! Who else would have heard?

"She is a comely creature and in something of a predicament at the moment. She is with child."

"My lord!"

"Yes," said the King ruefully. "This has happened and of course there would be a great noise about it if it were known."

"She is betrothed to Richard!"

"Richard of course must not know."

"But she is to be his bride!"

"That marriage may never come to pass. You know how it

123

is with these betrothals. There was the betrothal of John to that other Alice. What a pother there was about the castles I gave him. Why, that started a war. And now look you, that little Alice is dead and John has no affianced bride."

"They were but children, but Richard and Alice . . ."

"Yes, yes. But the fact is she is with child and I do not wish this to be known."

"How then, my lord, can this matter be kept secret?"

"Oh come, Rosamund, it is not the first time a child has been born in secret."

"At Westminster!"

"Nay, she must leave Westminster. There is the Bower here. That once proved a secluded spot. It could again."

"You are sending Alice to the Bower?"

"And I wish you to go with her to care for her and keep her company. You will do this, Rosamund?"

"If it is your wish."

"God bless you, sweetheart. I knew I could trust you with my life."

"And she is to be kept here in secret?"

"You will know how to do that. I shall let it be known that she has left the palace for a while to journey to the North. She will set out and come here and stay here. You will look after her and have with you but a few of your most trusted attendants. Those who once guarded our secret well. Let them know discreetly that they act so for the King's pleasure and that if they should chatter or act with indiscretion they will rouse his anger. Keep her here. Cherish her. And let her bear her child in peace."

"And when the child is born?"

"You may leave that to me. I shall arrange for it to be brought up in a state worthy of it. You will do this for me, Rosamund?"

"As you know, I live to serve you."

"Oh, it was a happy day for me when I came to your father's castle."

He did not stay long. He had to get back to Alice, to let her know that he had made arrangements for her. She had nothing to fear. His dear good friend Rosamund Clifford would care for her; and he trusted Rosamund as he could none other.

As he rode back to Westminster he felt elated. There was no situation he could not master. Even this one of getting his son's betrothed with child was not beyond him to solve.

He wanted to marry Alice. He would then legitimize the child, for it was unlikely that the marriage could take place before the birth. He must marry Alice, for the time was coming nearer and nearer when Richard would demand his bride and how could he go on making excuses to retain her?

Back at Westminster he sent a secret message to Rome inviting the papal legate Cardinal Huguzon to England. There were certain matters which he could discuss only in person. Mainly there was the conflict between the Archbishops of York and Canterbury. Of late there had been some controversy as to which should be regarded as the primacy of England. It was a matter which only the King and the Pope's emissary could work out.

This matter Henry would discuss but the real reason for his desire to see the Cardinal was of course a possible divorce from Eleanor that he might marry Alice.

Rosamund had successfully hidden her feelings from the King but she was a very sad woman.

How different everything might have been if the King had not come riding to her father's castle on that fateful day. Then she had been Alice's age and she had thought him the most wonderfully perfect knight she had ever beheld. And so she had continued to regard him.

Before she had met him she had believed a husband would be found for her and she would be married and bring up her children as her parents had theirs. How different it was to be the mistress of a king.

And of course the time must come when she would be discarded. She had always feared that, although Henry had sworn eternal fidelity. It had come now. She had understood by the manner in which he had spoken of Alice and of his great concern for the Princess, that she had been displaced.

It was a fearful situation. Alice was so young and already with child by him, and she, the daughter of the King of France and betrothed to the King's son Richard! What would happen if this secret were discovered?

She knew that she must do everything in her power to prevent that. She must suppress her jealousy; she must look after the child, who was innocent enough. Did she not know how easy it was to succumb to the wiles of Henry?

And here she was, no longer young, the woman who had sinned and had not even the love of her partner in sin to sustain her.

He cared for her still, in a way, but that would only be as long as she served him well, she knew. Once he had loved the Queen and now he hated her.

She must repent of her sins and the only way she could do this was to go into a nunnery. She had been thinking of this for some time. Her children were growing up. They were no longer of an age to need her. The King would do well by them for he was fond of his children, and more so of those born out of wedlock for they had been more faithful to him than his legitimate sons. She would care for the Princess Alice, bring her safely through her pregnancy and when the child was born and the Princess able to return to Westminster, Winchester or wherever she could appear with grace, Rosamund would tell the king of her decision to retire from the world.

He could not deny her this when she had done so much for him. Nor she was sure, would he wish to. Sadly she acknowledged the fact that he would doubtless be glad to see this neat end to their romance.

The King received Cardinal Huguzon with many honours. He was determined to show him that he had the utmost respect for him and his master.

How good it was, he said, of the Pope and the Cardinal to accede to his request to have this troublesome matter settled. As the Cardinal knew there had been conflict between Canterbury and York since the sainted Archbishop Thomas à Becket had gone into exile. The King believed that it was time the matter was settled.

The Cardinal was gratified to find the King so agreeable. It was pleasant to be so luxuriously housed and to be given costly presents.

It was clear to him that Henry was very eager to placate Rome and that was always comforting, for a man of such power could cause a great deal of trouble to the Papacy if he had a mind to.

That he should be so concerned over the supremacy claims of York and Canterbury was unexpected. His great concern had always been to curtail the power of either and make them subservient to the crown. So the Cardinal, while he discussed this matter, was asking himself what other problem was disturbing the King. That it was one for which he needed the Pope's help was obvious.

"Canterbury has long held the primacy in England," the

King was saying. "During the absence of Thomas à Becket the Archbishop of York performed duties which would have fallen to the lot of Canterbury. You see the dilemma in which we stand. York does not now wish to give place to Canterbury."

The Cardinal expressed his understanding, but it seemed to him that if Rome decreed that the Archbishop of Canterbury should be the Primate, then so it should be. He would take the King's problem to the Pope and there should be a formal pronouncement. It was clearly the King's wish that full honour should be returned to Canterbury.

The King nodded. "There is one other matter . . . since you are here, my lord Cardinal."

Ah, thought the Cardinal, we are coming to it now.

"As you know," went on the King. "I have been severely plagued by my wife, the Queen."

"She is now your prisoner, I know."

The King lifted his hands in a hopeless gesture. "What can a King do when his wife turns his own sons against him and incites them to rebellion?"

The Cardinal nodded gravely.

"As you know, my lord Cardinal, I have recently been engaged in fighting a war in which my sons were on the opposing side. Their mother brought them up to hate me. She was caught—in the guise of a man—making her way to join them and in person make war on me. Have I not been over lenient in merely holding her in one of my castles where, though she is a prisoner, she is treated as a queen?"

"You have, my lord."

"Many a king would have put her to death."

The Cardinal coughed slightly. "I am sure, my lord, you would never be guilty of such folly. The Queen is the Duchess of Aquitaine. I believe the people of that land would have risen in revolt if she had been harmed in any way."

"I keep her under restraint," said the King, "but she lives like a queen. She suffers no hardship except that she may not travel abroad, and when she leaves the castle she is with an armed escort. In view of what she has done and tried to do, I must keep her under restraint. It is tragic, my lord Cardinal, when a man is deprived of his natural rights."

" 'Tis so, my lord."

"I have long thought that I would put the Queen from me.'

"You mean divorce the Queen? That would not be possible."

"The Queen and I are closely related. We could be divorced on grounds of consanguinity."

The Cardinal sighed. The perpetual request. Grounds of consanguinity! It was possible if one searched long enough to find some blood connection between the nobility of England and all Europe. The trouble was that in granting the request of one side one offended the other.

The Cardinal then swore that he would carry the King's request back to the Pope and the King could assure himself that the Cardinal would do all in his power to make the Holy Father aware of the difficulties of the King of England.

Richard de Luci, the King's Chief Justiciar, had always been a man whom the King could trust. Ever since Harry had taken the crown Richard de Luci had held a high position and never once had he failed to serve the King. There had been moments when he had angered the King, but Henry was wise enough to know that Richard de Luci clung to his opinions solely because he believed them to be for the good of England and the King. A shrewd ruler did not think the worse of a servant who opposed him for his own good.

Richard de Luci was the King's man, and because he now came to Henry in consternation, Henry was ready to listen to him.

Richard after his manner came straight to the point.

"The visit of the Cardinal Huguzon has not been brought about simply to solve the controversy between Canterbury and York I know. My lord, you are contemplating divorcing the Queen."

"It is irksome to be bound to one who has shown herself an enemy."

Richard agreed that this was so.

"My lord, what would happen to the Queen if you were to divorce her and re-marry?"

"She would remain my prisoner. By God's eyes, Richard, do you think I would allow that woman her freedom that she might go back to Aquitaine and plot against me?"

"Nay, I do not think you would, my lord. But I beg you consider this matter with great care."

The King looked exasperated but Richard had more than once ignored the rising signs of temper.

"Do you imagine I have not considered this matter with the utmost care!" cried the King.

"I know it has been your great concern for some time. But I beg of you, my lord, to consider afresh what this divorce would mean."

"It would rid me of a she-wolf who has plagued me and turned my sons against me."

"And more than that, my lord. It would rid you of Aquitaine."

"I should hold it."

Richard shook his head. "She is the Duchess and your son Richard has been proclaimed Duke."

"It is a vain title. Aquitaine is mine."

"You received the title when you married the Duchess but the people would never accept you. They have ever been loyal to the Queen and regard her as their true ruler. If you rid yourself of the Queen you will rid yourself of Aquitaine."

"By God's eyes, Richard, you would keep me tied to a woman I hate."

"I could do nothing, my lord, if you wished it otherwise. My duty is to remind you of what this divorce would mean. She is a great heiress. Aquitaine would rise against you. What of Normandy?"

"My sons have sworn not to take arms against me."

"My lord, we know what these oaths mean in cases of emergency."

"A curse on you, Richard. You disquiet me. I had made up my mind. But, my good friend, I know you say what you say out of love and loyalty to me."

"Then I have achieved my purpose."

"So you believe that there is no way of getting a divorce without strife that could well continue for the rest of my life?"

"I do believe that, my lord."

"But I want to marry again."

"My lord, could you not content yourself with a mistress? You have long made this compromise."

"It is not so easy now. Tell me truthfully, Richard, have you heard rumours?"

"I have, my lord."

"Then it has been spoke of."

"With discretion and only in certain quarters. We must see that it is not generally known."

"But what can I do, Richard?"

"The lady has been removed from Court. She has been travelling to the North for her education. When she returns it would be well if you did not see her again."

"That is impossible."

"She should be married without delay."

The King hit his left hand with his right clenched fist. "No," he said. "I will never agree to it."

"If she were not the daughter of the King of France . . ."

"It is because she is, that I could marry her."

"The affianced bride of your son!"

"Such betrothals often come to naught."

" 'Tis so. It is the matter of the divorce that must give us cause for thought. My lord, you must consider whether you will have marriage and the loss of your dominions, or keep your hold on them and remain married to the Queen."

"The Cardinal hints that a divorce would be possible."

"Indeed so, my lord. Would not his master like to see your power curtailed?"

"You are determined to frustrate me."

"I am determined to serve you with my whole heart and strength and if I offend you in doing that, so be it."

The King slipped his arm through that of Richard de Luci.

"My good friend," he said, "I see that I must go away and brood on this matter."

He could not sleep; he rode through the forest, he returned his sweating horse to his grooms; he lay on his bed and stared into the future.

He pondered; he made up his mind and changed it.

And all the time one thought kept hammering in his brain: Alice the one he loved and the loss of Aquitaine. Alice and conflict. And to keep Eleanor, the Queen he hated, or to lose his grip on his empire.

He thought often of his great-grandfather the Conqueror and it seemed to him that the man visited him in his dreams. He saw the scorn and contempt on that stern face. For William the Conqueror there would have been no problem. He would never have been able to contemplate a woman's being more important than power. In the same dreams he saw his grandfather Henry I. There was a man whose needs of women had been as great—if not greater—than those of his grandson. He too gravely shook his head. It was unthinkable that their descendant should contemplate possible disaster to the empire they had left him for the sake of ridding himself of one woman and taking another as his wife.

It was a conflict between love and power. And Henry Plantagenet was a King and descended from William the Conqueror. There was really no need to consider the matter. He knew what he would have to do.

In the Bower at Woodstock Alice's time grew near.

Rosamund tended her with care and grew quite fond of the girl. They were alike in a way which was perhaps the reason why they had both attracted the King.

Rosamund would sit by the Princess's bed while she stitched at her needlework and Alice would ask her about the trials of childbirth.

They would pray for an easy labour, said Rosamund. She doubted there would be one. The girl was young and perhaps not yet ready for childbirth. Rosamund trembled, thinking of the King's wrath if anything should go amiss with Alice.

She dedicated herself to caring for the girl. It was the last service she would perform for him. She had definitely made up her mind that as soon as Alice's child was born and the girl was recovered she would go into her convent. She had chosen the one at Godstow and had already made gifts to it; and she knew that when the time came she would be welcomed.

In the meantime there was Alice.

The girl was beautiful and she believed the King to be all powerful. She was innocent in a way and did not seem to guess at the King's previous relationship with Rosamund. Perhaps that made it easier.

Alice talked of the King for even she was aware that Rosamund would know he was the father of the child.

He was a great good man, she told Rosamund, who was married to a wicked woman. The Queen was an advocate of the devil and the King was going to put her from him and marry Alice.

"My dear," said Rosamund, "are you not betrothed to Prince Richard?"

"I was, but it has no meaning now. The King says so and the King knows."

So young Alice thought that she would soon be Queen of England. Once he had promised her the same. He had long hated the Queen. How often he had discussed getting rid of her! Divorce would not be difficult, he had said, for there were certain to be blood ties. He had then promised to make Rosamund his Queen.

And now it was Alice and here was Alice about to bear his child tended by her, Rosamund, the discarded mistress.

The months passed. They walked in the gardens; they talked; they stitched baby's clothes and Rosamund brought out those which her own children had worn—half-brothers to this little one who was about to be born. Alice's child should wear them. Why not, since there would be a strong tie between them?

"The King is good to all his children," said Rosamund.

"Is it not wicked of his sons to turn against him?" cried Alice. "They have been ruined by their mother. But soon she will be put away from him. She has not long to bear the title of Queen of England."

Rosamund was older and wiser; she had heard promises which had now been forgotten. There was no point in hinting to Alice that the King might not find it easy to gain his divorce.

In due course Alice was brought to bed and delivered of a girl-child who died a few hours after its birth.

Alice was heartbroken. When the King came to visit her he pretended to be also, but he could not help thinking to himself that perhaps it was all for the best.

"When you are recovered, my love," he said, "you must return to the Court. And if you should appear a little wan, we will say that it was an exhausting journey to the North and the climate up there did not agree with you."

Rosamund said quietly: "I have a mind to go into a convent."

He answered: "I fancy it has been your wish for some time."

"I feel the need for solitude and meditation. I think the time has come for me to seek forgiveness of my sins."

"Rosamund, my rose of the world, you are a good woman. God will forgive your transgressions."

"All would not agree with you. I have heard that in some circles they speak of me as *Rosa-immundi*, the rose of unchastity."

"There will always be those to cast stones at others."

"Yet I feel my guilt heavily upon me and would spend my last years in repentance."

"Where would you go?"

"To Godstow. I have already made arrangements. They are prepared to receive me."

"When they do I shall bestow gifts on them. They shall not lose when they take you in."

She said: "You are as ever good to me." But she saw the relief in his face. It was what he wanted her to do. He would make gifts to Godstow because the convent offered sanctuary to his mistress. He no longer needed her, but he had loved her enough to wish to see her settled.

So with sadness in her heart Rosamund retired to the convent and Alice returned to the palace.

The King knew that he could not hope to divorce Eleanor, but at the same time he was determined not to give up Alice.

The Queen Comes to Court

The young King Henry was restive. It was too much to be borne. He could scarcely move without his father's being aware of it. He was weary of being told he must do this and that and there was only one way to govern and that was the manner in which his father did.

He heard accounts of how men such as Philip of Flanders passed their time. Philip was a glorious knight, skilled in the joust and his fame was spreading throughout Europe. Soon he was to go on a pilgrimage to the Holy Land. Philip was rich, most sumptuously clad; his horses were richly caparisoned and men looked up to him.

As for Henry he had so little. The only way he could live in any comfort was to incur debts. That was not difficult to do since he was the son of the King and indeed himself a king. That was what rankled. He was a king and no king. The title was a word, nothing more.

Men feared his father so they had little respect for his son; and when he rode beside that square figure with the garments which were worn for use rather than ornament and looked at those hands often roughened by weather, he wanted to scream out his frustration.

His friend William the Marshall no longer pleased him as he once had. Oh, William was an excellent knight, a faithful friend, but he was not like Philip of Flanders. Indeed, sometimes Henry thought that William believed it was good for him to be so guided by his father.

Thinking of Philip of Flanders he wondered whether he too might go on some sort of pilgrimage. Anything to escape from his father.

He remembered the stories his mother had told him of how her father, desirous of getting a male heir, had decided to take the road to Compostella and ask help at the shrine of St. James. The road was rough, the conditions terrible and the Duke had fallen sick of a virulent fever. He had known his end was near but had been carried in his litter and was buried before the main altar in the Church of St. James at Compostella.

What more natural than that his grandson feel the need to make a pilgrimage to the shrine of St. James and the grave of his maternal grandfather?

He told his father what he wished to do.

"Why so?" asked the King.

"I have committed the great sin of taking up arms against my father."

"Your father has forgiven you so God will."

"It weighs heavily on my conscience."

"Then," said the King, "I rejoice, for so it should and you can best expiate that sin by working hard and learning quickly all that I would teach you."

"I feel the need to go to Compostella."

"And I, my son, feel the need to keep you here, and I can assure you that my need is greater than yours."

"I am treated as a child," said Henry sullenly.

"Behave then like a man and earn the right to be treated as such."

"Others make such pilgrimages."

"Mayhap, they do not have kingdoms which they must learn to govern."

"Philip of Flanders plans to go to Jerusalem."

"Let him. It will keep him out of mischief."

"He will thereby earn remission of his sins."

"Doubtless it is necessary, for I believe he has committed many. Now I will hear no more. You cannot go to Compostella. You are to stay close to me that I may make you ready for the crown when it comes your way."

"But, Father . . ."

"I have spoken," roared the King; and when the angry lights sprang into his eyes it was no time to continue the argument.

The King was disturbed as he always must be when he heard news of Richard.

His son was coming to England as he was alarmed by the risings in Aquitaine and he wished to consult his father.

It was almost certain that he would demand that his bride come to him and that was something the King would not allow to happen. He was frequently with Alice now and his passion for her did not abate. He loved the girl and as she grew a little older the deeper was his devotion. He was determined not to part with her, yet could he not go on saying that she and Richard were too young?

If Richard came to England Alice would have to go away. He could have sent her to the Bower again, but Rosamund was not there now. He could not bring her out of Godstow to care for his mistress. Still he could send Alice to the Bower and those good attendants who had served Rosamund well and whom he, with some foresight, had kept there, could take care of Alice. Of one thing he was certain: Richard and Alice must not meet.

He would be pleased to see his son, for he had some admiration for him. The boy was proving a valiant commander, an excellent fighter and one who had genius for battle. He was different from young Henry and Geoffrey who thought only of pleasure and of getting power the easy way.

And now Richard was due to arrive in England with his brother Geoffrey and the King decided that he would show his subjects in what amity he lived with his sons. The feast of Easter was approaching, and they should spend it all together, and where better than at his castle of Winchester? However, young Henry wished that he might leave for Normandy and as the need arose for some member of the family to show himself there, the King said he might go. Young Henry was overjoyed at the prospect of escape from his father and made immediate preparations to depart.

The winds, though, were against him and as Easter was upon them the King commanded him to join the festivities at Winchester so that the original intention of all being together could be carried out.

Thus the King had his four sons with him which pleased him well. He had advice to give Richard and Geoffrey, and he looked forward to having young John with him—the only one of Eleanor's sons in whom he could hope to breed affection. He had come to the conclusion that he must allow young Henry a certain freedom or the young man would break out and rebel. It was for this reason that he had agreed to send him to Normandy, but while he was there a stern watch should be kept on him that he did not get into any mischief.

What pleasure it would have given him to have discussed his affairs with them, with no reservations because there need be none. If they had been loyal sons that should have been the case. Now, although they feigned friendship, suspicion was there.

Richard was the most frank of them all. He said what he meant without subterfuge and what he wanted was help in Aquitaine. He was not as popular with the people as he would like to have been.

"The fact that you and I are friends," he said bluntly, "turns them against me. They think that I am my mother's enemy."

"They surely know that not to be the case."

"They reason that if I am your friend I cannot be hers. I have a request to make."

Henry felt a fearful apprehension. Now he was going to ask to see Alice and demand when his marriage was to take place.

But he was wrong. What Richard said was: "I want to see my mother."

"Your mother is at Salisbury Castle."

"We are all gathered here. She should be with us."

"You forget that she has been a traitor to me."

"Could you not say that of your sons?"

"I could—to my misfortune."

"Yet you have forgiven us. Why should you not forgive her?"

"Because she it was who turned you from me. She fed you slander against me with her mother's milk. But for her there would not have been these troubles. I should have been a father with good and loyal sons."

"She did not change our natures."

"What mean you by that?"

"We rose against you because you gave us titles and then refused to make them meaningful. My mother had nothing to do with that."

"You may go to Salisbury to see your mother but you shall not be alone with her."

"Nay," said Richard. "She must come here. If you invite her here and she comes, then in Aquitaine they will know that it was I who demanded to see her and that I am her friend. Only then will they receive me."

The King was thoughtful.

"Let my mother return to Aquitaine with me," went on Richard.

"Never," said the King.

"I should go back with her and my bride."

The King's lips tightened. He said suddenly: "Your mother shall come here to Winchester. She shall stay for a few days and then be returned to Salisbury. The people of Aquitaine will then see that she has been brought here because you pleaded for her. They cannot then say that you are not her friend."

Richard bowed his head.

"There is the matter of my bride," he went on.

"Subdue Aquitaine," said the King, "and then it will be time for you to think of marriage."

"I would see the Princess Alice. She will be of marriageable age now. My brother Henry tells me that the King of France is asking why the marriage has been so long delayed."

"The Princess is touring in the North. If she returns while you are here of a certainty you shall meet. Settle your affairs in Aquitaine and then we shall see whether there shall be a marriage. In the meantime I promise you this: You shall see your mother and it shall be here at Winchester."

Eleanor laughed aloud when she heard that she was to travel to Winchester. What joy to see her beloved Richard! She would be pleased to see Henry and Geoffrey too, and perhaps young John. Best of all perhaps would be meeting her husband. Already vituperations were forming in her mind. She longed to tell him what she thought of him, to have one of those verbal battles which had always excited her.

She sent for her seamstresses. It was her good fortune that she lacked none of the amenities of life here in Salisbury; if she was a prisoner she was a queenly one. There was little to do in her prison and her attendants made gowns for her and as she had always been noted for her elegance she doubted anything at the King's court could compare with garments of her designing.

In high spirits she set out on the journey from Salisbury to Winchester surrounded by the King's guards. She was exultant when she saw the towers of the palace and as she rode forward she laughed aloud in her triumph.

The King received her and for a few moments they regarded each other appraisingly. She tilted her head and laughed.

"So at last we meet, my lord," she said.

The King waved a hand to those who stood in his chamber. "Leave us," he commanded.

"Well, we are alone," she said. "By God, Henry, I see grey hairs and deep lines on your countenance."

"I have had much to concern me as you well know."

"I know that your sons do not love you."

"Their thoughts having been poisoned by their mother."

She lifted her shoulders. "It is their father's own actions which have turned them from him. Why did you allow me to come here?"

"That you might see your sons."

"So indulgent! Come, Henry, there is a reason other than the love you bear them . . . or me."

"I bear none to you."

"I feared it," she mocked.

"But you are the mother of my sons and they have asked to see you."

"So we shall meet. I rejoice. And you brought me here to please my subjects of Aquitaine, did you not? If they learn that I am here this Eastertide they will hate you the less and realize that Richard is my friend. That is statecraft, Henry, my husband, and I will say that you are very crafty at it."

"Thank you."

"And now that Richard is here we have a matter to discuss . . . he, I and perhaps you."

"And that matter?"

"His marriage of course." She was studying him closely. "And where is our dear little Princess? I confess I expected to find her here."

"She is gone to the North . . . for her health."

The Queen raised her eyebrows. "She is sick then? Not sick of love . . . for Richard? But she has not seen him in the prime of his youth, has she?"

"She had already departed when he arrived."

"Churlish of her! Is she not eager to see her bridegroom?"

"I should have thought that after your seclusion you would have had other matters to discuss than this betrothal of Richard's."

"I might ask for my freedom. Would you be prepared to give it?"

"If I did, how should I know that you did not plot against me as you did before?"

"It is something you could never be sure of."

"Then you see why you must remain my prisoner."

"I thought we might strike a bargain."

"Why should I bargain with a prisoner?"

"You want a divorce."

"Who tells you this?"

"There are rumours."

"You should not trust rumours."

"Oh, it depends on the source. And suppose I agree to a divorce, would you release me?"

He said: "There is to be no divorce."

"I have heard that you have already decided on your next Queen."

"Tell me who gave you such news? I'll cut out their tongues for I'll not suffer such lies to be told of me."

"So 'tis true is it not?"

"If it were true that I wanted a divorce why should I not bargain with you as you suggest?"

"I doubt not you have your reasons."

"Nay," he said. "I have not asked for a divorce."

"You presented Cardinal Huguzon with rich gifts. Was this merely to settle the dispute between York and Canterbury?"

"I did not bring you here to discuss my actions with you."

"Nay. I know full well why you did that. You act always out of ambition. It is necessary for Richard to show my people that he is my friend and not yours. So you allow it to be known that he has prevailed upon you to let us meet here. Do not think that I am not aware of your ways, Henry Plantagenet."

Henry shrugged his shoulders. "I would have you know that if you do aught to harm me here you shall be sent back to even more rigorous imprisonment."

She nodded slowly. "What do you plan to do to me, husband? To murder me? That would leave the way clear without complications, would it not? But you must wait of course until Aquitaine is subdued and accepts Richard as the Duke. Then if you can keep him as your vassal—which I doubt—Aquitaine will be yours as you always intended it to be. It is a long time to wait and time is important to you. What do you hope to do? To get an heir by her? You have your heirs, Henry, and look you, what trouble they have brought."

"You talk nonsense," he said.

"Nay, nay, good sense and you like it not. What think you the King of France will say when he hears his daughter has been debauched?"

"*What* is this?"

"Such ignorance! Poor child. Scarce out of the cradle. But they say ageing men whose senses are satiated look for new excitements. Children is it?"

He advanced towards her, his hand upraised.

"That is it, Henry. Strike me. That will be good hearing for Aquitaine. I will let it be known that I goaded you, taunted you with seducing the daughter of the King of France."

He paused, fighting to keep control of his rising temper.

"Get out of here," he shouted. "Before I kill you with my own hands, get out."

"I wonder how I should feel if you laid hands on me. You once did in most tender fashion. Do you remember?"

"I know only that I curse the day I ever met you."

"That was before the Princess of France was conceived. But there was Fair Rosamund was there not? I shall never forget her terror when her skein of silk led me to her lair. And you were the traitor. It was attached to your spur. But are you not a traitor to us all?"

"If you do not leave me I shall not answer for my actions."

He was right. She could see that although he had fought hard for control, his temper was getting the better of him.

He would forget diplomacy. All wisdom would desert him if once that demon rage got the upper hand.

She had no wish to die yet; she gave him a mocking bow and retired.

When his rage had worn itself out he faced the facts.

So she knew. The she-wolf knew that Alice had been his mistress. What would she do? He could be certain that whatever she did would bring him the greatest mischief.

The King of France would hear of it. Richard would know and soon the whole world would be against him. He had had some experience of what condemnation he could expect. He had so recently emerged from the trouble his connection with the murder of Thomas à Becket had given him. And at what cost to his kingly dignity! It must not be known that he had taken Richard's bride and that she had had a child by him. But Eleanor knew, and Eleanor's great joy in life was to work against him.

What could he do?

Alice *must* not go to Richard. It was not only that he wished to keep her for himself. She was too young, too lacking in guile to be able to keep her secrets. Alice must remain and he must find some means of staving off Richard. If Eleanor started rumours he would declare that she had invented them out of her venom.

He believed he had made headway with young Henry; the boy had seemed almost affectionate to him in the last months. Richard would always be his enemy, he knew. He was too much his mother's son for anything else. Geoffrey was inclined to follow his elder brother. They could both be more easily swayed than Richard.

He must do everything in his power to stop her passing on this information to Richard and if she attempted to turn Henry and Geoffrey from him he would let them know that she herself had led a far from exemplary life. After all, when he considered the scandals Eleanor had created in her youth how could she judge him because he had fallen in love with a young girl who happened to be affianced to one of his sons?

It was a pity it had seemed necessary to let her out of her prison. Although he realized that it was good policy, he deeply regretted the need for it.

Her period of freedom should soon be at an end, and he would be very slow to allow her to emerge again.

Eleanor quickly found an opportunity of being alone with Richard. They met in the new herb garden where they could enjoy a certain amount of privacy.

She said: 'My dearest son, we must say what is in our minds in some haste because I do not think your father will allow me my freedom much longer. I have spoken with him and he has made me aware of his hatred. He is particularly wary of you, my son. It is because of Alice.'

"The Princess Alice? My betrothed."

"I have news for you, Richard. She has become your father's mistress and it is for this reason that he keeps her from you."

"He is welcome to her. I do not want his cast-off mistress."

"Nay, nor do you. But, my son, he must think you do. You must ask him where your bride is. You must give him no peace. The King of France must agitate for your marriage with the Princess Alice. It is the best way of harassing him. I never saw him so put out as when I mentioned her. He is crafty. He can outwit his enemies. He will lie, make promises he has no intention of keeping; but he could not hide his lust for that girl. And he is more alarmed at what the betrayal of his relationship with her could mean than he would ever be at going into battle."

"How long has it been going on?"

"A year or two I believe. I have heard a rumour that she has had a child by him."

"By God, and all the saints! I will let the whole world know of this."

"Not yet, Richard. Not yet. Feign ignorance for a while. Let him be plagued. If it were widely known, what would happen? There would be a scandal, but he would free himself in time." There was grudging admiration in her voice. "Consider what happened at Canterbury. Who else could have humiliated himself and have come through with honour almost? To be publicly whipped! Nay. What will disturb him most is the fact that there will be attempts to take her from him. So, my son, ask Louis that your marriage be celebrated. Tell him you are impatient for your bride. Let your father be fretted by continual demands that the girl be released, for depend upon it he will want to keep their liaison secret for as long as he can."

"I would go to him and confront him with his villainy."

"I know you would and your bluntness is a trait in your character which gives me some cause for alarm. I have heard of your new nickname, 'Richard Yea and Nay', they say, because with you it is always 'It shall be' or 'It shall not be.' You will have to learn that it is sometimes necessary to prevaricate and you could not have a better teacher in that art than your father."

"Would you have me behave as he does?"

"I hate him and I love you. But hating him as I do yet I see there is a certain greatness in him. His lust will destroy him, as it has destroyed our marriage. Yet do not underestimate him for he is a formidable adversary. Fight him with subtlety. Make sure that the revenge you take is the one which will hurt him most."

"I will do as you say, Mother. I will not let him know that I am aware of his seduction. I will not have her but I shall let no one know this and it will only be when she is brought to me that I will refuse her."

"For the foolish girl I care not. All I wish is to humiliate him."

"How you hate him!"

"Do you not also?"

"From my earliest days you showed me what he is."

The Queen laughed, well pleased. A very uneasy time lay ahead for the King.

It was difficult for Richard to keep his disgust to himself. Not that he was shocked at his father's seduction of a young girl; Richard's own morals were not so very stern; but that his father should have dared take the bride who was affianced to him was a personal insult.

He would be revenged, but what his mother said was true. For the time, he must do his best to feign friendship with the King, for he needed help to suppress the rebellions in Aquitaine. He had to face the fact that he was not popular there. For all that he was his mother's favourite and it was her wish that he should be crowned Duke, they did not want him. He was not of the South. One look at that long-limbed golden-haired young man was enough to proclaim him a Norman. So many of the Viking characteristics had come out in him: his blue eyes, his golden hair, his tall figure, the manner in which he sat his horse, his immense strength. True he was a poet and loved the troubadours, but even his songs had a northern flavour. They were more like those which Rollo and his men had sung when they came sailing down the Seine to ravage France than the voluptuous ballads of the South.

The people of Aquitaine could not entirely accept him. They suspected that immense energy. He could be fierce in battle, and they were suspicious of him. They wanted Eleanor back. They understood her. They admired her elegance; and her adventurous spirit appealed to them. They had been cheated of their Duchess and although they had been assured that Richard was her beloved son they did not trust him any more than they trusted his father.

Therefore he needed help. The best thing that could have happened would have been for him to take his mother back with him.

That was something the King would not allow.

He sent for his two sons, Henry and Richard, and told them what he wished them to do.

He had solved two problems at one stroke.

Henry should accompany Richard to Aquitaine and help him keep order there.

Henry did not protest. His great desire was to get away

from the leading strings which he declared his father had put him into. Once let him get away and put the sea between them, and he would be free.

So Eleanor went back to Salisbury and Richard prepared to sail for France. Before they left, Henry's wife Marguerite went to Canterbury to pray at the shrine of St. Thomas à Becket. She longed for a child and asked the saint to intercede for her.

Then the brothers with Marguerite left England.

The Young King

There was a difference of opinion between the brothers. Richard wished to return to Aquitaine as quickly as possible for the prospect of battle always excited him. But Henry was in no such hurry. He was free of his father, or so he believed, and he wanted to make the most of his good fortune.

Marguerite expressed her wish to see her own father and Henry said that before accompanying Richard to Aquitaine they would call on the King of France.

Louis received them with pleasure and as usual treated Henry as his own son. He loved all his children dearly and he always took great pleasure in the company of any of them. When he heard that Marguerite had been to Canterbury to pray at St. Thomas's Shrine, he applauded what she had done.

"A saint whose death was one of the great tragedies of Christendom," he commented. "I shall never forget the day I heard of his murder. I am sure your prayers will be heard and answered."

He himself gave special services for the couple and they were convinced that soon their great wish would be granted.

Young Henry took pleasure in the knowledge that if his father knew he had come to the King of France he would be furious. Although recently he had feigned affection for his father and had perhaps sometimes felt a little, now that he was no longer with him, all his resentment was aroused, and the hatred, revived, was as strong as ever.

He told Louis that they had seen their mother. Louis could never be quite indifferent to Eleanor and wanted to hear how she was faring under her imprisonment.

"There is little change in her," Henry told the King.

"She would come through any adventures unscathed," said Louis admiringly.

Henry then brought up the matter which his mother had suggested he bring to the notice of the King of France.

"Richard envies us our married happiness," said Henry. "He is wondering when his bride will be given to him."

"I wonder that also," said Louis, frowning. "I do not understand why there should be this delay. Alice is now sixteen years of age. Surely that is an age for marriage."

"And Richard is almost twenty. It is only right that he should have his bride."

"Why should there be this delay?" demanded Louis.

"It is some devilment of my father's," answered Henry. "Depend upon it."

"It makes no sense," said Louis. "The King of England wishes this marriage and so do I. Yet the Princess is kept at the Court of England and is neither returned to her father nor given to her husband."

"What·do you intend to do about it?" asked Henry.

"It would seem that the King of England has some intentions which are not clear to us. I will send a messenger to the Pope and ask his help in the matter."

Young Henry left the King of France and travelled to Poitiers, that beautiful capital city of Aquitaine set on a hill. It seemed to the young King that to go into battle was a foolish thing to do. There was so much which was more entertaining. Aquitaine, so called because of the abundance of springs, streams and rivers, was a beautiful land. In such well watered territory there were many vineyards and the vegetation was lush indeed.

It was a land made for song and pleasure and to give oneself to fighting and discomfort was not young Henry's idea of enjoyment. What was the use of being a king if one must continually be on the march and live in discomfort like a common soldier?

The fair city of Poitiers suited him and he would have liked to linger there, but Richard pointed out that they had not come to Aquitaine to pass the days in idleness. There was trouble in Angoulême and to Angoulême they must go.

Richard set out and Henry followed him, but he regretted leaving the city where he had had such a pleasant time; and as he was riding into Angoulême, he received a message from his old friend, Philip of Flanders.

Philip had, some time previously, sworn that he would go on a crusade to the Holy Land and Henry was surprised that he had not already embarked upon it. Philip wrote that he had a reason for remaining in Flanders which he would explain when they met. In the meantime he wanted Henry to join him and take advantage of a round of pleasure for he was staging a series of tournaments and he knew how Henry enjoyed such entertainments.

Henry wavered. He should, of course, stay with Richard, for his help would be needed and this was what his father had commanded. But Richard was capable of fighting his own battles as he was such a renowned warrior and why should he, crowned King of England, always have to consider what his father wanted? He soon convinced himself that he had every right to go where he wished and shortly after he received Philip's message, he set out for Flanders.

Philip was delighted to see him and Henry enjoyed enumerating all the wrongs he had received at his father's hands and declaring that he would never fall into them again.

He had been a puppet, nothing more.

Philip commiserated. It was monstrous that one who was a crowned King of England should be so treated.

"My father greatly regrets he ever allowed the crown to be placed on my head."

"Then if he regrets such important acts which were performed at his bidding does it now show he is unfit to govern?"

The friends were in agreement.

Those were days of immense pleasure.

"This is the life," cried Henry.

Tournaments were mock battles. They provided the utmost pleasure without the discomfort of war. Excitement and the ability to cut a fine figure were stressed. What could be more stimulating?

Philip of Flanders was greatly experienced in these affairs, and because he was such a skilled performer everyone watched him with awe and admiration. Henry longed to win such glories.

The arrival of Henry must be celebrated with a grand tournament, said Philip, and he sent heralds throughout the land to let all the knights know that they were invited to test their skill.

Then there was the pleasure of selecting the judges, and lofty towers and scaffolding of wood were erected. Counts and their Countesses, Dukes and their Duchesses, knights and their ladies were seated in accordance with their rank; and it was the custom for each man to wear a favour from his wife or mistress. Often the tournaments continued for days and there were various kinds of engagements—sometimes several knights were involved in an action, at others there were examples of single combats.

At the end of the day the judges gave their verdict and the ladies led the victors into the hall where they were divested of their armour and clad in beautiful robes. The minstrels played and verses were recited and songs sung praising the glories of jousting.

To indulge in this pastime was clearly a costly matter and although the King of England might supply his son with certain monies necessary for the conducting of war against his enemies, he would not do so that it might be squandered in tournaments.

But Philip of Flanders was a good friend and he assured Henry that he must not think of the expense. Such a small matter must not deter him from enjoying the occasion. Philip would provide the fine garments, the horses, the lances and spears.

Henry accepted the gifts and swore to Philip that he should one day be repaid with estates in England. He would never forget his very good friend.

He admired Philip, and as his skill at the joust improved he was very content.

Philip began to have a great influence on him. A ruler must be strong, said Philip. He must take his pleasures where he would and must allow none to condemn him.

Philip showed Henry how he dealt with those who betrayed him, when he told him why he had not gone on the proposed crusade after all. It concerned his wife.

Philip was married to the beautiful Isabel of Vermandois who was related to young Henry, for her mother was the sister of Queen Eleanor. Eleanor's sister Petronelle had become enamoured of the Count of Vermandois soon after Eleanor's marriage to the King of France. The Count had been something of a philanderer and had first cast his eyes on Queen Eleanor herself. He had made his feelings clear by sitting at her feet and sighing while he sang of love. At that time Eleanor, newly married to the King of France and hoping for an heir, had not indulged in active infidelity and the impatient amorous count had turned his attentions to her sister Petronelle. Not having the same reasons for preserving her chastity, Petronelle allowed herself to be seduced. She was, however, the sister of the Queen of France and marriage was considered necessary. Therefore the Count divorced his wife on the well-worn consanguinity excuse and he and Petronelle were married. Two daughters were the result of their union and of these Isabel was the younger.

Isabel had inherited the nature of her parents and although Philip was a virile husband she could not prevent her attention straying.

The young King listened to an account of the troubles between Philip and his wife. Both of them were related to Henry, for while Isabel was his cousin, Philip was descended from Fulk of Anjou; Philip's grandmother, Sibyl, daughter of Fulk, was the sister of Henry's grandfather, Geoffrey of Anjou. Hence the relationship.

At this time young Henry admired his kinsman Philip more than anyone he knew and he applauded everything he did with such an uncritical devotion that Philip could not help regarding him with great affection.

"You have heard of Walter of Les Fontaines?" he asked.

"I heard he was dead. Was he not a knight of some fame?"

"He was said to be a kind of Sir Lancelot and the name fits him well if you consider me as Arthur and Isabel as Guinevere."

"You are not telling me that Walter is Isabel's lover?"

"Was, cousin! Was! You do not think I would allow my wife to be unfaithful to me, do you?"

"I believe you have not always been faithful to her."

"That is a different matter."

"Tell me of this Walter. I have heard there was a kind of legend about him."

"He was very handsome, very skilled. Few could stand against him at the tournament."

"You could, Philip."

"Few besides. Imagine my rage when I heard that Isabel had a fancy for him."

"She could not possibly have preferred him to you."

"She wanted us both it seemed. I suspected that when I was away he became her lover."

"What did you do?"

"I taunted him with it. He denied it. But then he would consider it would be the knightly thing to do."

"Did you torture him?"

"No. I asked him, merely. I said I trusted his word as a knight."

"But if he were protecting a lady . . ."

"Exactly so. I forbade him to enter my castle and made a

plan. Oh, a simple one which I doubt not many a suspicious husband has used before. I made a great noise about going away for some days. I went and returned by stealth."

"And you discovered them . . ."

"I caught him in her bedchamber. Now I had proved what I suspected and no one could blame me if I took action against him."

"What did you do?"

"I asked him why he was there when my express command had been that he was not to enter the castle. I knew she had invited him but he would not betray her. I had him beaten until he was nothing but a mass of bleeding flesh but still he was determined to protect her. He was a knight until the end. He was elegant, you know. His linen was scented and he was most careful in his person. I believe it was that which she found so appealing. It seemed a good revenge therefore to hang him over a cesspool and this I did. He stayed there until he died."

Henry's eyes gleamed. "So I would act towards a lover of Marguerite's if I should so discover him."

"And none could blame you. None blamed me. A betrayed husband has his rights."

"And Isabel? What was her punishment? You could have put her from you."

"What! With the rich lands of Vermandois at stake. I did not want trouble there. She is a beautiful woman and it was a warning to her."

Henry nodded and admired his friend more than ever.

"All this has delayed my departure for the crusade," went on Philip. "That is why I have not gone. I must remain a while because of it. But I shall go in due course. It will be an even greater excitement than the tournament and I have a few sins to ask pardon for."

"When you go, Philip," declared Henry, "I shall accompany you."

As the influence of Philip of Flanders grew stronger over young Henry, that of old friends like William the Marshall and his Vice-Chancellor, Adam of Churchdown, waned. William, for all that he was a knight who loved to take part in tournaments and did in fact shine in them, was of a serious nature and he was disturbed to see Henry becoming rather dissolute and more arrogant than ever.

He tried to remonstrate with him, pointing out that his

151

father had commanded him to assist Richard and would be most displeased when he heard that he spent his time in extravagant pleasure.

"By God, William," cried Henry, "it would seem that you are a greater friend to my father than to me."

"I serve you both with all my heart," answered William.

"The time is coming when it will not be possible to serve us both. Then you will have to make a choice."

"I pray that time will never come," answered William.

"I pray it will come very soon. I have been in leading strings too long. Am I the King of England or am I not?"

"You are King in truth for your father has had the crown put on your head, but it behoves us all to remember that he is the master of us all."

"God damn him, William. I'll not be his slave."

"It is not his slave he would make you. He wants you to learn kingship from him and then when the time comes, to take over from him. It is a fatherly concern."

"To the devil with his fatherly concern. He is a miser, and you know it, William."

"Hush, my lord, do not say that which could be construed as treason."

"Faint-hearted William!" taunted Henry.

"Nay, my lord. Strong-hearted and strong in the arm I trust when it comes to protecting you."

Marguerite was pregnant.

"St. Thomas has interceded for me," she declared. "Oh, how happy I am! I shall pray for a son."

"That son," said Henry proudly, "will one day be King of England."

"I trust he will never try to take the crown from his father as you have from yours."

Henry was angry. "Dost think that I would deserve such treatment? Besides," he added shrewdly, "he will never be crowned king while I live."

He was delighted. It was gratifying to become a father.

Messages must be sent to the Kings of England and France to inform them that they would become grandparents.

He thought of Richard, battling away in Aquitaine. He had always been a little jealous of Richard because their mother had doted on him so much. He wondered why, for Richard was not in the least like her. Richard was a throw-back to their Norman ancestors. Old Rollo must have looked a little like him.

Richard was succeeding in subduing Aquitaine because he was such a brilliant fighter but it was said that he would never be acceptable to the people, for he was alien to everything they were. He was so essentially of the North; he could be hard and cruel; and although he had some talents as a musician and poet he was very different from their mother's languorous people. And if they did not accept Richard might they not accept someone who was more like themselves, someone who was content to enjoy life and did not want to be continually going into battle, someone who was easy going, who would enjoy the comfortable and easy life?

Why not?

This was a good life but inactivity was becoming boring. Intrigue was exciting and nothing could be more exciting than intrigue against the one whom he most wanted to defeat: his own father. One of his most glorious dreams was that his father, subdued and penitent, came to him to beg his pardon and ask that there might be an end to the strife between them. He could never completely shut out the memory of that humiliating scene when he had gone to his father, knelt before him and begged to be allowed to pay him homage. And the aftermath, that public statement of his humility! He would never forgive his father for that.

Suppose he stirred up a revolt—in Normandy perhaps? There were always people ready to revolt. On the other hand suppose he put out feelers to Aquitaine? Would the people there rather have him than Richard?

There were several possibilities.

William the Marshall guessed what dangerous thoughts were going on in the young King's mind.

He wondered whether he could speak to Marguerite about his anxieties. The young Queen, since she had become pregnant, had become serene and more mature. She loved her husband. There was a great deal to love in Henry. He could be very charming when he wished and his appearance was very much in his favour. When he entered a room people would have known him for a prince if they had been completely unaware of his identity. He was said to be the handsomest prince in Christendom and if now and then he wore an expression of discontent this was not always the case.

William, who had known him from a child when he had

been knight-at-arms to the royal children, had until recently been closer to Henry than any of his friends; he was much older and infinitely wiser, and he deplored the way in which the young King's character was developing; and most of all he regretted his attitude to his father.

He went to Marguerite who was taking a little exercise in the gardens, as she had been advised to do, in order to ensure an easy confinement. When he joined her the two ladies who were accompanying her dropped behind and William walked side by side with the young Queen.

After inquiring about her health he brought up the subject of her husband and told her that he believed Henry was getting restive.

"But he is so delighted at the prospect of having a son," she answered.

"He is indeed. But I do very much fear that the conflict between him and his father will grow, and I would give a great deal to prevent that."

"The King is determined to prevent Henry from having any power, and that maddens Henry."

"In time the King might change his mind."

"Henry thinks he never will. He gets so angry that the King should treat him like a child."

"Will you try to placate him? I think if he will but be patient a while the King may change. In any case no good can be served by whipping up his anger against his father. My lady, will you try to make him see this? You can talk to him more easily than any. We both love him dearly and his good is our great concern. I know it is useless for him to plot against his father. That is not the way to achieve what he wants."

"I will try to speak to him," said Marguerite.

So earnestly were they talking together that they did not see the approach of Henry himself.

"How now?" he cried. "What is this I see? My friend and my wife sharing secrets!"

"I was inquiring for the Queen's health," said William.

"Which you see is good."

Henry fell into step beside them. "I long for the day when my son is born," he said; and the sulky expression was no longer on his face.

He is indeed the handsomest of princes, thought William. I would to God he were the happiest.

But he was happy enough walking with William and his

wife and talking to them of plans for the future of his unborn
son.

The prospect of becoming a father had by no means turned
Henry's thoughts from rebellion. Rather had it made him
more than ever determined.

Plans began to form in his mind and he was often in the
company of men who were known to be hostile to his father.

William the Marshall was not the only one who was
uneasy. Adam of Churchdown, a man of mature years, could
also see what was happening and asked himself what he
should do about it.

He owed his allegiance to young Henry's father. Moreover
he was fully aware that any insurgents whom Henry might
succeed in arousing could do little good for any length of time
against the superior forces and generalship of the older
Henry.

It occurred to him that if he could send a message of
warning to the King in England of what was happening, he
would know how to deal with it. He therefore called a
messenger to him, gave him a letter and told him to make all
speed to the coast and not give up the letter into any hands
but those of the King.

He had worded the letter carefully. He considered it was no
treason to young Henry; it was merely to put the King on his
guard and Adam knew that he would act in such a manner as
to curb young Henry's rebellious activities and thus save him
from disaster.

Alas for Adam, his messenger fell into the hands of one of
those knights who hated the King of England and was eager
to support his son in rebellion.

The messenger and the message was brought before the
young King and when Henry read what Adam had written
his rage was great.

"Bring Adam of Churchdown to me," he cried.

Adam, standing before him, realized what had happened.
This was disaster. Under the tuition of Philip of Flanders, he
knew that his master had become ruthless, and he could
expect little mercy.

"So you are a traitor," spat out Henry.

"Not so, my lord. I have only your good at heart."

It was the worst thing he could have said. How often had
Henry heard the words: "It is for your own good." He was

heartily sick of being treated like a child. He was a man and a king at that, he would have them know.

He thought of the knightly Walter of Les Fontaines and he cried: "Take this man out, divest him of his clothes and whip him through the streets. Let it be known that this is my way with traitors. Proclaim to all that he sought to spy for my father. I have trusted him in the past and I had counted him my friend but this is how I deal with traitors. And when he has been whipped through these streets take him to the Castle of Argentan and there cast him into a dungeon. But in every town through which you pass he shall be whipped in the street and proclaimed as a taitor to King Henry of England, Duke of Normandy and Count of Anjou."

When Adam had been taken away William the Marshall came to the young King.

"I beg of you to consider what you are doing."

"God's eyes, William," retorted Henry, "remember to whom you speak lest the like should happen to you."

William turned away with a shrug of his shoulders. "Oh, yes, I know full well," went on Henry, "that you are nobly born and the nephew of the Earl of Salisbury. I know that you will say that you have been my friend from childhood. But I will not countenance traitors. Adam is one and he shall suffer for it because he deserves it and because he shall show an example to all others."

"He did what he did for your good."

"Stop that!" screamed the King. "I am not your pupil, now, William Marshall. Take care I say. Take care of all traitors."

William went sadly away. The situation was becoming more and more dangerous. He thought, as many had before him, that the old King had made the gravest mistake of his reign when he had had his son crowned King of England.

Was it not inevitable that there must be disastrous conflict when two kings possessed the same crown?

The King's Strategy

Alice was back in Westminster; Richard was in Aquitaine; and she trusted the King to keep her safe with him.

As for Henry he found it very pleasant to be in England. There he could visit Alice frequently and see more of his son John. The desire to be a good father, and to have the affection of his children was becoming an obsession with him. He had lost almost all hopes of the elder ones but there were however the two younger members of his family—Joanna and John—and he was trying hard to win from them the love and regard which the others had denied him.

He could blame their mother and he did. Let her fret out her days in the prison of his choosing; she had shown that she only had to appear to make trouble. He was certain that the importuning of Louis for the marriage of Alice and Richard was Eleanor's work. He had been shaken as he rarely had ever been when he discovered that she knew of the relationship between him and Alice. Could it be that she had told Louis the truth? No, not that. He would have been horrified. That would offend his pious soul and he would never keep quiet about it. But she had prodded him in some way, he was sure.

The matter occupied him more than any other, for he made himself believe that his sons would be faithful to their promises. Richard was doing well in Aquitaine and was certainly a great fighter. Henry was too pleasure loving and extravagant and Geoffrey took after him. But Marguerite was pregnant and if she gave him a grandson he would be satisfied with her.

The great problem was how to keep Alice.

It was a pity that she was growing up. She was not seventeen yet but of course they would say she should be married at that age. Richard was a laggard; he had shown no great desire for marriage, thank God.

If Alice were any but Louis's daughter . . . oh, but he had

157

to admit that had given a piquancy to the affair. He liked to think he was making love to the daughter of that old monk. She would make a worthy bride for him too if ever it was possible for them to marry.

While he was brooding on this a letter arrived from the Pope. He shut himself alone in his bedchamber and with some trepidation opened it. Glancing hastily through it he saw that Alice was the subject of it and his heart sank.

The Pope wrote that his dearest son in Christ, Louis illustrious King of the French, was complaining because his daughter, who had long ago been sent to England that she might be brought up in the country of her betrothed, had neither been married nor returned to her father. The King of France was insisting that either one of these courses must be adopted.

Henry threw the letter aside and stared ahead of him.

What could he do? If it were not for Eleanor he could marry her. As it was, what was the alternative?

He stood up and clenched his fist.

"By the eyes, teeth and mouth of God," he cried, "I'll not give up Alice."

He went to see his children. He had news for them both.

He sat down on the window-seat and as they leaned against him he put an arm about them both; he could not help thinking what a charming picture they must make and he was resentful against Eleanor who had deprived him of the love his older children owed him. He was not a bad father. His illegitimate children were devoted to him. It was only Eleanor's brood who were against him. But not these younger ones. They were going to be loyal and loving. They were going to make up to him for what he had lacked with the others.

John was naturally his favourite because he was a boy. The others were going to realize how much happier they would have been if they had loved him. They were going to see what he would do for a loving son. John might not be the King of England, Duke of Normandy or Aquitaine, but he should have the richest lands his father could give him. Never again was John to be known as John Lackland.

"Now, Joanna, my daughter, what say you to this? How would you like to be a queen?"

Eleven-year-old Joanna opened her eyes wide. "A queen, my lord. Not a Queen of England?"

"Nay, my love. How could you be that? Marguerite will be the Queen. If you would be one, you must have a husband to give you your crown. That is why I have chosen a husband for you. You are to be the Queen of Sicily, for the King of that country is asking your hand in marriage."

"I shall have to go away," said Joanna.

"Of a truth you must go to your husband's country and there be married. You will be a grand lady and that is what I wish you to be."

She was a little puzzled and looked at John to see what his reactions were.

"What of me?" he asked. He was a year younger than his sister but he knew that as a boy he was of greater importance.

"Your time will come, my son, and before long I doubt not. But you will not leave us. Your bride will come to you for brides it is who must go to their husbands."

"When is Alice going to her husband, Father?" asked Joanna.

God's eyes, he thought, are they talking of it in the nurseries!

"All in good time, my love."

"She is an old lady," said John.

"Well, hardly that, but older than you, shall we say. Now you are going to have a wonderful wedding dress, Joanna. It will be specially embroidered and set with many sparkling gems. You will like that eh, my love?"

She clasped her hands and turned her eyes to the ceiling. "Oh, yes, my lord."

He kissed her. Poor child, he thought, reconciled by a wedding dress.

He went to see Alice. What if he should be forced to give her up? He couldn't. When he had found the perfect mistress he intended to keep her.

She was older now, of an age to understand, and he wanted to share the burden with her. He wanted to make her understand how much he cared for her since he would go to so much trouble to keep her.

"Alice, my love," he said, "they are plaguing me to give you over to Richard."

She clung to him. "I will not go. I *will* not! I shall stay with you. You won't send me away."

"Dost think I would ever send you away, sweetheart, if it were possible to keep you?"

"Then I am safe for it is only if you wish to be rid of me that I shall have to go."

He stroked her hair. She trusted him. How could he allow her trust to be betrayed?

"By God's eyes, teeth and lips, Alice," he swore, "none shall take you from me."

Then he took her into a fierce embrace and made urgent love to her.

Then he laughed aloud and whispered: "But we shall have to be crafty, Alice my love. We have to delude your father and Richard. Dost doubt I can do this?"

"I know you can do it."

"And the Pope as well, Alice. He is on our track."

"We shall defy them all."

"Can you do that, Alice, think you?"

"You can," she said. "You can do anything you wish."

That was how a mistress should be—loving, docile and with complete faith.

He would keep Alice. He had nothing to fear. He would outwit the Pope and the Cardinals. They were afraid of him in any case. It was merely a matter of whom they feared most—him or Louis. Louis was a feeble old man and young Philip was a weakling; whereas he was called the lion for his strength.

He would hold her no matter who came against him.

Little Joanna had gone off to marry William of Sicily, taking with her the promised wedding dress which had cost over a hundred pounds. Poor child, she was delighted with the dress. Her father hoped she would be happy and not too homesick. She would travel through France at the head of a brilliant cavalcade to St. Gilles where she would be met by the Bishop of Norwich, whom Henry had sent to Sicily some months before to negotiate the marriage. With him would be the dignitaries of Sicily waiting to conduct her to her future husband.

The King took comfort in the fact that William of Sicily was an old man and would therefore be kind to the child and Joanna herself was such a beautiful and engaging creature that he must be pleased with her.

It was no use being saddened by her departure. Her sisters had gone before her at a tender age: Matilda to the Duke of Saxony and Eleanor to the King of Castile.

And so one's daughters pass from one's care, and often do

much good; but he believed that his elder daughters had been brought up on the same bitter milk as his sons, which was not surprising since they had fed at the breast of the same she-wolf.

No matter. He had his son John and John must love him. He could not be deserted by all his sons. To compensate John for the loss of his sister he bought him two palfreys which he himself chose and it gave him great pleasure to take the boy out to see them.

They had cost fifty-two pounds and were worth it. He told John this for he wanted the boy to grow up with an appreciation of money. Young Henry was extravagant in the extreme and so was Geoffrey. Richard too seemed to have little understanding of the value of money, even though he wanted it for the maintenance of his dominions not to fritter it away as Henry and Geoffrey did.

His time was spent between John and Alice now. He was getting older. Perhaps he was lonely even though he was always surrounded by men and women. This craving for affection persisted. He supposed it was because his wife hated him and sometimes it seemed his sons only cared for what they could get from him.

Not so Alice. She loved him for himself. She bore no grudge because he had taken her when she was an innocent child; she never upbraided him because he had not procured the promised divorce. She always understood; she always set herself out to please and never to criticize.

He could be sure of Alice. He hoped he could be sure of John.

He was glad that John's marriage to Alice of Maurienne would not take place now. He had thought that to become Marquis of Italy would have been a fine solution to his problems, for such John would have been if her dower had come to him. He had already found estates for John in England. He had given him the Earldoms of Cornwall and Nottingham and he proposed to make him King of England.

Another idea occurred to him, and he saw a possibility of John's becoming the owner of very large properties in Gloucester.

Robert Earl of Gloucester, illegitimate son of Henry I and therefore Henry's mother's brother, had been her chief supporter during her claim to the throne and taught Henry himself a great deal that was good for him and had helped to make him the man he was. Henry remembered well his grief when the Earl had died. How strange it was that often the sons of good and faithful men turned out to be traitors.

Thus it was with the Earl's son, Earl William of Gloucester.

William, who had inherited vast estates from his father, had become involved in the rebellion against the King. When Henry considered this he became very angry indeed. How different he was from his father and considering that there was a blood tie between them the perfidy seemed more unpardonable than ever.

William was now in his power and the King had him brought before him.

Expecting dire punishment William came in trembling, but the King who was considering John's future had an idea which seemed to him a good one.

"William," he said reproachfully, "you have betrayed my trust in you. I wonder what your father would say if he were here and knew that you had played the traitor."

William was shamed at the mention of his father.

"I remember him well," went on Henry. "My mother never had a more faithful friend than her bastard half-brother; and when I was young nor did I. I shall never forget the day I heard of his death. It was as though a part of my life had ceased to be, and now you, his son, stand before me as a traitor."

"My lord," cried William, "what can I do to win your forgiveness?"

The King shook his head. "You have robbed me of my trust in you. 'Tis a sad thing when those of the same blood work against each other. Your grandfather was also mine. It is for that reason that I do not throw you into a dungeon. You see, I respect blood ties. Mind you, a king has his duty and he must guard his realm, no matter what conditions are demanded of him. Not only did my son conspire against me, but so did those whom I should have thought I might have trusted. There is, though, a way in which we could heal this wound. You have a young unmarried daughter and I have a son, John."

William was alert. Could the King really be suggesting a union between Price John and his daughter?

He had no sons and three daughters, two of whom were married. The youngest, Isabel, was one of John's age. He was slightly dismayed, for he hoped to have a son and if he did how could he be denied his heritage?

The King went on: 'Let your daughter become betrothed to

my son John and your earldom and land would fall to him through marriage with your daughter."

"My daughters who are married . . ." began William.

But the King waved his hand. "I have considered this. The Crown will compensate them. They shall each be paid one hundred pounds a year."

"My lord," began William, "this is a great opportunity for my daughter and I should be happy for her to grasp it with both hands but if I should have a son . . ."

The King had thought of that too. He said glibly: "Then the lands should be divided between him on the one side and John and your daughter on the other."

"Then I am happy," replied William. "But I have one fear. The blood tie between these children is a strong one. It may be that the marriage will not be possible on grounds of consanguinity."

"I will prevail upon the Pope to grant a dispensation. I do not think he will wish to go against my wishes. Let there be a betrothal and if by some ill chance the dispensation should not be given, then I will find a rich and worthy husband for your daughter. What say you to this, William?"

What could William say? He could, after all, be condemned as a traitor.

The King was well pleased. John was now happily settled and provided for. Never more would he be known as John Lackland. The boy would be grateful to his father. Now all his children were settled and provided with partners—except Richard.

It seemed that every way he turned he came back to Alice.

Louis was determined not to allow the matter of his daughter's marriage to be further shelved. There was some reason for it, he knew. It was a most extraordinary situation and knowing Henry he suspected some perfidy.

The Pope had acted in a somewhat lukewarm manner and he was determined to get satisfaction.

Alexander had no more desire to offend Louis than he had to offend Henry and he knew he must take some decisive steps in this matter. He therefore let it be known that unless the marriage of Richard and Alice took place without delay he would place an interdict on all Henry's lands not only on the Continent of Europe but in England itself.

Henry fumed but he did not on this occasion fly into one of his uncontrollable rages. There was too much at stake to fritter away his energies so fruitlessly. He had to think of a way to save Alice for himself.

When one was in the wrong it was always a good idea to turn the tables and accuse the one who had been wronged.

He now pleaded to the Pope that Louis had not given up the territories he had promised for Alice's dowry, implying that it was this default on the part of the French King which was responsible for the delay. Of course, he announced, he would agree to the marriage of Alice and Richard when these matters were settled. In the meantime he proposed to visit Louis himself and perhaps they could arrive at some conclusion.

Before sailing he went to spend a night with Alice.

She was frightened, poor child, because rumours of the conflict between her father and lover had reached her ears. But quickly he soothed her. Did she not trust him to see that nothing came between them?

Dear little Alice, was she not his beloved and had she not been so for a long time now? Hadn't she learned to trust him? Didn't she know that with him all things were possible?

Alice did know this. She was confident that all would be well.

So Henry would visit him. Louis was puzzled. He must be on his guard.

He was several years older than Henry but constantly seemed to be at a disadvantage with him. He must be some fourteen years his senior and Henry was forty-four. Louis felt his years sorely. Life had been difficult for him, but it had had some wonderful moments. The early days of his marriage with Eleanor had given him most of these. That was when he had innocently believed that they were going to be happy for the rest of their lives. The birth of his son Philip was another. What a joyous day that had been when he had learned that at last he had a son.

How different his life might have been if he could have followed a career in the church which had been what was originally intended for him; but his elder brother had been killed—a simple accident caused when a pig upset his horse by running in front of it—and overnight he became the heir to the throne. He looked back at that frightened boy with pity, but almost immediately Eleanor had been there.

Poor Eleanor, a proud woman, now a prisoner! Had she remained true to her first husband that would never have been her fate. No matter what Eleanor had done he would never have put her into confinement as Henry had done. Henry was a hard and ruthless man; and now he was coming to see him.

Louis loved his children. Sometimes he thought how happy he might have been if he could have been a simple nobleman with his family living around him. As it was he saw little of them. There were necessarily political marriages for all of them; and now what was all this mystery about Alice? She must be more English than French by now; he had not seen her since she was a child. And there was Marguerite who would one day be Queen of England; and with Alice her sister married to young Henry's brother, there would be such strong ties between France and England that surely there would be peace.

He was concerned about Marguerite now for her child was due and must be born any moment. He was pleased that she was brought to bed in Paris. He could see her and his grandchild when it arrived, and he could make sure that everything was done for her comfort.

He was fond too of his son-in-law who was so different from his father. There had been rumours lately of young Henry's preoccupation with those extravagant tournaments which were so fashionable, but all young men loved to amuse themselves. He believed he was a faithful husband and since Marguerite seemed happy with him, he was content.

A messenger arrived to tell him that Marguerite's child was born and that it was a boy.

He was delighted. He would go to see her. News must be sent to the King of England. This was a further bond between them.

Marguerite's son was christened William after the most illustrious of his ancestors—the Conqueror.

Alas, the child was puny and after living three days, in spite of every effort to save him, the little boy died.

On arriving in Normandy Henry was met by his two sons Henry and Geoffrey.

He embraced Henry warmly, expressed his regrets over the death of the child, and waited for the appropriate moment to warn him against devoting too much time to pleasure. He was surprised, he told him, that he had not stayed with Richard to help him in his campaign. Henry's answer to that was that Richard did not care for aid. He liked to be the supreme commander and it was difficult for a king to take orders from a duke, and that duke his younger brother.

"I trust," the King replied, "that you are not deeply in debt."

Henry's mouth was sullen as he replied: "It is necessary for me to live in some state."

The King had no wish to quarrel with his sons. The desire to be on good terms with them was great, longing as he did for their love and loyalty, but he was too astute not to know that they would turn against him should the opportunity arise.

Well, he had Alice and he was going to keep Alice. No one was going to take her from him.

He instructed Geoffrey on what should be done in Brittany and sent him off to begin operations there, and when Geoffrey had left Richard joined them.

There was a young man with whom he could talk sensibly on the strategy of war. Richard had done well in Aquitaine. But how different they were! Richard was a cold man. Henry had heard stories that he was not above a little debauchery now and then but he never lost sight of the objective. He was not like young Henry who might lose an advantage in battle because he wanted to make sport in a tournament.

They talked long of the difficulties of subduing and governing Aquitaine. "They regard me as a stranger," said Richard, "that is the trouble. They fear me. When I arrive in a town the trouble-makers disperse, but they call me your son rather than my mother's. I have tried to assure them that I am against her imprisonment but they do not accept that."

The King grunted. He was angry with Richard for raising this point but he knew it to be true.

"If you can subdue them, then that is good."

"They are not like the English," said Richard. "They must be considered from a different point of view. They love pleasure; they want to sing and dance and dream in the sun."

"Then it should not be difficult to keep them in order."

"They work in subtle ways. They arouse the anger of the people through their poetry. They sing songs of their Duchess lying fretting in her cell."

"Nonsense! She has her servants and is well looked after in Salisbury. The only restriction is that she cannot leave to go about setting people against me."

"They don't believe this. In the songs she is represented as the poor prisoner. They set her behind prison bars in those songs and you are represented as the tyrant who inflicts humiliation and torment."

"Then make songs to tell the truth."

"The prisoner is a better subject for pity than the jailer."

"A plague on their song-making. Make them aware of the sword."

"I have done so, Father, and have brought about a kind of compromise, but always there will be rebellions. Always the poets will sing of the wrongs of their beloved Duchess. Release her. Send her back to Aquitaine."

"To conspire with the King of France against me. Never!"

Richard shrugged his shoulders. "There will never be peace in Aquitaine while my mother is your prisoner," he said.

This was true; and with this uneasy thought Henry went on for his meeting with Louis.

Poor Louis, thought Henry. He was showing his age. He had never been much of a man in Henry's estimation, but now he was really feeble.

He was clearly surprised that Henry should have come to see him and was very suspicious as to what this could mean. He believed that it had something to do with the betrothal of Richard to Alice, about which he was beginning to think there was clearly some mystery.

Henry had sent Richard back to Aquitaine, for he did not want him to be present during the negotiations with Louis about the marriage, and Richard being such a fine figure of a man would bring home the point that there could not be any reason on his side why the marriage should not take place immediately.

It was disconcerting to find that Louis had assembled a cardinal and some of his leading bishops. Clearly they were going to attempt to force him to agree to the celebration of the marriage without delay.

He was in a very delicate position and he needed every bit of astuteness to avoid the issue. Of one thing he was certain: he was not going to let Alice go.

He embraced Louis as King to King and then did homage as Duke of Normandy to his vassal lord.

They talked sadly of their lost grandson and immediately after that the subject of Alice and Richard was raised and everyone waited to hear Henry's objections to the match.

Objections? The tawny eyebrows were raised, the nostrils flared. The lion was benevolent in his surprise. But of course the marriage would take place. Were not Richard and Alice betrothed?

"There has been much delay," Louis reminded him.

"My dear brother," answered Henry with a smile. "The Princess Alice is young still. As for my son he has his Dukedom of Aquitaine to protect. He has scarcely been in England for some time."

"But he is of age to be a husband and the Princess is no longer a child."

"There is truth in that and the marriage must take place," answered Henry.

The company was so taken aback for they had been expecting there would be some hint of the King's objection. Their prepared arguments had no point now as they had intended to stress the advantages of the match and to listen to the King's objections to it.

"Then it would seem," said Louis, "that we are in agreement on this matter."

Henry bowed his head.

"The question now is when can the marriage take place?"

"That," Henry agreed, "is the only question. I will suggest that as I am to have the honour of your company for some days, we discuss together the most appropriate time."

The Cardinal and the Bishops retired. It seemed to them that there had been no need for them to have come. The marriage was to take place at a suitable time. The King of England had raised none of the objections they expected; and it was true that Richard was busy protecting his dukedom.

At the very earliest moment the King would recall Richard from Aquitaine, the marriage would take place and everyone would be satisfied. It was only necessary now for the two Kings to agree on a date.

Henry was pleased with himself. He had come through the first part of the ordeal. Before the Cardinal and the Bishops he had promised that Richard and Alice should marry. But it would not be the first time he had broken a promise. All he had to do was stave off the arrangement of an actual date.

Alone with Louis he expressed great concern for the French King's looks.

"It has been an anxious time for you, doubtless," he said.

"A king's lot is always an anxious one," replied Louis.

"Ah, you speak truth, brother. And it is for each of us to remember this and do all in his power to help the other. It is a sad thing when Kings war together. The crown is a sacred thing—no matter whose crown—and dishonour to one is a dishonour to all."

"I can agree with you on that."

"The health of your son gives you some concern, I believe."

Louis nodded sadly.

"As you know full well, I have suffered great anxiety through my children," said Henry.

"There is the conflict between you and their mother. That is at the root of it."

"She is a perfidious woman, Louis. We both have reason to remember that."

"Yet she can be faithful. She is to her sons, I believe."

"Only because in supporting them she betrays her husband. She betrayed you once, Louis. Strange that you, the King of France, and I the King of England should both have suffered at her hands."

"Release her, Henry. It is not good for royalty to be imprisoned."

"I would I could. But how could I trust her? She it was who raised my sons against me. We have our troubles, you and I. Perhaps God is punishing us."

"For our sins—doubtless."

"Of which I have committed many and you a few, Louis."

"I wonder. I still hear the cries of innocent people in the cities and hamlets my soldiers have pillaged."

"There is one way to shut out those cries. You did it once and I doubt not your sins were forgiven you. But since then perhaps there have been others."

"I doubt it not."

"Have you ever thought, Louis, of going on another crusade?"

Louis was astonished but Henry realized he had struck the right note. Louis could not have many years to live and he had always been a very religious man. He would see as sin that which to Henry was an everyday occurrence. Henry doubted Louis had ever been an unfaithful husband. He had always tried to be just. He was weak of course but the best way to save Alice was to get at her father through religion.

It was a brilliant stroke because Henry had to come away from this meeting with no definite date arranged for the wedding of Richard and Alice.

"I myself have often thought that I would go on a crusade."

"You, Henry! I am surprised. I did not think you would be concerned with such matters."

"It is true I have had my lands to protect and to hold. You

are less harried in that direction than I am. But I have often thought of getting together an army and marching to the Holy Land in this most righteous cause."

"And what of your dominions?"

"I have sons."

"You would give young Henry the power he craves."

"It is his due," said Henry.

Louis looked at him squarely. His plans were falling into shape. He had supported young Henry against his father. It was Louis's belief that the King should give his son more power. It had been the reason for the war between them. Henry had won that round; but if he really went on a crusade and left young Henry to govern, with Louis's daughter Marguerite beside him, that would please Louis very much.

"You are right," cried Louis. "Let us ponder on this matter of a crusade."

"By God's eyes I see you are ready to join me in this. I was never more pleased. You and I banding together as others have done before us and going into righteous battle. We can raise the men and money we need for this enterprise."

"We can," agreed Louis, "and we will."

"We will take an oath together, for there must be no friction between us. This is God's inspiration. Do you not feel it, Louis?"

Louis was sure that he could. It was what he had always wanted to do, and now was the time to do it. It was the way to cleanse his soul of all sin; and if he died on the pilgrimage he would go straight to Heaven. Until the King of England had suggested this and talked of it as though there were no difficulties which could not be swept away he would not have thought it possible.

Henry went on to talk enthusiastically of the project. What fortunate men they were! They both had sons. Philip was young as yet—twelve years old—but he had good advisers and a king-to-be could not shoulder responsibility too soon. Look at the Conqueror—he who was referred to again and again as the greatest ruler of all time—he had been a child when the Dukedom was thrust upon him. Henry had sons; Louis had a son. They could both contemplate this exciting project knowing that it was not an impossibility.

"We must swear that we are friends and neither will do anything that could be harmful to the other," said Henry. "Let us take an oath on this. Let us show the world that this

170

enterprise is the most important event that has ever befallen either of us."

Louis was agreeable. "The world should know it," he said.

"And now we must plan our exercise. It needs much thought. The equipping of armies to undertake such an enterprise is a major matter. Dismiss your priests when they have heard what we intend to do, for I cannot tarry with you long and we have much to plan."

Louis could think of nothing but the proposed expedition. He had once before gone on such a journey. It had been a failure, but that was due to the fact that Eleanor had accompanied him. God had been displeased then, and looking back Louis was not surprised. At that time Louis had been so enamoured of Eleanor that he had allowed her too much freedom. And how she had rewarded him—by entering into an incestuous relationship with her uncle and, so it was said, taking a Saracen as her lover! It was at that time that she had begun asking for a divorce. Oh, yes, it had been a disaster and he could see that Eleanor with the fine clothes she had taken with her for the trip had turned it from a holy enterprise into a worldly display of splendour and immorality.

This would be different. Two ageing and serious men bent on serving God and so earning the redemption of their sins.

He could think of nothing but the means he would use to raise the money, what equipment he would need, whom he would take with him.

Henry shared his excitement and the rest of the time they spent together was given over to making these arrangements.

Henry said farewell to his dear brother with whom he had sworn oaths of friendship. It was true he had promised that the marriage between Richard and Alice should take place but the vital point had been eluded. No date had been given.

As for going on a crusade Henry laughed at the idea. Louis was a fool. Did he think Henry would hand over his realm to inexperienced boys? Louis was unworldly, he did not understand what power meant to a man like Henry. Nor did he understand the determination to keep to himself the woman who pleased him more than any other.

The Lady of Godstow

In the convent of Godstow, Rosamund knew that her end was near. It was just a little more than a year since she had arrived at the convent where she had been received with pleasure by the nuns. It was not only that the King had endowed the convent with gifts since she had come, which had made her popular; her gentle nature very soon made her beloved by all.

There was none more devout than Rosamund. She spent long hours in meditation and penance; so deeply concerned was she with her sins, which seemed to her to have been of such magnitude that no matter if she lived for twenty years she could never wipe them out, even if she passed those years in extreme piety.

Sometimes she talked of this to the nuns who sought to comfort her.

"I know that it was wrong. I should never have agreed to become the King's mistress. I loved him and could deny him nothing. I cannot describe to you the charm of Henry Plantagenet."

"Others have sinned in like fashion, my daughter," the Abbess reminded her. "They have sought and found forgiveness as you are doing."

But Rosamund was too heavily weighed down by her conception of sin to be comforted. If she had been seduced against her will, it would have been different; if she had given way to save her family from the King's displeasure there would have been some hope for her soul.

"But no," she said. "He came to my father's castle and was entertained there. We took one look at each other and the temptation was born. I remember well how I returned to my bedchamber and my heart beat as it never did before. I loosened my hair so that it fell about my shoulders and I put on my most becoming robe. I waited for the summons and when it came most willingly I went."

"You were but a child."

"A child who knew the difference between good and evil."

She could not excuse herself. She wept often; she sewed garments for the poor until there were deep shadows under her once beautiful eyes. And each day she grew more pale and wan.

Occasionally she heard news of what was happening in the world outside Godstow. It was said that there would soon be a royal wedding for Prince Richard and the Princess Alice of France.

Poor Alice! What would her life be? How could she go to her bridegroom when she had already borne the King a child? Few knew of that, and Rosamund hoped never would. One day would Alice feel the heavy weight of her sins as insupportable as Rosamund now found hers?

And the King? How would he feel about letting Alice go? Yet he had let Rosamund go and surely he had once loved her even as he now loved Alice.

It was a sad and sorry world and Rosamund was convinced that her sins were too great for heavenly forgiveness.

She was no longer a young woman so perhaps the King had tired of her for that reason. She would soon have seen forty winters. So many years it had been since the King had first sent for her. Yet she remembered that occasion in every detail and with her was the certain knowledge that if she were young again and the King was there, everything would have happened as it had before.

That was what made her feel so doomed.

The Abbess remonstrated with her. Should she not work a little in the gardens? That would give her a little fresh air, and she loved the plants.

"I love the gardens," answered Rosamund. "To tend the flowers would give me the utmost pleasure. From now on I want to turn my back on everything that pleases me. I have had pleasure enough in my life. It is now time for me to endure the pain."

Confined in her cell she would spend long hours on her knees, the hairy garment she wore tormenting her soft skin. And at length there came a day when the Abbess despaired of her life, so much had she neglected her health and so deeply enamoured did she seem of death.

She was unable to rise from her pallet and when the nuns brought certain comforts to her cell she scorned them. They sought to wrap her in warm covering but she spurned it; she had grown so thin that she was not recognizable as the beautiful penitent who had entered the convent only a year before.

"Rest easy, my daughter," said the Abbess. "Your sins will be forgiven for you have truly repented."

Rosamund shook her head and the tears fell down her sunken cheeks.

"Nay," she said. "Do you know the big tree in the gardens . . . my favourite tree?"

The Abbess nodded.

"When that turns to stone you will know that I have been received into Heaven."

"You have shown true repentance, and God is good."

But Rosamund could not believe that her sins were forgiven, for she only had to think of Henry Plantagenet and she knew that were he to come to her and insist on her going to him she would be unable to prevent herself doing so. How could one be forgiven a sin when in one's heart one knew that should the temptation occur again, there would be no resisting it?

The nuns wept for her when she was dead. She had been a good and gracious lady; and much good had come to Godstow because it had sheltered her.

The King came to the convent. He was deeply distressed. His dear Rosamund, dead! Fair Rosamund. The Rose of the World who through him had become the Rose of Unchastity.

"She was a good woman," he said, "and dearly I loved her. If she sinned it was in loving me. She was my comfort when I needed comfort. She gave me solace which as King I needed. Because of her I was a better man than I would otherwise have been."

He wished her to be buried with some pomp. Let her coffin be placed in the gardens of the convent she loved so well. The grave would not be closed. A tabernacle should be built above the coffin; then an altar should be created and the coffin placed on it. The coffin should be covered by a pall of silk; tapers should be kept constantly burning at either end and banners should wave above it.

Thus it would be seen that this was a shrine to one who had been highly valued by the King, and he had decided that one day a suitable monument should be built beneath which she would be buried.

Until that time let her lie in state and let the nuns of Godstow keep the tapers burning and pray constantly for the salvation of the soul of one whom the King had loved dearly.

The Court of France

Philip, son of the King of France, was leading a hunting party into the forest. He was not a very happy nor a very popular boy. From an early age he had been aware of his importance as the King's only son and there had been much fussing over his health. Now that he was fourteen years of age—soon to be fifteen—he was spoilt, peevish and arrogant. He despised his father but naturally he must accept the fact that he was the King; his mother, who attempted to restrain his selfishness, often angered him and he had more than once warned her to take care, for one day he would be the King and then she would have to obey him.

He was sickly and caught cold easily and when he was not feeling well—which was often—he would be irritable. He had few real friends and his attendants counted themselves lucky when their duties did not bring them too close to him.

At this time he was more arrogant than ever because his father had told him that he was arranging for his coronation.

"You see, my son, I am no longer a young man," Louis explained. "I waited a long time for a son and married three wives to get you."

"I know this," said Philip impatiently. "All know it."

"It meant great rejoicing when you came. I had the bells ringing throughout France."

Philip inclined his head. He was not averse to hearing the often repeated tale of his much heralded arrival into the world.

The thought of the coronation delighted him. Then he would be King of France beside his father; and the old man was ageing fast. It could not be long before he was sole ruler of the country.

The more he thought of this the more impatient he became; and on this day when he rode out with his band of huntsmen he was thinking of the great day ahead in the Cathedral at Rheims. He was already putting on the airs of a King, seeing himself in his coronation robes, the crown on his head. King of France, what a glorious title!

They had sighted the deer and he wished his to be the arrow that killed it. There would be feasting that night and he would be at the head of the table. There was extra deference for him now that his coronation was in sight, and he was not so much the sickly boy to be cherished, as the future monarch to be placated. He liked the change.

He spurred his horse and immediately those knights whom his father had commanded to guard him came level with him.

He gave an angry glance to right and left.

"Keep off my tail," he growled, and they immediately fell back; he spurred on his horse and took great delight in leaving them behind.

On and on he galloped. He was sure the deer had gone this way. He wanted to be the one who cornered the animal. When he had killed it he would shout to the others and they would come hurrying up at his command and compliment him on the finest buck that had ever fallen to arrow. It would have to be because the King-to-be had shot it and even if it was the veriest baby of a deer they would have to see it as the finest. That was the joy of being a king. His father was a foolish old man. He talked about honesty and turning from flattery, and how a king's best and staunchest friends were often those who criticized him. No one was going to criticize Philip II of France.

He galloped on through the forest, leaving the others far behind. This was unfamiliar country to him, but he knew the direction in which he had come. Where was the deer? He drew up and looked about him. There was no sign of it.

He shouted and listened for an answer. None came. His attendants had obeyed his order to get off his tail, and he must have left the party far behind him.

He rode on. The forest had become more dense. He pulled up and called again. There was no answer. He listened for the sound of horses' hoofs, but there was only the faint sighing of wind in the thick August leaves and the crackle of undergrowth as some small animal scuttled along.

There was something sinister about the forest when one was alone. The tall dignified trees implied they would bow to no one and that a king was of no more importance to them than a woodcutter. Overhead through their leaves he could see the hot summer sky.

He was a little tired and thirsty. His throat craved cool

soothing liquid. Perhaps there was a woodcutter's hut nearby where he could ask refreshment. He liked the idea. Those stories—and there were many of them—in which some great personage visited a humble cottage and was given refreshment and treated as an ordinary traveller and then suddenly announced, "I am your King"—or some such phrase, greatly appealed to him.

He rode on. He was getting deeper and deeper into the forest and he was not sure what direction he should take. He tried calling again but when he raised his voice it cracked and the words were a mere croak.

He began to feel a little dizzy.

As he could not sit steadily on his horse, he dismounted, loosely tied it to a tree and lay down on the grass. He felt better lying down. He must have dozed a little for he awoke suddenly and his horse was no longer there.

Could someone have stolen it? Could it have broken loose? Or was he dreaming?

He staggered to his feet. There was no doubt that the horse had disappeared.

It could not be far off. He called it by name. There was no answering whinny, and suddenly the realization came to him that he was lost in the forest.

He looked up at the sky. There was a touch of evening in the air. He must have dozed longer than he thought. Night would soon be on him.

The thought frightened him. It was alarming to be lost by day, but by night it was terrifying.

The trees took on odd shapes. They seemed to come alive and their branches swayed towards him like avenging arms. He stood up and tottered uncertainly forward. Bracken caught at his garments as though it were trying to hold him back. The light was quickly fading. The breeze had now dropped and there was an unearthly stillness about him.

Night was almost upon him.

The members of his party would be anxious because he was lost. They would tell his father and the poor old man would be frantic. Search parties would be sent out to comb the forest . . . every part would be searched. They must soon find him. His father would be angry with his guards. Serve them right! But they would say that he had been left unattended at his own command and his father, always lenient, always wanting to be just, would believe them.

"Come and find me," he called out.

There was no answer, only a flurry in the branches as some startled creature, alarmed by the noise, made off.

He was frightened, for it was now dark. Would they never find him? His body was burning; the fever was on him. He knew it well for it was an old enemy. With it came delirium.

He thought he had died and had gone to hell. This was hell. There were devils all about him and they were trying to catch him and carry him off to eternal damnation.

"Let me alone!" he cried. "I am the King of France. My coronation is to be soon and then you will see."

It was as though he heard mocking laughter which implied: Where you are there is no difference between a king and the humblest serf.

It could not be so. Kings endowed abbeys; they went on pilgrimages; they fought crusades. Humble serfs could not do that. That must bring the rich and noble some merit.

But he had never done these things. And here he was lost in the forest with death beckoning him. Where was his father? Where were his guards? Where even was his horse, for he would have given him some comfort?

He tripped and fell; the grass seemed damp as he lay for a while. It seeped through his clothes and he started to shiver.

"Mother of Mary, help me," he prayed.

He felt the tears on his cheeks. He was not the future King of France now; he was merely a very frightened boy.

He rose again unsteadily and stumbled forward. Was he dreaming or were the trees less thick? He was not sure but the thought comforted him. He wanted to get out of the forest, for the forest was evil.

His clothes were wet, or was that the sweat now the fever had passed a little? He was cold now, shivering, with cold as well as fear.

He would die if they did not find him. When he was ill the King his father would send for the best physicians in the country to attend to him; prayers would be said throughout the country. But now he was alone and none knew of his dire need.

"Only God can help me now," he muttered. "Oh, God, forgive me my sins. Give me a chance to redeem my soul."

This was one of the rare occasions when he experienced humility.

As though in answer to his prayer he saw through the trees a small clearing in the forest and a dim light. His heart leaped in joy. "Thank you, God," he whispered. "You have heard my prayer."

He stumbled towards the light. It came from a cottage which was little more than a hut. He managed to reach the door and beat on it with his fist and as it opened he fell at the feet of an old man.

"Help . . ." murmured Philip.

The old man knelt down and looked at him. Then he dragged him into the cottage.

Philip lay on the floor and the old man put warm soup to his lips. He could see by the manner in which he was dressed that he was a nobleman.

"My lord, you are ill. Your clothes are damp. You should rest in my humble cottage until you are well."

Philip allowed his cloak to be taken from him. He felt better, partly because of the soup but mainly because of the human company.

"Tell . . . the King," he stammered.

"My lord."

"I am the King's son," he said.

"My lord. Is it so then?"

The old man knelt.

It was the old story in which he had wanted to play a part but how different this was from what he had imagined.

"I was lost and I am ill. Pray send to the King without delay."

"My son shall go at once, my lord," said the old man. "You should stay here and warm yourself. I can only give you old garments which it would not be becoming for you to wear, you may think."

Philip said: "Let me shelter here and send word to my father."

"We are but humble charcoal-burners, my lord," said the man, "but we are good and loyal servants of the King. I will send my son without delay."

Philip nodded and closed his eyes.

It was not until the next morning that guards from the castle arrived. Philip by that time was delirious.

The charcoal-burner was given a purse full of gold coins for his part in the adventure which made him richer than he could have been through a lifetime's work, and Philip was taken back to the castle.

His constitution was not strong enough to endure such an

ordeal and he was very ill, so ill in fact that it seemed very likely that he could not survive.

Louis was frantic. It was true that he was being punished for his sins; he needed to go on that crusade with Henry. This was his only son whom he had planned should be crowned with the pomp he considered necessary to such an occasion, and God was threatening to take him from him.

He wept; he entreated; he consulted with his kinsman, the Count of Flanders, who himself had recently returned from a crusade, after which he believed his sins had been washed away. The Count was a comparatively young man and had plenty of time to commit more and redeem the fresh lot, so he was in a particularly ebullient mood.

Louis could not sleep, so great was his anxiety. He sent for his ministers and said, "I am no longer young. I doubt I can get more sons and if I had one now he would be but a baby when I was called away. God is punishing me. I sense it. Why should he do this to me? Philip was never strong as I could have wished and that something like this should befall him is what I have always feared."

His ministers reminded him that young Philip still lived and the doctors were caring for him. There was a good chance that he would survive.

But when Louis saw the doctors they were very grave. The King's son was in a high fever. He was delirious and kept calling out that the trees were his enemies and they were seeking to catch him and turn him into one of them.

The King's advisers warned him that he must look to his own health. If he did not and he died while his only son was in such a condition that could be disastrous for France.

Louis deplored the fact that he had not yet gone on the crusade which he and Henry were planning, and thinking of Henry, Louis was reminded of Thomas à Becket, that great good man who had been so cruelly done to death on the stones of Canterbury Cathedral. His physicians gave him a soothing draught which they said would give him peaceful sleep and as he lay on his bed, between sleeping and waking, he had a strange experience which he believed to be a vision.

Thomas the Martyr was in the room.

"Is it indeed you, my friend, Thomas à Becket Archbishop of Canterbury?" asked the King.

"It is," said the shadowy shape.

"You come from Heaven where you have a place of honour?" said the King.

"I come to you from God," was the answer. "Go to Canterbury, humble yourself at my shrine there. Confess your sins and ask forgiveness. If I intercede for you, you will be given back your son."

The King sat up in his bed. He was trembling. He was alone in his bedchamber.

He was convinced that St Thomas à Becket had visited him and would save the life of his son.

Go to Canterbury! His ministers were disturbed. Go into the realm of his old enemy the King of England!

"You forget," said Louis, "that we are now friends. We have sworn an oath to this purpose and we are planning to go on a crusade together."

"It is unwise to put too much trust in the King of England," advised his ministers.

"I trust him now," replied Louis. "Moreover St Thomas has told me to go. If I do not my son will die. Even if I suspected perfidy on the part of the King of England I would still go to save my son."

They could see it was no use attempting to dissuade him.

Philip of Flanders was excited by the prospect. He was inclined to agree with the King's ministers that it was not very wise for Louis to go to England but the prospect of excitement always exhilarated him. Life had been a little dull since his return from the crusade and he was now trying to ingratiate himself with young Philip for he could see that Louis was not long for this world and the journey over the sea would surely be a great trial to him.

"My lord," he said, "I trust I may be allowed to accompany you."

"I would be glad of it," answered Louis.

His ministers remained dubious. Did he think that he could endure the crossing of the sea? He knew how unpredictable that stretch of water could be.

Louis was well aware of this but his mind was made up. All that remained to be done before he set out was to tell his good friend the King of England of his desire.

When Henry heard that Louis wished to visit the shrine at Canterbury he was uneasy for it occurred to him that while the King of France was in England he would surely wish to see his daughter. He would have to impress on Alice, if this meeting took place—though he would do his utmost to see

that it did not—that she must in no way betray her feeling
for him. Reference would certainly be made to Richard and if
so she must feign to accept him with pleasure as her husband. She could trust Henry to see that the marriage would
never take place. But time enough to prime Alice, if a
meeting took place between father and daughter. Louis was
at the time a very anxious man, concerned with one thing—
the preservation of his son, so it might well be that he would
forget the predicament of his daughter.

He sent a messenger to Louis with an effusive welcome.
The King of England would be honoured to receive the King
of France. He understood his great grief and his desire to
intercede through St Thomas. He would add his prayers to
those of Louis and Louis could be sure of a safe conduct.
There was absolutely no need for those in France who wished
him well to fear for his safety. The King of England would
personally make himself responsible for it.

Assembling a brilliant cavalcade Henry travelled to Dover
to await the arrival of the King of France. People gathered at
the roadside to see him pass and there were many to witness
the meeting of the two Kings.

Poor Louis, racked with anxiety for his son and the misery
he had endured during the crossing, looked his age. Have I
aged as much in the last few years as he has? wondered
Henry. He could still spend a day in the saddle without
tiring; he was as active as he ever was and men still marvelled
at that tremendous energy which showed no sign of abating.
He had never cared for his appearance. How Eleanor had
reproached him for that, calling him a peasant in some of her
rages, jeering at his chapped hands and his manner of dressing,
calling him a barbarian because he said clothes were meant
for use and not for ornament. Barbarian indeed! Some of
them loved their finery. What about her Saracen lover for
one? Why should he think of Eleanor after all this time?
What did he care for her opinion? Alice loved him. Alice
thought him the most wonderful being that had ever lived.
That was all that mattered. His hair was getting thin and he
had been proud of his tawny curling locks. They had perhaps
been his greatest personal vanity. Even now he combed them
carefully in an attempt to hide the baldness.

He had aged a little then, but gracefully, as was to be
expected. But poor Louis was an old man. He must be nearing
sixty—quite an age; and he did not look as if he would last
much longer.

Henry embraced him. "My dear, dear friend. Welcome. It rejoices me to see you here."

There were tears in Louis's eyes. "Blessings on you, Henry. How good it is of you to make me so welcome on your shores. My heart is sick, my dear friend, sick with anxiety. My beloved son . . ."

"I feel for you," said Henry, "and I have made it known that there shall be no delay. When you have rested from your voyage we will go together to the shrine at Canterbury and there mingle our tears and our prayers. I doubt not that they will be answered. Be of good cheer. St Thomas is the good friend of us both and he will intercede for you. I know it."

Louis thanked his kind host and the next day they set out together for Canterbury.

The Kings rode side by side along the road to Canterbury. They talked, Louis of his son's misadventure in the forest and how the night in the damp and lonely place had brought on a bout of the fever which often plagued him. "He is my only son," wailed Louis. "You my good friend are more fortunate, you are the father of several."

More than you know, thought Henry; and odd as it is I get more comfort from those who were born outside wedlock than those born within. Perhaps that has something to do with their mothers.

"I have had my trials with my brood," said Henry.

"You have never had anxieties as to their health."

"Nay, but they're a fighting breed, I fancy. I trust my young John will not turn against his father as the others have done. At least, Louis, you have not suffered that kind of ingratitude."

Henry thought: There is time yet for Philip to give you cause to suffer it, for I'd not trust him. At least my sons are handsome, boys to be proud of, although rebellious. I would hate to have a peevish weakling like your Philip.

"We are close," said Louis. "Bound by the marriages of our children. What a bitter blow that Marguerite should have lost her child. Our grandson would have made a greater tie between us. But I am the father of your son Henry even as you are of my daughter Marguerite. And so it will be with Richard and Alice . . ."

"Yes, yes, yes," said Henry hastily. "You must have heard of the numbers of miracles which have been performed at St Thomas's shrine. The blind have been made to see, the lame to walk. I believe with all my heart that this time tomorrow when we have said our prayers, Philip will begin to get better."

"You comfort me, my friend. I am beginning to believe, too, that it will be so."

The bells were ringing a welcome as they passed through the walls of the city. Louis went at once to the crypt and knelt by the tomb of St Thomas. There he prayed all through the day and night refusing food, pleading with St Thomas to intercede with God for the life of his son.

Nor was he content with prayer. He promised that the convent there should receive its wine free every year from France.

Henry expressed his thanks and insisted on taking his guest with him to Winchester that he might have a brief respite there before making the arduous journey across the sea. He was determined to show friendship for Louis. It was no use offering him a banquet. Louis was more interested in churches. Henry however took him to his treasure vault and there asked him to take something as a pledge of their friendship.

Henry trembled with anxiety as Louis handled some of his most precious gold, silver and jewel-studded ornaments, for he could not bear to part with any of his possessions; he need not have feared. Louis chose something of small value and again they pledged their friendship.

Henry said that he would have begged the King of France to prolong his stay, there was so much he wished to show him in England, but he knew full well how eager he would be to get back to his son. His great anxiety during the visit was that Louis might ask to see Alice or Eleanor. Either could have proved fatal. Alice would have done her best to keep their secret, but would she have been able to? And the fact that Eleanor knew of it often set him sweating with fear. He wondered why she had not made it known. He could only believe that she thought she could plague him more by keeping him guessing.

With skill he avoided either issue and it was with great pleasure that he accompanied the King of France to Dover. Louis embarked on the waiting vessel and sailed back to France.

There, joyous news awaited him. Philip was recovering his health. The doctors swore that it must have been precisely at the time when Louis lay prostrate before the tomb of the martyr that Philip began to revive.

Louis went at once to see his son and the change in him was remarkable. It could only be a miracle, declared the King; and how gratified he was that he had defied his ministers and put his trust in the martyr and Henry of England. He felt it augured well for the future and their new friendship which was to take them together to the Holy Land.

"Your coronation will not be long delayed," he told Philip. "We will make preparations without delay."

He was delighted when his son-in-law, the younger Henry, arrived at the French Court with his wife Marguerite.

Louis embraced them both warmly. Henry looked well and very handsome though Marguerite was a little wan after her ordeal.

"How glad I am to see you, my son and daughter," he said, and he added to Henry: "I want you and my Philip to be friends always. Your father and I have taken an oath of friendship and one day you two will stand in the same position as we hold today—Kings of France and England. I want there to be amity between you. Remember that, Henry, for there is nothing but misery in war. I would to God I had never taken part in it. I would be a happier man today if I had not."

Wars were a necessary part of a King's life, Henry supposed, but he did not bother to contradict Louis. The poor old fellow was looking older than ever and his skin had taken on an unhealthy tinge.

Henry was glad to renew his friendship with Philip of Flanders but he was less influenced by him than before, for he was more experienced of the world than he had been and although he remembered how generous the Count had been when he was initiating him into the joys of the tournament, he no longer seemed quite the glamorous person he had once appeared to be.

Nor did Henry greatly care for the young Prince of France. No one did; he was not a very attractive character. It was only his father who doted on him, and of course the ministers of France realized his importance, for he was the heir and if he had died after that mishap in the forest there would doubtless have been so many claimants to the throne that there would have been inevitable civil war.

Louis decided that there should be a thanksgiving service

at St Denis to commemorate the miraculous recovery of Philip; and this should take place as soon as possible.

He did not wish Thomas à Becket to think he was ungrateful for his intercession.

The date was fixed. Young Henry would ride side by side with Philip to show everyone that the friendship between France and England was firm.

When his attendants helped Louis on to his horse they were struck by his pallor and one of them asked the King if he was feeling unwell.

"A little weary," replied Louis.

"My lord, should you not perhaps rest?"

"Nay," replied the King. "I would not miss this ceremony for anything."

But he did miss it, for as the procession made its way to the Abbey the King startled everyone by falling forward. He would have slipped to the ground had not one of the knights, who had been inwardly noting his pallor, hurried to save him.

The King was taken back to the castle, and soon his doctors were at his bedside.

He had suffered a seizure and could neither speak nor move.

In a few days he was slightly better. His speech returned but one arm and leg were paralysed.

There was one thing Louis was determined on. The coronation must not be postponed again. Now more than before it was necessary for Philip to be crowned King of France.

He sent for Philip of Flanders and begged him to watch over young Philip. The Count was one of Philip's god-parents he reminded him and it was his duty. "My son is clever but so young," said the King. "He has much to learn but is shrewd enough to learn it. I trust that those who wish me well will be good friends of his."

Philip of Flanders swore that he would serve Philip with all his strength.

So he would, he promised himself, if the boy would be influenced by him. The Count pictured himself growing more and more powerful as his influence grew. It was clear that Louis had not long to live; the new King would be very young, and if he would accept his godfather's guidance, Philip of Flanders would be very content. It should be as Louis wished, only young Philip should serve the Count of

Flanders instead of the other way round. When that happened there would be amity between them and they would work together for the good of France and the Count.

Louis's wife Adela came to his bedside and he talked to her of his anxieties.

"I would our son were a little older," he said.

"He will soon grow older," she soothed him.

"Not in time."

"There is going to be time," she told him. Her eyes were sorrowful. He had been a kind and gentle husband. She had been afraid when she came to Paris to marry him and be Queen of France. Her family had been naturally delighted with the match and she was thinking of her brothers now, for if Louis died she would need their help. Philip was too young to rule and could well become influenced by those who were no good to him.

"Adela, my dear," said Louis, "you have been a good wife to me and I can never thank you enough for giving me my son."

She knelt down by his bed and kissed his hand.

He muttered an endearment.

"You must get well," she told him.

He nodded his head to comfort her, but he did not believe he would ever leave his bed.

On the day of the coronation he lay there still and longed to be at Rheims. There the crown would be placed on Philip's head by his uncle—Adela's brother—who was Archbishop of Rheims. He was a good man and a strong one. Her brothers would stand beside Adela and soon the boy, whom everyone must admit was clever, would be of an age to stand on his own.

If only Philip were a little older he could die in peace. Not that he was any use now except as a symbol; he was, though, still the King of France and men respected him as such, but this day there would be another King, a young boy who, he prayed fervently, would grow up to be a great king.

He felt that although he lay in Paris and his son was in Rheims he was with him in spirit.

He knew that Philip of Flanders would carry the golden sword and the young Henry of England would hold the crown, and the ceremony would be conducted by Philip's uncle.

He could hear the music. He could see it all and he prayed: "Holy mother, care for my son. Give him the wisdom I lacked. Make him strong to stand against his enemies and show him how to be merciful to those who wrong him. If you will do this I am ready to depart in peace."

And in the Cathedral of Rheims young Philip was exultant. King of France at last. Young Henry watching him wanted to say: The fact that you are crowned does not make you a king. You will have to wait until your father is dead but that will not be long doubtless.

Heaven knows how long I must wait.

Everywhere the young King of France went the Count of Flanders accompanied him. The wily Count was now trying to be to Philip what he had once sought to be to Henry. The two young people were in similar circumstances; both had been crowned while their fathers still lived; both bore the title of King without the power.

The Count marvelled at the folly both of the King of France and King of England that they could have had so little foresight as to raise their sons to this eminence while they still held the crown. It was asking for trouble. In the case of Louis, who could not live much longer, there was some reason; but that Henry Plantagenet should have been so unwise was a mystery.

However, the Count was now far more interested in the new King of France than he was in Henry. Henry's father had many years left to him; he was a strong man against whom few could pit their wits and fighting skill and come out victorious. It was quite different in the case of Philip.

So he brought all his wiles to bear on the young man.

Philip of Flanders was just the type of man it was natural for young Philip to admire. His flamboyance, his subtle flattery, his extravagance, his wealth, his generosity, all this enchanted the young King.

Queen Adela could see the effect the Count of Flanders was having on her son and she deplored this. She tried to remonstrate with him.

"Philip, your father still lives," she reminded him. "Remember he is still the King of France."

"He can do nothing. He lies in his bed and cannot move. France has to be governed."

"Your father has always said that a king needs good ministers to govern well."

"My father was always afraid to rule."

"Have a care what you say, my son. Your father is a good man and the only thing he feared was to do wrong."

"A king must be bold. A king has to make decisions whether others like them or not. He must take only that advice which seems good to him and it is he who has the final word."

"He also needs experience. I have asked your uncles to come to Court."

Philip flew into a rage. His uncles! Her brothers. These men of the house of Blois had too grand an opinion of themselves. The Count of Flanders said so. Since their sister had married the King of France they thought they had a right to rule.

"Then," cried Philip, "you may cancel that invitation."

"I shall do no such thing," retorted the Queen. "Your father is pleased that I should do so. He understands that you will need their guidance."

"I certainly do not need them. Nor will I have them."

"Philip," said his mother earnestly, "remember this. You have been crowned King but that does not make you ruler of this country. France already has a king and while he lives the crown, and the authority which goes with it, belongs to him."

"He is dead . . . or almost. He cannot think; he cannot act."

"Philip, how can you talk so! He is your father and King of France. He is stricken with a terrible affliction. Are you going to bring sorrow to his last months of life?"

"I am King of France," said Philip, "and everyone must know it."

"You are but a boy."

There was nothing that infuriated Philip more than to be reminded of his youth. He flew into a rage and cried: "You shall know . . . all shall know . . . what it means to cross the King of France, even though he be what you call a stripling."

"You must always curb your passions, Philip. You have been crowned as your father wished. He wants France never to be without a crowned King. That is why he commanded your coronation. Remember you owe your crown to him; you owe your life to him. No good ever came to those who did not honour their fathers. His is the crown. His is the seal of office. Loyal Frenchmen owe their duty to him and him only . . . as yet."

Philip raged out of the apartment.

In the gardens Philip of Flanders was walking with Henry and Marguerite. There was still a friendship between Henry and the Count, who observed with some pleasure that Henry

189

was a little jealous of the attentions he was now paying Philip.

Philip joined them.

"What black brows!" said the Count of Flanders lightly as he looked at Philip. "It would seem that there is thunder in the air."

"It is my mother," said Philip. "She will bring my uncles here to help me govern."

The Count was alert. The last thing he wanted was to have those brothers at Court. The House of Blois had too high an opinion of itself. It was very closely connected with royalty for one of the Conqueror's daughters, Adela—after whom the present Queen of France was named—had married into it. It was for this reason that Stephen her son had become King of England; and Stephen's brother Theobald was the father of Adela Queen of France. Adela had four brothers: one the Archbishop of Rheims who had crowned young Philip; Henry, the Count of Champagne, and Theobald, Count of Blois, who had married Marie and Alix respectively—Louis's daughters by Eleanor; and the fourth was the influential Stephen Count of Sancerre.

It was small wonder that at such a time these men should consider themselves the rightful advisers of the young King of France, and the Count of Flanders must prevent their getting influence over the young Philip.

"You will of a surety not permit that," said Philip lightly.

"I will do my best."

"Your best! But you only have to say you will not have them. Are you not the King?"

"Well yes, but as my mother pointed out, the crown and the seal of office still belong to my father."

This was true. Adela could talk to old Louis and get him to bring her brothers to Court. It had to be stopped. Philip of Flanders could see his dream of power being ruined if they came and took charge of this rather impressionable young boy.

"We will put our heads together," said the Count lightly. "Henry will help us, will you not? He knows what it means to be frustrated."

"I do indeed. My father has bound me not to take action against him."

"And you are restive under the yoke," replied the Count. "We must see that we do not allow them to put a yoke on your fair neck, my dear Philip."

Marguerite frowned at her half-brother. She did not like him very much. She thought it a pity that boys should be treated with such honours. She and her sisters had never been made as much of as Philip had, simply because they were girls. Moreover she loved her father dearly. Louis had always been good and gentle to his children and she was very upset that he was now lying on what everyone believed to be his death bed.

She said: "I do not wish to listen to such talk. My father . . . *our* father, Philip . . . is lying sorely afflicted. For pity's sake let us not talk as though he were dead already."

Henry laid a gentle hand on her arm.

"It is not of him personally we speak, Marguerite," he said. "We love him dearly. He has been a good father to me. Kinder than my own. But Philip must make sure that he is not robbed of his rights."

"Philip is but a boy."

Philip flushed and glared at her. "I am a man. I am capable of governing and by our lady I will govern."

"Spoken like a king," said the Count of Flanders. "I like to hear you speak thus. But it is action that counts. You must be ready when the day comes."

Marguerite turned away, a glaze of tears in her eyes. She would not stay and hear them talk as though her father were already dead. She saw William Marshall in the garden and went and joined him. The Count watched her. He believed she was telling William why she was upset.

The Count did not greatly care for the influence William Marshall had over Henry and Marguerite. He had been the knight-at-arms in the nursery when they were children and being such an old friend was too important to them. They both admired him far too much. William Marshall was one of those honourable men whose actions were predictable. He did not seek honours for himself; he was the sort of knight whose value Henry Plantagenet was aware of and the kind he liked to see beside his son. William Marshall and Count Philip of Flanders were as different as two men could be.

He turned his attention to the two young men and drew Henry out to talk of the wrongs he had suffered at the hands of his father.

"You are in a different position, Philip," said the wily Count. "Poor Henry here is the son of a forceful man who will never give way. You are the son of a dying one."

"There is a great difference," Henry agreed. He was watching Marguerite and William the Marshall. The Marshall was obviously soothing her. *He,* Henry, should be doing that. He, too, hated to hear them talk as though Louis was dead. He had always said Louis had been a father to him. But at the same time he had been in leading strings and he did understand Philip's resentment.

"A great difference," went on the Count. "There is little Henry can do at this stage. His father is too strong for him. It will not always be so. Then we shall pledge ourselves to help him, shall we not, Philip?"

Philip agreed earnestly that they would.

"But right at the start, we must not allow Philip to be put into leading strings from which we shall find it difficult to extricate him."

"I'll not allow it," cried Philip shrilly. Then his face clouded. "She is right though. He has the crown still and the seal of office."

"You have been crowned, remember," said the Count. "And where is the seal of office?"

"He keeps it in his bedroom, under his pillow."

The Count smiled. "If we could lay our hands on the seal . . ."

"What mean you?" said Philip.

The Count looked from the young King of France to Henry. Henry however was watching his wife and William the Marshall who were walking together towards the courtyard.

"If you had the seal, if it could appear that he had given it to you . . ."

"He will not give it to me. Should I ask for it?"

"No. The Queen will have told him that he must not give it to you. If you slipped your hand under his pillow. If you took it . . ."

"I could!" cried Philip. "But he would say that he did not give it to me."

"His word against yours! He is a sick man. He is often delirious. If you held the seal in your hands it would be yours."

"I will do it," breathed Philip. "It will be easy and when I have it I shall forbid my uncles to come to Court."

The Count of Flanders walked in the gardens alone with Henry. He liked to walk there not because he admired the flowers—he scarcely noticed them—but because out of doors it was possible to talk without being overheard.

He was succeeding well; a born intriguer, he was in his element. Life must for him be a continual adventure. He had returned from the Holy Land where he had lived excitingly and nothing would please him better than to rule France through its weak young King.

He had once thought he could hold a high office in England if he could have established young Henry there, but he was not so stupid as to think he was a match for Henry Plantagenet and he knew that the old lion was going to cling to power as long as there was breath in his body. His roar grew none the less menacing nor his claws less to be feared as he grew older. Philip, with a dying father, was a much better proposition.

He still must not lose sight of the old lion across the water. The vulture had to make sure he was not cheated of his prey. Young Henry was easy to handle. He was so resentful towards his father that he would always be ready to go into action against him if ever the opportunity offered. It was hardly likely that there would be much hope of success in that direction. But if old Henry died and young Henry was King, he would then be a subject worthy of the Count's attention.

In the meantime, he must make sure of his position in France, while keeping an eye on Henry. He had been watching William the Marshall and he believed that he was making an attempt to influence Henry against him, the Count. This could not be permitted. He would feel very much happier if William the Marshall were somewhere else than in the service of young Henry.

Watching him with Marguerite recently an idea had occurred to him and he thought it a good one.

Marguerite was a beautiful and attractive girl and there was no doubt that Henry was very pleased with his wife. He was not given to the pursuit of women to such an extent as so many young men were, and he was a faithful husband.

The Count said: "The Marshall is a handsome fellow."

Henry agreed. "And what a knight! No one can succeed in tournament as well as he can except you, cousin."

"An attractive fellow," said the Count. "The ladies think so too, I believe."

"I daresay. But he has never been one much interested in women. It is all part of his knightly qualities to respect them. He's the kind of knight they sing about in Aquitaine . . . the troubadours you know."

"I do know. They fall in love and adore their lady. They are chivalrous and would die for her. It seems an odd way to profess one's devotion by offering to die. Marguerite's half-sisters I believe are poets and songsters."

"It's natural," said Henry. "They are my half-sisters too, you know. We share the same mother."

"And our William the Marshall is such a knight. It is clear that Marguerite shares her half-sisters' admiration for these notions."

"What do you mean?"

"She and the Marshall are . . . good friends, are they not?"

Henry flushed. "Why . . ." he stammered, "we . . . have known William since our childhood. He . . . he was appointed our knight-at-arms."

"Some sentimental attachment," commented the Count of Flanders. "Well it is fortunate that you are not a jealous man, Henry. How different I am! I did tell you the story, did I not? Do you remember how I had my wife's lover beaten nigh unto death and to finish him off had him hung over a cess pool?"

"You are not suggesting . . ."

"My dear Henry, I certainly am not. But women are frail, and Walter of Les Fontaines was a knight who had won admiration wherever he appeared, for his chivalry and knightly ways. They did not prevent his getting into bed with my wife during my absence. I believe in fact that she lured him there. He would not admit it. Knightly to the end you see! But that is what I always thought. Nay, you are not a jealous fellow, as I am. But let us talk of other matters. Did you know that Philip has his father's seal?"

"Nay," said Henry, his thoughts far from Philip's seal. He was thinking of William and Marguerite. He didn't believe it really. It couldn't be true. And yet they were friendly. He remembered how when she was upset she had gone to him and talked to him.

"Yes," went on Philip, "he visited his father and was there alone with him. When he left the sick chamber he had the seal. Now of course he has the authority. The seal is in his hands so it must be his father's wish that he should have it. Depend upon it, those scheming uncles will never come to Court. They and the Queen will learn that Philip may be young but he has good men to advise him, and he is determined to be King of France."

From a turret of the castle Henry watched William the Marshall ride into the courtyard. No one sat his horse quite as well as William. He was indeed a handsome knight. Henry narrowed his eyes. Of course William was seeking to become Marguerite's lover and Marguerite was indeed taken with him.

He it was who offered her such affectionate sympathy over the rapidly deteriorating health of her father. Why should she go to William instead of to her husband? Perhaps because he was too friendly with Philip of Flanders and she had never been able to see how attractive he was. She thought he was a bad influence on Henry, no doubt told so by William the Marshall.

He shouted to one of his attendants: "Send William the Marshall to me."

In a short time William appeared.

Henry narrowed his eyes and said: "There is something I have been going to say to you for a long time."

William met his gaze steadily. "My lord?"

"You offend me with your censorious manner," replied Henry.

"I do not understand."

"And," cried Henry, "I find that you are too friendly with Queen Marguerite."

"My lord, I trust I am the good friend of you both."

"And particularly hers, eh?"

"I do not understand these insinuations."

"Do you not? Then you are indeed a fool. I will say it plainly. It has come to my ears that you see a great deal of my wife. I will not have it. Were it not for the fact that you have been my friend for so long I would punish you as you deserve. However, I will be lenient."

Henry quavered. It was so difficult when face to face with that steadfast gaze to believe these things. William had always been so honourable, so eager to serve him; and when in the past he had seemed to side with someone else, it had always turned out to be for his good.

"Get out of my sight," he said. "I will not have you near me. You must leave my service. Go back to England."

"You mean that you are in truth dismissing me?"

"I do mean it. Get out before I am tempted to do you some harm."

William the Marshall bowed with dignity and left.

Before the day was out he was on his way to England.

* * *

Marguerite was sad and angry.

"To dismiss William," she cried. "You are mad. He is the best friend you have."

"You would surely think so."

"Of course I do. As you must if you think sensibly about the matter."

"I know he is very friendly with you."

"He is the friend of us both. I know he loves you well and always has. He has tried to bring about a better relationship between you and your father. He is a better friend to you than ever Philip of Flanders would be. That man thinks only of his own advancement."

Henry began to feel uneasy. The Count was more or less telling young Philip what to do. And there lay Louis powerless to help. The Queen's brothers had already been forbidden to come to Court and the Queen herself was being treated churlishly.

Feeling that he had been foolish he sought to blame Marguerite.

"I know full well what has been going on between you and the Marshall."

Marguerite looked puzzled.

"He is your lover . . . or aspires to be."

"Henry! You are indeed mad."

"Nay. I have seen."

"What have you seen?"

"You both together."

"When?"

"Well . . . there was the other day in the garden . . . when you were upset about your father. He comforted you."

"Why should he not? I will not stand and hear the Count and my brother speak of my father as though he is dead. I thought you might have expressed some resentment. But you did not. Instead you imagine . . . nonsense . . . about me and William."

Henry said: "He is gone. I will not have him here. I have no intention of playing the cuckold."

"Oh, Henry, how can you say such things? You know them to be false. William is your very good friend. I am your faithful wife. You are misled by wicked people."

Henry did not like to feel that he had been so deluded so he pretended to believe that there was some truth in the rumour concerning William and his wife. He felt it would be too humiliating to ask him to return and offer him an apology.

He was sulky and went on with the pretence that he was a suspicious husband, much to Marguerite's exasperation.

He was relieved when Queen Adela asked if she could speak with him privately.

She told him she was very anxious and she believed he could help her if he would.

"With all my heart," he said. He went to her private chamber and there she told him that she was a very unhappy woman.

"My husband is dying," she said, "and my son has turned against me. My brothers are refused permission to come to Court and they—and I—are threatened with confiscation of our lands."

"The King will not allow that," replied Henry.

"How could I go to the King in his present condition and tell him what his son is trying to do and that he is listening to evil counsel?"

Henry bit his lip in mortification. Philip was not the only one who had done that.

"If I could do aught to help you . . ." he began.

"You can and it is for that reason that I have asked you to come."

"What do you wish of me?"

"Slip away to England. Seek out your father. Tell him of the position in which I find myself. He will help me I know."

Henry considered. He would be pleased to leave the Court of France, for he was feeling more and more ashamed of himself.

If he went to England to see his father that would be a way of escape from a delicate and embarrassing situation.

The King was in good spirits when he went to Westminster. There was dear little Alice eagerly waiting to greet him.

"The news is mixed, good and bad, sweetheart," he said. "For your father is grievously ill."

Alice tried to look dismayed but it was so long since she had seen her father that she could not remember what he looked like.

"So sick," went on Henry, "that it seems he will not last long. That is the bad news. The good is that while he is in this condition there can be no question of a marriage between you and Richard."

"It is as though God looks after us," said Alice, forgetting that while He cared for them He was being rather unfair to the pious Louis.

"I know that St Thomas à Becket is my friend. Now, sweetheart, we can put aside our fears."

He wished that he could put her into Rosamund's Bower, but that was not possible, for she was a princess and recently there had been so much talk of her marriage.

He stayed with her awhile and when he left to make a tour of Oxfordshire a messenger came to tell him that his son was in the country and on his way to see him.

Father and son met at Reading and there young Henry told the King why he had come in such haste.

"The Queen of France is asking your advice, Father. The King lies near to death and young Philip is in the hands of the Count of Flanders who seeks to rule France through him."

"The foolishness of youth!" said Henry in a way which made his son redden. "No doubt the Count is flattering young Philip as he well knows how to."

Remembering it was the Count who had been responsible for his dismissal of William the Marshall which he now saw was folly, he said: "The Count is in fact ruling France at this moment, for Philip obeys him in all things and now that Philip has filched the seal he is in command."

"This cannot be allowed to go on," said the King. "For all I know they may be planning an invasion of Normandy. It is just the thing which would occur to them. Philip of Flanders would doubtless like Normandy. By God's eyes, the upstart shall never have it."

"The Queen of France asks for your help."

"She shall have it."

"She will be very grateful to you if you go to her aid."

"She should be, for Flanders will make of young Philip nothing but a puppet to serve his ends. It is a sorry thing when a son flouts the authority of his father." Young Henry looked uncomfortable because it was a similar state of affairs which had arisen in France to that which had existed in England when the sons of Henry Plantagenet sought to take the power which their father would not give them while he lived. So was Philip taking power while his father was still on his sick bed.

The King was determined to bring home the lesson.

"When my sons turned against me," he said, "they went to the King of France for aid and he gave it to them. Yet when

198

the son of the King of France seeks to rob him of his authority, his wife the Queen asks my help. I am prepared to give it."

"It is noble of you, my lord," said young Henry.

His father burst out laughing. "Noble! Kings cannot afford to be noble. Kings must consider what is good for their kingdoms and if nobility is, then so much the better. If not, then that King who served his country ill in order to be noble would be a fool. Nay, I shall go to the aid of Louis and Adela, because I am determined to curtail the power of the Count of Flanders and his minion the King of France. I am going to make sure that Normandy is safe. So I will go to the aid of my erstwhile friend Louis and forget the ill service he did me when I was in like case. Your hold on the crown must be your first consideration, my son. Keep it firm. Then you will be a good king and however noble you are, consider it not."

"Shall we set out at once then?"

"We shall. Alas, you will not be accompanied by your good friend, William the Marshall. You sent him back to England when you could ill afford to lose his services."

Young Henry was silent. As usual his father succeeded in humiliating him.

When Philip of Flanders heard that the King of England had landed he took fright. This was not what he had wanted. He knew very well that he and young Philip could not stand out against that doughty warrior. Another thing he knew was that Louis's ministers were becoming a little uneasy and that if it came to war they would not be ready to support him.

The Count cursed young Henry for going to his father; it was some sort of revenge he supposed because he had advised him to get rid of William the Marshall. Ill luck again. He had failed to dominate young Henry and if he were not careful he would fail with Philip. Once Henry Plantagenet arrived with his armies in defence of Queen Adela and her brothers, he would find no one ready to face them with him. One thing was certain, the Count must not lose his influence over Philip.

The boy was foolishly blustering when he heard that the King of England had set sail.

"Let him come," he cried. "He will find my armies waiting for him."

The Count nodded but he was very uneasy. But he did see a way in which he could keep his influence over the King.

There was never any event which secured an alliance more firmly than marriage. Count Philip had often cursed the barren state of his wife but never more than at this time. If only he had a daughter whom he could marry to Philip. Then he would be the father of the Queen of France and could in truth call himself the King's father.

He did however have a niece. She was only a child but then Philip was not very old.

"Now you are indeed King of France you should have a queen," he suggested.

Philip considered the idea. It appealed to him.

"My niece Isabel is a very charming girl. What would you think of such a marriage? You would have Flanders in due course and Vermandois."

Philip said he would like to see Isabel.

"You shall," said the Count.

When the meeting was arranged, Philip expressed himself agreeable to the prospect, for Isabel had been well primed by her uncle to behave in a manner to please the young King, which was of course to be overawed by him and behave as though she were in the presence of a young god.

It was not difficult then for the Count to arrange an early marriage and coronation.

Here there was a difficulty, as naturally the one to perform the ceremony should be the Archbishop of Rheims, Queen Adela's brother, who was in the same position in France as the Archbishop of Canterbury was in England.

Count Philip found himself getting deeper into a troublesome situation. With the two Henrys of England on the march, and the people of France becoming restive, young Philip might soon begin to realize that he had not been as wise as he thought he had in placing his fate in the hands of the Count of Flanders.

The Archbishop of Sens must be made to see that it would go ill with him if he did not perform the coronation of Queen Isabel and no sooner had he done so than the Archbishop of Rheims saw his chance of breaking the influence of the Count of Flanders. The right to crown the Queen of France was his and although his sister Queen Adela and his brothers were being treated so badly, the Pope could not fail to support him over this last piece of folly.

In the midst of the upheaval caused by this matter, Henry of England arrived.

Such was the reputation of Henry Plantagenet that when he came at the head of an army terror filled the hearts of all those whom he considered his enemies.

It was therefore with great relief that Philip of Flanders received a message that the King of England wished to speak with him and Philip of France before he went into battle against them.

"We should meet the King of England," said the Count.

"Why so?" demanded young Philip. "How dare he come over here threatening me! I am the King, am I not?"

"You are, but soon might not be if Henry moved against us. Louis still lives and we have many enemies. Let us be cautious. We should certainly not go to war against Henry Plantagenet if we can help it."

"Young Henry is with him. I thought he was my friend and he is false . . . quite false."

"Do not think too harshly of him. He will one day be the King of England and it will be well to keep on good terms with him."

"My father never really trusted the King of England."

"Nor should you. We will meet them and outwit them, which is a cleverer way of dealing with an opponent than fighting in battle."

But Henry refused to allow the Count of Flanders to join them. He now wished to speak to young Philip alone, he insisted; and the Count was forced to accede to the wishes of the King of England.

When the meeting took place Henry studied the young King of France. A poor creature, he thought, and could not help comparing him with his own sons. There was not one of them who was not handsome. Poor Louis! He had staked everything on this boy and what had he got? A stripling so eager for power that he was snatching the crown from his father's head before he was dead. His own were as bad, he knew; but at least they looked like men.

And Philip of Flanders . . . an ambitious man! Well, he could understand that. The Count would have liked to be a king, and since he was not he was doing his best to make himself one. He would have to be watched. Henry had more respect for him than he had for the young King.

"My lord King," he said kindly, "I would speak to you as a father. I beg of you take care how you act. Your mother is sorely distressed. Your uncles too. These people wish you well. You cannot treat them churlishly as you have been doing. This is not worthy of you."

Young Philip glowered. Who was this man? To whom did he think he was talking?

He said: "The Duke of Normandy is somewhat bold."

The King burst out laughing. "I come not to you as the Duke of Normandy to pay homage to my overlord, but as the King of England who is brother to the King of France and at this time sees that brother in sore need of help."

"I understand you not," replied Philip.

"Then let me explain. My good friend King Louis of France lies on his sick bed. While he lives there can only be one King of France in fact although another—and rightly—bears the title too and when the time is ripe should take the crown. There are worthy men in your kingdom who do not care to see the Queen and her family humiliated."

"Is it for them to like what I do?"

"Kings rule by the will of the people."

"It surprises me to hear the King of England speak so."

"A strong king rules his people and if he does it well, however strict his laws, if they be just the people will accept them and welcome his rule. A strong good king is respected by his people and without that respect the crown sits uneasily on his head."

Philip lowered his eyes. He knew that he was no match for the King of England.

"Now," went on Henry, "you should become reconciled to your mother. The people do not like to see you harsh with her. The mothers of the nation will turn against you and they may persuade their sons to do the same. You need the services of men such as your uncles. Bring them to Court. Listen to what they say. A king does not necessarily take the advice of his ministers but he listens to them."

It was not easy for young Philip to withstand Henry's arguments and before the interview was over he had decided to call back his mother and receive his uncles at Court.

When the Court of Flanders heard what had taken place he knew that he had lost and must temporarily retire from the field.

It was at this time that Louis's illness took a more serious turn.

On a September night he became very ill and it was obvious that the end was not far off. Adela was with him at the end and that seemed to comfort him. Philip knelt by his bedside and wept with remorse, for now that he had been obliged to accept the return of his uncles and was friendly with his mother again he realized how rash he had been and what a bad impression he had made on his subjects by trying to take the crown while his father still lived.

As for Louis he lay back with a smile of serenity on his face.

This was the end. He was not sorry, for it had not been an easy life. Ever since he had known that his destiny was to wear the crown he had been afraid; often he had longed for the peace which he believed would have come to a man of the Church. The way had often been stormy. He would never forget the cries of men and women dying in battle. He had been haunted by them throughout his life. There had been good moments—with Eleanor in the beginning; with his children and particularly with Philip.

But it was all over.

"My son . . ." he murmured.

Philip kissed his hand.

"God bless you, my son. A long and happy reign. Farewell, Philip, farewell France."

Then Louis closed his eyes and died.

Berengaria

Side by side with his good friend Sancho, Prince of Navarre, rode Richard, Duke of Aquitaine. It was rarely that he took time off from the continual battle to hold the Dukedom, but he considered this a political mission for he had a favour to ask of the King of Navarre.

Sancho, that Prince known as the Strong, had invited him to a tournament which was being held in Pampeluna and Richard was noted for his skill in the joust; moreover he and Prince Sancho had a good deal in common, for besides being brave warriors they were also poets.

In the court of Sancho the Wise—father of Sancho the Strong—the troubadours flourished as they did in Aquitaine. So as the two young men rode south they had much to talk of.

Richard made a fine figure on his horse being so tall and with those blond good looks which were rare in this part of the country. Although he suffered periodically from a distressing disease known as the quartan ague he was otherwise very strong and healthy. He had picked up this ague when he was in his early teens and it was no doubt due to sleeping so often on the damp ground when in camp. His limbs would tremble and the effect was extraordinary for the fierceness of his cold blue eyes belied this trembling. It was said among his soldiers that when the ague was on him he was at his most fierce, and those who did not know him well, thinking it might be the outward sign of some inner weakness, soon learned to the contrary. There seemed to be a compulsion within him to belie the trembling. His ruthlessness increased, and he became noted for his cruelty. If a prisoner was brought before him and showed signs of believing he might take advantage of him because he was seen to tremble, that man would be condemned to have his eyes put out that he might never more look on Richard's trembling. The people of Aquitaine were beginning to fear him, and he had not yet understood that, although they were not by nature warlike and their love of soft living and poetry and song was their main characteristic, they were not of a nature to accept tyranny; and resentment, fanned by the verses of their poets, was smouldering and ready to burst into flame. There was trouble brewing in Aquitaine. The people did not want this Norseman to rule them—for although his mother might be their own Eleanor and his father the son of Geoffrey of Anjou on his mother's side he was descended from the Conqueror and those barbarians who had sailed from the Northern lands to pillage and conquer.

Richard himself knew that the only way to establish peace in Aquitaine was to bring back his mother. She was their Duchess. In their eyes her marriage to Henry Plantagenet had been a disaster. She had made him their Duke, a fact which they had never accepted; and borne sons—such as Richard—who brought to Aquitaine a way of life which was unacceptable.

There would be no end to conflict; and because he realized this, he had decided to accept this invitation to Pampeluna, that he might get away to think more clearly of the situation which faced him.

As they rode side by side, their followers behind them, they sang, often songs of their own composition. Sancho's songs glowed with the warmth of the South; but those who listened detected as others had before them, a hint of the North in Richard's songs. Those of the South were languorous, those of the North filled with vigour.

Even those closest to Richard thought: He is not one of us.

When they came into Pampeluna travellers were already arriving for the tournament which was to take place in a large meadow outside the castle walls. The inns were overflowing; beggars stood by the wayside, pathetic and cunning; thieves and vagabonds mingled with the respectable citizens, all looking for a picking. Stalls had been set up on which were all kinds of wares: girdles and buckles, purses, laces, brooches, razors, dice, rasps for scratching itchy skin, otter skins for making pelisses, and furs made into garments, pestles, wine, wool, barley—in fact goods of all kinds were laid out for show.

People stood in awe as the cavalcade passed. They gazed at their handsome Prince Sancho and they felt a little apprehensive at the sight of Richard of Aquitaine. There was something repelling about him, while yet fascinating. He was so tall; they rarely saw such a tall man in these parts and hé sat his horse as though he and the animal were one—some strange being from Heaven or hell. His reputation had travelled ahead of him. Richard, son of Henry Plantagenet and Eleanor of Aquitaine, a man who had set the whole of his Duchy up in arms, a man who sought to subdue them by terror.

There had been many rumours. He was as great a fighter as his father and his father was a great-grandson of the mighty Conqueror whose name continued to reverberate through the land even though it was years since he had died. It was said of Henry Plantagenet that he had many sons. There were four born of Eleanor and many more he had got on other women. Rumour had it that they were not indeed sons of the Plantagenet but of the Devil. To see this tall man with the hair which was not exactly red nor yellow but somewhere in between and the eyes that were blue and cold as ice was to believe there could be some truth in the story.

It was said that when he sacked a town he took the women and indulged in debauchery and when he had had enough of them he turned them over to his men. It was hard to believe this of the cold-looking man and it was well known that a man's enemies would tell any tale to discredit him. That he was cruel they could well believe.

The women smiled at Sancho warmly. How different was their handsome young Prince! It was true he seemed insignificant beside the other, but they loved him all the more for that. He was Sancho the Strong, who had excelled in battle and gave them such pleasure in the joust.

"Long live Sancho the Strong," they cried.

The King of Navarre greeted Richard warmly. It delighted him, he said, to have the son of King Henry and Queen Eleanor at his Court. His son Sancho had told him often of Richard's talents and he had wanted to meet him.

The tournament would begin on the following day and he trusted that Richard would add to the pleasure of the spectators by taking part in it. Richard declared his intention of doing so.

"This night," said the King, "we shall feast in the hall and later I hope you and your attendants will enchant us with some of the melodies for which you are renowned."

Richard replied that he was eager to hear the songs of Navarre which he was assured equalled in charm and beauty those of Aquitaine.

"You shall be our judge," said Sancho. "My son and my two daughters shall sing for you."

Sancho, King of Navarre, was by descent Spanish, his ancestor being the Emperor of Spain. He had married Beatrice who was the daughter of King Alphonso of Castille. He was extremely proud of his family—his beautiful wife, his son named after him who already had a reputation for valour and had earned the soubriquet of "The Strong," and his two lovely daughters Berengaria and Blanche.

Richard as guest of honour sat on the King's right hand and next to Richard sat the King's daughter, Berengaria. She was very young, dainty and with a promise of beauty.

They feasted and drank while Richard watched the lovely young girl at his side. She was a child in truth but her intelligence astonished him and later when she sang he was enchanted by her and found it difficult to withdraw his gaze from her.

Her father, watching, was aware of this and he thought that if Richard were not betrothed to Alice of France there might have been a match between them.

Richard sang songs of love and war and somehow it seemed he sang of war more frequently than he did of love. Sancho the younger was different. This hero who had distinguished himself in battle against the warlike Moors made all aware by the trembling passion of his songs that he was also a lover.

The King remained at Richard's side and he told him that he knew of the state of affairs in Aquitaine and was sorry for them.

"The people want your mother back. There is no doubt of that."

"I know it well," replied Richard. "I would to God my father would see the reason of this."

"It seems so unnatural . . . a husband to make a prisoner of his wife."

"My father can be a most unnatural man." There was a venom in Richard's voice which startled Sancho. It was true then, he supposed, that the sons of the King of England hated him. He looked at his own handsome Sancho and his lovely daughters and thanked God.

"Yet if he realized that the people of Aquitaine will never settle while she remains a prisoner, it might be that he would see the wisdom of releasing her."

"They hate each other," said Richard. "They have for years. I was aware of it in my nursery. He brought his bastard into be brought up with us. It was something my mother's pride would not stomach."

"That is understandable."

"Indeed it is. When they married my mother's position was higher than his. Then he became King of England. She would have been beside him to help him . . . but he spoilt that . . . with his lechery she used to say. I used to listen to them, taunting each other."

"You love your mother dearly, I believe."

"I would do a great deal to bring about her release. I plan to reduce my father to such a state that he will have to listen to my terms and the first of these shall be the freedom of my mother."

Sancho nodded sympathetically but he thought: You would never bring Henry Plantagenet to his knees.

"At this time it might be better to persuade him what her release would do for Aquitaine."

"I have done this. He will not listen. He sees me as my mother's partisan and he believes that she is only capable of treachery towards him."

"Perhaps if another were to put the case to him."

Richard's heart leaped with joy. It was for this he had come to Navarre.

"You mean . . . you would?"

"I mean I could try."

"By God's teeth, he would listen to you."

"Then let me try. I will send a message to him. I will tell him that as an outside observer I see how matters stand in Aquitaine and that the people there will never be at peace while the Duchess is a prisoner."

"If you could do this, you would be of great service to me and to Aquitaine."

Sancho the Wise said: "Then I shall do my best."

That night Richard exchanged tokens with young Sancho and took the oaths of chivalry with him. From this time on they would be *fratres jurati*, sworn brothers.

On the dais beside her father, young Berengaria sat watching the brilliant array in the meadow before her. The trumpets sounded, the gay pennants fluttered in the wind, and her heart beat fast with the excitement of watching for one particular knight. She would know him at once, even though according to practice his visor would be down. There was no one among the company so tall and straight, who sat his horse with such distinction, no one but this most perfect of all knights.

She had told Blanche that she had never seen anyone to compare with him. Blanche agreed that he was indeed a handsome knight. He was so different from all the men they had ever seen, most of whom were dark haired, dark skinned and of smaller stature. But Richard, Duke of Aquitaine, was of a different race it seemed.

So had the gods looked, Berengaria believed—those who had once inhabited the earth.

She glanced at her father; he was in his jewelled crown today, for it was such a great occasion. He would not ride into the lists. Her brother would do that for the honour of the crown. She hoped Sancho would not tilt against Richard for then she would be torn as to whom she must pray for, and hope to be the conqueror.

"They will not," she whispered to Blanche, for she had spoken her thoughts aloud. "They are sworn brothers. So they would not tilt against each other on this day."

" 'Tis not a battle," replied Blanche. "Only a tournament."

"Yet they will not," said Berengaria.

What a glorious day with a cloudless blue sky and a dazzling sun shining down on the colourful scene! How the armour of those gallant knights glittered and how the eyes of every lady shone as they rested on the knight who wore her colours, proclaiming to the world that she was his lady and his valiant deeds that day were done in honour of her.

What excitement when the first of the matches was heralded and the contestants rode into the lists. They seemed to be clad in silver and how gay were the colours of the ladies' dresses as they sat gracefully on their dais, their eyes never leaving the colourful field stretched out before them!

And there he was—outstanding as she had known he would be—different from all the others because he was so tall. She was sure his armour shone more brightly than the rest.

She felt faint with joy, for upon his helm he wore a small glove with a jewelled border. She knew that glove well for it belonged to her.

What ecstasy! This wonderful godlike creature had this day taken the field in honour of her!

Of course he was victorious. It would have been embarrassing if he were not, since he was their guest of honour. But there need have been no fear of that. He was more bold, more skilled, more daring in every way.

He rode to the dais where the King sat with his wife and two daughters. He bowed on his horse, and Berengaria took one of the roses which adorned the balcony and threw it to him. He caught it deftly, kissed it and held it against his heart.

It was a charming knightly gesture; and from that moment Berengaria of Navarre was in love with Richard of Aquitaine.

He could not tarry long in Navarre. His absence would give his enemies the opportunities they sought. Yet he was attracted by Berengaria. She was but a child but she would grow up. He had no wish for marriage yet. He could wait. She adored him and thought of him as some superior being. That was pleasant.

He talked to her as they sat side by side at table of the beauties of Aquitaine; he told her of his growing desire to go on a crusade to drive the Infidel out of the Holy Land.

She listened, hands clasped, eyes shining. He was certain that if he married her while she was so young and innocent he could make her into the wife he wanted.

He talked to her father.

"You have two beautiful daughters," he said, "and in particular the eldest. I would I were in a position to ask you for her hand."

"If you were to do so I should not deny you," answered Sancho.

"You know my position. For years I have been betrothed to the daughter of the King of France."

"I know this. But the marriage has been long delayed."

"My father said it was to take place. But I have heard no more since."

"You wish for this marriage?"

"Not since I have seen your daughter."

"Since there has been this delay, your father must have some reason for it."

"My mother says that he has and that it plagues him when there is insistence on its taking place."

"Do you think it would please him to forgo an alliance with France for the sake of one with Navarre?"

"We have alliances with France. My elder brother is married to the daughter of the King of France."

"You are in a very strange position, but I am honoured that you should admire my daughter."

Sancho was thoughtful. He was not called "The Wise" for nothing.

At length he said: "As yet let us say nothing of the attraction you feel for my daughter. The Princess Alice has been long withheld from you. Why should you not if she should be offered withhold yourself from her? Excuses have been offered to you. Why then should you not offer excuses? If you do not wish to marry the Princess Alice you can avoid it."

"I will do that and in time . . ."

"Berengaria is young yet . . . too young. Perhaps in due course . . ."

Richard thanked Sancho fervently.

"I will wait," he said. "And in the meantime you will speak to my father . . . not of a possible marriage but of my mother's imprisonment?"

"This I will do," said Sancho. "I give you my word on it."

Richard strummed his lute. Berengaria sat beside him, her eyes shining.

The song was of love and although it held the northern strain it throbbed with passion.

"I will return," said Richard. "I shall find you here . . . waiting."

He laid down his lute and smiled at her.

"You are but a child, Berengaria."

"I shall soon grow up."

"Then we shall meet again."

"You will not forget me?"

"Never will I forget you. I shall return and will you be waiting?"

"Yes," she answered, "until I die."

"Long before we die we shall be together."

"Richard, I have heard that you are betrothed to a French Princess. Is it true?"

"I was betrothed to her in my cradle."

"She is very beautiful, I have heard. Do you find her so?"

"I cannot find her beautiful for I know not what she looks like. Although we were betrothed she has been withheld from me."

"Does that cause you sorrow?"

"Now it causes me nothing but joy."

"What if your father arranges a marriage for you?"

"It will not be the first time he has found me a disobedient son."

"You will in truth refuse to marry her?"

He smiled and nodded. "There is only one whom I would marry."

"And who is she?"

"Her name is Berengaria and she lives at her father's court of Navarre."

"Can it really be so?"

He took her hand and kissed it.

"Does my father know?"

"We have spoken of this."

"And what says he?"

"That when you are of an age and I am free of my entanglements it could come about."

"I am so happy," she said.

He pressed her hand and took up his lute again.

When he rode away she was at the turret watching him.

"His coming has changed my life," she told Blanche. "I shall pray for the day when we can be together."

He turned and waved a piece of silk—a scrap from one of her gowns. He knew she would be watching.

"Soon he must come back," she whispered.

The Devil's Strain

Henry could not help congratulating himself. Louis was dead, and therefore the controversy over Alice's marriage must necessarily be put aside. He knew of course that it would only be a temporary respite, and that young Philip would probably very soon be wanting to know what was happening to his sister.

But Philip was only a boy, and Henry had already implied that he wished him to look upon him as a father. That he was a headstrong boy was clear, but Henry had an uneasy feeling that when he had a little experience he would not be as weak as his father had been. Henry would have to keep a sharp eye on what was happening in France.

There was news from Aquitaine that there was revolt everywhere. The people wanted Eleanor freed, and sent back there. That should never be.

Sancho of Navarre had sent him a message telling him that he was disturbed by events in Aquitaine and how it was his belief that there would never be peace until Eleanor returned.

He had thanked Sancho for his advice and had told him that although he could not free Eleanor at this time, for Sancho must understand how dangerous to him that would be, he would allow her a little more freedom. For instance if visitors came to England she could come to Court to see them, or they might visit her. But to have her roaming the world free to harm him, was something to which he could not agree.

While he was pondering these matters, a message arrived from the young King of France to tell him that Philip of Flanders had turned traitor and had made a pact with the King's uncles who were now threatening to march against him and take the throne from him. As Henry had assured him that he might regard him as his father, that was what he was doing now. He begged a father's help.

Henry smiled. Of course he would help young Philip. The

Count of Flanders had too big an idea of himself. There was a man who must be watched.

Henry would send his sons to the aid of the King of France. Young Henry should go with Geoffrey and because military skill would be needed he would send Richard too. Young Philip must be shown that he could trust Henry Plantagenet and then perhaps he would not make demands for the marriage of his sister.

Young Henry arrived in Paris followed shortly by his brothers Richard and Geoffrey.

With Richard came a troubadour warrior, Bertrand de Born. He was the castellan of Hautefort and a man whose reputation as a poet was beginning to equal that of Bernard de Ventadour.

His songs it was said were an inspiration to any who were about to go into battle and were considered to be an important part of any campaign.

Young Philip welcomed them warmly and there was a feast in the great hall followed by songs of love and war. Philip had changed already from the petulant boy he had been at the time preceding his father's death. It was as though a sudden realization had come to him of the hazards of his position, and he seemed to have grown wise in a few months. He listened intently to Richard's advice for he realized quickly that Richard was the one who knew how to succeed in battle. None could deny the social graces of the young Henry and Geoffrey too, who was a shadow of his elder brother, but it was Richard whom he needed now.

What a man Richard was with those cold blue eyes and that wonderful light coloured hair! Most of all he was to be admired for his great stature, and the fact that he was sometimes in the grip of that strange ague rather added to his essential virility.

Philip was attracted by Richard.

While Philip was admiring Richard, Bertrand de Born was watching Henry. Bertrand thought he had never seen such a magnificent specimen of manhood as the young King of England.

Henry was known as the handsomest Prince in Christendom and rightly so. His countenance was as fair as any woman's; his manners were graceful and charming. He was not a fighter as his brother Richard was. He was a man to win through his charm rather than his sword.

How much better for Aquitaine, thought the troubadour, if Henry had become its Duke instead of Richard.

Richard was animated, talking of the campaign they would wage against Philip of Flanders and the house of Blois.

Philip listened gravely.

"I give you command," he said, "for I have complete trust in you."

He was right to be trustful. They went into action riding side by side and it was as Philip had known it would be. Philip of Flanders, driven to his castle, remained there besieged until he was forced to beg for mercy.

The revolt was put down.

There was no doubt whose military genius was behind this.

Bertrand de Born found an opportunity of talking with Henry.

"I have written verses to you, my lord. May I have your permission to sing them to you?"

Henry, who could accept any amount of flattery without suspecting an ulterior motive, was ready enough to listen.

He knew he was handsome; but it was pleasant to see himself through the eyes of the poet. The poet was in love with him. That was amusing, but Henry had never been interested in passionate attachments with members of his own sex. He liked women.

Then Bertrand made a remark which immediately caught his attention.

"How different you are from your brother Richard. The people of Aquitaine will never accept Richard, but they would accept you."

"How so?" asked Henry.

"If you were their Duke . . ."

"I am the Duke of Normandy, Count of Anjou and King of England. Richard was given Aquitaine."

"The people of Aquitaine prefer to bestow themselves."

"Do you mean they would bestow themselves on me?"

"If you came to take Aquitaine they would give it to you."

"How could I take what is my brother's?"

"How can Aquitaine be your brother's, if the people reject him?"

"It is my father they reject . . . and his sons with him."

"They do not reject your mother."

"Richard is her son. She chose him for this inheritance."

"And where is she now? A prisoner! The people would accept you if they were led to it."

"Who would lead them?"

"There is something more powerful than the sword. You may not believe me. But I know that my people are swayed more by poetry than by battle cries."

"It could be so."

"It shall be so, my lord, if it is your wish."

Henry was excited. He wanted the thrill of adventure without the discomfort. It would delight him if the people of Aquitaine begged him to come to be their Duke. He would say, "What can I do? We must have peace in Aquitaine. The people want me. They are demanding me. They will not have Richard." How amusing! Richard who was the great fighter! Richard, who could not keep Aquitaine in order!

Bertrand de Born crept a little nearer and touched Henry's sleeve.

"You could try it," said Henry.

"I will do it," cried Bertrand de Born. "I will have all Aquitaine in arms, demanding that Henry be their Duke."

Henry hesitated a moment.

"Why do you do this?" he asked.

The poet bowed his head. "Because I love you," he said.

Henry smiled—not entirely displeased.

Philip said to Richard: "So now will you go away?"

"I am needed in Aquitaine."

"They are still in revolt against you?"

"It is ever so. While I am there I can keep some sort of order. When I go away they become overbold."

"They say you are ruthless, Richard, a cruel ruler. Is that so?"

"I am determined to keep order if that is what you mean."

"Ever after I shall regard you as my brother. You have saved my throne for me."

"I do not think you will have more trouble with your rebellious subjects."

"Nay. Philip of Flanders knows himself for a defeated man."

"Beware of him."

"Indeed I shall."

Philip raised his eyes to those of Richard. How tall he was, how magnificent! he thought. He had never seen a man who gave such a feeling of power.

"It grieves me," said Philip, "that you must go. I would have banquets, tournaments to entertain you."

"Alas, my lot is not for such entertainments."

"You must protect your Duchy. But know this, I am your friend and brother."

"I shall remember it."

The King laid his hand on the Duke's arm.

"I shall look to see you soon," he said; his voice shook a little. "Nor shall I be content until I do."

Their eyes met and for a few seconds they looked at each other. Then Philip took Richard's hand and kissed it.

The King had no wish to leave England, but when had he ever been able to follow his own wishes? His presence was needed across the water and he must say farewell to Alice. How she had grown up in the last year! She was no longer a child. He had loved her fresh young innocence but in one way he was glad to see her mature; he was as enamoured of her as ever which might be a sign that he was growing old. Even the lustiest men were slowed down by the years, and fidelity to one woman was something which came with age.

His determination to keep her was as strong as ever. He told himself that he could not in honour allow a woman who had borne his child to become the wife of his own son. Moreover he could be sure that someone would have discovered the secret and be prepared to use it against him. The truth was that he wanted to keep Alice for himself. He wanted to settle down with Alice. He wanted his family around him—a loving gentle wife as Alice would be to him and his sons eager to support him in all he did. Those were the family joys which all men—be they kings or serfs—had a right to. Was he asking too much?

Always statecraft came between him and his desires. He must always ask himself what was good for England or for his dominions overseas before he considered his own personal needs. Now he wished to stay with Alice and he must cross the sea, for there was work to be done. It was imperative that he keep on good terms with her brother, the King of France, and he could best do this by bringing about some sort of treaty between young Philip and the Count of Flanders.

Flanders was in no position to dictate terms and it proved to be not difficult to get a promise from him to make good the damage he had caused.

Aquitaine was very much on the King's mind and while he

was dealing with the French agreement Geoffrey arrived from Brittany. Geoffrey was suave and noted for his gracious manners and it occurred to the King that he would be a good mediator between Richard and those Knights who were making trouble in Aquitaine.

"Go to Aquitaine, my son,' said the King. "Talk to these nobles, study their grievances and try to bring about some understanding between them and your brother Richard. Point out to them that only if there is friendship between them can there be peace in Aquitaine."

Geoffrey set off. He was a born intriguer and was constantly considering how everything could be turned to his advantage. He had heard some of Bertrand de Born's songs and believed that the people of Aquitaine would not have Richard but would be willing to set up his brother Henry as their Duke in Richard's place, so it seemed to Geoffrey that Henry had a good chance of triumphing over Richard and he, Geoffrey, wished to be on the winning side. So instead of following his father's commands, he intrigued on behalf of Henry, extolling his brother's virtues and explaining to the nobles of Aquitaine how much happier they would be under Henry than Richard.

The King, meanwhile, having completed the treaty between the King of France and the Count of Flanders turned his attention to Aquitaine. He marched into the Duchy, and called a meeting of those who were in rebellion against Richard for the purpose of coming to terms with them. Since these rebels believed that they were about to depose Richard and set up Henry in his place they refused to come to the meeting.

So it was that because of the intrigues of young Henry and Geoffrey neither side knew what the other was aiming at and there was complete confusion. In the meantime, young Henry had arrived at Limoges where he was greeted as the new Duke. He accepted the people's homage and then marched on to join his father and Richard, who had no idea what he had done.

Face to face with his father Henry found it impossible to explain that he had been accepted as Duke and when the King told him that he had arrived in time to take part in suppressing those who were in revolt against Richard, he could not find the courage to do anything but join with them.

The people of Aquitaine were naturally bewildered. Henry, whom they had believed was to be their new Duke, was now fighting with his father and brother Richard whose object could only be to put Richard in command.

Young Henry knew it would always be thus. He could never stand up to his father and it was only when the King was far away that he believed he could. He was in a state of great anxiety fearing what would happen when his father discovered his perfidy.

It seemed like a miracle when news reached them that his sister Matilda, who was married to the Duke of Saxony, was on her way to Normandy.

She was in great distress because her husband had been involved in a dispute with the Emperor Frederick Barbarossa who had confiscated his lands and sent him into exile. She and her family had nowhere to go and she implored her father to come to her aid immediately.

The King, desperately seeking affection from the members of his family, was happy to be called on.

He sent for his sons. "The rebellion in Aquitaine is crushed," he said. "There should be little trouble now. I will leave you here and go to Normandy to see what can be done for Matilda and her family."

Young Henry congratulated himself that he had slid out of a very awkward situation. The King had left for Normandy and young Henry was now free to indulge in secret negotiations with the knights of Aquitaine whose passions and resentments were being whipped up by the songs of Bertrand de Born.

The King was briefly happy to be reunited with his daughter. She needed him, and he longed to be needed. She and the Duke of Saxony had three children—Henry, Otto and Matilda. The King grew sentimental watching them. He played with his grandchildren, and they crawled all over him, tweaked his hair and called him Grandfather. He remembered his mother's telling him how *his* grandfather King Henry I had loved him and his brothers—but particularly him; and how men trembled in his grandfather's presence while he, the baby grandson, had pulled the great man's nose and had no fear of him.

I would, he thought, my sons had loved me.

As he played with the children he thought of the days when his sons and daughters were in their nursery. What a beautiful child young Henry had been! And he was still very handsome. In spite of all that had happened Henry was his

219

favourite son. How could he help but be proud of such a handsome young man? Henry could charm him when they were together to such an extent that he would forget the promptings of common sense against his better judgement and believe in his son's affection. Geoffrey was the same in a slightly less charming way but still a boy to be proud of. Richard? Well, there had always been animosity between them, but Richard too was a son of whom any man must be proud. And there was John—no longer so young, being nearly fifteen.

He was growing sentimental with the years. He wanted to believe in them and as he had made a habit of getting what he wanted he kept his belief. But his shrewdness often got the better of his great desire for affection. Then he would ask himself which of them was going to betray him next, and whether, when John grew older, he might not be as false to his father as his brothers had been.

He needed this short respite with his grandchildren. They were too young to be aught but honest with him.

When his father had gone, young Henry's ambitions grew.

He was no longer a boy. It was twenty-eight years since he had seen the light of day. Oh, God, he cried, shall I be treated as a child until I die?

Bertrand de Born was singing songs describing Henry's beauty and valour. He wrote of the yoke under which the people of Aquitaine suffered. Richard the ruthless and cruel had put that there, this harsh son of a harsh father, this Viking man, with his yellow hair and steely blue eyes. Yet there was one whom the whole world loved, a beautiful gentle man, who hated wars and loved song and poetry. Richard did too, but this man would sing of love not war. Henry loved pleasure. He was generous hearted; he excelled at the tournament—Richard did too but Richard would rather indulge in actual warfare. He could see no glory in the mock battle. Henry was waiting to take Richard's place. Let them welcome him with open arms.

Here they were waiting to receive him, thought young Henry, and his father treating him like a child!

He wondered whether news of what was happening in Aquitaine had reached his father's ears. Of course there was a little explaining to be done about his accepting the acclaim of the people and then joining Richard and his father and acting as though he were in their camp.

Before his father could hear of his conduct he took up an offensive attitude and wrote to the King imperiously demanding to be given control of Normandy.

The King's answer came back promptly. He was holding his dominions while there was life in him, was the answer. Suffice it that a good and obedient son should honour his father and be prepared to serve under him. Must he remind Henry that once he had taken an oath in which he had sworn to follow this course?

Young Henry stamped and swore with rage when he received his father's reply.

"It is no use, Henry," soothed Marguerite. "Your father will never give up anything while he lives."

"Then I shall perforce take it," cried Henry.

She smiled at him soothingly. He knew as well as she did that he could never take anything that his father did not wish him to have.

"There is nothing for me to do but take Aquitaine," declared Henry. "If I have it and the people acclaim me my father must perforce allow me to keep it."

Marguerite was uncertain but she knew that it was no use trying to oppose her husband.

An opportunity arose at that moment and it was brought to his notice by Bertrand de Born who had written a song which troubadours were singing all over Aquitaine.

A castle had been built near Mirabeau which was close to the frontiers of Poitiers but which was actually in Anjou. Anjou was of course that territory over which young Henry would have held sway had he been allowed to. Richard had built this castle and in doing so he had strayed beyond Aquitaine into Anjou.

Would the young King allow this insolence to go unchecked? He must be most displeased that the tyrant Richard had encroached on his land.

When young Henry heard the news and the song which was being sung in every hall where knights gathered together he was angry. He would have to do something about it or people would jeer at him. Bertrand de Born would not go on loving a man and writing enchanting verses about him if he proved himself to be too meek to stand up against his insolent brother.

He sent a message to his father demanding that Richard give him the castle since it was on his land.

* * *

When the King received the message he groaned aloud. Who would have children? He had gone wrong somewhere. No one could call him a weak man and yet he had failed with his family.

This time Richard was at fault. He should never have built a castle outside Aquitaine.

He sent a message to Richard, saying that it had come to his ears that the castle built near Mirabeau was in fact in Anjou. This had understandably offended his brother Henry and it was only right that having committed the offence he should pass the castle over to his brother.

Richard's retort was that he would not yield the castle. It was necessary for the defence of Poitiers because the city was unprotected on its north flank.

Henry could always more easily be roused to anger through Richard. Of this son he was unsure. That he was steadier than his brother, more honest and reliable he could not fail to know. That he was a great soldier and a man dedicated to duty he knew too. But between them was an emotion so fierce that it could not be quelled and it was largely made up of hatred. Richard hated him for what he had done to his mother; and he disliked Richard who had turned away from him as a child and that dislike had turned to hatred because he had wronged him through Alice.

He sent a message back at once. "Hand over the castle or I shall come and take it from you."

The last thing Richard wanted was war against his father. He needed his help badly. He could not hold down Aquitaine and fight his father at the same time.

"I shall not give the castle to my brother Henry," he wrote, "who is working against me here in Aquitaine. I will give the castle to you if you will judge whether it should be in my hands or not since it is necessary to the defence of Poitiers."

When the King received this message he was very disturbed. Henry working against Richard! Oh, no, Henry could not be such a fool. He sent back a message at once to Richard. It should be as he wished. He would make the decision as to whom the castle should belong and he wished his son to come with all speed to Angers for he had something of importance to say to him.

Henry met his three sons at Angers, whither he had summoned them all.

"I have brought you here because there is something of

great moment which I must say to you. It has been brought to my notice that there is some conflict between you, and I command you to end this strife. You must understand that all your strength is in your union. We have great dominions and if we are to keep our grip on them we must stand together. When there is trouble in our midst then do our enemies rejoice. There must be no such jubilance among our enemies. In our discord is their triumph."

Young Henry looked bland enough although he was secretly smiling. What would Richard say if he knew that Aquitaine was ready to turn him out and accept his brother Henry?

"Once," went on the King, "you swore to serve me all my life. Sometimes I think you have forgotten that, for the way you can serve me ill is to war against each other. I am going to command you to swear fidelity towards each other now . . . here this moment."

Young Henry was not deeply perturbed. His father broke his word continually and men respected him. There was no reason why he should not follow him in that.

"Henry is my eldest son," went on the King, "and as such he will be King of England and hold rights over those lands which are mine. Richard and Geoffrey you will hold Aquitaine and Brittany through the grace of your brother. You will therefore swear fealty to him."

Young Henry smiled, well pleased with this arrangement. Not so Richard. His eyes were cold as steel and if his hands trembled slightly it was with the ague and as his family knew they must not misconstrue the reason for the tremble.

Unlike his brother Henry, Richard was not capable of deceit. Had he not been nicknamed "Richard Yea and Nay" because he would give a clear confirmation or denial to any question and he would mean it? He was not afraid of the truth.

He said now: "I shall not do homage to my brother for Aquitaine. It was my mother's wish that I should inherit her lands. I do not owe it to you, and it has nothing to do with your dominions. Henry may be your eldest son but I am your son also and the son of my mother. I will give homage to no one for Aquitaine save the King of France which custom and tradition demand."

Curse you, Richard, thought his father yet half admiringly. You are right of course. Aquitaine is not Normandy nor Anjou. But why cannot you be an obedient son!

"You will obey my wishes," he shouted.

"I shall do no such thing."

The King whipped up his rage but he felt no real anger, only fear of this son who was the betrothed of Alice. He could not help even at this moment wondering what he would say if he knew that she had been seduced by his father and had already borne him a child.

Richard turned away.

"Come back," cried the King; but Richard took no notice.

The King stood looking at his sons Henry and Geoffrey.

"By God's eyes," cried the King, "I'll not be flouted by my own sons."

"Richard declares he will be curbed by no one," said Henry.

"You have seen him defy me," replied the King. "What will you do about that?"

"Methinks," commented Henry, "that your son Richard should be taught a lesson."

"Then we are in complete agreement," said the King.

Young Henry was exultant.

Richard had played right into his hands. If he were going to teach Richard a lesson how could he do it better than by taking Aquitaine?

Richard meanwhile was riding back to his Duchy.

Young Henry, with Geoffrey beside him, exultantly rode towards Aquitaine.

"Now," he said, "we will show our father of what stuff we are made! Richard too. They have had enough of him in Aquitaine. They like not these stern men who call themselves just. Richard with his warlike ways and the fierce punishment he metes out to offenders has lost their regard. They want to be rid of him. I know how the people of Aquitaine wish to be ruled and it fits in very well with what I want."

He thought of himself presiding over the great tables in his castles. There would be song and laughter; he would delight his subjects with the tournaments he would devise. He saw himself riding into the arena and the ladies would smile at him from the dais. All would vie with each other for his favours. Marguerite would be proud of him. He would wear her colours.

That was the way to rule. That was the way the Provençals wanted it. Richard had no understanding of them.

What great good fortune for him that Richard was hated so much.

When he reached the borders of Aquitaine many nobles were waiting for him and with them their followers.

He would have a great army. He could not fail.

Very well, Richard, he said to himself, you would not swear fealty to me. I can do without your oath. I shall simply *take* what you will not give.

When the King heard what was happening in Aquitaine he was filled with anxiety.

Brothers fighting against each other! It was the way to disaster.

What kind of men have we bred between us, Eleanor and I? he asked himself. Why was it that the sons he had had by other women had been his good and loyal subjects? Was it, as Eleanor had said, because they had no rights and all their benefits came from him, whereas those who had been born in wedlock believed what was his became theirs by right. Was it because his union with Eleanor had always been doomed?

There were rumours about his ancestors. It was said that one of the Counts of Anjou when riding in the forest met a woman of such beauty that he was captivated by her and married her. Her beauty was such that all marvelled at it; however she was reluctant to enter a church and when she did always left before the consecration of the Host. This puzzled her husband and several years after their marriage one day just as she was about to leave the church he caught hold of her cloak and he would not release it.

Suddenly she was said to have floated upwards, holding two of her children by the hand. She disappeared, leaving her bewildered husband holding her cloak. It was said that she was a witch and a servant of the devil. Although she had taken two children with her she had left two behind and one of these became the next Count of Anjou.

This legend lived on and because of it many said that there was a satanic streak in the blood of the Angevin Counts.

Was it true? wondered Henry. Had it come down through him? Was it this in him which had made him seduce his son's betrothed? Was it this that set his sons warring against each other and their father?

Nay, he told himself, it is from their mother that they get their natures.

What was his sin in taking Alice compared with Eleanor's incest with her uncle?

And what could be expected of the offspring of two people such as himself and Eleanor?

But he must stop this brooding. There was work to be done. He would go with all speed to Limoges where Henry was encamped and put a stop to this attempted fratricide without delay.

On the way he met Richard who welcomed his coming.

With his father on his side against his brothers he could not fail to succeed.

"This grieves me greatly," said the King. "Does nothing I say have any effect on you?"

"You have always favoured Henry," Richard reproached him. "Yet he has deceived you right and left, and shown quite clearly that he is unfit to govern."

"He is my eldest son and you have all defied me. My sons are a bitter disappointment to me . . . except John."

"John is as yet too young to have a mind of his own," replied Richard.

"I trust in his affection."

The King decided that he would have to parley with Henry who was in Limoges.

"I will accompany you," said Richard, "and we will take a company of troops with us."

"Nay," said the King. "I'd have them know I come to talk in peace. They will recognize me and no harm will come."

"I trust them not," said Richard.

"You will remain here while I go forward to the town and I shall take with me but a small company of knights."

"I do not like it," replied Richard.

"My son, you will have to learn that I do as I will."

As he rode forward he was thinking: Oh, Henry, my son, why cannot you be the affectionate little boy you were in the nursery, before your mother changed you? Why did your ambitions have to rob you of your sense of honour? How can I give you what you ask? I *must* rule. I am experienced in the ways of rulers. You do not understand. To rule is not to enjoy a life of pleasure. What pleasure I have had has been snatched in between forays here, punitive expeditions there and all the cares that beset a king who has wide-flung dominions. If you understood you would rejoice that I am here to rule and you to learn from me so that in time you can keep your kingdom in your hands.

They were approaching the town. He rode at the head of

the company. Above his head fluttered his pennant proclaiming him as the King of England, sovereign of them all.

Suddenly a stream of arrows shot up in the air. One of his men shouted: "The King comes."

There was another flurry of arrows. One pierced the King's cloak.

"My lord," said his standard bearer, "they know who you are and they are trying to kill you. We are not fitted to meet their attack."

"You are right," said the King. "We will turn back."

He withdrew the arrow from his cloak.

He looked at it. It could so easily have pierced his heart. And Henry's men had sent it.

Back in his camp he told Richard what had happened.

Richard's cold face expressed no fear for what might have happened; there was only scorn for his father's folly. Had he not warned him? Why did he go on trusting his eldest son when time after time he had been proved to be of a light nature capable of playing the traitor to his father and brother?

Henry sat ruminating, the arrow before him.

My son wishes me dead. So does he long for my crown that he would hasten my end to attain it. There was a sadness in his heart, and more than ever he yearned for the affection of his family.

As he sat brooding a messenger came in to tell him that his son Henry was without and begging to be seen.

"Send him to me," he said.

Henry came in; he took off his helmet and his beautiful fair hair fell about his face; he knelt before his father.

"Well, my son," said the King.

"Oh, Father, when I saw what had happened . . ."

"You saw the arrow did you? You saw it pierce my cloak?"

"I rejoice that it was nothing but your cloak."

"St Thomas was watching over us . . . you and me. He saved me from death and you from becoming your father's murderer."

"Oh, God help me," murmured Henry.

He lifted his face to his father's and there were tears in his eyes. The King stood up and drew his son to his feet. He embraced him.

"My son, my son," he said, "let us put an end to this strife."

"Oh, Father, you forgive me then?"

"I know it was not you who shot the arrow."

"Nay, but it was those who thought to serve me."

"We must put an end to this strife, Henry. It will destroy us all."

"I know it, Father. And this day . . . when I thought you could have died . . ."

"We will forget it. You are my son and I must love you. You know full well how I have always deplored this rift between us."

"If you would but give me some authority . . ."

"I shall . . . in time. I grow old and because I have lived many years I can control my territories. There is so much to learn and when you have learned, all that is mine will pass to you."

"Oh, Father, give me your blessing."

He knelt and the King laid his hands on his head.

Afterwards they talked awhile. "It would seem," said young Henry, "that you have sided with Richard against me and Geoffrey."

"It is you and Geoffrey who have made this unfortunate affair. Richard is Duke of Aquitaine by his mother's wish."

"But you commanded him to swear fealty to me."

"I want no war between you. I want you to stand together. It is imperative that you do."

"Father, I have influence in Aquitaine. The people want me as their Duke—not Richard. You know how harsh he is. He calls it justice. He has inflicted terrible punishments on those who had worked against him whom he calls traitors. They will not accept Richard. But I could persuade them to accept you."

"Would you do this?"

"I would, Father, for I now see that it is the best course. Richard they will not have. But if you offered to mediate with them and let them decide whom they would accept as their Duke there could be peace. Let me return to them as your emissary."

"Go then," said the King.

Young Henry went and the King continued to regard with the utmost sadness the arrow which had pierced his cloak.

Geoffrey was waiting for his brother in the town of Limoges.

"I talked to the old man," said Henry. "He forgave me. There were tears in his eyes. How is it possible that a great king can be such an old fool?

"What now?" said Geoffrey.

"We have the people with us. We shall win. My father will

228

see that he can do nothing here. He will have to take Richard back with him. Once they called our brother John Lackland. Perhaps they will now say the same of Richard, once Duke of Aquitaine. We will now set about fortifying this town. The King will then understand that it is not his for the taking."

The King was the first to see that he had once more allowed himself to be deluded by his son. What had been Henry's motive in coming to make his peace? To gain time perhaps for the fortification of Limoges?

"I have bred a nest of vipers," said the King. "But at least I am their father."

He had decided what he would do: he would ride boldly into Limoges and demand to speak to his sons.

He came this time with an even smaller company; there was merely his standard-bearer and two other knights.

As he approached close to the city walls a shout went up and he saw his sons Henry and Geoffrey watching from the battlements.

Then as before came the shower of arrows; this time his horse fell to the ground taking him with it.

So now they have done it! thought Henry.

He was surprised to find that although his horse had been killed, he himself was unhurt. The knights had leaped from their horses.

"I am unhurt," he said. And he thought: And never so bitterly wounded. They are bent on my death. God help me and God help them.

Someone was riding up to him. It was his son Henry.

He laughed bitterly. "What?" he said to him. "Failed again?"

"What mean you, Father?"

"You have killed my horse. Had he not reared at precisely the moment he did, the arrow would have gone where it was intended to go, through my chest."

"Oh, my father!" Tears once more in the beautiful eyes! Oddly enough the King was touched by them. He did not believe in them but still he was glad to see them there.

This was an enemy, this son. Where his children were concerned he might be a sentimental old man, but he was not so foolish as to refuse to admit the truth when it had stared him in the face for so long.

This son of his whom he had loved—more than any of the others—was a traitor to him. He wanted him dead. On two occasions in the space of a few days he had been nearby when an attempt had been made on his life.

No more sentimental father! he warned himself. No more forcing yourself to believe what you want. No more turning from the truth because it is ugly.

You have four sons born in wedlock. Two of them work against you; they are your enemies; they have looked on while their men attempted to murder you. The other, Richard, you cannot like. He is too cold, aloof, he has been brought up to hate you and will never do anything else; you can never be fond of him; he is his mother's son, he hates you for imprisoning her and you hate him because he has never cared for you and—since we are facing the truth—because you have wronged him by seducing his betrothed and stopping his marriage. That leaves John.

My son John, my beloved son John. All my hopes are in you. You were never in that nursery made sour by a mother's hatred for the father of her children. You I have loved; I have changed you from John Lackland to John of many possesions. *You* will love me. I must turn to you to give me all that I have missed in the others.

In the meantime he must make peace in Aquitaine and when his son Henry came to him with tears in his eyes, he would not be deluded a second time. He would play Henry's game; he would pretend to be reconciled, while all the time he knew that Henry and Geoffrey were his enemies.

He allowed himself to be helped on to the horse which was provided for him; he rode with his son into Limoges and there he sat with him and listened to his plans for bringing about peace in the country.

He was not surprised at what followed.

Geoffrey had left his brother and father in Limoges while he went out to rally more forces to his brother's banner. After a few days the King rejoined Richard to discover that young Henry and Geoffrey had raised forces throughout Aquitaine and Philip of France was sending help to them.

"The ingratitude!" cried the King. "How long ago was it when I saved his crown for him?"

Not only that, there were murmurs that the time had come to attack Normandy.

The King was incensed. He would lay siege to Limoges and when he took that town he would show no mercy to any, be they his own sons.

Young Henry however had taken the opportunity of slipping out of the town before his father realized his intentions and while the King was besieging Limoges he was ranging far and wide causing havoc in Richard's domain.

Young Henry was no great soldier. He had no real love of battle. He longed for the round of tournaments to which he had become addicted. It was so much more enjoyable to indulge in mock battles, to succeed in the lists, to be led triumphant into the hall by beautiful women, to sit with them and listen to the songs about love and bravery. Real fighting was quite different. It was not so much the risk of death; that was an excitement to him; it was the discomforts that accompained actual warfare which did not please him.

Still he was determined to get what he wanted. It was humiliating in the extreme that he, a man of twenty-eight, and crowned King of England, should be kept short of money and be absolutely powerless, always held in check by a dominating father.

His quarrel was not really against Richard; it was against his father. It was not that he particularly wanted Aquitaine; he wanted power and if his father saw that he could take Aquitaine, might he not be prepared to give him Normandy or England? The old man wanted to have complete power, which was ridiculous. Couldn't he see that it was impossible for him to hold sway over Normandy, Anjou and England all at the same time?

Why did he not delegate some of the rule to his sons? That was what the battle was all about.

Henry was too fond of luxury; he was over generous; he had always greatly enjoyed handing out gifts to those who pleased him. To him that seemed a confirmation of his power. It was kingly to act so and since all knew he was a king without power he had to be constantly reminding people that he was at least a king.

What could he do for money?

One of his captains had come to him telling him that the soldiers were demanding their pay.

"They must wait," he had cried.

"My lord," was the answer, "they will not wait. If they are not paid they will desert."

"Traitors," cried the King.

But what was the use. He had to have money.

Money. It haunted his dreams. He had to find it somewhere. He was beginning to wish he had not started this war. This was not the way to do it.

He began to have uneasy dreams. He remembered how his father had come into the nursery—a powerful figure who liked to play with the children. He could get very angry though and when he was angry all the attendants crept away to be far out of reach of the storm. They were all afraid of him. He knew how to inspire fear if not love. They had never loved him, any of them, except perhaps Bastard Geoffrey who had been introduced into the nursery much to his mother's disgust. Bastard Geoffrey had thought their father wonderful; he had done everything he could to please him. He tried to shine at lessons, horse-riding, chivalry, archery, everything that would please the King.

Richard hadn't cared about pleasing their father. He had been coolly aloof. But he had loved their mother dearly. There would be warmth in the cold eyes when they rested on her. But Henry had loved neither of them. He had wanted most of all to be King and when he was crowned he had been so pleased with life until he realized that it did not mean power after all. It was only a symbol. It meant nothing. The crown was a hollow bauble while his father lived.

But money? Where was he to get money?

They had halted at an abbey and there they paused to rest. The monks welcomed them and invited them to the refectory.

Henry and his captains sat down with the monks; they partook of the simple food which had been prepared; and when they had eaten their fill they admired the rich ornaments of gold and silver which decorated the Abbey, and the wonderful gem-studded gifts to the Madonna.

Henry studied these ornaments through narrowed eyes. So much that was beautiful was worth a great deal and all hidden here in the abbey!

"By God's eyes," he declared to his captains, "we could feed an army on a few of those silver chalices."

The captains avoided his eyes but he insisted on pressing his point. Of what use were these ornaments hidden away in an abbey? How much more useful they would be to supply him with the money he so desperately needed.

As the beautiful objects were taken from the shrines of saints, the monks protested. Young Henry however waved aside their protests.

His soldiers were hungry, they wanted their pay. He was determined to feed his army and go on with the war.

He laughed at the squeamish attitude of some of his men. They feared reprisals from the saints.

"Nay," cried Henry, "this is a just cause." Providence appeared to be proving this was so, for news had come that several important knights and their accompanying men were ready to join him in marching against Richard.

Henry was delighted. Nothing was going to deter him now. He knew how to come by the money he needed. There were so many rich abbeys in the neighbourhood. Why should they not provide the means of feeding and equipping his army?

A feverish excitement possessed him. His sleep was haunted by strange dreams. Often he tossed on his pallet and his father dominated those dreams.

Now when his armies came into sight the monks tried to close their doors against him. He would not have this. Sometimes it was necessary to batter them down.

He was rich now. Robbing the shrines was a seemingly never ending source of providing for his needs.

Terror spread through the land. There were fearful stories of drunken soldiery storming the abbeys. The monks kept a look-out for the approaching armies and sought to defend themselves, but they were helpless against Henry's men.

He was like a man possessed by devils. He would call out in his sleep that his witch ancestress was after him. His attendants thought he was ill, but in the morning he would be up and ready to march on.

His cheeks were flushed and it seemed that he had a fever. He was advised to rest awhile but he would not hear of it.

"What! When we are winning. Give my father and Richard a chance to outwit me. Nay! I am going on to conquer Aquitaine and one day the monks will rejoice for the part they have played in my victory."

On they marched. Close by was the most famous church in France, well known for the shrine of Roc Amadour. The treasures in this shrine were worth a fortune. Pilgrims came to it from all over the country. It was said that miracles had been performed there and that the Virgin herself was often present.

Henry noticed that his attendants were afraid. He felt the fever burning through his body and a recklessness seized him.

"Why think you we have come to Roc Amadour if not to help ourselves to the treasures of the shrine?" he demanded.

Perhaps no one believed he would commit this deed of

sacrilege. Perhaps he did not believe it himself. He saw the looks on the faces of the men—frightened faces—and he laughed aloud. Something was urging him on. He did not know what. He was going to prove to them all that he feared nothing . . . neither his father nor God. Then they would understand why he was so angry to be deprived of the power that was his by right.

"To the shrine," he cried.

He looked at them witheringly. "Let those who are afraid, go back to their firesides. They are not worthy to come with me to Aquitaine. I would not have them at my board for I like not cowards."

Then he went forward into the church and there was scarcely a man who did not follow him.

What riches! What treasures!

"These spoils will take us through our campaign to Aquitaine," cried Henry.

That night the fever was on him. He was delirious and those about him trembled. They could not forget that he had descrated the shrine of Roc Amadour.

In the morning he was a little better. They would march on, he said.

He told the Duke of Burgundy who had joined him and put several hundred men into his service: "Last night I thought I would die. I dreamed that Our Lady came to me and told me that my days were numbered. 'Repent,' she said, 'for there is but little time left to you.' I thought I was dying."

"My lord, should you not rest?" asked the Duke.

"No. I have a desire to go on. Send one of my messengers to me. There is one I wish to see and I want him brought to me without delay for it may well be that there is truly little time left to me."

"Who is this?" asked the Duke.

"It is William the Marshall. I have a fancy to see him. I wish him to come to me with all speed."

In the next few days young Henry had become so ill that it was impossible for him to go on. He lay in a merchant's house for some days, talking a great deal to himself and now and then seeming to know where he was and asking if William the Marshall had come.

At length William arrived and when he went into the bedchamber in which Henry lay, the young King gave a cry of welcome.

"So you have come, my friend."

"As soon as I received your message," answered William.

"Good William, we have always been friends have we not?"

"Aye," answered William.

"You were with me in my childhood, so it is good that you should be with me at the end."

"The end. What mean you?"

"Do you not know it then, William? I do. I am a sick and most sorry man for I shall go to my Maker with my sins on me—and what sins! You know that I have desecrated sacred places."

"Why, my lord? Why."

"It was necessary to find money for my soldiers."

"In such a way!'

"Nay. It was my way. You know that I have a devil's witch for an ancestress. It was as though she took possession of me."

"My lord, you should repent."

"I will. I wanted to see you, William."

"I knew it my lord. And now I am here I shall not leave you again."

"You will not have to stay long."

"Nay, you will recover."

"William, I never believed that you were Marguerite's lover."

"I know it."

"Some devil got in me. The same devil who was in me when I sacked the shrines."

"Philip of Flanders was your evil genius."

"Nay, I was my own, William. Now I am free of that evil, I see that I am indeed wicked and that I must repent."

"Shall I send for a priest?"

"Later, William. As yet stay with me. I have a little while left."

"You should make your peace with God."

"I will, I will. Now you have come to me, everything seems different. I am as a child again. I admired you so much, William. You were the perfect knight. You could do everything better than any other. You were too good."

"I am a sinful man, even as you, and none could be too good. But rest now. Let me call the Bishop."

"If there were time, William, I should ask you to accompany me on a crusade."

"Later when you have recovered perhaps."

"Later? There will be no later for me. You know it, William. Why do you pretend now? You were always such an honest man."

"Then if there is little time, repent, my lord King."

"Aye, I must repent. Bend down and see what lies on the floor, William. It is a crusader's cross. I took it from the shrine."

"My lord!"

"Nay, cease to be shocked. What I have done is done and there is no taking it back."

"Then repent, my lord."

"Send the priest to me then, William. And tell me you forgive me. It was an ill day for me when I sent you away."

"That is over. I am back now."

"William, take care of Marguerite for me. I fear she will be a widow ere long."

William turned away. He could not bear to look at the once handsome face now pallid and flushed by turns, the beautiful eyes wild and bloodshot.

He should have stayed with him. How could he when he had been sent away? But he should have come back and not waited to be sent for. He should have warned the young King that the way he was going could only lead to disaster.

The Bishop of Cahors came and gave him absolution.

It was clear now that he could not live many more days.

He asked that William the Marshall stay with him.

"The end is very near now," he said. "See here is the crusader's cross. How can I expiate my sin in taking it from the shrine? If I were granted my health I would go on a crusade and take it to Jerusalem. There I would place it on the Holy Sepulchre and pray for forgiveness. Oh, God, grant me the gift of life that I may in time find forgiveness for my sins."

William turned away. He knew that Henry would never go to Jerusalem.

"I must see my father before I die. I have lied to him and wronged him. I must ask his forgiveness," he cried.

"I will send a messenger to him without delay," William promised. "I will tell him in what state you are and beg him to come to you."

"Pray do that."

He seemed to revive a little. It was as though he must see his father and ask his forgiveness before he died.

The King did not come to his son's death bed. Henry had

lied to him before; how could he be sure that he was not lying now and that he would not be walking into a trap? He sent one of his Bishops with a ring which had never before left his finger so that his son would know that the Bishop came with his blessing.

Henry held the ring in his hand and held it against his heart.

"You will take a message to my father," he said. "I am dying and would fain have seen him and I know full well that he would have come to me."

"He was prepared to come," said the Bishop, "but was advised against it."

Henry's face twisted in painful grimace. "I know. I know. I had lied to him so many times. He could not trust me now. That was wise of him . . . but this time I happen not to be lying. Pray ask him to look after the Queen my wife. I would send a message to my mother. I think of her often and I would ask my father to be kinder to her. I have committed terrible sins. I have robbed sacred shrines. I would wish my father to repay what I have stolen as fast as he is able. Ask him to forgive his erring son."

The exertion of talking was proving too much for him but he seemed more contented now that he had sent word to his father. It was almost as though he had prepared himself for death.

He asked again for William the Marshall.

"Take the cross," he said, "and if the opportunity arises carry it to Jerusalem in my name."

"If I go there I will do this," said William.

"Let them make for me a bed of ashes on the floor and bring me a hair shirt. Put a stone for my pillow and one at my feet and let me die thus, that God and all his angels may know that I come in all humility. I am deeply stained with sin but most truly I repent."

William gave orders that this should be done and then tenderly the young King was lifted from his bed and placed on the ashes.

He lay there in great bodily discomfort but he seemed to have found a spiritual peace.

A few hours later he was dead.

The Painting on the Wall

When the King heard that his eldest son was dead, for a few days he felt nothing but grief; but he could not for long give way to his sorrow. Henry's death raised many problems. Most important, it meant that there must be a new heir to his dominions.

Richard!

The King's expression hardened. If there is aught I can do to prevent that, prevent it I will, he told himself.

And yet it was dangerous to depose the rightful heir and set up another in his place. Richard had never cared much for England. Aquitaine had been his passion. That might be because it was his mother's and he was close to her. In spite of his Norseman's looks he loved the southern land.

My sons! thought the King. What affection have they ever given me? Henry! Richard! Geoffrey!—my enemies all of them.

There was one who had so far been his obedient son—John.

Why should he not make his heir the son who had been loyal to him? He would show traitors, be they his own sons, that he did not forget injuries.

Richard? He must confess that Richard had never been anything but straightforward. If Richard was planning to act in a certain way he did not feign otherwise. He was not like Henry had been or Geoffrey was. Those two he had never been able to trust. But he could not like Richard.

How ironical was life—and particularly a king's life! He craved for sons and when they came they made his life a burden.

Henry had lied to him and stood by when one of his men had shot arrows at him. What had been his son's true feeling when the arrow had merely pierced his cloak, and his horse, not himself, had been shot down?

He was a shrewd man in all but his family affections. He

should have known long ago that his sons had no love for him, only for his crown.

He wished that he could love Richard. Richard was perhaps the one in whom he should have put his trust. But he was uncomfortable to be in his presence; he always feared that a subject would be referred to which would make him very uneasy, even might make him betray something which must never be told.

"Oh Alice, my sweetheart," he murmured, "you have much to answer for."

He longed for home . . . and Alice. He thought of her in Westminster or Winchester or Woodstock. Dear, beloved Alice, who never complained that he could not marry her; who was content to remain in comparative seclusion; who was content merely that he love her and keep her from Richard.

He had Alice, but he desperately wanted his sons' affection too. He had visualized when they were in the nursery how they would grow up and work together and how happy they would be to do his bidding. He had seen them as a formidable family of strong men with himself at the head. None would have dared come against them. Four sons who would marry into Europe and bring more and more rich lands under the Plantagenet crown. How sad, how disillusioning, with his sons warring against each other and against him and making allies of the King of France!

And now Henry dead—and most ignobly had he sacked sacred shrines before dying and something must be done about that or there would be no good fortune for the family. The saints must be placated.

Henry, the most beautiful Prince in Christendom, with his charm of manner which drew men to him—dead. What a waste of a life!

My son, whom I wanted so much to love and who wanted nothing from me but my crown!

And Richard? No, not Richard! He could not have him beside him, the future King of England. How could he? And what of his marriage? It would be expected now.

I will send for John, thought the King.

John came riding in from the hunt when the news was brought to him that his father wished to join him.

John was now seventeen years old; very conscious of being the youngest son, he had been determined to exert himself.

His brother Henry had been tall and handsome, so was Richard. John however took after his brother Geoffrey. They were both of small stature though their limbs were well formed. Their father, who was of little over medium height, seemed to tower above them both. Geoffrey and John were very much alike in features and also in character. Both of them could acquire knowledge without much difficulty and were more interested in book learning than either young Henry had been or Richard was. Geoffrey had always been able to express himself with lucidity and to put forward a good case when this seemed a difficult thing to do. John was like Geoffrey in this. He was bland and full of soft words when he wanted something. He was deceitful and seemed to take a delight in deceit. For the sheer joy of getting the better of someone he would go to great lengths and perhaps achieve nothing in the end but the pleasure of deceiving someone.

Gerald of Wales, the priest who had been sent to John to help further his education, realized that it was no use attempting to go against his nature. John had long been dissolute. He had been seducing women from a very early age and often rode out into the country with a band of lusty followers indulging in seduction or rape, whichever came to hand.

He was in the charge of the justiciar Ranulf Glanville, a very able man who had distinguished himself on the battle-field and won the King's favour to such an extent that he was content to overlook his peculations which were numerous, even when they were proved against him.

That his son John should have been put in the charge of such a man was strange even though he was a justiciar of England and one of the most important men in the country.

John admired him and saw nothing wrong in his shady dealings.

At seventeen he was very much aware of being the youngest son and he never forgot the fact that when he had been born his father had called him John Lackland.

Now his brother Henry was dead and Richard was the heir with Geoffrey next and then himself. It seemed there was no hope for him with two strong brothers to stand between him and the crown; but there was this in his favour: his father was fond of him.

John was amused. Henry had perhaps been the favourite because Henry was tall and beautiful and knew how to charm people, even his father. It seemed he could shoot an arrow at him which could have killed him if it had not pierced his cloak instead and still he could talk himself out of such a situation.

John admired that in his brother, but Henry was a fool of course. He had died of a fever, and that was the end of him. Richard was always going to war so he would doubtless meet a violent end one day.

That left Geoffrey. John had a great deal in common with Geoffrey—they looked alike; their characters were similar. John was the more dissolute. He had surrounded himself with companions of similar tastes. Geoffrey was a sedate married man in comparison; he had a wife, Constance of Brittany, and a daughter Eleanor named after their mother. John, too, had inherited the Angevin temper. He was as ready to flare up as his father was and then his rage could be terrible. He was naturally not so feared as his father, but his attendants always kept well out of the way when John's temper was about to rise. There was a sadistic streak in him, too, which Geoffrey lacked. And, although on the surface he appeared to be a pleasant young man with a charming manner, beneath that façade there were traits of character as yet unsuspected even by those who were close to him.

When he received the news that his father wished him to join him in Normandy he sent for Ranulf de Glanville to tell him the news.

"You see what is happening, Ranulf, I am to be my father's favourite now."

"Good news, my lord. Good news."

"The poor old man must have one son on whom to dote."

"And fortunate, my lord, that Richard and Geoffrey have displeased him so much that you are to be the chosen one."

"The chosen one! What do you think it means?"

"It means that it depends on you, my lord."

"What do you mean, 'depends on me'?"

"How you play your part. You could have England."

"I . . . King of England, with two brothers to come before me!"

"Richard loves not England. He is for Aquitaine. Geoffrey is out of favour. He stood by while someone shot the King's horse from under him and made no move. Think you the King will forget that?"

"King of England, Ranulf. I like that. I like it mightily. Think what sport we would have . . . you and I . . . and others . . . roaming the country . . . received everywhere with acclaim. Riding into the towns, picking the most likely women . . . and all coming running when I beckoned."

"There might be some who repulsed you."

"So much the better. A little resistance is amusing. One does not seek submission all the time. If that were so what would become of the delicate art of rape?"

"My lord, you must curb your language when you are in the presence of the King."

"A rare one to talk! What about him? In the days of his youth no woman was safe from him and it seems he can even now give a good account of himself."

"Alice contents him when he is in England."

"That makes me laugh, Ranulf. Richard's betrothed is my father's mistress! I have heard that she bears him children. Is it so, think y ?"

"We should not believe all we hear, but if Alice is fruitful it is no more than must be expected."

"Methinks he loves not Richard."

"And Geoffrey has displeased him."

"And so," said John, "that leaves his youngest son—his good and dutiful John who will love him and obey him and prove to him that he will be his very good son. Do you think I can play that part, Ranulf?"

"My dear lord, I think you can play any part you have a mind to."

"I have a mind to this one. He must make me his heir, Ranulf, before he dies; and once he has done that I shall be very ready to take a tender farewell of the old man." John began to laugh.

"My lord is amused."

"I think of my father. Great Henry Plantagenet before whom men tremble. His sons have been a disappointment to him . . . all but John. He does not know that John is the most wicked of them all. 'Tis true is it not, Ranulf?"

"It may well be. But let us please keep that interesting fact from your father."

"You may trust me, Ranulf." He fell on his knees and raised eyes moist with emotion to Ranulf's face. " 'Father, I am your youngest son. I would I were your eldest. But young as I am there is time for me to show you that I will bring to you that which my brothers failed to. Your sons have disappointed you . . . all but John. It is my mission to prove to you that there was one in the nest whose coming shall repay you for all the ingatitude of the rest.' How's that, Ranulf?"

"It could be improved," said Ranulf.

"It shall be, my friend. It shall be."

Henry received his son with open arms.

"My son John! It does me good to see you."

He looked into the young face and John raised eyes as full of emotion as they had been when he acted before Ranulf.

"Father, you have suffered much," said John. "I rejoiced to receive your summons. I wanted to come to bring some small comfort to you."

"My blessings on you. I need comfort. Your brother, John, my handsome son Henry, to die as he did! He was so young."

"He was twenty-eight, Father, and was it true that he had desecrated shrines before he died?"

"We must pray for his soul, John. He repented at the end. William the Marshall has given me an account of his last hours. When he died he was lying on a bed of ashes in a hair shirt."

"I thank God," said John.

"You know, my son, that I am sore pressed. Your brothers are warring against each other one moment, against me the next. Henry was engaged in war against me when he died. That grieves me sorely. But he sent a message to me and I forgave him. We were friends then. Would to God we had never been anything else. These battles in the family, John, they are no good to any of us."

"No, Father."

"You are now of an age to be taken into my confidence."

"I rejoice in that. I want to be beside you. I want to help you. I must learn quickly."

Henry's eyes were emotional suddenly. Could it really be that in this son he was going to find the one who would make up for the disappointments the others had brought him?

"Your brother's death has made great changes," went on Henry. "The King of France will now be demanding Marguerite's dowry back. I cannot give up the Vexin, it is so important to the defence of Normandy."

"My brother Richard is now the heir to England, Normandy, Anjou . . ." began John.

The King was silent.

"He will have to marry the Princess Alice now," said John slyly.

"We shall see," said the King.

"People are saying that there is something strange about

the Princess. So long she has been betrothed and still there is no marriage."

"People will always make mysteries where there are none," said the King.

"Mysteries, yes. There are no real mysteries because some-one always knows the answer to them."

The King allowed that to pass.

"I have sent for your brother Richard," he said. "He is unacceptable to the people of Aquitaine and I am going to make him give up the Duchy."

"Who will take it then?" asked John.

"You, my son."

John nodded. The idea pleased him. He was going to be King of Ireland; he had several estates in England; and now Duke of Aquitaine.

He could see that his brother's death had benefited him greatly. He must keep his father's good will and much more that was good would flow his way.

Richard wondered what his father could wish to say to him. The trouble in Aquitaine had been settled favourably with the King's help, and he could now say that he had established his position there.

That there must be change, he knew. The heir to the throne was dead and he was the next. He believed that his father had many years left to him and one thing was certain: no one would be allowed to take the crown of England or have the slightest sway in Normandy and Anjou while he lived. Aquitaine was different. That had been passed to him by his mother and he could be said to have won it over the last years by the right of his own sword.

If he became the heir to the throne of England and his father's dominions of Normandy and Anjou, what of Aquitaine?

The King received Richard with accustomed restraint and wished that it had not been necessary for them to meet.

The two brothers surveyed each other with suspicion. John felt a pang of envy, for the blond giant had an air of kingli-ness which he knew would never be his. He had always disliked Richard, though not as much as he had Henry, for Henry had been even more handsome, as tall, and had a charm which delighted almost everyone.

Well, he was dead now and Richard was heir to the throne and large dominions overseas, and it was better to be King of England than Duke of Aquitaine.

"My sons," said the King, taking them to his private chamber where they could be alone to talk. "We meet at a time of great bereavement."

"Henry was a fool," said Richard in his usual blunt way. "He knew he had a fever and he refused to care for himself. He brought on his death."

The King bowed his head and John said: "Hush, Richard. Do you not see our father's grief?"

Richard said: "Since they were at war together and Henry was behaving with the utmost folly I doubt not our father remembers that."

The King was thinking: Richard is right. I mourn my son but I cannot forget that he was my enemy. He would have seen me dead and not lamented. Yet I loved him and always hoped he would change towards me. But John is affectionate. Richard is a brilliant soldier, but John is kindly. He will be a good son to me. And that is what I need to comfort me.

"Let us not brood on the past," said Henry. "We are met together for a purpose. Your brother is dead and that has changed so much. I have brought you here Richard that you may retire from Aquitaine. Your brother John will be the Duke and you will now surrender the Duchy to him."

Richard's eyes were as cold as ice: the ague showed in his hands.

"Aquitaine is subdued now," he said. "Ever since my mother had me crowned its Duke I have fought for my place with my sword. I have won it. You would not ask me to give it up now."

"I am not asking," replied the King. "I am commanding."

Richard did not speak. His brother Henry had been crowned King of England and had never had any power at all. He was Duke of Normandy, Count of Anjou—and much good that had done him.

Young Geoffrey Count of Brittany ruled that land. He as Duke of Aquitaine would rule his territory. He would rather be a ruler in fact than have the promise of high-sounding titles which could be nothing until his father's death. Not that the King had talked about making him heir of his dominions. It was presumed he must be because he was the eldest living son, but his father had not said so. And by the way in which he was beginning to dote on John, who knew what was going on in his mind?

Richard did not trust his father, particularly now that he had sent for John.

He did not therefore, as he might have done previously, give his definite refusal to hand over the land for which he had fought. He said that the proposal was such a surprise to him that he needed time to brood on it.

The King was agreeable to this but he added that he would need a reply—and the reply must be agreement . . . within the next week.

Richard rode back to Aquitaine. From there he sent his answer to his father.

As long as he lived he would rule Aquitaine and no one else should.

The King lingered in Normandy. He kept John with him and his youngest son played the part he had intended to. He listened gravely to his father's advice; he feigned wonder at his wisdom; and he was determined that he was going to remain the favourite son.

Henry was no fool. He often wondered about John, but he was so anxious to be loved that he continued to deceive himself—half of himself warning him to look out for treachery while the other half assured him that at least he had one son who cared for him.

There was much to keep him abroad although he longed to return to England.

There was a meeting with Philip when they wrangled over the return of Marguerite's dowry. They settled this by arranging that Henry should pay her an income of over two thousand Angevin pounds. Henry was never reluctant to enter into such agreements for he promised himself that if payment became difficult he would simply let it slide.

It was inevitable that Alice should be mentioned.

"Her marriage with Richard is long overdue," said Philip.

"There has been so much to occupy me and Richard," replied the King.

"And now you are having trouble with him, I believe."

"He is a disobedient son."

"You have been disappointed in your sons, brother."

"They have caused me trouble. It will be different with my youngest. John will be a good son."

Philip paused ironically as though he were listening. What for? wondered Henry. The ironical laughter of the gods?

They agreed on Alice's dowry.

"You might decide that if she is not for Richard she could be for John," said Philip. "Geoffrey is settled in Brittany."

"John is betrothed to the Earl of Gloucester's daughter."

"Such betrothals are often forgotten. Do not forget, brother, that Alice is a Princess of France."

"I shall do my utmost to see that she is well cared for," said Henry.

Philip did not press the point. Sometimes Henry wondered how much was known about him and Alice.

Henry planned to leave Normandy in the early summer and to take with him the Duke and Duchess of Saxony. His daughter Matilda was pregnant and he thought it would be a good idea for the child to be born in England. He had been thinking a great deal about Sancho of Navarre whose advice had been that he should show a little leniency towards Eleanor.

She was sixty-two years of age—hardly likely at her time of life to start rebellions. But of course she must not be judged by ordinary standards. There was nothing ordinary about Eleanor. It seemed incredible that she had been imprisoned for eleven years, but this was the case.

The last time they had met she had proved to be not in the least contrite. It was impossible to imagine her ever so. She had done her best to make trouble between him and his sons; and for so long that had been the great purpose in her life.

Yet perhaps it would be advisable to give her a little freedom—not much, but enough to show those who watched the situation between them, that he was ready to be indulgent if only she would make it possible for him to trust her. Richard was defying him in Aquitaine and there could be trouble there. The people of that province would be pleased if he showed them that his attitude was softening towards Eleanor. Their daughter Matilda would be in England and it would be a pleasant gesture to let mother and daughter meet.

He would consider granting Eleanor permission to leave Salisbury for Winchester where she might be with her daughter during the latter's confinement.

The more he thought of the idea, the better it seemed. It could do him no harm, for he would have Eleanor closely watched, and it would show that he was ready to be tolerant if only she would meet him half way.

Eleanor found imprisonment irksome rather than uncomfortable. To a woman of her nature it had been galling to be shut away from events, and to be unable to take part in them, but she had managed to keep herself aware of what was going on. She would not have been Eleanor if she had not managed to organize a system whereby letters could be smuggled in to her and naturally those who brought them took out letters from her.

She knew what was happening in Aquitaine and she longed to be there. She heard of her children's adventures and was deeply gratified at their hatred of their father.

She had taken care of her appearance and for her years looked remarkably young. She had determined to maintain her elegance and a great deal of time was spent on making her clothes; she herself designed them, for then she could be certain no one else should look exactly as she did.

Sometimes she recalled sadly that in the days when she was married to the King of France she had made her Court the most elegant in the world. She often sighed to remember all the men who had been in love with her. Louis had loved her to the time of their divorce; she liked to believe he had till his death. Henry was the only one who had eluded her. He could not desire her, or he would never have kept her locked away so long. It was his infidelity which had given existence to this hatred which consumed her and which had led her to turn his sons against him.

Often she thought of the death of Henry. She had had an uncanny experience before he died. She had dreamed that she found herself walking on the cold stones of what she believed to be a crypt. There had been a faint light in the place which she had followed. Suddenly it had stopped. She approached and saw that it was shining down on a man who was lying on a couch. She had caught her breath with horror, for the man was her son Henry. He lay like an effigy on a tomb and on his head were two crowns—one was the crown of England and the other a kind of halo. Henry was smiling, although his eyes were closed, and she was struck by a look of peace in his expression such as she had never seen in him before. She had awakened with a start.

"Oh, my God," she had cried, "what did that mean?"

Then had come the news of his death and her dream came vividly back to her.

Henry was dead—that bright and beautiful boy was no more. That was what her dream had told her. He had died in conflict with his father. It was a terrible story of hatred, betrayal and disloyalty. She heard how he had sacked sacred shrines; how he had plundered villages and how people had fled before him and his soldiers. And the end . . . the terrible end . . . when fever had taken hold of him and death had come. He had repented. So many repented on their death beds, and his was a bed of ashes, his pillow a stone.

My son, she thought. Oh, my God, where did we go wrong?

Why did she ask? She knew. These sons of theirs were bred in hatred, against the violent emotion of a lecherous father and a vindictive mother.

We considered our own emotions, she reproached herself. We did not restrain ourselves. We were obsessed by ourselves and did not pause to think what we were doing to our children.

We are the ones who should make our beds of ashes. Ours was the sin.

She thought of her son Henry who had been their eldest since the death of little William. Henry, the most handsome of a handsome bunch. She remembered how excited they had been at his birth and how delighted to have another boy because at that time little William's health was failing. Such a bright boy! How proud his father had been of him. He had always been Henry's favourite as Richard had been hers.

Richard had noticed his father's preference and been sullen and resentful because of it. And she had made up to Richard for his father's neglect of him and between her and Richard there had grown a passionate attachment which she believed was stronger than any emotion either of them felt for any other person.

It was in the nursery that the rot had begun. The children were reared to hate their father and she had done this.

Then Henry Plantagenet had made the mistake of crowning his son Henry King of England. He had made few mistakes in his government of his dominions, although his family life had been one long misjudgement; but nothing could have worked more to his undoing than the coronation of young Henry—to make an ambitious man a king in name and then deny him the power to be one. Oh, Henry, Henry, wise Henry Plantagenet, what a fool you are!

She wept, for although Richard was her favourite she loved all her children. Their progress had always been of the utmost interest to her. She loved the two daughters she had by Louis. And when she thought of the last months of Henry's life she trembled for him. She herself had sinned, Heaven knew, and so had Henry Plantagenet, but they had not been cut off in their prime with all their sins upon them.

He had repented at the end. He had given William the
Marshall the cross to take to Jerusalem; but that very cross
he had taken from a shrine. And he had asked his father's
forgiveness and Henry—she granted him that—had readily
given it. He had not been with his son at the end although he
could have been. His knights advised him against going for
fear of treachery. Treachery between father and son!

Oh, what a lot we have to answer for!

She prayed for forgiveness, that the sins of her sons might
be averted from them to her.

Ours was the fault, oh, God, she prayed. Blame not our
children.

She spent several days in fasting and praying for Henry's
soul.

But she was a born intriguante and the thought which
must keep recurring to her was: Now Richard is the heir to
the throne and the next king will not be Henry the Third but
Richard the First.

The Archdeacon of Wells came to see her on behalf of her
husband. He told her that the King wished her to prepare to
leave for Winchester and her future would depend on how she
behaved when she was there. The King himself was in
Normandy but he hoped soon to be in England.

"Did he say he wished to see me?" she asked.

"He did not, my lady," was the answer.

She was amused and intrigued. This was release . . .
temporarily, the King stressed. She was to be free because
her daughter was coming to England. Was that the real
reason? Henry was sly. Why should he feel it so important to
make an impression on the Duke and Duchess of Saxony who
were merely exiles? There was another reason. Aquitaine.
Her people hated him because he kept their Duchess prisoner. She knew him well. His motives were always suspect.

What excitement there was at the castle when gifts from
the King arrived for her. What had happened that he should
send gifts? How long was it since she had received anything
from him?

Her women crowded round her. They believed the King
was going to take her back. Rosamund had been dead for
some time and Rosamund had been one of the main causes of
their discord. Now the Queen would be the Queen in truth.
They would all leave Salisbury and go to Winchester or
Westminster wherever the Court was. The sequestered life
was over.

A beautiful dress of scarlet was revealed as it was taken from its wrappings.

Belle, the youngest and prettiest of the attendants, exclaimed with pleasure.

"Look, my lady. It is lined with miniver."

The Queen took up the dress and held it against her.

"It is long since I have worn a dress so fine," she said. She would have it altered a little to suit her individual taste and it would be perfect. The fur was of the highest quality and the red cloth most excellent.

The following day another gift arrived from the King. It was a saddle ornamented with gold. Her women danced round her with glee. Eleanor watched them thoughtfully.

The King was staying longer in Normandy than he had intended. There was so much for him to settle. Eleanor heard that he was meddling in the affairs of France. He was afraid of Philip; and no wonder, when he had treated Philip's sister as he had.

What was happening about Alice? There she was, still kept at Westminster and Richard continued to be denied his bride.

Eleanor smiled grimly wondering what would have happened if news of what had actually taken place between Henry and Alice had been brought into the open. So many times she had wanted to divulge the secret. What trouble it would have made—but only temporarily! Henry could be trusted to find a way out. No, she had had more sport keeping him on tenterhooks. He would have extricated himself from that embarrassment as deftly as he had from the murder of Thomas à Becket. She was sure that the best way to harass him was to keep silent, and every now and then give him a little fright that the affair might be exposed.

Richard would not take Alice now, but she had advised him not to let his father know that. Let Henry go on worrying as he had for years. How devious was Henry Plantagenet! It relieved her conscience to revile him in her mind. If she was in some measure to blame for the conflict among their sons, he was even more responsible.

She longed to see him and when she heard that he was considering his return to England her spirits rose. He was on his way and with him came their now heavily pregnant daughter Matilda and her husband. It was time for Eleanor to leave Salisbury.

* * *

With what joy she greeted her daughter!

Matilda was twenty-eight years old, her husband, the Duke, many years older; and now Matilda was pregnant and she told Eleanor how comforted she was to see her.

They spent much of their days together and Matilda often marvelled at the youthful looks of her mother.

"I have spent so many years in confinement that I have been able to preserve myself," laughed the Queen.

"You will see changes in the King when you see him," Matilda warned her.

"Shall I see him. I wonder? He has said nothing about our meeting."

"He is very upset over the death of Henry."

"Has it changed him?"

"The loss of a son would not change him very much. Only the loss of his crown would do that."

"So he shows the years?"

"You know that he was never one to care for his appearance. I am sure he is often mistaken for the humblest of his servants for it is only on rare occasions that he pays heed to his dress."

"He was always so," said Eleanor. "I used to tell him that he looked like a serf,"

She wanted to hear so much of him but she had to curb her curiosity. She did not wish even Matilda to know how much she thought of him.

They sat together, Matilda embroidering a garment for her baby and Eleanor singing or playing the lute.

"When I was in Salisbury new songs were brought to me," she said. "So much of the news came to me through them. Minstrels would sing to me of what was happening to your father and your brother."

Eleanor loved the children—Henry, Otto and little Matilda. She watched Matilda's health with maternal care and herself made many of the preparations for her confinement.

What was going to happen in Saxony? she asked Matilda, but Matilda could not say. Her husband, known as Henry the Lion, had not wished to make war on Italy as the Emperor Barbarossa wanted him to and for this reason the Emperor had turned against him. The result—exile. "How thankful I am that we could turn to my father," said Matilda.

Her husband was so many years older than herself, Eleanor pointed out. Was she happy with him?

Matilda was as happy as royal princesses could expect to be, she answered.

"Perhaps I expected too much," commented Eleanor. "I married your father for love you know."

"And look where it ended," pointed out Matilda. "You were soon hating each other and all these years he has kept you a prisoner."

"At least it was love at the start. And although I never loved Louis, he loved me, I believe, until the day he died."

"But you are different from the rest of us, Mother. You guide your own fate. Ours overtakes us."

"And as you say I was overtaken by imprisonment in the end. Perhaps it is better to have our marriages made for us and be good docile wives. Is your Henry a good husband?"

"He is jealous."

"It is often so with older men. With older women too. I was twelve years older than your father and I think that was one of the reasons which began the discord between us. He was unfaithful and I could not endure it."

"Yet you were unfaithful in your first marriage."

"That was Louis. It was different. Louis could have been unfaithful to me and I would not have cared. But perhaps I lie. I can say that, because he never would have been. No, I do not think I would have tolerated infidelity in either of my husbands, and when I discovered it in Henry that was the start of the trouble between us."

"My Henry was angry over Bertrand de Born," said Matilda. "He wrote love poems to me. Henry discovered and banished him from the Court."

"He is a great poet," said Eleanor. "He is compared with Bernard de Ventadour. I would not have his verses sung in Salisbury though because he did much to harm your brother Richard."

"You know why. He fell in love with my brother Henry."

"I thought he was in love with you?"

"He made verses to me but it was Henry whom he loved. If you had seen the verses he wrote to Henry you would have realized how much he loved him. He thought my brother the most beautiful creature he had ever seen and you know how these poets worship beauty. When my father had taken his castle and he stood before him, his prisoner, my father goaded him with this much flaunted cleverness and asked him what had happened to his wit now. Do you know what he replied: 'The day your valiant son died I lost consciousness, wits and direction.' "

"At which your father laughed him to scorn I doubt not."

"Nay, Mother, so deeply moved was he, that he restored his castle to him."

"He can be sentimental still about his sons," mused Eleanor.

"He loved Henry dearly. Henry was always his favourite. Again and again Henry played him false and every time he forgave him and wanted to start again. He wanted Henry to love him. His death was a great blow to him."

Eleanor played the lute and Matilda sang some to the songs which had come to Normandy from the Court of France and Aquitane. They told of the conflict between the King's son's and the love of knights for their ladies.

In due course Matilda's child was born. The confinement was easy and the little boy was called William.

Eleanor, who loved little babies, delighted in caring for him.

Christmas was approaching.

To Eleanor's amazement and secret delight, a message from the King arrived. He was summoning his sons to Westminster and he invited his wife to join them there. Matilda with her husband and children would accompany the Queen and it should be a family reunion.

The grey mists hung over Westminster on that November day, and in the palace there was an air of expectancy. This was an occasion which would be remembered by all concerned for as long as they lived. The King, the Queen and their sons would be together there.

When Eleanor came riding into the capital the people watched her in silence. This Queen had been a captive for ten years. She amazed them as she had in the days of her youth. There was something about her which could attract all eyes even now. She was an old woman but she was a beautiful one still; and the years had not robbed her of her voluptuous charm. In her gown of scarlet lined with miniver, adjusted to her special taste and with that unique talent which had stylized all her clothes, she looked magnificent.

The watchers were overawed.

Then came the King—so different from his Queen, yet, though he lacked her elegance there was about him a dignity which must impress all who beheld him. His cloak might be short and worn askew, his hair was greying and combed to hide the baldness, although by his garments he might be mistaken for a man of little significance, his bearing and demeanour proclaimed him the King.

She was waiting for him and they studied each other for some moments in silence.

By God's eyes, he thought, she is a beautiful woman still. How well she hides her age!

The years have buffeted him, she thought gleefully. Why, Henry you are an old man now. Where is the golden youth who took my fancy? How grey your hair is and no amount of dressing it can hide the fact that it is thinning. Does your temper still flare up? Do you suffer the same rages? Do you lie on the floor and kick the table legs? Do you bite the rushes? But what was the point in mocking? She knew that he was still the King and that men trembled before him.

He bowed to her and she inclined her head.

"Welcome to Westminster," he said.

"I thank you for your welcome and for the gifts you sent to me."

"It is long since we have met," he said. "Now let it be in amity."

"As you wish. You, my lord, now decide in what mood we meet."

"There must be a show of friendship between us," said the King. He turned away. "Grief has brought us together."

They stood looking at each other and then the memory of Henry, their dead son, seemed too much for either of them to bear.

The King lowered his eyes and she saw the sadness of his face. He said: "Eleanor, our son . . ."

"He is dead," she said. "My beautiful son is dead."

"My son too, Eleanor. Our son."

She held out her hand and he took it and suddenly it was as though the years were swept away and they were lovers again as they had been at the time of Henry's birth.

"He was such a lovely boy," she said.

"I never saw one more handsome."

"I cannot believe he has gone."

"My son, my son," mourned Henry. "For long he fought against me, but I always loved him."

She might have said: If you had loved him you would have given him what he most wanted. He asked for lands to govern. You could have given him Normandy . . . or England . . . whichever you preferred. But no, you must keep your

255

hands on everything. You would give nothing away. Even as she reproached him she knew she must be fair. How right he was not to have given power to the fair feckless youth.

"We loved him, both of us," she said. "He was our son. We must pray for him."

"None understands my grief," he said.

"I understand it because I share it."

They looked at each other and he lifted her hand to his lips and kissed it.

Their grief had indeed brought them together.

But not for long. They were enemies, natural enemies. Both knew the bonds must loosen. They could not go on mourning for ever for their dead son. It was not for mourning that Henry had allowed her to come. She quickly realized that. He had not released her from her prison because he wished to show some regard for her, because he had repented his harshness towards her. No, he had his motive as Henry always would.

He had brought her here for varying reasons that did not concern her comfort or well being.

In the first place she had heard through Richard that Sancho of Navarre had requested it and he wished to be on good terms with Navarre. The main reason, though, was that Henry's death had made the reshuffle of the royal heritage necessary and he needed her acquiescence on certain points, mainly of course the re-allocation of Aquitaine.

She was overjoyed when Richard arrived at Westminster. Her eyes glowed with pride at the sight of this tall man who had the look of a hero.

They embraced each other and Richard's eyes glowed with a tenderness rare in him.

"Oh, my beloved son!" cried Eleanor. "How long the years have been!"

"I have thought of you constantly," Richard told her, and because she knew her son so well she could believe him. Her dear bold honest Richard who did not dissemble as the rest of her family did. Richard on whom she could rely; whose love and trust in her matched hers for him.

"We must talk alone," she whispered to him.

"I will see that we do," he replied.

He came to her bedchamber and she felt young again as she had when he was but a child and she had loved him so dearly and beyond her other children, as she still did.

"You know why your father has brought me here?"

He nodded. "He wants to take Aquitaine from me and give it to John."

"You are the heir to the thone of England now, Richard, England, Normandy and Anjou."

"He has said nothing of making me his heir."

"There is no need for that. You are the eldest now and the rightful heir. Even he cannot go against the law."

"He is capable of anything."

"Not of this. It would never be permitted. It would plunge the country into war."

"He is not averse to war."

"You do not know him. He has always deplored war. He hates wasting the money it demands. Have you not seen that if there is a chance to evade war he will evade it? He likes to win by deceit and cunning. He has done it again and again. That, my son, is what is known as being a great king."

"I would never stoop to it. I would win by the sword."

"You are a born fighter, Richard. A man of honesty. There could not be one more unlike your father. Perhaps that is why I love you."

"What think you of him? He has aged has he not?"

"Yes, he has aged. But I remember him as a young man . . . a boy almost when I married him . . . not twenty. He was never handsome as you and Henry and Geoffrey . . . and even John."

"We get our handsome looks from you, Mother."

" 'Tis true. Although your grandfather of Anjou was reckoned to be one of the most handsome men of his day. Geoffrey the Fair they called him." She smiled reminiscently. "I knew him well . . . for a time very well. A man of great charm and good looks but no great strength. Not like his son. But what has your father become now? An old man . . . a stout old man. He always tended to put on weight. That was why he would take his meals standing and in such a manner as to suggest he did so out of necessity rather than pleasure. Of course that unrestrained vitality of his, kept down his corpulence in his youth but it was bound to catch up with him. I notice he often uses a stick when walking now."

"One of his horses kicked him and he has a toe nail which has turned inwards and causes him pain now and then."

"Poor old man!" mocked Eleanor. "He should have taken better care of himself. He is never quite still. One cannot be

257

with him long without sensing that frenzied determination to be doing something. In that he has not changed. And how untidy he is! His garments disgrace him."

"He never cared for them. 'I am the King,' he says, 'and all know it. None will fear me the more because I wear a cloak of velvet and miniver.' "

"In the days of his love for Thomas à Becket when Thomas was his Chancellor and they went about together one would have thought Thomas the King and he the servant."

"Yet Thomas died and he lives on and now he proclaims that Thomas loves him even more than he did when they were young and that he keeps an eye on him in Heaven."

"That is like him," said Eleanor, not without a touch of admiration. "He would turn everything to his advantage. But we waste our time talking of him. We know him so well, both of us, and that is good for we are aware of the man with whom we have to deal. What of Aquitaine, Richard?"

"I shall never give it up."

"You have had a troublous time there."

"But I have brought it to order. They think me harsh and cruel but just. I have never murdered or maimed for sport. I have meted out terrible punishments but they have always been deserved."

She nodded. "In the days of my ancestors and during my own rule life was happy in Aquitaine. We were a people given to poetry and song."

"Poetry and song have done much to inflame the people. You know that Bertrand de Born made it possible for Henry to come against me?"

"I know it. They loved me. They would never have harmed me. Why could they not have accepted my son, the one I chose to follow me?"

"They never really believed that I was on your side. They hate my father and they look on me as his son, not yours. But I have won my place by my sword and I shall keep it. I would rather be Duke of Aquitaine than King of England. I shall never give up Aquitaine to John."

"He has made John his favourite. That is reckless of him. Do you think John will love him any more than the rest of you did?"

"I know not. John is like him in one way. He has that violent temper."

"That speaks little good for him. Henry would have done well to curb his. I wonder if he has inherited his lust?"

258

"I hear it is so."

"Let us hope that John has inherited his shrewdness too or it will go hard with him. But it is of you I wish to speak, Richard. You will be King of England when Henry dies."

"And Duke of Aquitaine, for I shall never give it up. And when I am King, Mother, my first concern will be for you. Before anything else, you shall be released and beside me. I swear that."

"God bless you, Richard. There is no need to swear. I know it will be so. There is another matter. You are no longer a boy and still unmarried. What of your bride?"

"If you mean Alice, she is still in the King's keeping."

"Still his mistress! How faithful he is to her. What has she told him? She's another Rosamund, I'll swear. You'll not take your father's cast-off, Richard?"

"I will not. I am determined to tell him that he can keep his mistress and make his peace with Philip. I know not how. There could be war over this."

"I doubt not he would find some way out. He has the cunning of the fox and slithers out of trouble with the smoothness of a snake."

"Mother, I have seen a woman I would marry."

"And she is?"

"The daughter of the King of Navarre. Berengaria. Her father has intimated that if I were free of Alice he would welcome the match. Berengaria is very young. She can wait a while."

The Queen nodded. "Say nothing of this. We will continue to plague him over Alice. I would I knew whether he clings to her because he finds her so irresistible or whether it is because he fears what might happen if it were known he had seduced his son's betrothed and is afraid she might betray this. Oh, Richard, this is an amusing situation. You and I stand together against his marriage with Alice. If neither of us was here he would marry her and take her dowry and the matter would be settled. I wonder if he would be faithful to her? It is possible that he might now that he is so fat and walks with a stick and has trouble with legs and feet. Morality sets in with disabilities."

"You hate him still, Mother."

"For what he has done to you and to me, yes. It could have been different, Richard. All our lives could have been different. If he had not betrayed me with other women I would

259

have worked for him and with him. I would have made sure that my sons grew up respecting and admiring him. He has himself to blame. But perhaps that applies to us all. Oh, Richard, how good it has been to talk with each other."

"One day," said Richard, "we shall be together. On the very day I am King, your prison doors will be flung wide open and I shall let all men know that there is no one I hold in higher esteem than my beloved mother."

The King announced that Christmas should be celebrated at Windsor and that the Queen should be of the party. Eleanor was delighted. It would be the first Christmas she had spent out of captivity for a good many years. She was in high spirits. It had been wonderful to see Richard again and while she mourned for Henry she must be aware of the turn in her fortunes, for Richard was to be trusted. What he promised he would do. He was Richard Yea and Nay. God bless him! He would always be his mother's friend.

For Christmas they must forget their enmities. They must join with the revellers. There would be feasts and music and for once the King would be forced to sit down and behave as though this was a festival and that they were not on the verge of a battle.

Eleanor and he had watched each other furtively. Neither trusted the other. That was the nature of their relationship and it could not be otherwise. He was planning to rob Richard of Aquitaine and give it to John. John was going to be as well endowed as any of them. Why not? John had never taken up arms against his father as the others had. A man must have one son to love.

What an uneasy family they were. In his heart he no more believed he could trust John than he could any of the others. There they were all at the same board, and all ready to work against one another.

What strength would have been theirs if they had worked together! And there at his table was his Queen. How did she remain so young-looking and elegant? Was it through witch-craft? That would not surprise him.

How beautifully she sang—songs of her own composing. She sang of love. She should know much of that. How many lovers had she had including her uncle and a heathen Saracen? All those troubadours who had surrounded her when she kept court with him, how many had been her lovers?

And how often had he strayed from the marriage bed? So many times; there were numbers of women whose names he could not remember. Two he would cherish for ever—Rosamund and Alice.

Oh, Alice, fair Alice. A woman now. Twenty-three years of age. She had been but twelve when he had first taken her. And she had been his ever since. He had loved Rosamund and he had loved Alice—only those two had he truly loved. What it had been with Eleanor he was unsure. There had always been conflict between them. What exciting conflict though, in the beginning when no other woman had satisfied him as she had. And of course there was Aquitaine which went with her.

With Alice there would be the Vexin, that land so vital to the defence of Normandy. God in Heaven, why would not Eleanor die! She was old enough to be dead. She had lived long enough. Did she want to go on in captivity? For by God's eyes he had seen enough of her to know that after this spell of freedom she must go straight back to her prison.

He would never again trust her to roam free. It would be foolish to give her the opportunity.

The King sent for Richard. "Are you determined," he said, "that you will never give up Aquitaine?"

"I am," answered Richard.

"Then go back there."

Richard was astonished. This could surely only mean that the King had decided not to interfere with his control of the Duchy.

When he said farewell to his mother she warned him to beware of his father. His promises were not to be trusted and if he agreed now to let him keep Aquitaine he might change his mind the next week.

Richard left, assuring his mother of his devotion which would never change.

Next the King sent for his son Geoffrey.

"You will return to Normandy," he said, "and keep peace there." He then proceeded to give Geoffrey more power than he had ever had before.

Eleanor was watchful. What did this mean? Was he saying that if Richard was so determined to hold on to Aquitaine he could forgo the crown of England?

What a devious mind that was! And he had never liked Richard. It occurred to the Queen that if the King could take from Richard what was his by right and give it to his other sons, he was capable of doing that. What was he planning to give to John?

Finally he sent for his son John and told him to prepare to take over his dominion of Ireland. John seized the opportunity with alacrity. He would be ready to leave in the spring.

The King then set out with the Queen and his Court for Winchester.

Winchester—the palace of many memories, second only to that of Westminster. Here he had kept Rosamund for a time when he had ceased to keep their liaison secret. Here Alice had been with him. And now Eleanor came.

She was delighted with the place; she always had been. She admired the herb garden which had recently been made and picked many of its contents which she declared were the best of their kind.

She wondered how long she would be allowed her freedom. She knew in her heart it would not last. How could it? Their interests must certainly clash. Nothing could stop her intriguing with Richard against him when the time came, and he would know it. Well, she would rather go back to her prison than allow him to think that he had subdued her, or that she would cease to demand her rights for the sake of freedom.

He had had many decorations painted on the walls of this castle. He was rather fond of allegory, and they were adorned with scenes from his life. He would want future generations to know that he was the one who had restored it and made it beautiful.

One day when she walked through the castle she came to a room and went silently in. To her amazement she saw that the King was standing there.

The light from the narrow slit of a window showed his face drawn and sad. His carelessly donned clothes, his slovenly stance, the manner in which he leaned on his stick made her feel half sorry for him while at the same time she thought: It will not be long before Richard is the King of England. My beloved son you and I will be together. And yet she was conscious of a sadness. Ever since she had known Henry she had never wished to contemplate a world without him. She could never forget the first time she had seen him—the son of her lover, for she had shared his father's bed once or twice.

Geoffrey the Fair had never been the most beloved of her admirers though he was an exceptionally good-looking man and a virile one too. But when she had seen the son, she wanted no more of the father. Henry, lover, and husband for whom she had divorced the King of France, father of their troublesome brood, the lion and the cubs who from their earliest days had planned his downfall.

He was aware of her and without taking his eyes from the walls he said: " 'Tis you then?"

"This room has changed since I knew it long ago."

"I have had it newly painted."

"And you admire it evidently."

"Come and look at this picture."

She went and stood beside him. "An eagle and four eaglets," she said.

"Yes. Look closer. See how the young prey on the old bird. Do you see anything familiar in their faces?"

She turned to look at him and she saw the glaze of tears in his eyes.

Henry Plantagenet in tears! It was impossible.

"I am the eagle," he said. "The four eaglets are my sons."

"You have caused this picture to be painted."

He nodded, "I look at it often. See how they prey upon me. My three sons, Henry, Richard and Geoffrey. And see the fourth poised on my neck. That is John. I tell you this, that he, the youngest, the one I love so tenderly, is waiting for the moment when his brothers have laid me low; then he will pluck out my eyes."

"I am surprised that you torment yourself with such a picture."

"There must be somewhere where I face the truth. I feign to believe them. I am their father. I have been over tolerant with them. I let them deceive me and I deceive myself that they must love me because they are my own sons."

"You should never have put a crown on Henry's head."

"I know it well."

"You did it to spite Thomas of Canterbury. You wanted a coronation in which he should not partake."

"Yes. But I did it too because I feared God might take me in battle and I wanted no bloodshed. I wished it to be that when the King died, there was a new King ready waiting."

"It was a foolish act."

"Unworthy of a shrewd king," he agreed. "And here I look at this picture and face the truth."

"It is not too late. Trust your sons. Take Richard to your heart. He is your heir. Give him the power he needs."

"That he might take my crown from me?"

"He will not take it until it is right and proper for him to do so."

"The eaglets are impatient," he said.

"Because the eagle has kept them in the nest too long."

"You turned them against me," he accused. "You are at the source of all my troubles."

"Had you been the husband I wanted, I would have loved you to the end."

"You wanted to rule."

"Aye. We both wanted it."

"And between us we bred the eaglets."

He turned away at the door and looked back at her.

"This painting will be copied and I shall have it in my chamber at Windsor. There I shall look at it often and I shall remember." His voice shook slightly and he said suddenly:

"Oh, God, Eleanor, why was it not different? What would I not give just for one loving son."

Then he was gone. She listened to the sound of his stick on the stone flags.

She laughed quietly. Poor Henry, the great King, the seducer of women, the lover whom none could resist. He had failed where she had succeeded for she had one son who loved her.

The Curse of Heraclius

News reached the King at Winchester that Heraclius, the Patriarch of Jerusalem, had arrived at Canterbury and that he had made the journey to England to impart news to him which he was sure would urge Henry to action.

Fearing what the visit meant, Henry could make no excuse to avoid seeing the Patriarch for his subjects must never doubt that he was a deeply religious man. He remembered with misgivings that at the time of the murder of Thomas à Becket he had taken an oath to go to Jerusalem on a crusade. He had vaguely thought he might go when his kingdom was in a fit state to be left, knowing deep in his heart that it never would be.

Now here was the Patriarch and there could be but one reason for his coming. He would be wanting to raise men or money for the preservation of the Holy City. Eager to hear what news he had brought Henry immediately granted an interview to Heraclius and Roger du Moulin, the Grand Master of the Hospitallers, who had accompanied him. The Patriarch's first action was to offer the King the keys of Jerusalem and the Holy Sepulchre.

"I bring ill news," cried Heraclius. "Queen Sybil of Jerusalem craves your help. Her son who is but a child is the heir to the crown and her brother Baldwin is close to death. He is sick of leprosy and his flesh is shrivelling from his bones fast. He cannot live long and the Saracens are ready to take the Holy City. It must be saved and Queen Sybil implores you to come to her aid."

"We shall certainly give her aid," said the King. "I will levy a tax without delay for this is a very worthy purpose."

"It is not money that is needed. It is a Prince to lead an army against the Saracens. You are the man, oh, King, for at the time of the death of Thomas à Becket you swore that you would go to the Holy City."

Oh, Thomas, thought Henry, shall I never escape from you? I did my penance. Was that not enough?

It was true that he had taken such an oath, but he had meant of course when the time was ripe and he had always known that the time would never be ripe. How could he, a king with far-flung dominions, ever leave them to go to the Holy Land?

"You are the most powerful of kings," went on Heraclius. "God will bless you if you do this. If not . . ."

The King said quickly: "To leave my dominions would be a matter not so much for me to decide but for my ministers. I should first be obliged to ask their opinion. If they considered that I should go, then go I should. But it may be that they would be against it and I must needs bide by their decision."

"Why so, my lord? You are a king who makes his own decisions. The whole world knows it. None would dare go against your will."

"Nay, a king governs through the grace of his people. Rest assured I shall do all in my power to meet your wishes. The Holy Land must not be allowed to fall to the Infidel. Allow me to put this matter to my ministers and I will give you their answer."

"My lord, you should not let your response depend upon them. You should remember the oath you took. You should remember your duty to God. You are no longer a young man. You may be closer than you think to the throne of judgement."

What an uncomfortable man this Heraclius was! Henry disliked him. As if he had not enough with which to concern himself without bringing this up to plague him. He was not going to Jerusalem. How could he? He could imagine the chaos which would ensue if he did. His sons at each other's throats and at his. Eleanor who must be watched! Certainly he could not leave.

He insisted that he would put the matter to a council which he would call at once.

This he did, letting them know first that they would be brought together to discuss whether or not he was to raise an army to go and fight a crusade for the Holy City; and he made it clear that if any of them should vote for his departure they would forfeit his favour. They had to decide that on no condition could he leave his dominions and that to do so now would be to act against the wishes of God.

Eleanor was amused when she heard. She understood him

266

so well. Go to Jerusalem! Leave Alice! Endeavour to wash away his sins! Nay, she thought, they are too numerous for that. He would need twenty such missions.

Would he go? Of course he would not. Odd as it was, although he had spent most of his life near battlefields, he was not enamoured of the fight. He had ever held that battles were wasteful and rarely brought the victor what he had been fighting for. It was so much better to discuss and manoeuvre one's enemy into a bargain. He was adept at making bargains which proved to be advantageous to himself.

And what of her? What were his plans? She did not know. But still she remained at Court. She was not allowed much freedom. If she rode out she was always well accompanied by attendants of his choosing. Did he think she would make for the coast and take ship to France?

She had often thought of it, it was true. If she could reach Richard, together they would hold Aquitaine against all and if Henry were indeed planning to give it to John, then by God, she would do her utmost to reach him.

She thought of how excited she and Louis had been when they set out on their crusade. There was something about such a mission which fired the blood. One imagined oneself riding to glory carrying the cross. Of course it was very different on the battlefield. Death was death—not glorious, but bloody and horrible. And men were men whether they were Christian or Saracen, as she had discovered.

Ah, Saladin. What a lover he had been. And now there was another Saladin. Was it his son, his grandson? And he was threatening to take Jerusalem from the Christians!

Suppose she had married Saladin as she had once thought she might, suppose through this marriage a peace had been brought about between Saracen and Christian. If Saladin had become a Christian old Heraclius would not be here now begging Henry to go to the aid of poor leprous Baldwin.

But life did not work out like that. Instead of Saladin she had married Henry Plantagenet.

Henry meanwhile was preparing the members of his council. Considering how affairs stood in Aquitaine, Normandy and Anjou he did not feel it was the moment for him to go far away. He asked them to visualize the troubles which could arise if he were out of the way. A crusade was an expensive venture. The people would have to be taxed and how would they react to that? It was bad enough when they had to pay to keep their own country safe. He himself might win personal glory but what of his country? He had ever thought to serve his subjects and make it possible for them to live peacefully in a just community. If he were absent he did not see how he could preserve the laws of England which had been set up by his great-grandfather and strengthened by himself; and he knew that the members of his council, being wise men, would never permit him to embark on such an undertaking.

The assembly met in London; the English nobility were present with high ranking members of the Church and on a dais Henry sat side by side with his guests, Heraclius and Roger de Moulin.

The King told the assembly the reason for the mission and what great honour had been done to him. The Holy City was in peril; King Baldwin was dying of a dread disease; there was but a child to take his place; and the keys of the Holy Sepulchre had been offered to him, Henry of England. Here was an opportunity for him to win great glory to himself and wash away the sins of his lifetime. He was a king, however, who had always considered first his people. He had no will but theirs and he had summoned them thither that they might decide for him whether or not he should undertake this pilgrimage.

Heraclius rose to his feet and told the assembly that Jesus Christ and the godly throughout the world were asking the King of England to save Jerusalem. He would tell them how Saladin, the leader of the Saracens, those heathens who were the enemies of Christ, were preparing to take Jerusalem. Could true Christians stand aside and allow this to happen. Nay! For those who could do this were not true Christians.

Henry replied that he would do all in his power to save the Holy City.

He then called upon the assembly to tell him what they wished him to do.

Richard, Archbishop of Canterbury rose to his feet. "My Lord King," he said, "your duty lies in your dominions."

Heraclius turned on the Archbishop.

"My Lord Archbishop," he cried thunderously, "I call on another Archbishop, a saint, a martyr. He was done to death on the stones of his Cathedral and at that time the King swore an oath that he would go to Jerusalem."

"If it was in his power to do so," replied the Archbishop. "But our lord the King swore another oath at his coronation. In it he declared that he would always watch over the welfare of his subjects. That oath, my lords, being the tenure of the crown, supersedes all other oaths. A crusade to Palestine cannot be compared with the duties of a king. And for this reason my lord King, and my lord Patriarch, the King must stay in his own dominions."

Henry nodded his head slowly.

"I see that the members of my council speak with good sense. My heart will go to Palestine but I must perforce remain here. My duty must be done." Heraclius was about to burst forth in his indignation when Henry said: "I will give fifty thousand to the cause and if any of my subjects desire to join a crusade I shall do all in my power to help them."

"I have not come for money," cried Heraclius. He turned on Henry in his fury, for he knew full well that these men would never have dared to decide against him unless primed by the King. It was Henry's decision and Henry's only. "As for you, sir," he went on, "You have hitherto reigned with an abundance of glory, but know this: God whose cause you have abandoned is now about to abandon you. You will see what happens to you as the result of your ingratitude. You make excuses. You say you must stay and protect your subjects. You murdered the Archbishop of Canterbury and you refuse in expiation of your guilt in that crime to undertake this Holy War."

At the mention of Thomas à Becket the colour flamed into the King's cheeks and his eyes gleamed murderously.

"Do not believe that I dread your fury," cried Heraclius. "Cut off my head if you will. Treat me as you treated St Thomas à Becket. I had rather die by your hand in England than by the Saracen in Syria. I esteem the Saracens more than I do you."

Henry trembled with rage. He could never listen unmoved when Thomas was mentioned. For a few moments he was on the point of shouting to those about him to seize the Patriarch, throw him into a dungeon and there put out his eyes.

Heraclius showed no fear. He was sick at heart though. He must find a noble prince, rich and strong, who would come with him and save Jerusalem.

"Give me one of your sons," he pleaded. "If you will not save your soul yourself, let one of them come on your behalf."

"I need my sons."

"God needs them."

Henry thought: Richard? Geoffrey? John? No, never. He

must keep them close to him. He must know what they were doing. He could not trust one of them.

"God gave me great lands to defend," said the King. "I must needs defend them. If I left my sons would fight among themselves. My duty lies here."

The Patriarch knew that he was defeated.

"You and your sons . . . you came from the Devil and to the Devil you will return. No good will come to you, Henry Plantagenet, for you have turned your face from God."

Henry left the chamber. There was only one who could soothe him and make him forget the Patriarch's dismal prophecies: Alice.

Henry was shaken. Was it true, he asked himself, that God had forsaken him?

His sons were not to be trusted—even John, his youngest, his beloved now. What was the use of pretending? Could he trust John? What sort of man was he growing up to be?

He sent for him and John came readily. The boy knew that now his brother Henry was dead he was his father's favourite son.

John, sly, well versed in villainy, for his tutors had seen which way his inclinations lay and encouraged him, was looking for the advantage. He despised his father with the contempt of the young for the old. John believed he was on the threshold of a life of power and adventure and that his father was nearing the end of his.

In the past he had watched his father in the castle, seen his eyes linger on women, watched him fondle them and take them away to his bedchamber. It was not long before John was experimenting in this game which men said had been an obsession with his father. John understood his father's inclinations in that direction. They were his own.

And now, who knew what was in store for him? Geoffrey had offended his father beyond forgiveness because his men had actually shot arrows at the King while he looked on. As for Richard the King had never liked him. That left John.

The old man could be quite maudlin at times.

John had heard the appeal of Heraclius and one of his cronies had told him of his mother's adventures in the Holy Land when she had been old Louis's wife. His mother had known how to enjoy life even as his father did! John thought he would like to go to the Holy Land. Nothing could be more amusing than to lead a riotous life on the journey and then get your penance at the shrine.

So when he presented himself to his father, he began by kneeling and telling him that he wished to go to the Holy Land.

"Let me go, Father," he said. "There I shall gain redemption for your sins as well as my own."

"Nay, my son. There is too much to be guarded here," replied the King. "I could not let you go."

"But, Father, Heraclius has cursed you."

"God will not listen to his curses."

"Is he not a good man—the Patriarch of Jerusalem?"

"That is a title. He comes to me because he wishes to save his own position. He cares not what would happen here. And what do you think would happen if I went away?"

"You have sons, Father."

"Ah, John, that should be a comfort to me should it not? But is it, think you? Geoffrey, Richard . . . When have they ever been good sons to me?"

"You have another."

"You, John, my youngest. All my hopes are in you now."

"Father I shall do my best to show you that your trust is not misplaced."

"I count on you, John. You are to go to Ireland. Your dominions there need you. As you know I sent Hugh de Lacy to hold Ireland for me, but I no longer trust him. He has married the daughter of the King of Connaught. He did not ask my permission for this marriage but tells me it was contracted in the manner of the country. I recalled him but found it expedient to send him back, for there was no doubt that he had great knowledge of the country and seemed the best man—and this was helped by his marriage—to hold it for me. He is an ambitious man and I believe thinks to set himself up as King of Ireland. That, my son, is an honour which I have reserved for you."

John considered this. Ireland seemed a good exchange for the Holy Land. Ireland would be his. He was King of Ireland. If he went to the Holy Land it would be as the King's son; he would be at the head of troops but there would doubtless be others of higher rank. In Ireland he would be King.

"Father," he said, "my spirit longs to go on a crusade. I am young but I have committed sins and would wish to receive forgiveness for them. I know that you have been deeply affected by the curses of Heraclius and I wished to pray for you at the Holy Shrine. But you have decreed that it is not to be this time. I will do my duty as you show it to me. I will go to Ireland and pray God that I may act in such a way as will please you and make you rejoice that you have one son who will obey you without question."

The King embraced John.

This was indeed his beloved son.

John then set about preparing for the journey and before the month was out sailed from Milford Haven with sixty ships in which were three hundred knights and a company of archers.

Within a day they had landed at Waterford.

If only his other sons were as obedient as John!

Geoffrey was of little account. Geoffrey was pleasure-loving and more given to sporting at tournaments than on the battlefield. This was a pity, for Geoffrey had a ready wit and was quick to assess a situation. His marriage was successful; he had a daughter, Eleanor, and his wife would most likely bring him more children. He should hold Brittany satisfactorily.

The son who caused him most concern was of course Richard. The question of when he was going to marry was continually being brought forward. It was becoming farcical. Alice was now twenty-five. All those years she had been his mistress and still was. She seemed young to him because of the great difference in their ages and she had become a habit. If he were not so passionately desirous now as he had been, he still cherished her; and in his desire for her was a certain amount of hatred against Richard and the King of France. He had to keep Alice. If he let her go now the story of her seduction would surely be discovered. Alice was mature; she had borne him a child. She was not going to be mistaken for a virgin. Then the scandal would break. His enemies would revel in it, magnify it. He could imagine what old Heraclius would do with it.

He had survived one scandal, the murder of Thomas. How would he fare if the story of Alice's seduction at twelve, her life with him for thirteen years when he had held her in spite of the importunings of Richard and her family, was known? What would the world say to that?

They would say he was a monster. They would recall that

his ancestress was a witch; they would say that the Anjou family was born of the Devil.

He had been young when Thomas was murdered; his sheer vitality and quick mind had brought him through that. Now sometimes he felt an old and beaten man. And every time his sons rebelled against him he felt a little more vulnerable.

His presence was needed in Normandy and he left England beset by many problems. He was thinking a great deal about Richard who had defied him when he refused to give up Aquitaine. As he saw it now, Richard would be King of England. He could not have Aquitaine as well. Richard must give up Aquitaine to John.

Suddenly it occurred to him that there was one person to whom Richard *would* relinquish his Duchy: his mother.

He sent for Eleanor to come to Normandy, selecting a suitable escort for her.

Eleanor was excited.

What did this mean? It must be a change in her fortune. It was years since she had crossed the Channel. Henry must be realizing at last that he was making too many enemies by keeping her captive.

When she arrived he received her with courtesy and she was very eager to hear what he had to say.

"My lord, to what do I owe this honour?" she asked as soon as he granted her a private audience.

"I want to talk to you."

"I knew you would want something," she mocked. "I did not expect you would have brought me here otherwise. Why, Henry, you look perplexed. Has old Heraclius been bothering you with his curses?"

"He bothers me not."

"They say he is a very holy man."

"He is a man who, like most, has his own interests at heart."

"As you say, who has not? And what are yours this moment?"

"I would have you remember that you are here by my clemency."

"I am not likely to forget it. You and your servants constantly remind me."

"I have sent for you as I wish to discuss Aquitaine with you."

"Ah?" She raised her eyebrows. "I am all attention."

273

"Richard refuses to give it up."

"Rightly so. He has fought for it."

"There should have been no need to fight for it."

"Nor would there have been if my people had seen me treated in accordance with my rank."

"Your people if they have good sense will know that you played traitor to your husband and because he is a king he has a way of dealing with traitors."

"They like not to see me in capitivity."

"Then mayhap they will be pleased to see the land restored to you."

"What mean you, Henry?"

"That I am commanding Richard to give back Aquitaine to you."

"To me." Her eyes were alight with excitement. He watched her closely. This was the way to act.

"Richard must by nature of his age be my heir. He will have England, Normandy, Anjou, all that Henry would have had, had he lived. We have another son, John. I would have my dominions divided equally."

"So you want Aquitaine for John."

"I want Aquitaine for you."

"And I shall return to my country." For a moment her emotions were too much for her to control. "Oh, my God, how I have longed to be there. How the cold of Salisbury Castle has seeped into my bones. I long for the sun."

He was silent, watching her. If Aquitaine were hers and she was the only one to whom Richard would give it, and she was his prisoner, he it was who would have control of that land.

She was aware of his eyes upon her and she thought: Once it is mine I will bestow it on Richard again as I did before. Aquitaine is for Richard. He belongs there as he never did to England. He is my son and Aquitaine shall be for him.

"This will be the way to restore order to Aquitaine," she said.

Eleanor had not felt so excited for years. At last her imprisonment was over. She was going to be free, free to hold her own Court, to gather round her the troubadours of the South, to intrigue with her beloved Richard against his father.

The Fatal Joust

Henry's plan had succeeded. Richard, who had refused to hand over Aquitaine to his brother, at once agreed to give it to his mother. This was done.

When Eleanor was making her preparations to depart for Aquitaine she received a shock.

Henry came to her. "I see that you are ready to leave," he said. "That is good for I wish there to be no delay."

"In a few days I shall set out. Soon I shall be in Poitiers."

The King raised his eyebrows. "Nay," he said, "that is not what I intend."

She stared at him unbelievingly.

He said: "You have forgotten one thing. You are my captive. How could I trust you in Aquitaine? What would be the first thing you would do? Plot against me. Do you take me for a fool? You are going back to England. At your castle they will be waiting to receive you."

"No!" she cried.

"But yes. I am glad you will soon be ready to leave.".

"You have given me back Aquitaine."

"In name only. That will keep the peace."

"You . . . cheat!"

"Call me rather the guardian of my dominions."

"I should have known you never kept a promise."

"Well, you had many years to make my acquaintance, so could be expected to know me well."

"It is small wonder that your sons all hate you."

"You brought them up to that. A bad task well done. Do you think I shall ever forget or forgive you for it? If you think that, you do not know Henry Plantagenet. Moreover, how could I ever sleep easy if I thought of you in Aquitaine plotting against me, stirring my sons to rebellion?"

"I . . . hate you," she said quietly.

He shrugged his shoulders. "You have done that for years but I have managed to survive."

"What a liar, what a cheat, a lecher, a breaker of promises; it is small wonder as Heraclius says that God has abandoned you."

He was suddenly afraid of her. With her loosened hair and her eyes blazing she looked like a witch prophetess.

He turned and left her.

John proudly stepped ashore on Irish soil. His land! Lord of Ireland! King of Ireland! The titles rang in his ears and the feeling of power it brought with it was as intoxicating as any wine.

What did a king do in his own land? He made sure that everyone was aware that they were his subjects. What he wanted of them they must give. A wonderful situation. Lands, women, everything he wanted was his. He kept reminding himself of that. He had chosen his special friends to accompany him, young men who were very like himself. They strutted, they drank too much, they boasted of their conquests of women and they never forgot to give their Prince what he constantly demanded: flattery.

The dress of the Irish amused them and, when dignitaries came to receive him, John roared with laughter at their costumes and his followers immediately joined in his mirth. The Irish were bearded. It was one of their customs. This seemed comical to John and he and his friends tweaked the beards of those who came to greet them in a most insolent manner.

Naturally enough the chieftains were insulted and were not going to endure this.

Hugh de Lacy tried to restrain the irresponsible young men, pointing out to John that the Irish were a quarrelsome and warlike people and would not endure such treatment.

"They will endure whatever treatment I care to impose on them," retorted John.

Hugh de Lacy groaned. Why had the King, usually so shrewd, risked the loss of Ireland by sending this stupid arrogant youth?

Worse was to come. John and his band marched through Ireland. Whenever they fancied anything, they took it. They plundered the towns, they coerced the women and if these were unwilling they were raped.

It was hardly likely that the Irish would quietly allow such desecration of their land. As John proceeded through the country he was met by armies. and as he was more proficient in plundering defenceless towns than in fighting, he was very soon in desperate straits.

After five months he was so impoverished and his forces so depleted that he had no alternative but to return to England.

He came to his father who received him with affection and great consternation when he heard how badly everything had gone in Ireland.

"How could such disaster have befallen you?" he wanted to know.

"The answer, Father," replied John, "is the traitor Hugh de Lacy. He has stirred up resentment against us all over Ireland. You know he plans to be Lord of Ireland. He wants to be the King."

Henry studied his son closely. There were signs of dissipation on his face, young as he was. He had heard stories of the women he had seduced. A young man it was true must follow his natural instincts, and Henry was the last who would blame anyone for being fond of women. He himself had fathered two illegitimate children before he was eighteen.

Little doubts came in his mind but he refused to see them. He could not endure to have another son whom he could not trust. There must be one in the brood who would love him and serve him well.

He thought of the picture of the eaglets and the youngest of them waiting to peck out the old eagle's eyes. Why had he caused that picture to be painted? If he believed in John why should he have said that the youngest of them was standing aside waiting to peck out his eyes?

What had really happened in Ireland? Was John power-drunk? Had he behaved in such a manner that the Irish had turned against him?

Shrewd Henry who had come so far because he had understood the ways of men, said: Discover. Ask those whom you can trust. Know this son of yours.

But he was a tired old man, longing for affection. It could not be possible that all his sons would betray him. There must be one who loved him; and who could it be but John?

There was news from Ireland.

Hugh de Lacy had been murdered.

"A just reward," said John, "for his treachery to his King."

Henry listened to the news. The Irish had done this. They had cut off his head. No doubt they had grown tired of his pretensions, thought Henry.

He sent for John.

"Hugh de Lacy had many estates in Ireland. They must be seized without delay. You should prepare yourself to leave for that country."

John was nothing loth. He looked forward to further merry sport.

Before he had time to leave, though, there was more news, this time from France.

Geoffrey had presented himself to Philip of France, ostensibly to do homage to his seneschal and Philip had welcomed him with such honours that it seemed suspicious. Philip had insisted that Geoffrey stay awhile at the Court of France, and there grew up such friendship between Philip and Geoffrey that those who wished the King of England well felt he should know of it.

Henry did wish to know of it. He did not trust Philip who was no weak vacillating Louis.

Strangely enough Philip had grown from the spoilt boy into a ruler who was not to be lightly ignored. He was becoming a very ambitious man. His dream was obviously to extend his dominions. Philip would have liked all the vassal states to be entirely his, and like Henry, he was wise enough not to want to go to war if he could acquire what he wanted through diplomacy and shrewd dealing.

Henry had for some time been aware that he must keep a watchful eye on Philip of France.

If Philip was making much of Geoffrey then he was doing it for a motive. Had he got his eyes on Brittany . . . or worse still, Normandy?

Henry must be very watchful of what was happening at the Court of France. He might need all the forces at his disposal, in which case it would be unwise to send his son John to Ireland. So the Irish expedition should be temporarily postponed.

How right he was. It was said that at their secret talks Geoffrey and Philip were discussing the invasion of Normandy. And what of Richard? How was he feeling? He had handed over Aquitaine to his mother only to find that she had promptly been sent back to captivity.

Oh, yes, he must be very watchful indeed. The eaglets might well be poised to fall on the old eagle.

Geoffrey was enjoying his sojourn in France and one reason for this was that he knew the effect his being there would have on his father.

Geoffrey loved mischief. It had always been so since his nursery days. If he could make trouble he was happy. He had a grudge against his father and another against his brother Richard, because he had been denied power by the one and shown to be inferior in battle by the other.

Moreover, it was pleasant to be treated with honour by the King of France. The fact that Geoffrey was clever, quick-witted and able to express his thoughts with an uncommon lucidity made him more dissatisfied with his lot. There was some greatness in him but he was marred by the flaws in his character rather than his ability. He could be persuasive and eloquent but he rarely meant what he said; people had begun to recognize him now for a hypocrite with a talent for decep-tion. They simply did not trust him any more.

He was content with his marriage to Constance, the heir-ess who had brought him Brittany and so far one daughter. She was at this time pregnant and they were both hoping for a son.

Since he had been introduced to the tournament through Philip of Flanders he had become obsessed by it. What was it but a mock battle? It was certainly suited to his tempera-ment. He loved the show and ceremony, the occasional dan-ger, for it was dangerous and many a knight had lost his life in the jousts. Now he was known for his skill and when he rode out it was one of the highlights of the day.

The King of France, knowing his love for the sport, had arranged that there should be one tournament after another so that his guest might realize how his host wished to please him.

Invitations were sent out and those of rank such as Geof-frey gathered together their followers with the intention of staging mock battles against other men and their knights. These battles were conducted in the same manner as actual warfare and one of the favourite practices was to separate a knight from those of his party and if possible ground him and capture him. There were casualties often enough and if any knight were taken prisoner his captors would hold him to ransom. This kind of action made the battles more exciting. There was of course many an example of single combat but it was the massed battles which thrilled both spectators and participants.

Geoffrey had heard that his father was deeply perturbed because of the hospitality the French King was showing him and that he was planning to come to Normandy. That was a pity. It would have been so much more satisfactory to have launched an attack on Normandy before his father had a chance to appear. Perhaps Philip was not as eager to do that as he pretended to be. Was Geoffrey himself all that eager? No, it was more amusing to attack his father by rumour than actual fact. The tournament was the thing.

He was preparing to go into action when his wife, only just sure of her pregnancy, came to put her favour in his helm.

It was a piece of bright-coloured satin cut from her dress.

"I shall be watching," she said, "and that is all I shall know you by."

"When the battle is over I shall expect you to be waiting to lead me into the hall," he told her.

Out into the field he rode that day with no premonition of danger. Surrounded by his small company of knights he was thinking of the triumph that would be his when the fight was over. Life was full of promise. The King of France was his friend. His brother Henry was dead and only Richard stood between him and the crowns of England, Normandy and Anjou. He already had Brittany. He had a daughter and his wife was pregnant. His father's youth was passing fast. How many years could he live? Richard belonged more to Aquitaine than he ever would to England. And the next in order was himself, Geoffrey.

Suddenly he realized that he was surrounded by attacking knights. What had happened to his allies? They had been thrust aside, and there he was facing them alone. They crowded round him.

He was about to strike when his horse suffered a blow from a lance and fell to the ground. Geoffrey went down under the horse.

"Yield! Yield!" was the cry.

Yield! *He*, the son of the King of England to yield to a French knight! It was not to be thought of.

"Never," he cried and as he spoke the hoofs of one of the knights came down upon his head.

He lost consciousness and lay there.

When it was discovered that the knight who had fallen in battle was Geoffrey Count of Brittany he was carefully carried into the castle, but it was then too late.

His wife Constance came and stood by the bier. She saw that the piece of satin from her gown was still in his helm and she knelt and covered her face with her hands, for he was dead and she thought of the child she carried and wondered what would become of them.

Henry heard the news with grief.

"We are doomed," he said. "Why has God turned his face from me? Two of my sons cut off in the prime of their youth. There was only John left to him now . . . Richard was there of course, but Richard was his enemy.

Now he must torture himself with memories of Geoffrey as a boy. He could not say that he had been his favourite son, but nevertheless, he had been his own flesh and blood. What mischief had got into them that they must always be at war? Why had they not stood together as a father and his sons should do? William first as a baby, then Henry and now Geoffrey. Three sons lost and of the others . . . he could put his faith only in John.

He turned to John now.

"John, my beloved son, I have lost your brothers. You must be a comfort to me now."

"I will, Father," promised John. "I will serve you with my life."

It was comforting to remind himself that he had John.

In her castle fortress Eleanor mourned her son.

Her Geoffrey, she had called him in contrast with that other of the same name whom Henry had brought into the nursery—his bastard Geoffrey.

Such a bright boy her Geoffrey had been, so beautiful, though always overshadowed by his brother Henry because Henry had been more handsome. But Geoffrey was the cleverer of those two. Geoffrey had been the schemer, the plotter, the one who charmed while he plotted to do mischief.

Neither of those sons would ever have ruled a kingdom as their father did, but she had loved them as she did all her children. If she could not be a faithful wife she could be an affectionate mother.

Now she thought of Geoffrey as he had been when she had known him. He had been a boy then and she hated Henry afresh who had kept her all these years shut away from her children.

Her beloved Richard was safer, for Geoffrey had been no friend to him. It might be that Richard's position was more secure since the death of his brother.

So while she mourned Geoffrey she thought of Richard. He

was the son on whom all her hopes were fixed. Henry knew this. Was this one of the reasons why he was doing his best—as she suspected—to displace Richard and set John up in his place?

That should never be.

Oh, God, she cried, is there no end to the strife in this family?

The King now doted more than ever on John, and John played up to the situation with all the guile of which he was capable. It amused him that he who had been born John Lackland should now be in sight of possessing great dominions. All he had to do was delude his poor old father into thinking that he was a good and obedient son; he could do that easily enough and his nature was such that he enjoyed the deception.

The King liked to walk with him or ride with him and to initiate him, as he said, into the duties of kingship. Henry behaved as though there would be no question of his having the crown in due course. If he mentioned Richard it was to dismiss him as though he were of no importance, the younger son instead of the elder.

"I could never really love your brother Richard," said Henry one day. "He hated me from the days of his childhood. His mother did that. I thank God, John, that you were too young to be influenced by her."

"I never would have been," replied John unctuously. "I should have seen the truth."

"Would you, my son? I sometimes think your brothers didn't. They all gave me trouble."

"I never shall," declared John.

"Thank God that one of my sons gives me some affection."

"I will make up to you, Father, for what you have suffered."

Christmas was approaching and the King decided to spend it at Guildford castle. In the Norman fortress the King commanded that there should be revelry, for he wished all to know that his beloved son John was high in his favour. John was beside his father for the two days they spent there and it was seen that the King took great pleasure in his company. They would be seen walking round the castle wall deep in conversation, the King talked earnestly, John eagerly listening as though determined not to miss any of those words of wisdom.

John was delighted when early in the new year a bull

arrived from Pope Urban in which was set out his approval of Henry's desire to make his son John King of Ireland. The royal party travelled to Westminster to receive Cardinal Octavian who was bringing a crown of gold and peacock feathers with which the Cardinal would crown young John.

But once again John's pretensions did not come to fruition for before the coronation could take place there was disquieting news from France. Philip was very different from Louis. He was not easily deceived. If Henry wanted to keep the peace, he said, the two Kings must meet for there were certain matters which Philip must discuss with Henry.

Henry knew of course that one of these must concern Alice. That he had kept her so long was something of a miracle. Who else but Henry Plantagenet could have done that?

It could not last though.

He would have to postpone John's coronation and sail for France.

John was a little put out by the deferment. His inclination was to scream his disapproval and lie on the floor and kick everything near him. But he knew that he must show no displays of temper; and the game of deluding his father into thinking he was the good and dutiful son was so intriguing at the moment that he managed to get the better of his rage.

He told himself that if he could go on winning his father's favour, if he could supplant Richard, if he could become King of England, he could have as many rages as he liked. In the meantime he had to remember what was at stake.

So with docility and a show of affection he set sail with his father for France.

A meeting was fixed when the differences between the two Kings would be discussed and Philip hoped settled so satisfactorily that there would be no need of a conflict between them.

Before the confrontation could take place there was news from Brittany. Constance, the wife of Geoffrey, who had been pregnant at the time of her husband's death, had given birth to a child. This time it was a son.

Henry was delighted. A grandson! His sons—with the exception of John—had failed him and now that he was looking for family affection might it not come to him through the younger generation?

He wrote congratulations to Constance of Brittany and he was thinking: I shall have to find another husband for her ere long. As soon as she had recovered from the birth he would do so.

He would regard it, he wrote, as a compliment to himself if his grandson received the name of Henry.

Alas, it seemed that everyone was determined to flout him. Even the people of Brittany.

Constance wrote that the bells had been ringing throughout Brittany to herald the birth of a boy. The people would not hear of his being christened anything but Arthur. They wished him to be called after the great King who was the deliverer of his people.

That seemed ominous to Henry, and he was annoyed that his wishes had been disregarded. Still it was a matter which, in view of his present precarious position, he must ignore.

So Geoffrey's son was christened Arthur as his future subjects wished him to be.

Philip and Richard

Henry was feeling ill. He had an uncomfortable and humiliating internal disease. Long hours in the saddle tired him. It was irksome. Always before he had had ten times the energy of other men but he was not young any more. He was fifty-four years of age. It was true Eleanor was twelve years older, but she seemed indestructible and during the years of captivity she had led a peaceful life occupied only with keeping herself young and beautiful and dabbling in intrigue whenever it was possible. Whereas he had fought a perpetual fight to keep Alice with him, to keep at bay the young sly King of France. It had been so much easier when Louis had been alive. Gentle Louis had been so different from his shrewd young son. Who would have thought that the spoilt boy would have turned into a considerable ruler? and he had to face him now.

They were going into battle against each other. The conference had failed as Henry had feared it would. Philip had had no intention of doing anything but humiliate him. He had never wanted battle. He had always preferred to win through shrewd diplomacy. Louis had been of like mind; but how easy it had been to fob Louis off with promises he had no intention of keeping.

Philip, sly young Philip, how different he was!

God help me, he prayed. Forget my sins until the battle is over. Then I will go on a crusade to the Holy Land.

He smiled wryly. That was how he had wheedled his way out of difficult situations with Louis. Poor Louis, who had always been pious and could be deluded by such talk. Did he think that he could delude God as he had Louis?

Nay, he would never go on a crusade. How could he? He had lands to govern.

At least on this occasion he had his sons with him. Richard the fighter and John the beloved. That was a mercy. At least they stood together against the King of France.

Richard was uneasy. He had wondered lately what his
father's intentions were. There was so much talk about John,
and John gave himself such airs of superiority even over his
elder brother, that Richard wondered whether he was privy
to some plan of his father's. Always when Richard was in his
father's presence the antagonism was there. Both of them
were aware of it; Richard continually wondered whether his
father was deceiving him.

While Richard was brooding one of his servants told him
that a knight was without and asking to have word with him.
To Richard's surprise Philip of Flanders was brought in to
him. This ambitious, adventure-loving man who had at first
sought to dominate the King of France and had later taken
up arms against him, now served in his army, and this meant
that he had risked considerable danger in coming into the
enemy's camp.

"Hail, cousin," said Philip of Flanders.

"What do you want here?" demanded Richard.

"I came to have a word with you."

"*You* to come here!"

Philip laughed. "I was ever one to take a risk."

"What is it you wish to say to me?"

"To warn you. You are preparing to fight against the King
of France. Have you forgotten that the Duchy of Aquitaine is
held under him? So . . . you would be fighting your suzerain."

"I stand with my father."

"With a father who is planning to disinherit you."

"That is not true."

"What of your brother on whom he dotes? I would have you
take care, Richard. You are a better warrior than your
brother or your father. Think. Do not be rash."

"What would you have me do? Turn on my father? Join the
enemy?"

"Nay, I would not ask that of you, but the King of France
would see you and speak with you."

"Does he wish to make a truce?"

"He wished only to speak with you."

"When?"

"Now."

"You have come to take me to him."

"Come as you are. In your armour. He does not ask you to
come humbly. He would wish to receive you as a friend . . . a
cousin."

"Should I tell my father?"

"Nay, that is the last thing. He wishes you to come with me now."

"How do I know that I may trust him?"

"He gives his word. As I give mine."

Richard did not look for deceit in others. He said: "I will come."

"Then let us leave at once."

Together on horseback they went through the lines and when they came to the French camp Philip of Flanders led Richard to the quarters of the King of France.

The King of France came out of his tent and looked up at Richard seated on his horse. Few men could sit a horse as Richard could. He looked magnificent, godlike almost in his shining armour seated on his splendidly caparisoned horse.

"Richard," said the King of France. "Cousin, welcome."

"What would you have of me, Philip?"

"Friendship," answered Philip.

"Offer it to my father."

"I have none to offer him. Come into my tent. We will talk together." The King of France did him the great honour of holding his stirrup.

"Why, Richard," said Philip, "how tall you are. You are a veritable Viking."

"So I have been told. It comes from my ancestor the Conqueror."

"And proud you must be of him."

Together they went into the tent.

"Take off that of your armour which encumbers you. You may trust me, Richard. See I am unarmed."

"And I in the midst of the enemy's camp."

"By God, Richard, I believe you would give a good account of yourself if the whole of my army came against you. But it will not. I have asked you here in good faith. I would not allow aught harmful to touch you."

"Smooth words," said Richard.

"Spoken from the heart."

"Sit here where I may see you," said Philip.

Philip gazed at him intently.

"Did you have some matter to discuss?" asked Richard.

"You and I should not be on opposite sides."

"How could it be otherwise?

"It would be otherwise if you did not fight beside your father."

287

"I would not wish to fight against him."

"It would not be the first time he has fought against you. He has betrayed you, Richard, again and again. What of my sister Alice? Why is she not your wife?"

"My father has continually postponed the marriage."

"Why, Richard?" Philip laughed. "There have been rumours. She is my sister, a daughter of France. She is going to marry you, Richard, and then you and I will be brothers in very truth. You are the heir to England and we shall be friends, you and I. Wars between us destroy us both. Your father is my enemy, not you, Richard, and I have brought you here to tell you that if he is not your enemy he is not your friend. You are fighting beside him. For what reason? That he may disown you and set up another in your place? He deceived my father . . . again and again he deceived him. He won the battle against Louis VII not with sword and lance but with sly cunning; he shall not win against Philip II. I ask you to consider this. Should you and I not be on the same side?"

Richard said: "If that is all you wish to say to me, I shall be going."

"Nay, sit awhile. Have no fear. You shall be safely conducted back to your father's camp."

"I have no fear."

" 'Tis true, Richard. You are a great warrior. Never have I seen you without my spirits being lifted. This is why I want you for my friend."

Richard had risen to his feet and Philip stood up; Richard was the taller by far.

"Noble Richard," murmured Philip. "I know that you are to be trusted. Richard Yea and Nay. If you said I will be your friend, I would know you meant it. There are not many men on whom one can rely. I am eight years younger than you Richard—yes I have known but twenty-two winters and you thirty—but I am wise in the ways of the world and I respect you, Richard. I want you for my friend."

"You honour me," said Richard.

"If you gave me your friendship *I* should be honoured."

"I will go now and think of what you have said."

Philip lifted Richard's hand to his and kissed it. Than he helped him on with his armour.

"Such an honour," said Richard, "the King of France, my dresser!"

"It is I who am honoured," said Philip softly.

They stepped out into the night. Philip of Flanders who had been waiting stepped forward.

"Conduct my good cousin safely to his camp," said the King of France.

Richard thought of the strange interview and wondered what it meant. None could have appeared more friendly than Philip. And he was warning him against his father. Could it possibly be true that his father was planning to disown him? And why was Philip so eager to help him? Was it because Philip's sister was his betrothed?

Richard was puzzled.

As soon as dawn broke he went to his father. Henry looked haggard and ill in the harsh light of morning.

"Well come, Richard," said the King.

"You are not well, my lord."

"It is my complaint. Richard, I like not the position. It would seem to me that the King of France is determined on war."

"He was ready to consider a truce."

"But on what terms? He wants to humiliate me, force me to do this and that."

"You mean relinquish Alice."

"Alice," cried Henry. "The Princess Alice? But you are to marry her . . . when the time is ripe."

"The ripening has been so long delayed. Do you forget, Father, that I am thirty, and Alice is no longer young."

"She is of a good age for marriage and you were not ready before."

"Why should *you* be so concerned at relinquishing her?"

"I was not thinking of Alice. How I wish Louis were alive. I could reason with him."

"Philip is stronger than his father."

"He is a headstrong young man."

"I think he is more subtle than his father; he will be a clever ruler."

"I fear so. That is not good, Richard. I want to avoid a direct conflict. I see no good in fighting a war in which much blood could be shed to no purpose."

"It could be that there will be no alternative."

"I have thought of something. I am getting old, Richard, and my sins sit heavily upon me. It has often occurred to me that I should go to the Holy Land after all. You remember Heraclius, the Patriarch, and the ill news he brought us. It has sadly disturbed me that at the time I refused him, although it was on the advice of my ministers."

"I know full well," said Richard coldly, "on whose commands they advised against your going."

"My son, I had my dominions to govern. A king cannot forget his duty to his people for the sake of his own sins."

"That is what you wish to do now."

"Nay, nay. I will go on a crusade and ask Philip to give me a truce for two years while I am away. I believe he is a cynical young man but even he would not dare attack my dominions while I was fighting a holy war."

"I have always felt an urge to fight the Infidel," said Richard.

"I know it, my son. We will go together. I shall send envoys into the French King's camp and tell him of my intentions."

When Philip heard Henry's request he smiled slyly.

He sent for Philip of Flanders.

"Do you know, Count, what the King of England suggests? That I give him two years' truce while he goes to the Holy Land."

"He will never go to the Holy Land."

"I know that well."

"He is old and sick."

"Though a lion still."

"A mangy lion."

"He can still growl fiercely and has some of his teeth. Let us not forget that, Count."

"What will you do, my lord King?"

"Accept the truce. Let him go to the Holy Land and we will see what happens to his dominions while he is away."

"You would attack them? While he was away on a crusade?"

"Let us say that I would have no hesitation if I saw the opportunity. But rest assured, Count, he will never go on a crusade. That is what he told my father. He merely wants to postpone a battle. He has no intention of going to the Holy Land."

"What do you wish then?"

"To say yes. There shall be a truce for two years. Now let him go to the Holy Land! It is time Henry realized that I see right through his schemes. Let them go. I cannot wait to hear what the King of England has to say."

* * *

Even before the envoys returned Henry was in despair.

He sent for Richard whose knowledge of warfare was so much greater than John's.

"I wouldn't trust Philip." he said. "If I went on a crusade how should I know what was happening to my country? He is not like his father."

"Nay," agreed Richard, "he is indeed not like his father."

"It occurs to me that he may accept my terms. If he did, how could I go on a crusade? How could I, Richard?"

"You would risk losing all if you did."

"Then how could I go? And the other alternative is war. I will take you into my confidence, Richard. All those years when Philip's father was King there was conflict between his country and mine. Sometimes I think there always will be. What am I to do? I must have a truce. I must avoid war."

Richard looked at his father. He could not believe that this was the great Henry Plantagenet speaking. How grey he looked, how drawn! He was more ill than he would admit.

"Richard," he said, "you must see the King of France. Ask him for new terms for a truce. I am not prepared to go to war. The King of France is eager for it now, which can only mean that he is aware of his strength."

"*I* . . . see the King of France," cried Richard. "You would ask *me* to go . . . as a suppliant?"

"I would ask you to go in all honour but to see if you can bring him to terms."

"You have offered him terms. You will go on a crusade for two years' truce."

"I cannot go on a crusade! I dare not. Nay Richard, there must be other terms."

"And you think he would offer those terms to me?"

"You are my son, my eldest son . . ."

"Methinks that is something you often forget," said Richard quietly.

"Bring about this truce and I will remember it always."

Spoken from the heart but what did that mean with Henry Plantagenet?

"I see I must needs go," said Richard. "I must be humble and I like that not."

"Sometimes momentary humiliation is necessary for glory to come."

"Then," said Richard, "I will go to the King of France."

* * *

Philip waited to receive him.

How beautiful he was! thought the King of France as Richard rode into his camp. Those cold blue eyes, that hair that was neither red nor yellow, the strength of the countenance and the tall straight figure!

How proud the King of England should be of such a son and how foolish he was to put his faith in John. The King of England's folly was the gain of the King of France.

Ceremoniously Richard handed his sword to Philip. He was bareheaded as he knelt.

Philip put out a hand and touched the curling hair.

"Rise, Richard," he said gently.

He took him into his tent as he had before.

Richard said: "I come in humility. My father asks for a truce."

Philip smiled wryly. "That he may go on a crusade?"

"He cannot go on a crusade. He wishes for a truce that you might parley together and come to terms."

"Come to terms with your father! But he does not know how to keep a promise. My father was continually coming to terms with the King of England and what good came of it for France?"

"Still he asks for terms."

"Then I will meet him. Why Richard if I went into battle with him now I would defeat him."

"He has never been defeated."

"He is eager for a truce now because he knows that the time has at last come for him to face defeat. I am going to be lenient with him, Richard. You would fight with him. I would not wish you to suffer the humiliation of defeat . . . or possibly death. For your sake, cousin, I will consider this truce."

"What are your terms, my lord?"

Philip looked at that proud handsome face.

"That the King of England gives me his son to stay with me a while that we may talk together of our difficulties."

"You mean . . . a hostage?"

"I would not call it that. You will be treated as an honoured guest. I would not have you think that I would make a prisoner of you. I want your friendship, Richard. Aye, so much do I want it that I am ready to consider giving your father a truce—when I all but have him at my mercy—for the sake of it."

A hostage! thought Richard. For that was what it was. He liked that not. And the alternative? Defeat in battle.

He must give way.

Philip took great pains to treat his guest with the utmost courtesy. He wanted Richard to know that it gave him great pleasure to have him at his Court.

They hunted together and when they sat at table they ate from the same dish. This was how the most honoured guests were treated and Philip implied that that was how he regarded Richard.

He was not happy when Richard was not at his side. His voice was frequently heard demanding the whereabouts of the Duke of Aquitaine.

He said to Richard: "It is a custom that the greatest honour we can show a guest is to ask him to share our bed. That is what I would wish you to do, my beloved cousin."

And so it came to pass. The friendship between Richard and the King of France was one of passionate devotion.

Richard began to learn much of the affairs of France from Philip and in his turn he talked of his own difficulties. The two trusted each other during this time for there was a deep bond of love between them.

When they rode together in the forest they talked of their affairs and sometimes when they lay in bed together Philip would tell Richard of his plans.

"You must watch your father, Richard," he said. "I have seen that he is no friend of yours. He favoured your brother Henry although he would give him no power and when Henry died he turned to John. I know that he plans to set you aside for John."

"I shall not allow it."

"And I shall be beside you."

"Why should he treat me thus?"

"Because he fears you in some way. You are so noble to look at. So different from him. What a coarse creature he is! His clothes are so often soiled, and his hands . . ." Philip shuddered. "My beautiful Richard, it seems impossible that you could be his son. But then regard me. And I had a monk for a father . . . or so he would have been if he could have chosen. You were born to rule and he fears you. That is at the source of it. He has prevented your marrying my sister. He will try now to disinherit you."

"He cannot do it. I am his eldest son."

"He will try. He wants John to have what is yours."

"I shall not allow that. Nor would the people."

"We must see that they do not. You and I will work together, Richard. Always . . . you and I together."

Henry was puzzled. What was this strange friendship of his son with the King of France? They were seen often together. It was said that the King of France was peevish when Richard was not at his side.

It was disconcerting. Henry did not like to think of Alice's brother and Alice's betrothed putting their heads together.

Sometimes he suffered intense pain. Then he only wanted to be at peace. If he could be with Alice he would be content. Alice had become a symbol to him; she was more than a mistress. When he lost Alice he would have lost the battle. He felt somehow that would be the end.

This was a folly. He was a great king. He had been known as the most feared in Christendom. It was simply because he was old and ill that he felt this.

He kept John beside him, and thanked God for him. The poor old man he had become needed John, needed his affection, needed to know that he had not failed with all his sons. The old Henry that he had been seemed a separate part of him, another being who stood aside and watched mockingly. John, that Henry said, do you trust John? Have you forgotten the eaglet who was waiting the moment to pluck out your eyes.

Richard and Philip . . . together. His son and the King of France!

It was a dangerous friendship.

He wrote to Philip.

He knew that one of the differences between them was the betrothal of Alice to Richard. That marriage had been long delayed. Richard had never shown any interest in it. Now he, Henry, had other plans. Suppose he gave all his lands—with the exception of England and Normandy—to John, and John married Alice.

Henry had lacked his usual shrewdness. Full of deceits himself, he had judged Philip to be the same.

Philip however was in love. He was also trying to prove to Richard that he was making a mistake in trusting his father.

He immediately showed Henry's letter to Richard.

Richard was furious. He cared passionately about Aquitaine. He had subdued it by the sword and had only allowed his mother to have it because he knew that she was his faithful ally and that in due course it would be entirely his. He would not give up Aquitaine.

He said: "By God's eyes, Philip, I must defend what is mine." Philip nodded sagely.

Then he added wistfully: "It seems I must let you go."

"I must fortify my castles. I must be prepared against my father."

Philip had to consider. He must either lose his friend or keep him very much against his will. He loved Richard and did not want to lose his regard. If he let him go, he would prove indeed the depth of his feeling.

He decided that he must make the sacrifice.

"It grieves me deeply to see you go, Richard, but you are right when you say you must defend your castles against your father. At any time he could take them from you, for that is his intention. So I will not say good-bye but *au revoir*! Soon we will meet again. Perhaps when the time is ripe you and I will go on a crusade to the Holy Land."

"By God's eyes," cried Richard, "Little could please me more."

Then he rode away to Aquitaine.

Richard had made his castles strong and was thinking of going off to the Holy Land in the company of Philip. He could think of nothing that would better suit his mood. To ride out with Philip beside him, two good friends bent on a righteous mission. Before he had left Philip they had talked of little but their adventures in the Holy Land.

"Side by side," Philip had said. "That would give me greater pleasure than anything I have ever known."

News reached him from Jerusalem. Heraclius had prepared the world for what was happening. Had he not begged King Henry to come to their aid? He had told them of the terrible disease which had overtaken King Baldwin and how the flesh had fallen from his bones and he was in such a sorry state that he could not live much longer.

Now he was dead; his nephew had succeeded him—a young boy who himself was but little more than an infant. Moreover the boy was not robust and he had quickly followed his uncle to the grave.

Saladin, the leader of the Infidels, a man of action who knew no fear, was as determined to drive the Christians out of the Holy Land as they were to preserve it. He was fierce and courageous; he gave no quarter and asked none. This man Saladin was fast becoming a legend and Christians trembled at his name .

Heraclius had forseen this. He had come to plead to the King of England to save Jerusalem because Henry of England had the reputation of being a strong man.

They had been mistaken in his father, thought Richard. Henry was no longer a strong man; he was a feeble old one. It was not he who would be the saviour of the Holy Sepulchre.

But he had a son; and there was born in Richard then a great desire.

He went to Tours and there took the cross and swore that he would join a crusade and save the Holy Land.

Now that Richard was gone Philip was determined to bring Henry to terms. He knew that Henry had written to Richard and that Richard only half believed in his father's treachery. Richard was after all Henry's son and he could not entirely believe that his own father wished him ill. It seemed to him wrong that he should be in league with another against his own father, even though that other was Philip.

Philip was well aware of Richard's character and his great aim now was to prove to him how treacherous his father was. So while Richard was putting his castles into a state of defence and swearing allegiance to the cross at Tours, he decided to take action.

Henry, who was lulled into a sense of security, believing that Richard had brought about a temporary peace with Philip, planned to return to England. He longed to escape to a certain amount of peace. He would go and be quiet with Alice for a while. She could nurse him, for he needed to be nursed; and there in the peace of one of his palaces he would grow stronger and ready for anything that Philip might be planning.

Christmas was not very festive. How could it be with the King's security in jeopardy and his temper so uncertain for he was in sporadic pain? All the company looked forward to being in England where the King would feel more at peace. Alas, Philip had no intention of giving Henry an easy way out.

Let Henry go to England if he wished. Then Philip would invade Normandy and stand a very good chance of success with Henry out of the way. On the other hand, if Henry preferred to stay and fight, let him.

Henry sighed and knew that he could not make the longed for visit to England.

A message came from Philip. He pointed out that Henry had taken possession of Alice's dowry but there had been no marriage. When was the marriage to take place? Either he must return the lands he had taken or Richard must marry Alice without delay.

It had begun again. The old question.

Oh, Alice, he thought, what am I going to do? The decision is getting nearer and nearer. Louis, why did you have to die and give me this son of yours to deal with?

They must meet at Gisors which town Philip was demanding he return.

Was the time approaching when he would have to surrender Alice?

God was on his side. Or was it Thomas à Becket? In any case a way out was shown to him.

Before the conference at Gisors could be started the Archbishop of Tyre came riding into the city. He had heard that the Kings of France and England were there and he had sorry news for them.

Almost three months before, Jerusalem had fallen into Saladin's hands. The little King was dead as they had already heard. His mother who had remarried had appointed her second husband King of Jerusalem. Now Saladin was in Jerusalem and he had taken possession of the Holy Cross.

Christians all over the world must be plunged into deepest mourning. King Guy was captured and the true Cross was in Saladin's hands. All good Christians must rise and wrest the holy relics from the Infidels.

It was impossible in the face of such an overwhelming calamity for the two Kings to discuss their differences. They seemed petty enough now . . . to all except Henry.

Philip, who had planned in any case to go on a crusade with Richard, knowing that Richard had already taken the cross, declared his intention immediately. And the Archbishop of Tyre in a moving ceremony presented him with the cross. There was nothing that Henry could do but take it also. He doubted though that he would ever carry out his vows. He could only regard this as a temporary way out of his difficulties. Their men followed them and so numerous were they that crosses of different colours had to be handed to the different nationalities—red for the French, white for the English and green for the Flemings.

Philip and Henry now conferred not as enemies but as allies and vowed together what they would do to enable them to set out on their crusade together. They would need time to prepare and they decided that it would take a year to get together the money they would need and to assemble their equipment. They planned to leave at the Easter of 1189.

They discussed together how the money could be raised and Henry suggested that each man who did not accompany them should give one-tenth of his possessions to the cause and those who did should set aside a tenth of theirs to provide themselves with what they would need.

This seemed fair enough and in great relief Henry set out for England.

He found Alice in a state of anxiety, for news had reached her that the King of France was determined on her marriage.

He embraced her with fervour. The very sight of her revived his youth.

"What news, my lord?" she asked anxiously.

"All is well. God is with me. It is St Thomas I think, for it was like a miracle. Your brother is a hard man, Alice. He is so different from your father. He is sharp and sly and I think he is doing his best to destroy me."

She shuddered.

"Have no fear, sweetheart, I'll be a match for him . He's but a boy and I am a man of great experience. He was going to demand you for Richard, and then the Archbishop of Tyre appeared with the terrible news. How could we discuss our affairs then? There was only one thing for us to do and that was band together and go on our crusade."

"It will come to nothing. Many times in my life has there been talk of crusades and never have I been on one yet. Nay. Something will happen, depend upon it, and I shall be prevented from going to Jerusalem. I have my duties here. I can see no virtue in leaving my own lands to disaster and rebellion maybe, while I go fighting to bring the Holy City back to Christendom. Now if I were a man without responsibilities . . . but I am not, Alice. So fear not. We are together and there is only one who could part us two."

"Who?" she asked.

"Death," he replied, She shivered and he said: "Now I have made you fret. Smile, Alice, smile for me. You do not know how I have longed to see you do that."

So she smiled and they forgot all these alien forces which sought to part them, chief of them all Death.

Richard was delighted to hear that the conference between Philip and Henry had been abandoned that they might join together and plan a crusade.

His nature was such that, much as he disliked his father and much as he was drawn to Philip, he could not forget that he was Henry's son and that the kings of France were the natural enemies of the kings of England. He did not wish to be disloyal to his father and if only Henry would have met him half way he would have been prepared to strive for harmony between them.

The fact that Henry was now pledged to go on a crusade pleased him. It made hopes of a reconciliation between them possible.

He wrote to his father asking him to supply him with money for his crusade. Also as he was to go on such a dangerous venture he thought he should ask that the knights and bishops of England swear fealty to him as his father's eldest son and heir.

This was the crux of the matter. It was tantamount to asking Henry to deny the rumours that he was planning to disinherit Richard in favour of John.

He was no longer a boy. He was a man who needed assurance that his future was secure; and this matter of the crusades had brought the question to a head. Everything depended on Henry's reply. If he agreed that Richard must come to England and receive the oaths of allegiance then rumour had lied. The King must mean him to be his heir and once the oaths had been sworn he would be accepted.

Henry's reply was characteristic of him but it was an indication to Richard of the true state of affairs.

They would not go separately on the road to Jerusalem. Richard need not concern himself with raising money, for the King and his son would share everything together.

And no mention of the oath that should be sworn to secure his inheritance.

When Richard read the reply his eyes were as cold as steel and fury raged within him which was none the less fierce because he did not show it in a furious outburst.

This was the end of all hope of harmony between them.

By his reply and more by his omission the King had shown Richard that he was against him.

"And he will find," said Richard, "that those who work against me will discover in me a bitter enemy."

It was inevitable that conflict should break out between Philip and Henry. When the excitement about the crusade had died down, as it must do for the preparations were long and enthusiasm could not remain at fever pitch, Philip remembered that the greatest goal of his life was to drive Henry out of France and bring every province under one crown; Henry on the other hand was determined not to lose his inheritance and that land which he had added to it through his clever diplomacy. Each was firm in his purpose and as they were completely opposed so there must be conflict.

Philip was again calling for a conference. He knew that Richard was wavering. He had become involved in hostilities against the Count of Toulouse, a matter which did not greatly upset Philip for it gave him an opportunity to reproach Henry with his son's conduct. He was however obliged to go to the assistance of the Count of Toulouse which meant that for a time Richard and Philip were on opposing sides. Philip had no intention of letting this affect his relationship with Richard, but the fact that, as Henry saw it, there was trouble between Aquitaine and France, meant that he could no longer stay in England and he prepared to cross to Normandy.

He was beset by great anxieties. He knew that the brief respite was over. Philip would not allow it to last long. Moreover the people of England, who had long been satisfied with his rather stern but just rule, were now complaining of the Saladin Tithe which he had imposed for the crusade. If asked they would declare that they were true Christians and that the thought of the Holy Relics being in the hands of the Infidel was distasteful to them; but when it meant that one-tenth of their possessions must be given up for the sake of an attempt to retrieve them, they were less enthusiastic. Life in England was not too comfortable that it could not be improved on; and it seemed that the money which would be taken from the country was needed within.

There had long been a murmuring discontent against the forest laws. Like his Norman ancestors Henry was devoted to the hunt. It brought him comfort and solace as it had to the Conqueror and there was no relaxation like it for a man as active as he had always been. To preserve the forests for his use—again like his ancestors—he had found it necessary to keep to the harsh laws they had introduced. He had brought out a legal system of his own devising; and the main objects of this were to keep order and at the same time to replenish continually the royal exchequer. In the governing of a country there was a constant need for money and it seemed an excellent plan to him to gain as much by imposing fines as by gathering taxes, although of course the latter was necessary too.

Determined to restore the order which had been lost through the reign of mild Stephen, wrongdoers were punished by death. Many were hanged and many broken on the wheel and it was a common sight to come upon a dead man hanging from a tree or gallows.

This the people accepted because it did mean a suppression of crime and was a benefit to the law-abiding members of the population. What they would never agree to was the punishment meted out to those who infringed the forestry laws. Any man trespassing in the King's forest or killing a deer or wild boar when his family might be starving invoked terrible penalties. For offending against these laws, arms, feet or hands were cut off; eyes were put out; men were castrated; and if the crime was considered to be a great one, they were boiled alive.

Many of these sad victims would be seen begging by the roadside and people shuddered at the sight of them for they knew that fate could have befallen so many of them. It was merely a sign that they had invaded and made free of the King's forests.

Because of the King's good laws they accepted this; but when what they considered unfair taxes were levied, they remembered. They remembered now.

So there was a further anxiety for Henry. The people of England who, up to this time, had given him little cause for anxiety were restive and complaining of his rule. With this to torment him and the discomfort of his ailment together with the awareness that his body was losing its exceptional vitality, he set out for France.

It was necessary to talk with Philip; if the two Kings could come to some agreement, their ministers told them, they could avoid the consequences of a bitter war, which at heart neither of them wanted.

Philip was eager to talk. His great aim was to prove to Richard that his father was deceiving him. He wanted to force Henry to admit this. But he was young and Henry was old and crafty as a fox; he was an adept at making promises with apparently genuine honesty only to have no intention of ever keeping them. Each King knew the goal of the other; Philip to take back everything and Henry to hold on to it.

They met under an old elm tree at Gisors which was well known as that tree beneath which the kings of France and England had often met to attempt to sort out their differences. The English arriving there first took the shady part and the French were obliged to wait in the sun, and as it was August and the heat intense, the sun-drenched French could scarcely bear it. No satisfactory conclusion could be reached and Philip was so angry because he and his men had been obliged to endure the sun's heat while his opponents enjoyed the shade, and shifty Henry had apparently got the better of him, that in a rage he ordered that elm to be cut down so that no more conferences could be held beneath it.

He sent for Richard and, as his over-lord, commanded him to come to him without delay.

When Richard arrived he embraced him warmly.

"We have been apart too long," he said.

Richard replied, "My lord, I love your company but I am my father's son and I cannot with a good conscience work against him."

"Can you not, when he works continuously against you? Has he not denied you your inheritance?"

"He has not said this. He has merely implied that he will give me no power and that I must wait until his death."

"It is not what is in his mind. I am going to call a conference and you shall be there. I will make my demands in such a manner that he is forced to betray his true designs to you. Then you and I will stand together against him, the friends we were meant to be, as I knew when you came to me as my guest. Tell me, Richard, can you bear to know the truth?"

"I wish to know the truth more than anything."

"Then wait and I will confront him with my terms and we shall see."

The two Kings faced each other. Richard was with them.

"I offer you," said Philip, "all the lands I have taken in this last conflict. Richard shall keep what he has gained. I ask that he be given my sister the Princess Alice as his wife and you command your nobles, Archbishops, bishops and all men of authority to swear fealty to Richard as the heir of your dominions."

Henry was cornered. He was asked to give up the two things he had sworn never to give up. The first Alice. She was his and he was going to keep her his. Moreover, he did not wish Richard to rule after him. England and Normandy were for John. Richard could keep Aquitaine but it was England for John.

What could he do? This was not a time for prevarication. He was caught at last.

The French King was smiling mischievously; Richard was looking at him steadily, and Henry remained silent.

"You have heard the King of France, my lord," said Richard. "Swear to me that I shall have my bride and that I shall be acknowledged as your heir to which, on account of my being your eldest living son, I have every right."

In vain Henry sought a way out. There was none. He could promise, yes, but he could see by the purpose in the eyes of Philip and Richard that he would be forced to carry out his promised without delay.

He cried out suddenly: "No. I will not."

Richard looked at him in some amazement. Then he said quietly: "Now at last I see that you mean this. I would not believe it could be possible, but now I know it is."

He turned to the King of France and unbuckling his sword he gave it to him.

"My over-lord and suzerain, I offer you my allegiance," he said.

Richard had taken Philip's hands between his and Philip stooped quickly and kissed Richard's.

Their eyes met and those watching marvelled at the tenderness between them.

Henry was thunderstruck. Before his eyes his own son was swearing allegiance to his enemy. Philip was his liege lord of course on account of Aquitaine, but this was a pledge to stand with the King of France against his own father.

Philip said quickly that he would agree to a truce until January when they would meet again. In the meantime perhaps the King of England would consider his demands and if he could not agree to them, then war could not be avoided.

Philip had achieved his purpose. He had proved to Richard

that his father would not accept him, had decided to disinherit him and set up John in his place.

When the conference was over Henry had the mortification of seeing his son ride away side by side in most affectionate manner with the King of France.

The Death of the Eagle

Christmas came. Henry was still in France and spent it at Saumur. He was feeling very sick and old and was in constant pain. He knew that Richard and Philip were together. Several meetings had been suggested but he had been able to plead illness with good cause. He had great comfort from young Henry's old friend and knight-at-arms, William the Marshall, and his own bastard son Geoffrey who had shown him more genuine affection than any of his sons ever had.

"I cannot understand," he told William, "why my sons have turned against me. Think of it, good Marshall, Richard is with my enemy."

"It is because he is your eldest son, my lord," answered William, who was always truthful, "and he believes that you are trying to rob him of his inheritance."

"I shall bestow my crown where I please," answered Henry stubbornly. "Aquitaine was always for Richard."

As the winter passed he grew a little better and when in June Philip suggested a further conference the two Kings met at La Ferté Bernard. With Philip came Richard, for the two were inseparable, and as Philip was going to insist on Richard's recognition as heir to the throne of England and Normandy he brought with him several men of the Church so that if Henry could be forced into making an oath there would be plenty present to witness it.

"We want peace," said Philip. "We bicker over our petty quarrels when the Holy City calls to us. Let us make peace, brother. You know my terms. The marriage of Richard to Alice and your acknowledgement that he is heir to your dominions as is his right as your eldest living son. Richard has sworn to go ere long to the Holy Land. Your son John must take the cross and accompany him."

Henry narrowed his eyes. John accompany Richard! He knew what that meant. They did not trust him nor John and they wanted to know where John was and what he was doing.

If he were taking part in a crusade to the Holy Land he could not seize the crown of England on his father's death.

"No," thundered Henry. "I will not agree. I will give my consent to Alice's marriage to John."

He looked at one of the Cardinals whom he had bribed to stand for him. He had wheedled his way into the man's confidence explaining that while the King of France was hostile to him he could not go on the proposed crusade to the Holy Land. He dared not. If he could be proved right in this argument between them, if the King of France would accept his terms, then there would be no more delay.

The Cardinal had been tempted by the rich gifts of the King of England and now declared that Philip should accept Henry's terms. What mattered it if the Princess Alice took Prince John instead of Prince Richard, particularly as it was clear that Henry would make John his heir?

Philip was furious. "How dare you come here," he cried, "stinking of the King's gold. Dost think I do not smell it. Nay, I will not accept the King of England's terms. It is he who, in honour, should accept mine. And I tell you this: if he will not agree to the marriage of my sister and Prince Richard and will not command his knights and men of the Church to swear fealty to Richard then there can be no peace between us. He turned to Henry. "Will you swear?"

The red blood showed in Henry's eyes. He thrust one clenched fist into the palm of his other hand.

"No," he cried. "Never. Never."

The conference was over and once more it had ended in deadlock.

Henry had always loved the city of Le Mans. Perhaps it meant more to him than any of his continental possessions. His father was buried there and as soon as he came back he went to his tomb to pray.

How old and tired he felt, how sick and weary of the battle. He thought of his father who had been so gay and handsome and who had quarrelled so violently with his mother. He remembered those quarrels, the contempt his mother had had for his father and his dislike of her. Of course she had been an overbearing woman and his father had been feckless and pleasure-loving; his own sons Henry and Geoffrey had taken after their grandfather.

Geoffrey the Fair they had called the man who now lay in this tomb. He was descended from the wild Counts of Anjou, those who were said to have come from the Devil. If the story about his ancestress who had turned into her true shape in church when faced with the Mass was true then they were descended from a witch and there could well be a devil in them all. Had he not seduced his son's betrothed when she was but a child? When his temper was at its height what deeds had he not done? How many men had he murdered? Yes, the Devil was in him; but with his satanic descent on one side and his forceful mother, a granddaughter of the Conqueror on the other, what could he expect?

His mother had worked for his success. She had loved him in her hectoring way. So had his father differently, more tenderly. Geoffrey the Fair, lover of many women! It was said that Eleanor had briefly shared his bed. Henry smiled wryly. Anything could be expected of Eleanor. That was why all these years he had kept her a prisoner.

He shrugged his shoulders. She deserved her fate. He would waste no pity on her.

He had come to this town to be quiet, to think of his father and to tell himself that all rulers were beset by anxieties. There was no peace in a crown. Why then did men seek it with such passion that they were ready to barter their lives—and those of others—for it? They did it for glory. And what did they come to in the end? The tomb.

He rose from his knees and as he made his way to his chamber a messenger arrived to tell him that Philip was on the march. Richard was with him and they were only a few miles from Le Mans.

From the top of the battlements he could see the armies encamped there. Philip and Richard were together in the same tent.

"What have I done," he asked himself, "that my sons should take up arms against me?"

I have one good son—Geoffrey—base-born Geoffrey whom I would trust with my life.

But there was John whom he must love best of all because he was his legitimate son. My youngest and my best, he assured himself.

By God's eyes, John should be his heir. If he defeated Philip, if he brought him to terms he would strip Richard of everything—even Aquitaine.

Some of his old ardour returned. He felt better. If only there could have been a conference. In the old days he had excelled at conferences. He could always get the better of his opponents by his agile brain and of course the old trick of agreeing to do that which he had no intention of performing. But people became wary. One cannot keep playing the old tricks.

"They shall not take Le Mans," he declared. "Not the city I love best, not that which holds the tomb of my father."

He hated the thought of a head-on battle. He had always avoided that. So much depended on luck and numbers and it always seemed to him senseless destruction. He who had always relied on strategy relied on that now.

He would start a fire and as the wind was in the right direction the flames would be carried into the French camp. At best it could destroy so much that it would disable them and prevent their fighting, at least it would cause confusion. He gave the order.

As he stood at the turret watching the blaze, he laughed to himself. Strategy was always better than hand to hand combat.

His glee changed suddenly to consternation. God was indeed against him for the wind had suddenly changed. It was like a direct order from Heaven. Instead of enveloping the French camp it was blowing back in the direction of the city.

Henry left the turret. His knights, seeing what was happening, were waiting for orders.

"The city will be destroyed," cried Henry. "The hand of God is against us. There is nothing for us to do but get away while we can."

He and his men left the city which was now beginning to blaze into a mighty conflagration as the flames driven by the high wind encompassed it.

Henry was sick at heart. This was the final disaster. Something told him that he could not survive it. The new vigour which had come to him had evaporated.

He rode to the top of a hillock and looked back at the blazing city.

His son Geoffrey was beside him and he said to him, "God has taken from me the city I loved most."

Geoffrey said: "It was a freak of the weather. Who could have guessed the wind would change so suddenly?"

"It is God's sign that he has deserted me. Geoffrey, my son, in my youth I spent many years in that city. My father's tomb is there. And he is reducing it all to ashes." In a sudden access of rage Henry shook his fist at the sky.

Geoffrey was afraid for his father and sought to pacify him. "I beg of you, my lord," he said, "consider. You need God's help as never before. You blaspheme. Should you not humbly pray to him?"

Henry laughed aloud and his eyes flashed with the old fury while the blood hammered in his temples.

"Why should I plead with One who is determined to destroy me? Why should I honour Him? What has He done for me? He gave me sons and turned them against me. In that camp is my son Richard. What have I done, Geoffrey, to be so treated?"

"God has given you much, my lord. He gave you a crown and the strength to hold it. Troubles have come to you perhaps to test you. They say God loves to test those whom He loves best."

Henry turned to look at his son and grasped his arm suddenly.

"You have been a good son to me, Geoffrey. I would you had been my legitimate son. How different that would have been. He gave me you, did He not, and He has given my my son John. My son John will be a good king for I am determined that he shall follow me. He is the only one who has shown me affection. I have my son John."

Geoffrey looked away to the burning city and he prayed to God that He would not let the King discover the true nature of his youngest son, for Geoffrey knew the boy to be dissolute, unreliable, hypocritical and far less worthy than his brother Richard whom the King was seeking to disinherit.

"My lord, thank God then for what he has given you and I beg of you let us ride on, for the enemy will pursue us and they must not capture you."

Even as he spoke William the Marshall rode up to the King.

"The French army is in pursuit," said William. "Ride on my lord with all speed. I and my company will hold your retreat but ride on as fast as you can."

The King in retreat! The King being protected by a rearguard! It was breaking his heart.

William the Marshall could see that they could not hold back the French. Richard rode at their head. He wanted to be the one to capture his father. He had not stopped to don his armour even and was unarmed.

Cold fury possessed him as he told himself what he would say to the old man who had done his best to disinherit him.

The smoking city was behind them, the air filled with acrid odour. Richard could see the retreating band of men in the centre of which would be his father.

With a shout he rode forward. He was talking to the old man as he rode. "What sort of a father have you been to me? Did you not always hate me? Why did you hate me? Because my mother loved me. You hated her so you hated me and you tried to take from me that which is mine by right. Unnatural father! Now you will see what happens when you are my captive."

A knight seemed to rise up in front of him. A lance was pointing at his troat.

"Halt, Richard of Aquitaine," said a voice which Richard recognized.

"It is William the Marshall," cried Richard. "Will you kill me then? That would be a dastardly thing to do. See you not that I am unarmed?"

"I will not kill you," said William the Marshall. "I shall leave that for the Devil."

"William . . . !'

"I have nothing to say to you," said William. "You are a traitor to your own father." And with those words he thrust his lance into Richard's horse.

The horse fell dying and Richard was thrown to the ground. William the Marshall turned and galloped away.

Richard was unharmed but since he was incapable of proceeding then he called his men to a halt. They returned disconsolately to the French camp.

The King and his band of faithful followers which included his son Geoffrey and William the Marshall came to rest at a small castle and as the King was too exhausted to go further they decided they must stop there awhile.

Geoffrey was beside the King and took off his own cloak to cover him for although it was June and warm Henry continually shivered.

While the King slept restlessly Geoffrey and William the Marshall talked with some of the King's knights, discussing the desperate position in which they found themselves.

William said: "We should make for Normandy. There we could rally many a faithful knight to the King's cause."

"Once there," agreed Geoffrey, "we could send to England for reinforcements."

"It is our only hope."

In the morning the King seemed a little better.

He refused to go to Normandy.

"Le Mans is destroyed," he said. "I can never forget it. I will stay in Anjou which is the land of my fathers. My son John will join me. He is a good warrior and he will put heart into our army and fear into the enemy."

William the Marshall did not meet his eyes. If the King had been stronger he would have had something to say, but Henry needed a spar to cling to. Let him believe that John provided that.

"Where is my son John?" he asked. "I am surprised that he has not yet joined me."

"There is no news of him yet, my lord," said Geoffrey.

"He will surprise us," said Henry. "I know him. He will arrive with men for our deliverance. You will see."

Neither Geoffrey nor William replied.

Philip's armies were taking every castle on their route. He sent a message to Henry. He was ready to meet him again and he thought Henry might now find it expedient to consider his demand.

"I would not wish young Philip to see me as I am now," said Henry. "In a few days I shall be better. Delay replying. Tell him I am indisposed. If only John would come. But he will soon."

The messengers returned with Philip's answer.

He did not believe in the King's indisposition. Henry had made so many excuses during his lifetime, had told so many lies that no one believed him now.

Philip went on with his march and castle after castle was falling into his hands.

Again Philip suggested a conference and again Henry replied that he was too ill.

The answer came: "The King of France wearies of the continual excuses of the King of England. He must come to the conference or risk the result."

So he must go. He could scarcely sit his horse.

"If my son John were here, he would go in my place," he said. "He would reason with my enemy and my traitor son."

* * *

It was difficult to remain on his horse. William the Marshall was on one side of him, Geoffrey on the other. They were ready to catch him if he should fall.

Oh, God, that I should come to this, he thought. Once proud Henry Plantagenet now a conquered King with a pain-racked body, deserted by my own son. Oh John, my beloved youngest, where are you now?

Philip's terms were read to him.

He must accept the counsels of the King of France and do homage for all his territory on the Continent. When Richard returned from Jerusalem he must be given the Princess Alice as his bride and be proclaimed heir to all his father's territories. Henry must pay Philip the cost of the war. If he did not agree to keep to the terms of this treaty his knights and barons were to swear that they would desert him and join Richard.

Henry bowed his head. The humiliation was more than he could endure. They were killing him.

Yet he must concede, for what was the alternative? They would make him their prisoner. He, proud Henry, prisoner of the young King of France and his own son!

It was unendurable.

He must accept. Then when his health returned he would find some means of evading those terms. How many times had he wriggled out of his contracts. It had been part of his policy. To this he owed his success.

He accepted. His humiliation was complete. But not quite.

Now that he had accepted the peace terms one more thing was required of him. He had behaved unfairly to his son; he had tried to rob him of his inheritance. There must be no recriminations. He would now give Richard the kiss of peace before all those assembled.

Richard rode to him—young, straight, beautiful with the sun on his fair hair, godlike. The King of France watched with love and pride.

Henry's bloodshot eyes fiercely hating looked into the steely blue ones of his son. They embraced.

Henry could not control his anger. "I pray God," he said, "that I may live long enough to take a fitting revenge on you."

Richard smiled coldly. The hatred between them was great.

They would take him to the castle of Chinon because it was near and he was in no fit state to endure a long journey.

Geoffrey ordered that a litter be brought and, protesting, but only a little, he allowed himself to be placed in it.

"My son John will soon be with me," he said. "Then I can begin planning my revenge. Richard shall never have the crown."

When he reached the castle he felt better. He would live to fight again. When he had been forced to give Richard the kiss of peace his anger had been so great that it had ignited the old spirit.

"I will have my revenge," he said. "I must."

He lay on the bed covered by Geoffrey's cloak, for he was too tired to take off his clothes.

"Geoffrey," he said, "there were many knights on the side of Philip and Richard who should have been on mine. They deserted. They left me for the enemy."

" 'Twas so, my lord. And many more have gone."

"I would know who they are."

Geoffrey nodded. "It is well to know traitors."

"Send a man to the King of France. Ask this favour of him. I would have a list of all those knights who left me. He cannot deny me that."

"It shall be done, my lord."

The King nodded and closed his eyes.

"Stay beside me, Geoffrey," he said. "You comfort me. It is good to know that I have faithful friends. I do not despair though it has never been so dark as this. I have faced some desperate situations but never one like this. But I shall emerge. Doubt it not, Geoffrey. My son John will be here very soon, and he and I, with you, Geoffrey, and William the Marshall and those whom I would trust with my life . . . we shall plan together. I want my son Richard brought to me, a miserable captive. He shall join his mother in prison. Think of it, Geoffrey. A wife and sons who turned against me!"

"Try to rest, mylord. You need to sleep."

"I'll try, Geoffrey. Wake me the moment John arrives."

"I will, my lord," answered Geoffrey.

The King started from his sleep.

"Is that John?" he asked.

"No, my lord. It is the list sent by the King of France," answered Geoffrey. "The list of knights who deserted your ranks and joined those of Philip and Richard."

"Ah. Now I shall know the traitors. Let the list be read to me."

There was a brief silence.

The King said: "I am ready."

Still there was no answer.

"What ails you?" cried the King. "Why do you not give me the names of these traitors?"

"The first on the list is . . ."

"What ails you, man. Who is the first on the list?"

"It is Prince John, my lord."

He lay sick and silent.

He could not believe it. He must see for himself. There it was plain to read. Prince John at the head of the list. So this was why he had waited in vain.

Why, John, why?

He could see the face of his son. He could picture the thoughts behind that charming countenance. Because you are finished. Father. You are vanquished. How could I be beside you when you have nothing to offer me? Richard is in the ascendancy. In a short time he will be King, I cannot afford to offend the new King of England, Father, even if the old one is you.

Alone, ill, deserted!

What do I care for now? he asked himself. Nothing. Let me die. I am a vanquished king. Oh shame, shame that this should come to Henry Plantagenet. Deserted by my best loved son, John. Was it not for you, my son, that I brought this war upon me? Richard hated me and made no secret of it. And you . . . you pretended to love me and I believed you. Did I believe? Deep down in my heart, did I not know?

He thought of the painting on the wall at Winchester. The voracious eaglets plucking their father to death and the youngest waiting his moment to pluck out his eyes.

That is what you have done to me, John. You have plucked out my eyes. I no longer have any desire to live. Nothing else matters now. I have lost everything. While I believed in you there was a reason for going on. But you have lied to me, deceived me, laughed at me behind my back, doubtless. John, you are a monster. Every one of my sons was against me. There was not one who did not lift up his hand and try to stab me in the back. Every one . . . and now that she-wolf in her prison, their mother . . . is laughing at me.

See to what you have come, Henry. You the proud one, arbiter of our fortunes, where are you now? We are laughing at you, Henry. You have no more power to harm us.

He was not sure where he was. It was cold suddenly. He was in Rosamund's Bower. Beautiful Rosamund whom he had loved so dearly. She had changed into Alice. Alice, Alice, what will become of you now? You will go to Richard, be his bride. He will never forgive you for having loved me, for having borne me a child. He is harsh and cruel. I know. I have looked into his icy eyes. Alice, my darling Alice, what will become of you?

Why was it so wonderfully cool? He opened his eyes. His son Geoffrey was fanning his face.

"Oh, Geoffrey, my good Geoffrey. Would you had been my legitimate son. What do you there?"

"I am keeping the flies away. It has turned so hot. Is there anything I can get you, my lord?"

"Call me not my lord. Call me Father. You have been a true son to me. Why is it that you were so good to me and the sons of my Queen deserted me? They have destroyed me, and the youngest most of all. He was here quietly waiting to pluck out my eyes. God will reward you, Geoffrey . . . my son."

"I want no rewards, Father," said Geoffrey. "If I have served you and won your love that is reward enough."

"There is a sapphire ring on my finger, Geoffrey. I never cared for such baubles, but I carried them for their worth. Take it. It is yours. Remember me by it, Geoffrey."

Geoffrey took the ring and kissed his father's hand.

"May God bless you, you who were truly my son."

Geoffrey sat by his bed while he grew more delirious.

"He should have a priest," he said, "for his end is near."

There was no priest. The priest had gone, so had most of the knights. There was nothing to be gained by staying with a dead and defeated king.

Geoffrey stayed by his side with William the Marshall, and as they watched, the King ceased to murmur and his eyes became glazed. Then he spoke. William bent near to catch his words.

"Shame," muttered the King. "Oh, the shame of a vanquished king."

Then they saw that he was dead.

They carried him to the Abbey of Fontevrault and laid him in the church. Only a few faithful men had remained with him. The rest had stripped him of his jewels and clothes.

Richard, the new King of England, came to look at his

father's corpse. He stared down impassively and none knew what emotions there were in his heart.

William the Marshall faced him across his father's body and Richard's expression did not change.

It is the end of me, thought William. He will never forgive me for what I did.

Then Richard spoke. "You were my enemy but a few days ago, William the Marshall. You killed my horse so that he fell under me."

" 'Twas so, my lord King, and so would I do again in such circumstances."

Richard nodded. "Now I am your King, do you seek to kill me?"

"Nay, for you are the true King. I served the King before and that is why his enemies were mine."

Richard said nothing but turned away and William the Marshall wondered what his fate would be. Death or the dungeons?

When Richard was leaving Fontevrault he called to William the Marshall to walk beside him.

"Go back to England," he said. "Guard my Kingdom till I come."

William was taken aback.

"*I* . . . my lord?"

"Aye, you," replied Richard. "I like men who are faithful to their Kings."

William the Marshall turned to Richard. He said: "The King is dead. Long live the King."

It was enough.

The news reached England. The King is dead. There is a new King. Richard the First.

In her apartments at Westminster they told Princess Alice. She was seized with a fit of trembling and shut herself into her bedchamber.

It was impossible. He was gone. She was alone. What would become of her?

They would marry her to Richard. She could not endure it. She had heard that he was cold, that her brother Philip loved him dearly and he loved Philip.

She was too stunned to weep.

All she could do was whisper to herself: What now? What will become of me?

In Salisbury Queen Eleanor heard the news.

He was dead. That vital man whom once she had loved and later whom she had hated and reviled. She could not believe it. Henry Plantagenet dead.

She heard of his last hours. They had all turned against him. Serve him right. He had tried to disinherit Richard, her Richard, her best loved son.

There was change in the air. Everything was going to be different now. She touched her face. She was an old woman. Sixty-seven years of age and so many of them spent in captivity. Her two husbands were dead, her lovers were dead, and she lived on.

She would have something to live for; but she always had had. She had always loved life. That was why she was young even at sixty-seven.

But it was a new life which was opening for her. Freedom! And she would be with her beloved son. She and Richard would stand together as she had always longed for them to do.

Soon she would be delivered. He had promised that it should be the first thing he would do.

All day she waited at the turret. Before sundown she saw a party of riders coming towards the castle.

She went down to meet them.

She was right. She knew that she could trust Richard.

Greetings from the King to his revered mother.

She was free.

Bibliography

Appleby, John T.	*Henry II, The Vanquished King*
Aubrey, William Hickman Smith	*The National and Domestic History of England*
Aytoun, William E.	*The Life and Times of Richard the First*
Dark, Sidney	*St Thomas of Canterbury*
Demimuid, Monsignor	*Saint Thomas à Becket*
D'Auvergne, Edmund B.	*John, King of England*
Guizot, M. Translated by Robert Black	*History of France*
Holbach, Maude M.	*In the Footsteps of Richard Coeur de Lion*
Hope, Mrs.	*The Life of St Thomas Becket of Canterbury*
Hutton, the Rev. William Holden (arranged by)	*Thomas of Canterbury. An Account of his Life and Fame from Contemporary Biographers and Other Chroniclers*
Morris, John	*The Life and Martyrdom of St Thomas à Becket*
Norgate, Kate	*England Under the Angevin Kings*
Norgate, Kate	*John Lackland*
Pernoud, Regine Translated by Peter Wiles	*Eleanor of Aquitaine*
Poole, A. L.	*From Domesday Book to Magna Carta*
Rosenberg, Melrich V.	*Eleanor of Aquitaine, Queen of the Troubadours and the Courts of Love*
Salzman, L. F.	*Henry II*
Stenton, F. M.	*The First Century of English Feudalism*
Stephens, Sir Leslie and Lee, Sir Sidney (edited by)	*The Dictionary of National Biography*
Strickland, Agnes	*The Lives of the Queens of England*
Wade, John	*British History*
Wilkinson, Clennell	*Coeur de Lion*

NEW FROM FAWCETT CREST

☐ **THE MASK OF THE ENCHANTRESS**   24418 $3.25
by Victoria Holt
Suewellyn knew she wanted to possess the Mateland family castle, but having been illegitimate and cloistered as a young woman, only a perilous deception could possibly make her dream come true.

☐ **THE HIDDEN TARGET**   24443 $3.50
by Helen MacInnes
A beautiful young woman on a European tour meets a handsome American army major. All is not simple romance however when she finds that her tour leaders are active terrorists and her young army major is the chief of NATO's antiterrorist section.

☐ **THE SEVEN CARDINAL VIRTUES**
OF SCIENCE FICTION   24440 $2.50
Edited by Isaac Asimov, Martin Harry Greenberg, and Charles G. Waugh
Temperance, Prudence, Justice, Fortitude, Faith, Hope and *Charity*—these are the seven cardinal virtues. In this anthology each virtue is illustrated by a classic science fiction tale.

☐ **EL DORADO**   24449 $2.95
by Maggie MacKeever
From the dazzling splendor of New Orleans to the intoxicating promise of the gold hills of California, this is a story of the lawless passion for money, power and love.

Buy them at your local bookstore or use this handy coupon for ordering.

COLUMBIA BOOK SERVICE
32275 Mally Road, P.O. Box FB, Madison Heights, MI 48071

Please send me the books I have checked above. Orders for less than 5 books must include 75¢ for the first book and 25¢ for each additional book to cover postage and handling. Orders for 5 books or more postage is FREE. Send check or money order only. Allow 3-4 weeks for delivery.

Cost $_____	Name_____
Sales tax*_____	Address_____
Postage _____	City_____
Total $_____	State_____ Zip_____

*The government requires us to collect sales tax in all states except AK, DE, MT, NH and OR.

Prices and availability subject to change without notice.   **8216**

CURRENT CREST BESTSELLERS

☐ **BORN WITH THE CENTURY**   24295 $3.50
by William Kinsolving
A gripping chronicle of a man who creates an empire for his family,
and how they engineer its destruction.

☐ **SINS OF THE FATHERS**   24417 $3.95
by Susan Howatch
The tale of a family divided from generation to generation by great
wealth and the consequences of a terrible secret.

☐ **THE NINJA**   24367 $3.50
by Eric Van Lustbader
They were merciless assassins, skilled in the ways of love and the
deadliest of martial arts. An exotic thriller spanning postwar Japan
and present-day New York.

☐ **KANE & ABEL**   24376 $3.75
by Jeffrey Archer
A saga spanning 60 years, this is the story of two ruthless, powerful
businessmen whose ultimate confrontation rocks the financial community as well as their own lives.

☐ **GREEN MONDAY**   24400 $3.50
by Michael M. Thomas
An all-too-plausible thriller in which the clandestine manipulation
of world oil prices results in the most fantastic bull market the
world has ever known.

Buy them at your local bookstore·or use this handy coupon for ordering.

COLUMBIA BOOK SERVICE
32275 Mally Road, P.O. Box FB, Madison Heights, MI 48071

Please send me the books I have checked above. Orders for less than 5 books
must include 75¢ for the first book and 25¢ for each additional book to cover
postage and handling. Orders for 5 books or more postage is FREE. Send check
or money order only. Allow 3-4 weeks for delivery.

Cost $_____	Name_____
Sales tax*_____	Address_____
Postage _____	City_____
Total $_____	State_____ Zip_____

*The government requires us to collect sales tax in all states except AK, DE,
MT, NH and OR.*

Prices and availability subject to change without notice.   **8215**